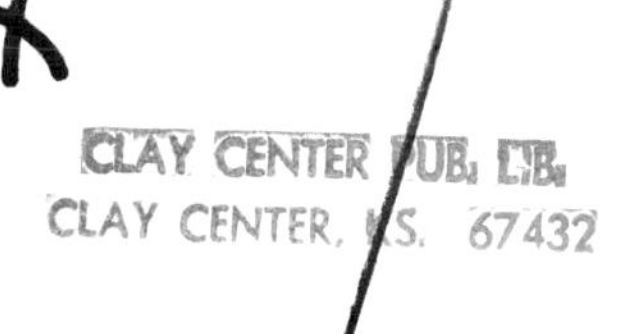

McCollum, Thomas $25.00

Tainted blood

TAINTED BLOOD

TAINTED BLOOD

A NOVEL

Thomas C. McCollum III

SHOJI BOOKS
Tokyo • Charlottesville • Wilmington

SHOJI BOOKS, INC.
An Imprint of Bookwrights Press

2123 Ivy Road
Suite B108
Charlottesville, VA 22903

PUBLISHER'S NOTE

This novel is a work of fiction. The medical data is based on fact, however, all names, characters, places, and incidents either are the product of the author's imagination or are used fictitiously, and any resemblance to actual persons, living or dead, events, or locales is entirely coincidental.

Printed in the United States of America

1 3 5 7 9 10 8 6 4 2

ISBN: 1-880404-11-7

LIBRARY OF CONGRESS CATALOGING-IN-PUBLICATION DATA

McCollum, Thomas C., 1939–
Tainted Blood: a novel / Thomas C. McCollum III.
p. cm.
ISBN 1–880404–11–7
I. Title.
PS3563.C3434T35 1995
813'.54—dc20

95–19726
CIP

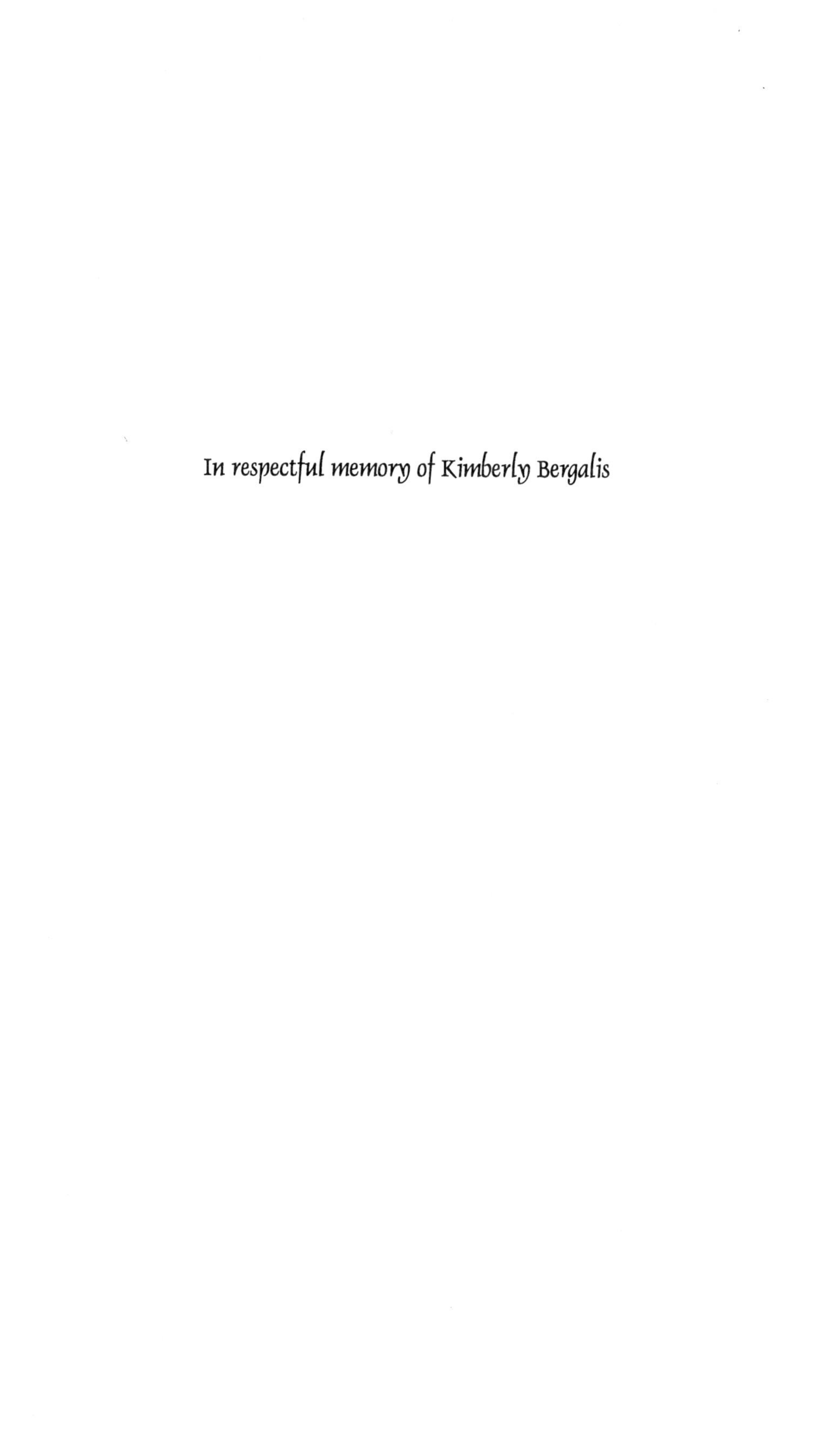

In respectful memory of Kimberly Bergalis

PROLOGUE

February 1, 1976
NAIROBI, KENYA

This was Doctor Adolf Troutmann's second trip to Africa. His first was almost twenty years earlier as a medical graduate doing research work at a British hospital in Tangier, Morocco. There he learned the mysteries and customs of the Arabic world of northern Africa; now destiny called and he was about to embark upon the desolate and exotic world of central Africa.

Troutmann could not get comfortable in the small, single-engine Cherokee Six aircraft. Before takeoff, the obliging pilot removed one of the second row seats so the seven-foot doctor could stretch his legs during the flight from Nairobi to Kasensero, Uganda.

Once airborne, Troutmann bent his head down to see majestic Kilimanjaro, snow peaked and cloud shrouded, directly to the south. Herds of roaming elephants plodded towards the cool mountain, seeking relief from the hot, arid uplands. Lake Victoria sparkled a light, silvery blue in the distance. Mount Elgon, where the U.S. Army scientists thought the dreaded Ebola and Marburg filoviruses originated, lay about three hundred miles to the northwest. A thousand feet below, a pack of hungry hyenas loped after a crippled gazelle and fat, muddy rivers curled like pythons. Off to the north, sugar-cane fields stretched for miles. Further in the distance he could see a rising verdant belt of jungle, which he was sure was full of the green monkeys he used in the National Cancer Institute (NCI) research lab back home.

The plane's cabin was warm and confining. Troutmann removed the jacket of his pinstriped blue and white seersucker suit. He wore no tie and quickly undid the top two buttons of his white Polo shirt. He was drenched in perspiration.

After an hour and a half they decended into the city of Kisumu to pick up a virologist who had been working for the United States Army Medical Research Institute of Infectious Diseases (USAMRIID) project at Kitum Cave, at the base of Mount Elgon. Troutmann had just gotten comfortable and didn't want to get out, so the pilot radioed the control tower and asked the new passenger, Major Alice Allen, PhD., to bring aboard cold Cokes for all.

Major Allen hopped aboard and laid a warm six-pack of bottles and an opener on the empty co-pilots seat. Her military-issue cap had brushed against the roof and tilted down over her nose, exposing close cropped, dishwater-brown hair. She pushed the cap up and set it straight. She secured it by pinning two gold-colored bobby pins into the cap and her hair; then heaved up into the plane a large black valise with a red Biohazard-3 symbol pasted on its side. Troutmann blanched and sat up straight. What the hell was going on? She was transporting lethal infectious waste!

The pilot and field crew topped the fuel tanks and they were quickly on their way. Troutmann was deep in thought. He stared at a fly on the face of the small rectangular window. He reached up and grabbed a Coke, then roughly flipped the top off the bottle with the opener. Fizzy foam shot up from the neck and streaked down his shirt. He swore beneath his breath and quickly sucked the rest of the foam from the top. The fly, instinctively triggered by the sweet smell, started buzzing energetic Immelmann loops under Troutmann's chin. He swatted it dead—then popped it in his mouth! For the remainder of the flight he made no effort to speak to the dozing Major Allen; however, he did sneak sideway glances at the graceful curves of her legs flowing out from her pressed, tan Bermudas.

The plane flew in a semi-circle around the northern shores of Lake Victoria, then headed southwest past the Sese Islands and into a grass landing strip at the fishing village of Kasensero. The circuitous trip was about six hundred and fifty miles and took them better than half a day.

Troutmann was stiff and exhausted. He had little rest in Niarobi during his layover from Washington, D.C. Disembarking, he unfolded like a concertina from the small, cramped quarters of the fueslage and stepped down onto the turf runway and into the sweltery central African landscape. He extended his hand to help the young doctor, carefully avoiding the black valise she was carrying. She frowned and refused to be helped. Probably a bull dyke, he thought. Troutmann then stretched his arms over his head and tilted backwards to get the kinks out. The skinny mongrel dogs who chased the plane as it landed, howled as the pilot wound the hot Lycoming engine to a halt. A cacophony of African sounds greeted him. Gibbons screeched eerily in the distant podo trees, cockatoos whistled and clucked from nearby indogo and bamboo thickets, cicadas rubbed their wings, droning their mating call from swamp reeds. The sun was a huge yellow glare and heat rolled in waves over the short landing strip. A dozen semi-clad natives sat quietly on their haunches under the shade of a tin-roofed quonset hut, staring at the tall man. Major Alice Allen ignored everyone, and with her Biohazard-3 bag bumping her sides, headed briskly for the building and her USARMIID companion waiting in the shadows. Troutmann wondered what she was up to, he shrugged his shoulders and picked up the sizable medical bag he had stashed on an empty seat and started walking towards the hut. Unbeknownst to Major Allen, or anyone else, Troutmann too was transporting a deadly agent. AIDS. He was a walking viral time bomb.

His gait was a crab-like waddle. He had long hanging arms, giant flat feet, size 20 AAA, and congenital scoliosis had curved his spine at an odd angle, so he appeared tilted to the right as he walked. Once off the runway, he stopped to put a khaki hat on his slightly balding head for protection against the beating sun. Sweat poured from his face. He removed his thick yellow-tinted glasses and wiped them clean with a white handkerchief.

The dogs were now nipping at his heels. He gave one a hard kick in its bony ribs and the pack scurried off, yelping. He then replaced his glasses by bending the pliable metal stems over his ears and turned towards the squatting, staring natives. His harelip and protruding teeth inadvertently grinned at the villagers, who giggled and pointed at his face. He had suffered similar reactions whenever he visited new places in his travels, so he pointed back at them and laughed. He could hear boisterous voices and the thumping rhythm of overhead fans in the quonset hut; stooping to get through the door, he entered the cool building.

Troutmann was greeted heartily by a group of beer-drinking medical colleagues from Washington who had been sent into Africa before him. He ordered a Heineken and quaffed the cold brew. Enthusiastically, they brought him up to date on the viral scare in the area while they shared a late snack—pieces of grilled crocodile tail—which he wolfed down. It seemed a young nurse named, Mayinga, had died of the deadliest known strain of Ebola virus yet discovered. She bled to death in Zaire, but they were able to save samples of her blood and tissue and a military courier was in the process of transferring those samples to Washington that very day. Troutmann, his distorted mouth hanging open and ringed with unwiped crocodile grease, took in every word. In his mind, the riddle of Major Allen was now solved. But he knew they hadn't seen anything yet. Finishing their beer, the group left the cool shade of the quonset hut and piled into a rusted-out Land Rover to drive to the local hospital.

Earlier, in December, when the new Mayinga strain appeared, the World Health Organization (WHO) and USAMRIID felt they had a potential epidemic and world catastrophe on their hands in central Africa. Numerous indigenous tribes, and a few foreigners in an isolated area around the northern shores of Lake Victoria in Kenya and Uganda, had also died suddenly of the dreaded Ebola and Marburg viruses. Viruses so insidious that you are usually dead within three weeks of exposure.

Your demise starts with a splitting headache behind the eyes, then a debilitating backache. By the third or fourth day you vomit until you get the dry heaves. Then your face is paralyzed, your eyeballs turn red as they fill with blood, your skin turns yellow and you grow demented. After a week, you start vomiting black blood, which stinks of internal rot. The virus then begins to liquefy the internal flesh of the body. Blood oozes from every orifice, from the tear ducts to the anus. Clots form in your guts and your brain starts rotting. Within the next week your visceral organs are rotten. You puke and defecate them out as blood and you die with horror and pain that defies description.

The USARMIID says that the victims "crash and burn" and they call these viruses, "hot viruses." BIOHAZARD MATERIAL! All personnel must be outfitted in Chemturion biological spacesuits before they enter any area where the viruses are being worked on. The scientists are terrified of these viruses because they can be airborne—the easiest and most lethal way to infect humans. One sneeze from a single infected individual could potentially generate a worldwide pandemic. At the USARMIID lab in Fort Detrick, Maryland, a desperate race is on to find a vaccine for these viruses. Marburg is stored in their BioSafety-Level-4, an area restricted to hot agents for which there is no known vaccine or cure. Ebola virus is so deadly that it has its own biocontainment area, known as AA-5, at the same laboratory. Most scientists think you're crazy if you go in there under any conditions.

Adolf Troutmann had risen to become one of the world's foremost virologists at the National Cancer Institute in Fort Detrick and had been working in coordination with the WHO and USAMRIID on a vaccine for the Ebola virus for a number of years. *He* couldn't wait to do research in AA-5.

Troutmann wanted to try one of the vaccines he had developed on African "subships"—i.e., human beings. It was a mixture of animal retroviruses, sheep visna and bovine leukemia, which in 1974 he had successfully grown in human tissue culture. He told superiors his theory: if he mixed his animal retroviruses, which change the genetic composition of the cells they enter, into any inoculating material, his vaccine could potentially create a change in DNA structure which would allow all newborns to be inbred with an immunity to whatever disease with which they were inoculated. If this turned out true, it would eliminate the logistical problem of vaccinating most of the population of the world against future diseases. At the time, his bosses thought Troutmann a genius. And since it was Africa where he would be doing the experimentation, they gave him the go-ahead.

Before Troutmann left for Africa he met with a former medical school colleague, Doctor Victor Zbrinski, then head of the New York City blood bank. He convinced Zbrinski to start using his mixture of animal retroviruses in Hepatitis B vaccine for gays suffering from this lethal disease. As the homosexual population of the world was being decimated by hepatitis, Zbrinski was only too happy to work with Troutmann. Especially after Troutmann informed him that Zbrinski would be coauthor on any publications regarding the test results and would share in any awards. Zbrinski was also led to believe that Troutmann had already done human experiments with his retroviruses, not just grown them in human tissue culture, and that Troutmann might be on his way to a Nobel prize in medicine.

Blinded by his desire for recognition, Zbrinski, immediately set up a voluntary program in New York City under Troutmann's guidance. He bypassed all normal rules, regulations and safety procedures regarding clinical testing of human subjects. He paid gays who were *non-monogamous* and between the ages of twenty and forty to be inoculated with the mixture of bovine leukemia and sheep visna retroviruses and Hepatitis B vaccine. Zbrinski then gathered data on the inoculated individuals over the next few years.

Upon arrival at the hospital in Kasensero, Troutmann unpacked his medical bag. He had brought along hundreds of small vials of his retrovirus mixture packed in

Styrofoam. Each snap-off glass vial contained enough doses of retrovirus to vaccinate fifty people. He used the hospital laboratory to mix the contents with the Marburg and Ebola vaccine he and the USARMIID laboratories had been working on. He immediately started injecting as many of the local inhabitants as he could, using the same needle over and over again. Over the next three weeks, numerous people still died of the horrors of Marburg and Ebola, and in a short time, the scientists realized they did not have a vaccine. The teams of scientists returned to the confines of their laboratories in America. However, Troutmann begged to stay on in Tanzania. He plead his case by saying that his statistics showed a gradual decline of Ebola outbreak in the populace he had vaccinated. Allowed to stay for the duration of 1976, he passed the time by injecting Africans all around Lake Victoria by the thousands with his vaccine.

Medically, it was acquired immune deficiency. He nicknamed it AID. A clever, helpful-sounding acronym he thought would encourage people to accept his Ebola vaccination. They did, in ever-increasing numbers. Unknowingly, destroying their T-cell system!

During the next two months Troutmann inoculated the entire villages of Kashenye and Bukwali in the remote province of Kagera, Tanzania, with his mixed vaccine. After finishing there, he went by boat, train and bus to the villages around the shores of Lake Victoria. He took the Kinshasa Highway from Kinshasa in Zaire through the sweltering jungles of the Congo to Kisangani and back to Nairobi for the remainder of 1976, inoculating everyone he could in every city and village he visited.

People were moved by Adolf Troutmann—thinking him an odd, but magnanimous soul, dedicating his life to helping mankind. Many Africans wept upon his departure in September. Worldwide health agencies expressed their eternal indebtedness for his tireless work. Gratefully, they sent Troutmann on to Brazil and Haiti to continue his vaccination program for another three months.

By Christmas of 1976, he returned in triumph to his laboratory in Maryland. Zbrinski was also a hero in the gay community for his compassion and relentless efforts. Privately, he worried because his test data showed no improvement with controlling Hepatitis B in homosexuals. Yet, he continued to inoculate gays in his paid-volunteer vaccination program until 1980.

In late 1980, an ominous occurrence transpired. A disease began appearing in Kasensero and wiped out most of the inhabitants. The villages of Kashenye and Bukwali in Tanzania were hit next. By early 1981, people all along the Kinshasa Highway were developing the same symptoms—which carried all the hallmarks of AIDS. In particular, an unexpected collapse of immune system defenses in young adults had allowed fungal and other infections to run wild. Deaths began. In New York, San Francisco and Los Angeles a similar health crisis, called gay-related-immunodeficiency-disease (GRID), started cropping up. Health organizations, the WHO, the Centers for Disease Control in Atlanta, doctors, nurses, UNICEF and voluntary workers rushed in to diagnose the problem in Africa and the United States.

Kenya, Uganda, Zaire, Tanzania, Zambia, Haiti, Brazil, New York, Los Angeles, and San Francisco suddenly became the epicenters of AIDS.

*Periodic outbreaks of Marburg and Ebola continue around the world. The Ebola virus surfaced again in Zaire and the Philippines around 1980. Even the U.S. had a scare in the late eighties in Reston, Virginia, when the "Ebola hot virus" somehow escaped from the USARMIID lab in Fort Detrick during a monkey experiment. The USARMIID now stores those same blood viruses in their laboratory under the name of "Ebola Reston" virus. Fortunately for mankind, the catastrophic epidemic never came about. The filoviruses seem to mutate, strike certain areas, weirdly die out, and just as mysteriously reappear again. The Marburg and the Ebola viruses have been basically forgotten by all but the scientific world, lying in some form of viral hibernation, waiting silently to one day strike again.

TAINTED BLOOD

September 17th, 1992
OMAHA, NEBRASKA

During the night a freak blizzard struck the city. In less than two hours, howling, gale force winds whipped blinding snow into drifts across ice-covered highways. Normally placid midwesterners, basking the day before in the warm autumn sun, had been thinking of nothing other than fall crops, pheasant hunting and the beginning of the "Big Red" football season. Yet within six hours, those hardy folks had the snowplows out and the city was starting to function for the work day as though disasters occurred like clockwork.

Even at the height of the storm, the air strip at Omaha's U.S. Strategic Air Command and the Eppley International Airport stayed open. The city's largest employer, Medical Reference Laboratories, Inc., was able to receive its usual airfreighted packages of blood samples. These sanguine vials of fluid were shipped in daily from around the world to be analyzed for various diseases by MRL scientists.

The blood samples were labeled by number only. A patient's name was kept private by the originating clinics, hospitals and physicians when the blood was sent to the laboratory. However, if a blood sample tested positive for human-immunodeficiency-virus (HIV), its number would then be matched with a patient's name. Medical Reference Laboratory contacted the clinic, hospital or physician with the positive test result and at the same time entered the data into a computerized government data base at the Centers for Disease Control (CDC) in Atlanta, Georgia.

When the vials of fluid were unpackaged, MRL technicians would code the blood samples in increments of odd 1000's. Numbers 1000–1999 were analyzed from nine a.m. to ten a.m. The next lot of 3000–3999 would be analyzed from ten a.m. to eleven a.m., and so on through 9000–9999, the last samples of the day, which were analyzed from three p.m. to four p.m. All the samples were analyzed in an upstairs laboratory using Medical Reference Laboratories' patented diagnostic test kits, along with the FDA-approved Western blot analysis. When the analyses were completed, the vials were spun in a centrifuge to prevent coagulation. They were then refrigerated to forty degrees Fahrenheit, hung on stainless steel racks, and put on a sterile conveyor belt to a downstairs laboratory.

The downstairs lab technicians manually cross-checked the previous test results, using different diagnostic tools. All blood samples were tested again for HIV. This time the diagnosis was made by a demonstration of antibody to the virus, using an enzyme-linked-immunosorbent-assay.

Acronymed, the ELISA method. This test for HIV had far greater accuracy than the Western blot test used earlier upstairs.

The downstairs lab technician fed the final analysis into a MRL computer, which should then show a match with the upstairs test results. However, if a sample tested positive for HIV or for any one of the Centers for Disease Control's list of complicating illnesses associated with HIV, the lab tech would also feed that same-numbered blood sample into the CDC's central computer in Atlanta. That data was then forwarded to the medical facility or physician which had ordered the test. They in turn would provide the Center's for Disease Control with the name of the individual who tested positive.

A simple and so far, safe and reliable method of testing.

The following morning at exactly nine-twenty a.m., samples 1000–1999 rolled into view downstairs on the metal conveyer belt. Lab tech Kim Yew, hairnet in place, put on her scrubs, goggles, surgical mask and rubber gloves. Medical Reference Laboratories took no chances on employees becoming infected with any of the diseases they tested.

Usually complacent, Kim Yew's mind was wandering. The message on her answering machine from her boyfriend had said it was urgent she meet him at MacDonalds for lunch. She was terrified that he was getting "cold feet" and was going to break off their relationship. Her eyes moistened at the thought.

Kim picked up blood sample 1021. She looked closer—no, it was 9021. Some niggling thought wavered in the back of her mind, then vanished. Images of Ron rose to the forefront of her thoughts. What could be so urgent? She thought worriedly ahead to their lunch date. Maybe the blizzard would prevent him from making it into the city to meet her and they could discuss the problem later.

On the tube she held in her hand, a tiny drop of fluid had spilled during the coagulation process and smudged the first digit—making the 1 look more like a 9. Normally thorough, Kim should have immediately spotted the error, but not on this day.

With a glass dropper she placed a few drops of the tainted blood in the augur gel and antigens of a perforated quantiplate, unaware that this sample had already tested positive for HIV in the upstairs lab. This test quickly verified that the blood was HIV positive. Its cluster designation 4 (CD4 helper) cell count was 400 parts per milliliter of blood. 1,100 to 1,800 was normal. A very high cytomegalovirus (CMV) index also showed. This was not at all unusual, for CMV was one of the most prevalent illnesses associated with AIDS. Yet this ratio for CMV was so exceptionally high, the highest she had ever recorded, that it made this particular test lodge in her memory.

What did not register in her love-distracted mind, was that it was then only nine forty-five a.m. and therefore the blood sample number could not have been 9021! Only numbers 1000-1999 came down from the upstairs lab between nine and ten a.m. Nonetheless, using her terminal's built-in high speed modem, she entered the HIV-positive test result under the number 9021 into the Centers for Disease Control's computer in Atlanta. A few more keystrokes entered the data in the Medical Reference Laboratory computer as well. Then she cued the computer to contact the physician who forwarded this blood sample for testing. A Doctor Franklin D. Nelsen—at the Berlinger Clinic.

The rest of Kim Yew's morning droned along uneventfully. She could see from the window that the blizzard was still raging outside. No other exceptional tests appeared and Kim gossiped happily with her bench partners as they worked. When lunch hour arrived, she ran through the storm to meet Ron. She could see his four-wheel drive Blazer, with its huge knobby snow tires, parked in front of the yellow, red and orange restaurant, and nervously rushed through the melting slush.

Ron greeted her, smiling nervously as she slid into the booth. He took out a small jewelry box and opened it.

" I just couldn't wait any longer. My little princess, will you marry me?"

Blushing, crying, and *relieved,* Kim said, "Oh yes, yes! But we have to wait until we can afford it!"

Excited, he nodded his head in agreement, then put a minuscule diamond engagement ring on her dainty finger then leaned across the table to plant a kiss on her forehead.

When Kim returned to the laboratory that afternoon she was in a daze of happiness. The only thing on her mind was the dull glint of her engagement ring under the translucent latex glove she wore. Right after three p.m., she plucked the real blood sample 9021 out of the sampling rack. But she did not yet recall the mistake of the morning. Absentmindedly, she examined the blood under her microscope. Again she recorded one of the highest ratios of cytomegalovirus she had ever tested. It was as high as the one she tested that morning. Yet, she still did not realize her error. It was only when she went to put her second results of test number 9021 into the CDC computer that she saw the green and black monitor screen highlight a warning—blood test number 9021 had already been recorded that day as having tested positive for CMV and HIV!

In a nanosecond she knew what she had done that morning. She quickly dialed the Centers for Disease Control in Georgia.

A male southern drawl answered. "CDC hotline. How can I help y'all?"

Kim said nervously, "This is the head lab tech for Medical Reference Labs up in Omaha." It was a little white lie. "We sent down a positive HIV on an early test today by modem. It was numbered 9021." Kim could hear the CDC technician key in the data on his computer as soon as it left her lips, but she continued talking, "By any chance have you recorded that entry yet?"

"We sure enough have, ma'am. Y'all be happy to know that we even forwarded the information to the Berlinger Clinic that the patient's blood sample had tested twice as HIV positive."

Icy panic raced through Kim Yew's veins. An error of this magnitude would certainly stifle any promotion. Company policy was that she could be terminated! She could not get fired. Not now. She was about to get married to an American citizen. She was sure she was ready for her promotion—maybe they would strip her of her green card and work visa and have her deported! Fear flooded her soul. She finally responded,

"Thanks. Thanks a lot. We were just double checking," and quickly hung up.

Other blood tests were now backed up and sat idle on Kim's lab bench. They needed to be completed before five o'clock.

She decided to cover up her mistake.

The laboratory had a waste refrigerator in the basement where they stored by-products left over from the daily testing before disposal. Kim's smile and personal security card got her by the guard on duty. She was shaking, not because it was almost freezing in the lab's refrigerator, but because she was terrified. She found the test tube numbered 9021 that she had analyzed that morning and examined it closely. Under the smudge, the number clearly should have been 1021. How she could have been so stupid! She realized that the person with number 1021 had high HIV titers and probably less than a year to live. *The other person behind test number 9021, Scott Reid, had only an extreme case of cytomegalovirus. He would be ill for some time, but he would live!* He would find out later that he did not have HIV and would in all probability be forever grateful to the doctor who informed him. Whoever Scott Reid was, why would he pursue the matter any further? It also seemed to Kim that it was highly unlikely that anyone could ever trace the mistake back to her as long as she registered the original blood test number 1021 as HIV positive. She did just that with both of the computers—the laboratory's own and the computer at the Centers for

Disease Control in Atlanta. She punched in test number 1021 as having tested HIV positive, then put some contaminated blood from test tube 1021 into vial 9021 and sent it upstairs for reanalysis. The company computer would match her findings on the real test 9021.

Scott Reid was now labelled as having tested positive for HIV. And Kim Yew wondered, who could really be harmed by her coverup?

September 25, 1992
BEVERLY HILLS, CALIFORNIA

Yaps echoed throughout the bedroom. A hand shot out from under a white satin sheet to press down a black button on the headboard console. A heavy pair of salmon-colored drapes hummed apart over the large glass doors, letting in the early morning light. By habit, Scott reached blindly over to the other side of the bed, searching the cold sheets for the warmth of Rebecca, even though it had been years since she had slept in his bed. His tabby, Ginger, curled up at his feet, and greeted him with a yawn and meow before scurrying hungrily down to the kitchen.

Scott woke up feeling terrible. He knew immediately that he was not going to make it to the office that day. The air conditioning had left him stiff-muscled and he grudgingly sat up to look out the window. The city below was choked with a thick cloud of grit. Smog hung in the sky like a damp gray blanket, casting a pall over the vast county. The Los Angeles summer had been miserable and the unhealthful air alerts had carried over into the autumn. The days had been hot and sticky, although many nights were cool enough for a sweater.

Scott Reid's home was on Coldwater Canyon Drive, hidden by a large coppice of scrub oak trees and oleander in front of the property, and by a National Forest which backed onto the rear. It was a comfortable two-story, rough-hewn wooden structure, with a log cabin guest house in the rear along with a swimming pool and a red clay tennis court, that Scott had built to his own specifications.

An invitation to his standing Sunday tennis match was a sporting event as cherished as a courtside seat at a Lakers game. His overly plump, live-in housekeeper, Rosa Martinez, would serve her homemade tacos to all comers. The players usually included the athletes, celebrities and politicians who made the entertainment business run.

Scott forced himself out of bed and sleepily eased through stretching exercises in front of the sliding glass door. As he watched, a chubby, black-masked raccoon and her four coal-eyed babies wandered into the back yard and knocked the lid off a metal garbage can. It was no wonder the dogs had been barking. The lawn was littered with brownish-yellow sycamore leaves and at the loud sound of the lid's fall, the raccoons scampered into the woods, leaving fluttering leaf debris in their wake. Scott always found it odd that amid the hustle and bustle and mass of humanity in southern California, the tree-filled canyons surrounding Beverly Hills were full of wildlife. As bad as he felt, he grinned as the lid rolled down the cement walkway by the guest house and clanged into the terra-cotta brick siding of the swimming pool. He used the remote switch on the television and resumed his leg squats.

Scott had been ill, on and off, for over three months. He had fevers, night sweats, mild diarrhea, exhaustion and a bronchial cough that would not go away. Half the time he felt disoriented. Today, he decided to imitate most of the population of Los Angeles and seek refuge by the ocean. He stopped stretching and rang for Rosa. As usual, he jokingly pleaded with her, half in broken Spanish and half in English.

"Buenos dias, Rosa. Desayuno, por favor. I feel horrible." Rosa grinned through her large, well-lipsticked lips. She adored her boss.

"Hola, buenos dias, Senor Scott. Si, I know jour seek. Jou want jour breakfast right away?"

"Si si si. I'll be down in an hour. I want to catch the news."

"Jou mean, no no no. Not, si si si. Un hora no es right away."

Rosa loved to put her boss straight. He liked it, too. She started singing and made his usual breakfast of toasted wholegrain bread smeared with creamy Jiff peanut butter, a lemon lowfat yogurt, and a steaming mug of Earl Grey tea.

After watching CNN's business news and weather report for September 29th, Scott put on swim trunks, jumped into a blue Fila track outfit and rambled downstairs to the large, country kitchen table. His yellow canary, Big Bird, happily hopping around his cage, whistled a cheerful good morning. By then Rosa was busy vacuuming the living room and ignored Scott, so he quickly ate his breakfast, poured a mug of tea to go and drove his black Porsche Turbo to Malibu Beach.

He lay all day like a lazy reptile, screened by a white canvas beach umbrella from the pollution downtown and from the hills which loomed around the valley where his office was located. Even the abundance of tanned, buxom, bikini-clad women parading up and down the sand did nothing to make him feel better. Nor did the greasy, foot-long hot dog smothered in chili that he bought from a strolling vendor.

As the sun started to head west and down for the night, Scott watched a flock of seagulls silhouetted against the flaming ball of orange. They shrieked as they hovered over a small fishing trawler that was dumping unused bait in front of Alice's Restaurant. Once the sun dipped behind the pier, an immediate chill drifted in over the waves. He slipped on his track suit and tennis shoes and hiked up the small, steep red sandstone cliff to where his car was parked. As he headed the Porsche onto Sunset Boulevard toward his house, he automatically punched the code for his home telephone on the mobile phone panel. The answering machine beeped endlessly; the tape was full. With a final raucous beep, the first message started. Scott smiled to himself and checked his teeth in the rear view mirror for chunks of greasy hot dog. He recognized the familiar Texas twang. But the familiar voice spoke softly, in long drawn-out words, almost in slow motion.

"Scott, you must know I didn't want to leave this news

on your goldang answering machine. I don't even like the things. But when you were back here for your tests last week, you told me if I couldn't reach you, to leave it on your tape. Well, I haven't been able to reach you at your car or your office all day, so please, Buddy, understand—I've double-checked what I'm telling you."

There was a long silence. The strangely nervous voice was his old college roommate, Franklin Nelsen, now a Berlinger Clinic internist. Scott could visualize his pal sitting in his office in an extra-large green hospital gown, with a surgical mask drawn up over his capped afro. Scott was now speeding, snaking down the winding boulevard toward home. Once past the UCLA campus, he downshifted hard for an upcoming corner just in time to spot a motorcycle cop parked ahead behind a clump of trees. As the speedometer fell, Nelsen's foreboding voice continued.

"Scott, I'll give it to you straight. *You checked positive for HIV.*"

Scott listened, nonplussed. This could *not* be possible. His mind raced through the facts. He never used condoms, but he'd relied on a knowledge of medical statistics that told him he had about as much chance of contracting AIDS as of getting hit by lightning. Immunodiagnostics was his business and he was educated about HIV and AIDS. Plus which, things like this did not happen to the Scott Reids of the world!

Scott floored the Porsche and the turbo impellers screamed into action. He turned the car up Coldwater Canyon Drive past the Beverly Hills Hotel, heading towards the Mulholland Drive shortcut to his office. As he passed his own house on the canyon road, the tachometer leapt towards 6,500 rpm and the red line. Nelsen had not stopped talking.

"I'm sorry. I'm truly sorry, Buddy. But listen, you can start AZT treatments right away. Potentially, you can live another twenty years with this virus if you take care of yourself. Look, Bud, it's not AIDS yet! What the heck, Scott, you've been in the medical business all your life, you know with all the funds the government's pouring into this disease there must be a cure just around the cor..."

The message ended and the machine beeped that a new recording waited on the tape. Scott was traveling so fast that he had almost reached his office. He pushed the "end" button on the mobile telephone's digital panel before the next message could kick in.

Suddenly, an old, hunched-over jaywalker, with a tattered black coat drooping heavily, staggered out into the middle of the block. Scott swerved to avoid hitting him, then, fishtailing, slammed the brakes hard in front of a redwood and glass office building. He could see the lights of Encino twinkling below as he turned and skidded to a stop in his parking space. A neat sign on a small post reserved it for the Chairman and CEO.

As Scott turned off the car's hot engine, he was sweating heavily. His keen mind was racing. Positive for HIV. That was absurd. He sat for a moment and reviewed his sexual pursuits over the past ten years, since his separation from Rebecca. At first he had tried a procession of relationships to forget the nightmare of his past and had a prolific sex life for years with a multitude of female partners—mostly beautiful, airheaded, Hollywood hopefuls. However, for the past three years he had dated only Pamela

Kramer, his best friend, Josh's, ex-wife—now the world's richest divorcee—a fact she never let anyone forget.

Like many other abandoned orphans, Scott spent a lifetime striving to find an identity and prosper. He replaced his unknown family by immersing himself in the security of an early marriage. Fatefully, it was doomed from the start. He regrouped by leading his company to success. Yet he lived as unpretentious a life as he could under vast financial circumstances. He did, however, indulge in a few material whims. He belonged to the Riviera Country Club. He had his Porsche for pleasure, but usually drove his red, four-on-the-floor, pristine '66 Chevy El Camino. It had 272,000 original miles on the odometer and a "Barry Goldwater for President" sticker on the bumper. It was Rebecca's wedding gift to him and he cherished the memories and the feeling of security the vehicle gave him over the years.

Yet no matter how unassuming Scott tried to make his existence, to most observers and especially to the press, he led a fairytale bachelor life. His romances and financial successes appeared in the pages of every business periodical and gossip column in the States, and for the past two years the tabloids had been constantly spiced with photos of Scott and Pamela Kramer.

Scott got out of the car and closed the door with a solid thump. He pushed the auto alarm button on his ignition key and it gave a reassuring beep. As he walked up to the front of his office building, he wondered if his previous promiscuity had finally caught up with him. His "dayglow" security card radiated a lime green hue as he inserted it in the slot by the laboratories' front door and let himself in. It was 7:30 p.m. and there was not an employee in sight. He was wondering where the usual company guards might be, when a security recording sternly broke the silence.

"Welcome to IMA Laboratories, Incorporated. You have just activated the main security alarm. This alarm is directly connected to the police department and internal security officers for an immediate armed response. Be sure that you deactivate the alarm with your individual authorization card before proceeding further into the laboratory. Thank you."

IMA Laboratories specialized in immunodiagnostic research and development. The rise in the corporation's common stock over the past twenty years had made Scott a very wealthy man. The company had grown to be the largest in the world in this esoteric field of medicine. IMA's sales, size and profits were on such a scale that Scott had ultimately appointed a president and management team to run the daily operations. During the last few years, Scott mostly attended board meetings and flew around the world promoting the company's image and products.

Scott shut off the security device and walked upstairs. His office juxtaposed the medical research testing laboratory and he walked over to a black metal fireproof filing cabinet and unlocked the sliding drawers. The file he pulled out was marked "Personal."

It had been around the first of June when he first started feeling ill. He had suffered for about two weeks before he asked his friend and head corporate physician, Milton Schwartz, to take a Western blot HIV blood test on him. Milton was close enough to Scott that when he found out his boss had once co-captained the Stanford football team, he nicknamed him "Captain."

They drew the blood in Scott's executive office. At the time, the doctor thought Scott was being paranoid, but he surmised that Scott had probably slept with a number of those dreamy-eyed starlets he had seen him with over the past several years. With all the scare talk about AIDS, Milton ran the test as a precaution.

Scott spread out the June test results over his glass-topped desk and aimed the beam of a coiled brass lamp onto the scattered pages. All blood counts were normal. All indexes and titer counts, but one, for cytomegalovirus (CMV), were normal. Basically, it was a clean bill of health. At the time, Doctor Schwartz had said he thought the slightly elevated ratio for cytomegalovirus was the probable cause of Scott's two-month-old symptoms.

It was only when Scott's symptoms worsened in September that he decided to see Nelsen at the Berlinger Clinic and have a complete checkup.

The Berlinger Clinic was renowned as the finest diagnostic hospital in the world. It had been founded in the countryside on the outskirts of Milwaukee at the turn of the century by the famous German inventor and physician, Gerhart Berlinger. He had single-handedly built his clinic into the largest private hospital in America. The chronically sick and the rich and famous from every country on earth came there for treatment and for their annual medical checkups.

Scott had avoided sex with Pamela for a number of months. So how could the Berlinger's laboratory have found him HIV positive? But he also knew that Franklin Nelsen did not make mistakes. Therefore, he had to re-check the June blood test that Milton Schwartz had run and compare it to the new Berlinger lab test immediately.

Scott took off his shirt and hung it on the back of his leather desk chair, then removed a twenty-two gauge needle from its paper packet and a ten cc syringe and suction tube set from a medical supply drawer in the filing cabinet and walked to the executive bathroom. He switched on the light and in the full-length mirror at the end of the room saw that he was covered in dripping perspiration. He could smell the acrid sweat and was visibly shaking. He swabbed a cotton ball of alcohol over the crook of his left arm, but could not work the needle into the vein. He slapped the syringe on the counter in frustration and analyzed himself in the mirror.

He was forty-eight years old, but looked much younger than his age. He was always tanned; crow's feet spread toward his temples and two weathered seams ran down the cheeks. Streaks of grey tinged his sideburns. The irises of his eyes were deep blue and the small black pupils were penetrating. His eyes were his best physical features and women found them irresistible. Now, the blue orbs just looked tired. His lips had a kissable pucker about them and he blew a sigh of air from between them.

He searched his body for HIV indications. He could find none. There were no signs of fungal infection around the mouth or any other mucous membranes. No blotches anywhere. He took off his shoes and socks to examine his feet. No purple spots around the toes or toenails—the deadly stigma of Kaposi's sarcoma. No macular rashes of any sort. He should have been relieved. Instead, he felt terrible.

He ran his hands through his damp hair. It had been receding for some time; he put a dab of mousse gel on his fingers and combed the brown strands straight back in the manner of most balding European men. Although he had lost about ten pounds during his recent illness he still weighed one hundred seventy-five and was slightly over six feet tall. The image in the bathroom mirror showed a small belly from too much beer after tennis and golf. No amount of sit-ups would alleviate the bulge.

He took a towel and dried himself off, then squeezed the towel as hard as he could in his left hand. A large, blue vein popped up in the forearm and he painfully inserted the needle into it. The blood flowed a chunky, dark red into the container. After it was full, he took the tube over to the refrigerator in the laboratory next door, then dialed his corporate physician at the doctor's home.

"Milton, Scott here."

"Top of the evening, Captain. What's up?"

"I need a favor. I'm leaving some blood in your lab's fridge tonight. I want you to run a new HIV test on it A.S.A.P. in the morning. Do it in private and get back to me immediately. I'm feeling lousy and want to see if we can find anything new."

Milton Schwartz was a sixty-year-old medical doctor, lifelong bachelor and closet homosexual. He was the first scientist Scott had hired upon opening IMA Laboratories and he was now the director of IMA research and development. His curriculum vitae read like a Nobel Prize winner's. Phi Beta Kappa, he had graduated with honors from Columbia and received his M.D. from the Johns Hopkins University School of Medicine. He was former head of research at the National Institute of Health and had seven patents to his credit in the field of immunodiagnostics. But Milton Schwartz was an oddball in the medical community. He constantly challenged protocol and the establishment.

When Scott called, Milton was sitting on his sofa watching a football game, puffing his ever-present pipe. He was thinking how much he missed Howard Cosell's acerbic analysis of the game.

"Captain, will do. Say, what did the Berlinger find out?"

Carefully, Scott said, "Nothing of any importance. Same as you did. Just a little CMV and Frank's going to rerun this last test. So I thought we should rerun our own test at the same time. I'd appreciate it if you keep the results between us. Good night, Milton."

As Scott locked the laboratory, the security recording droned its ominous warning.

"You are now leaving IMA Laboratories. Be sure to reactivate all systems or there will be an armed response from the police department. Thank you."

It was a little after eight-thirty when Scott drove home, coughing most of the way. Rosa, dressed in her crisp black and white uniform, was there to greet him. She said in her happy mixture of Spanish and English, "Hola, Meester Scott. Buenos tardes. Jour tamales es ready. They es on mesa."

"Muchas gracias, Rosa."

He was not hungry, but out of respect for Rosa's efforts, he picked at the food for a few minutes before going upstairs to his room to rest.

Before dozing off, Scott kicked off his shoes, lay down on the bed, put his hands behind his head and stared at the ceiling. Ginger jumped up on the bed beside him, nuzzling his chin.

An hour later, Scott got up from the bed with a throbbing head and checked his watch. With a two-hour time difference between Wochester, Wisconsin and California, Scott figured Nelsen had enjoyed enough time to have finished his dinner. He dialed Franklin's home number.

Nelsen answered his own telephone. He had not eaten, for he was worried about Scott and did not have his usual voracious appetite.

"Scott, good to hear your voice. I knew you'd call as soon as you got my message. I'm sorry, Buddy. But let's talk about what we're going to do about this HIV problem."

Having published innumerable papers on internal medicine over the years, Franklin was a luminary in the medical world.

"Frank, hold on a minute." Scott said. "I've got some tests I'm running in the morning to recheck your results. You see, I had a HIV blood test run on me in June and it was negative. I've had no sex between the time I took that test and the time I saw you. So I think there's something strange in your results and I want to see what my own tests show tomorrow before we discuss this any further."

Franklin sighed heavily into the phone. "Look, Buddy,

I know it's hard to accept this kind of news, but you're going to find out tomorrow that we don't make mistakes here at the Berlinger or at our lab in Omaha. I double checked with them down in Nebraska and your test result was still positive for HIV!"

His headache was killing him and Scott lay back on the bed, then raised his voice in protest.

"Maybe you didn't hear me, Frank, Milton's test in June was negative!"

"Heck, Bud, you know there's lots of reasons your June test could have been negative. Hey, I only want to do what's best for you. And I want to get you on a treatment program immediately."

Scott realized Nelsen was only trying to be helpful. He sighed.

"What did you have in mind, Frank?"

"Well, they've been having tremendous results with azidothymidine out at San Francisco General and I could get you in their program next week. As a matter of fact, I've already called for you."

Scott exploded. "Wait just a damn minute, Frank! Do you think I'm going to go into some general hospital with a bunch of homosexuals infected with AIDS and get treatment? After all, your test results only show an exposure to the HIV antibody, not that I have anything. Christ, I suppose you've also already put my name into the Centers for Disease Control's computer as an HIV carrier?"

Offended, Nelsen replied, "Scott, first of all, you as a man who knows medicine and as a benefactor to the AIDS cause, must know that worldwide AIDS is primarily a heterosexual disease. This homosexual thing is an aberration in America. We physicians don't seem to know why."

Scott sat up, holding his head and shouted into the telephone, "I damn well know why! It's a typical medical and governmental cover-up, but nobody out here in L.A. seems to know that! People have been duped for so long, everyone's going to think I'm some kind of closet queen who's been spending his nights in West Hollywood bars!"

"Come on, Scott," Franklin said gently. "Forget about your macho and let me help you get well. You know, Buddy ...one of the big problems with AIDS carriers is dementia."

"Frank, I'm not an AIDS carrier!"

"That's not the lab's opinion, Scott. You're getting me worried with this nonsense. I'm sure you can understand I didn't personally put your name in any government computer. My associates at the lab down in Omaha do that automatically when a test is positive after a double check. Calm down, Bud, and have a good night's sleep. Call me tomorrow when you get your blood results back. We'll work out what's best for you then."

Scott heaved another sigh.

"You're right, Frank. Sorry I was so short. But I want my name off that computer as soon as I forward my test results here in California. I don't want to be ostracized because someone's made a mistake!"

Nelsen lectured often, yet when it came to bedside medicine, he went through torment before he could tell anyone they had a potentially terminal illness. Giving the news to his best friend churned in his gut like a red-hot iron.

Franklin was one of life's true innocents. He was a member of the NAACP. He was a blind patriot and had joined the National Guard. He was a staunch Baptist who had never smoked or touched alcoholic drink. He believed in the system—the American way.

In the spring of 1965 he was drafted number one by the Pittsburgh Steelers, but he turned them down to go to medical school and to get married. After he married Matty Jones, they moved to Wisconsin so Franklin could do his residency in internal medicine at the Berlinger Clinic. They never left and had five sons in the next six years.

Franklin had seen the lab's report of the extreme drop in Scott's CD-4 cell count to around four hundred per milliliter of blood—about a third of normal. And he felt it might not take the HIV long to develop into AIDS unless Scott started medical treatment immediately. Although he was very worried about his friend, he reminded himself that with the proper treatment, Scott could lead a normal life for some years to come.

Balancing all of this, Franklin replied compassionately, "Scott, I'll do all I can if you can prove to me you're not HIV positive."

Scott grunted, "I'll get you the proof as soon as possible."

Franklin continued, "If you recall, when you were back here, I told you Matty and I are leaving at the end of the week for Kenya for two solid months of escape from humanity. I know it's not the best timing with the news I just gave you, so I'll cancel the trip and fly out to see you if you want me to help you get this straightened out."

Scott heard the call waiting beep. "Hold on a minute,

Frank. There's another call coming in. I'll be right back with you." He pressed the button on the phone and a soft voice chimed.

"It's me, darling."

"I'm sorry, Pamela. I'm on the other line. A bit of an emergency. I'll get back to you as soon as possible."

"Please. I'm at home and I'll be worried sick until I hear from you."

Scott jabbed the button again.

"Sorry, Frank. Look, Matty's been planning this trip for a long time. I'm telling you I'll be all right while you're gone and I'll have proof of my negative status before you leave. Don't you dare change your plans!"

Franklin did not believe that Scott was going to be able to refute the Berlinger Clinic findings, but he stilled the thought.

"Well, then, I could kill two birds with one stone, because first I'm going to stop in Nairobi at your African AIDS Center to catch up on what they're doing. Who knows, maybe they can be of some help to you."

"That's what I want to hear, Frank. What else is on your agenda?"

"Then we go on an elephant caravan safari. You'll be happy to know that I bought a new video camera, so I can show you the tapes of the hospital and of our trip when I get back. Now get some rest, Bud, and we'll decide what to do before I leave and have this problem straightened out by the time I get back."

Scott was perspiring and the telephone receiver felt slippery in his hand.

"I hope so, big fella. I still feel like crap. Thanks for

everything. Say, before I go, who does the blood testing for you down in Omaha?"

"We use Medical Reference Laboratories. They're terrific and they're now the biggest and best in the world."

Scott hung up disheartened. He reached over and scratched Ginger's head. He knew Medical Reference Laboratories was owned by Josh Kramer. Scott was a former shareholder of the company and had been ejected from two shareholders' meetings for voicing his concern that no percentage of the corporation's profits were being used for research and AIDS patient care. He had sold all of his holdings in August of 1991. Scott was always giving to charities. He felt he owed this to the world for his own good fortune, so he donated the five million he made from his sale of stock to build a non-profit AIDS research hospital in Nairobi.

There are no corporate taxes in Nevada, and for that reason, Gino Rigitinni, Medical Reference Laboratories' legal counsel, incorporated the company in that state in 1982. Its trading symbol on the New York Stock Exchange became MRL.

According to the Forbes 400 list of the richest people in America, Josh Kramer was listed as third wealthiest, worth over five billion dollars. He had put up the original seed money for MRL's capital base. Although that monetary infusion had given him majority control of the company's common stock and the chairmanship of the board of directors, he had nothing to do with the day-to-day management. MRL was just one of his many sizeable assets.

The Board of Directors was composed of a former president of the United States, a Nobel Prize winner in chemistry, five CEOs of major medical companies, and the lawyer, Gino Rigitinni.

The silver-maned Rigitinni represented a Netherlands Antilles offshore corporation named Zafra Limited, which held an eighteen percent equity ownership of Medical Reference Laboratories' common stock. He also represented the Mafia. He was wined, dined and invited to tennis by the Washington bureaucratic elite. The word on the street was that he even had the ear of the White House. He also had no scruples.

Although they were not friends, Gino Rigitinni had a tacit agreement with Josh Kramer. As long as the corporation was profitable they voted their shares together. Rigitinni made sure that each year MRL's common stock was split in some manner for the benefit of the shareholders. He made sure no preferred stock, or any other form of diluting stock was ever issued. He also made certain no cash dividends were ever going to be paid to shareholders, as dividends for offshore corporations are tax deducted at the source of payment at a rate of thirty percent. An offshore corporation pays no capital gains tax whatsoever on its U.S. common stock transactions. In other words, Zafra Limited paid no taxes on MRL common stock that it resold for capital gain—and it had done a great deal of that.

Kramer had hired Ralph Landen, a former Washington lobbyist for the pharmaceutical industry, to run Medical Reference Laboratories as President and CEO. Landen's wife, Joyce, and Josh's ex-wife Pamela were best friends, and the four of them had socialized a great deal during the Kramer's marriage. Landen ran a profitable, growing company. He was a strict disciplinarian in business and his political influence landed MRL one government contract after another. He became a protege of Josh Kramer's, and thought of himself as a man destined for bigger things.

Medical Reference Laboratories' most valuable asset was a patent for quantitative testing of HIV and AIDS blood titer counts. (A titer measures the extent to which a sample of blood serum containing antibody can be diluted before losing its ability to cause clumping of the relevant antigen.) Rigitinni realized that once AIDS became an epidemic in the public mind, MRL had a monopoly. He spent a fortune on advertising the danger of AIDS and Ralph Landen encouraged his cronies in Washington to do the same. Scare tactics became commonplace in public advertising for HIV and AIDS.

Testing blood for HIV and AIDS was big business for the insurance industry and Medical Reference Labs signed contracts with all the major insurers. Private clinics, hospitals and Medicare facilities flocked to use MRL's patient testing facilities in Omaha, Nebraska. Blood testing became a three billion dollar per annum business worldwide. One third of this business, one billion dollars per year, went to MRL. In a little over ten years, it became the largest blood testing facility in the world. Sales soared and the company's common stock was split in some fashion every single year in the decade. Lucky shareholders made fortunes and the corporation rapidly became the darling of Wall Street.

❧

The jacuzzi in Scott's bedroom sparkled and bubbled bright aquamarine as he switched on the power. It faced the giant screen television across the wood-beamed room. The Los Angeles Rams and the Raiders were playing the last of the meaningless preseason games. Scott muted the sound. While waiting for the water to heat, he took a Corona from the drawer in his nightstand, lit it, lay back on his king-size circular bed and dialed Pamela's home telephone number. Ginger was intently watching the bubbles surface in the jacuzzi like a spectator at a tennis match.

"Castle Rock, Hubert speaking."

Pamela Kramer *never* answered her own telephone in the main house.

Hubert was Pamela's manservant. He was a pallid, rotund, bushy-haired man who was always in formal attire. He was English, but pronounced his name like the French, with a silent "h" and "t".

"Ah, Hubert, nice to hear your voice. This is Scott Reid. Is Pamela available to speak with me?"

In a polished Belgravia accent, Hubert replied,

"Mr. Reid. So very nice to hear your voice. Mrs. Kramer has informed me that she is not to be disturbed until she has finished with her trainer. Would you like me to have her give you a bell later?"

"Yes, Hubert. Tell her I shall be home all evening."

The cigar relaxed Scott. He coughed and laughed to himself over Hubert's pompous ways. Before he could put the telephone down, Hubert replied.

"Mr. Reid, I shall inform her immediately of your call."

The jacuzzi was scalding hot as Scott went to hop in. He always seemed to forget about the temperature. It was only when steam started rising from the tub and accumulating on the face of the TV that he remembered to turn down the thermostat. He put his portable telephone on a towel next to the deep wooden tub and sat down gratefully with the water up to his neck. A thick purple bougainvillea vine curled around the stained-glass windows of his bathroom. He popped open an ice-cold can of beer and zapped the remote, cranking up the sound so he could hear the name of the kicker who won the game for the Raiders with a last-second field goal. He then turned off the television. The strong jets shot hot streams of pulsating water onto his aching body and he turned one onto the bruised inner part of his left arm where he had drawn blood. It was the first time in a week when he did not feel horrible. He sat for twenty minutes in bliss.

The ringing of the telephone brought him back to reality.

"Darling, it's me."

This was Pamela's standard opening line to Scott. She never announced her name.

"I've been through the mill with this new trainer. Thirty minutes on the Stairmaster. What a great butt I'm getting. God, I'm getting sexier by the workout, which since we don't seem to have sex anymore probably doesn't interest you in the least."

Scott knew that as soon as she finished talking about herself, she would get to the fact he had called her earlier.

"Speaking of you, my darling, what was your emergency all about? I was worried sick."

So worried that Hubert wouldn't let him talk to her earlier, thought Scott.

"It turned out to be nothing. Only business."

"I'm glad. And I'd like to get a little business from you. Are you feeling okay? Because I'm getting a little horny for that old body of yours."

The bubbles from the hot tub frothed around his shoulders, Scott took a quick swig of beer and said, "I'm starting to feel..."

Pamela rudely cut him off. "By the way, did you get the test results back from Franklin yet? I mean, you didn't call me to tell me you had AIDS or something, did you?"

She giggled over her own macabre humor.

The ephemeral state that the warm jacuzzi had put him in made Scott want to tell her everything that had happened. Common sense prevailed.

"Pamela, I'm only this minute feeling I'm going to live. I'm sitting here in my jacuz, having a cold beer and soaking like a lazy turtle. I'm also more than a little horny for your body. I just don't want to do anything about it until I get all my test results back from the Clinic."

Cunningly, while admiring her profile in the stage-lighted bathroom mirror, Pamela asked, "Pretty please?"

"My dearest little Arab, I don't want to give you something infectious just for a roll in the hay."

While brushing her hair with one hand, Pamela purred ruefully, "You mean you haven't heard anything at all from the Berlinger?"

Scott did not want Pamela to know there had been a mistake made. He decided to stall for time.

"Frank did call, but the tests were inconclusive about some bug he found and he's going to rerun them. Did you know the Berlinger doesn't use their own labs for testing everything and if this isn't ironic, they use Medical Reference Laboratories down in Omaha for most of their blood tests? You remember the lab Josh founded years back—and he's now making another fortune from?"

Laughing, Pamela said, "I remember they kicked you out of a shareholders' meeting and you sold your stock and then like a fool, spent all the money building that stupid AIDS hospital in Kenya!"

Scott rose to the bait with an indignant growl. "Don't be so small-minded regarding what I do with my money! And that episode with the MRL directors wasn't funny. Even though I was proud of Josh for sticking up for my right to be heard."

"Aren't we the touchy one tonight?"

"Pamela, I'd like you to know that the hospital I built appears to be the only charity doing anything constructive about the AIDS problem. So, my dear, in response to your inquisition, no, I don't have AIDS!"

Pamela felt better hearing that—and very hungry. She puckered her freshly lined lips and begged, "Darling, do you think we could ditch the papparazzi just once and sneak off to Mr. Chow's by ourselves for some smoked duck? I could meet you there in an hour."

"Sounds good to me, but it's almost ten. I'll have to call down and make sure we can get in. If you don't hear from me in five minutes, I'll see you there."

Pamela waited until ten minutes had passed, then had Hubert telephone her favorite paparazzo photographer regarding her upcoming rendezvous with Scott at Mr. Chow's. She prepared for her entrance by dressing in one of Chanel's sexiest black sequinned outfits, which she had purchased that afternoon on Rodeo Drive. Provocatively, she sprayed all the sensual parts of her anatomy with Dior's *Poison!*

Reservations being no problem, Scott slipped on a pair of Levi's, pulled a silk black crewneck sweater over his head, grabbed a black and white hounds-tooth cashmere jacket from a hanger and put on a black pair of suede boots. He topped it off with a black cowboy Stetson.

He felt exhausted and his skin was clammy as he walked down to the garage, got into the shiny El Camino and drove toward the restaurant. He stopped at a street-side floral vendor and purchased a large bouquet of red carnations for Rosa. Their smell reminded him of funerals but he knew Rosa loved them. He picked out a small blue primrose corsage for Pamela.

Forty-two-year-old Pamela Kramer had the looks of a movie star and the manners of royalty in public, but in private she loved acting like a whore. She often ran personal ads in an L.A. singles paper and would then meet men who answered in seedy hotel rooms for an afternoon of sex. Carrying a purseful of multicolored condoms, she would dress in a black leather S and M costume, complete with mask so she would not be recognized. She had a motto—a hard man is good to find!

She was regal, tall, and willowy. Six foot, with the figure of a fashion model, except for the fact that her breasts were too large for that profession. She was half Saudi Arabian and half British. Her parents died when she was a teenager, yet Pamela made it to the top of the social and monetary heap on her own wits and intuition. She had inherited smooth, olive, unblemished skin from her father. Her jet black hair, which she wore short, had the texture of silk. Her eyes were brown and almond-shaped. Her teeth were capped. They were perfectly white, but they were not perfect. They were too big for her mouth and she always looked as though she were smiling, when in fact, she was most of the time insecure and riddled with depression.

The truth was that, Pamela, whom all believed had no conscience, was suffering relentless remorse over abandoning her illicit daughter to boarding school. She desperately wanted to be loved by a man—but only on her own terms. She felt Josh had never really loved her, nor did Scott, and similar self-pitying thoughts about the absent Melissa looped like an endless tape in her mind. Ultimately, her limitless self-absorption drove her to drink, albeit in private.

Pamela was a clever woman. A meticulous and devious woman. She was half Muslim and half Christian. And a Gemini. It was a wicked genetic, religious, and spiritual combination that led her in relationships to either the starkest truth or total deception.

As Scott pulled up by the valet parking sign in front of Mr. Chow's, the paparazzi were waiting like glittering fireflies. He saw the back of Hubert's bushy head in

Pamela's yellow stretch Bentley by the curb in front of the restaurant. The car was adorned with Pamela's personalized license plates, "P. K." Hubert sat, tapping his fingers rhythmically on the steering wheel while he waited. Cameras flashed and Scott realized that as usual, Pamela was the center of attention. She waited for him on the sidewalk next to the restaurant's entrance. Arms open, breasts bulging and sequins sparkling, she gave him the European two pecks on the cheeks.

"Darling, it's me! Oh, I have the most awful story to tell you."

Scott gave her the corsage. She smiled weakly, and handed it to Hubert. Putting her arm through Scotts, she steered him to the restaurant door.

Dewey, the maitré d' who took Scott's call ordering the Peking duck ready upon their arrival, led them directly to their booth. The restaurant was crowded with celebrities who nodded to them as they passed. Jack Nicholson, Anjelica Huston, Johnny Carson, film director Steven Spielberg and the famous criminal defense attorneys, F. Lee Bailey and Robert Shapiro all dined regularly at this establishment.

Scott ordered *Tsingtao,* a Chinese rice beer for them both. They drank them quickly and ordered another round. The waiters then began to array the steaming food on the table.

Pamela tonged the smoked duck with her ivory chopsticks and daintily placed a few crispy pieces of Scott's favorite cuts on his plate. Scott loved the Arab in this woman, the one who served her man. He was fascinated by her unfathomable heritage and her ability to make him feel like a king with a devoted harem. Sometimes he thought that Pamela was the most loving and sensual woman he had ever met. Yet he knew, too, that like a pet reptile, she might bite him at any moment. He finally chose to be with her for what she was. But most of the time, he did not understand her at all.

As she took a sip from the green-labeled bottle of Chinese beer, she slowly told her sad tale to Scott.

"Darling, I have to tell you the dreadful thing that happened to me yesterday."

Scott could not help thinking, if only she knew what a dreadful thing happened to me!

"You remember Beauty, my prize-winning Black Belgian shepherd? Well, she had the most adorable puppies about ten weeks ago. They grew like weeds and got so fat and cuddly that I hated to think of parting with any of them. So I decided that the young Filipino couple who take care of trimming my botanical garden and who helped raise the puppies for me, should have the first pick of the litter. I asked them if they wanted a dog and they took the biggest and fattest of the lot. A male."

"That was nice of you sweetheart."

Pamela immediately broke into tears.

"Like hell it was! This morning as Hubert was driving me down to Rodeo, I rolled down the window and asked the Filipino boy how the dog was." Pamela really started sobbing. "And the little fucker said, 'Oh, he vely good madam. Vely tasty. We make last night with callots and onions and ginger, madam. Thank you vely much. Vely, vely good stew.'"

Scott held her hand to reassure her, then he started

laughing and coughing uncontrollably.

"Oh, Scott, how can you think that's funny! That dog must have been worth at least two thousand dollars and would have made some little boy a happy camper."

Scott noticed that she had released his hand across the table and he tried to stop laughing, but burst forth in hilarity.

"Your Filipino imitation is pretty good, but you sound awfully mercenary to me, not like an altruistic soul making some little homeless boy happy. Why not look at the bright side? The Filipinos certainly enjoyed your gift."

"Well, they weren't so happy when I fired them! If they want to eat dog, let them go down to the animal pound and eat some scruffy mutt! Not my prize shepherd."

Pamela pouted and continued ruefully, "Let's change the subject, darling. You still don't look a hundred percent. When are you going to get the rest of your test results back from Franklin? Didn't he tell you anything?"

Twinkling beams sparkled from Pamela's diamond earrings as she moved her head, looking Scott up and down like a curious witch doctor.

"My dear, what I think they found is not a topic for mealtime discussion. But scientifically, it's called cytomegalovirus, CMV for short, and there's no cure other than time and rest. The lab found a trace of it in my blood, so I assume that's the cause of my weight loss and other problems."

Between dainty bites of her white rice, Pamela mumbled, "God, for my sake, I hope it isn't catching. How in the world does one get sightoomugoolovirus, or whatever it's called?"

She really thought that Scott had picked up a dose of gonorrhea, or maybe even genital herpes. Scott had not had sex with her for some time and she felt that he was being too secretive. And because of her own sexual proclivities, it was beyond her comprehension that someone might be faithful to her. Scott answered her question.

"Just call it CMV. And you're not going to catch it from me. As I mentioned, the way one contracts it is not good dinner conversation. However, since you ask, Milton says I probably got it from eating human shit."

"You're disgusting. I may throw up at any moment." She opened her mouth and hung out her tongue, "Yuk!" then calmly said, "Pass me the snow peas, will you, dear?" Teasingly, she tilted some cleavage towards him.

Unconsciously, Scott stole a glance and said. "Pamela, CMV's not an uncommon disease, but as my body can tell you, it's not a pleasant one either. So until I get all the facts in the next few days, why don't we just drop this?"

Taunting, Pamela teased, "Aren't we still the touchy one! Is it possible you haven't kept your dick in your knickers lately, my dear?"

Scott frowned. And Pamela continued, "Oh don't look so upset. I'm not in the least bit jealous. I mean, if I have guests over to Castle Rock and I let them eat off of my fine china, after they're finished eating I don't throw out the china. I just have it washed up and eat off of it again. To me, a man's prick is the same way!"

Fuming, Scott removed a sharp sliver of duck bone from his mouth and put it on the side of his plate. Before he could reply, Pamela pouted, "What I really want to know is just who you are fucking because you're certainly not servicing me!"

Pamela gulped down another beer and while peeling off the labels, lined the finished bottle in a row on the table.

"I assure you, there's no other woman in my life and I've just about had enough of your pettiness tonight."

"You know Scott, you men are all the same. Josh is busy screwing his skinny, rug praying Wog secretary and he thinks I don't know, and you think I don't know you're out fucking every little starlet you can find, instead of me. Neither of you ever loved anything but your goddamn businesses!"

It was almost a religious habit with Scott to finish every meal with a snifter of Courvoisier and a Number 4 Monte Cristo cigar, but on this night he heatedly shot back.

"If you want me to be in your life in the future, don't ever speak of my friend Annie in such bigoted terms. Is that perfectly clear?"

Pamela puckered her lips and gazed at Scott with her eyelashes blinking and pleaded, "I'm sorry darling, please don't be angry with me. You're the only man I've ever really loved. You know I just don't have any control over my jealousy. These things always seem to pop out in anger. I don't really mean them."

Scott then blurted, "It's late and I've had a long day and you've had too many beers. Do you mind if we just go home now?"

As Pamela and Scott were leaving their booth, various diners gave sly, knowing grins. Her voice had carried to other tables. Scott stopped at the cloakroom and retrieved his Stetson and Pamela's floral Gucci wrap. When they stepped onto the sidewalk there was a flurry of cameras whirring and flashing.

The whole scene made Scott sick. He hurried home, his energy fading. Grabbing a blue and white patterned vase from the top kitchen cabinet, he took the time to arrange the bouquet of red carnations, placing it on the kitchen table for Rosa. Wearily, he climbed the stairs to his bedroom.

Hubert, humming to himself, steered the lumbering, customized stretch Bentley limo onto the 405 Freeway towards Mulholland Drive. He had pre-mixed a double Southern Comfort whiskey and orange juice in a large Georg Jensen crystal glass for Pamela's ride home. As she sipped it in the back seat, he could hear her talking on the cellular phone to Joyce Landen in Omaha.

"Hello darling, it's me. Joyce, my dear, so sorry to wake you up in the middle of the night like this, but I need a huge favor immediately."

Pamela knew there would be no argument. She had caught pudgy, but homecoming-cute Joyce in bed with a more than well-endowed Mexican soccer player the last time Joyce was visiting her in California. At the time Pamela said to Joyce that she certainly would say no word to anyone—especially her husband, Ralph Landen. It was repayment time!

"Joyce, you know every scientist at MRL's lab, so first thing tomorrow morning, I need you to go to the head of the blood testing division and discreetly get me the test results on Scott Reid. They were sent down last week from the Berlinger Clinic by a Doctor Franklin Nelsen."

Sleepily Joyce responded, "Pamela, my baby. Is this *your* Scott Reid I'm checking on?"

Giggling, Pamela replied, "Never you mind, busybody. Just please do me this favor. When you have the results, fax them to my private line in the house. Honey, I can't tell you how important this is, so please, please, get it to me before noon my time."

"What lovely intrigue! I'll have it to you *before* eight your time," Joyce promised. "Bye."

In the back seat of the Bentley, Pamela gulped the last drops of her whiskey as Castle Rock's security people let Hubert through the electronic gates. He then drove her to the private entrance of her master bedroom suite. She stepped outside into the cool mountain air and entered her domain.

Castle Rock was a mind-boggling phantasmagoria. Even blasé Los Angelenos, accustomed to all sorts of eccentricities, were in awe. Other than the Sultan of Brunei's palace, Castle Rock was considered the largest house in the world. The house was approached through a driveway lined with swaying, pencil-thin coconut palms. The facade was a gaudy, marble-pillared cross between the Taj Mahal and the White House. When the TV program "Lifestyles of the Rich and Famous" toured the property, the show scored the highest viewer rating ever.

The house held the world's largest private collection of Impressionist paintings—van Goghs, Bonnards, Manets, Gauguins, Renoirs, Monets and Degas hung like wallpaper in rooms around the mansion. One of Pamela's passions was her huge collection of Rodin sculptures. The main estate had ceilings twenty feet high, thirty-eight bedrooms, forty bathrooms with bidets in each (Pamela was fanatical about personal hygiene), thirty fireplaces, a movie theater, a bowling alley, a ballroom with stage and orchestra pit and an indoor ice-skating rink. It was furnished with every imaginable Louis XIV antique Sothebys could locate. The carpets came from the Shah of Iran's Palace in Teheran. There was a staff of thirty-two full-time employees, including security guards. On the property was an eight-thousand square foot guest house, two Olympic-size swimming pools, a stadium size tennis court, a private 7,000-yard Nicklaus-designed eighteen-hole golf course, a helicopter pad for her Bell Ranger and an eighty-space garage that housed her vintage collection of fifty cars. There were acres of gardens that Pamela designed herself which rivaled those of Versailles.

Acreage in this wealthy section of Los Angeles on Mulholland Drive averaged about one million dollars an acre. Castle Rock sat on two hundred acres with a 360-degree view of the valley, the Pacific, Los Angeles and the Sierra Nevada mountain range in the background.

Melissa Kramer was now ten. By mutual agreement, Pamela and Josh retained joint custody of the child and put the little girl in a boarding school in Switzerland. This never bothered Josh, as in his business pursuits, he spent as much time in Geneva and Glasgow as in Los Angeles. The arrangement actually gave him more quality time with Melissa, away from the interruptions of Pamela.

Although at first Pamela had begged Josh to let her have the child live with her, once the divorce was final, she selfishly chose to live alone at Castle Rock.

The Henry VIII canopied bed adorned with hanging golden tassels had been turned down and a fire was blazing in the ceiling-high rock fireplace. Pamela checked the top of her cherrywood Jeffersonian writing desk to see that her fax machine was turned on and then went over to the leather-topped bar and built herself another Southern Comfort and orange juice without ice. As she went to put the bottle back on the shelf, she quickly poured in another shot of the aromatic whiskey.

She slept soundly.

At seven thirty a.m. the fax machine rang only once, but it was loud enough to wake her. It clicked and whirred as it spat out a short note on Joyce Landen's letterhead. It read:

"You have an emergency. Test you asked me about is positive for HIV virus. I repeat, POSITIVE! You poor baby. Call me. Joyce.

P.S. For my own protection, you didn't sleep with Juan Carlos, did you?

P.P.S. Don't worry, Honey, I've burned the original of this fax."

A cold shower couldn't have awakened Pamela any quicker. She grabbed the telephone and punched in Joyce's number as if it were an enemy.

"Joyce, what do you mean—positive for HIV? Jesus, we're talking about my life here! When I asked you to check up for me, I was only thinking Scott had the clap or he'd been out fooling around. But Christ, HIV positive! I don't believe it."

"Maybe the rotten bastard's just been lying to you all this time," suggested Joyce.

"Scott's too straight, he wouldn't lie to me. He said he thought he had some other kind of virus. Site-omoogoolo something or other. He was going to have Franklin Nelsen recheck those results right away. Are you sure of what you're saying?"

"Pamela, sweetheart," Joyce replied haughtily, "I've been at the lab since it opened this morning and I personally talked to the head of the blood testing department regarding Scott's results. They double-checked his blood and it was positive *both* times. I even saw the papers the lab sent back to the Berlinger. My God, Pamela, you've got to get to a doctor immediately and get yourself checked. Oh, by the way, you didn't sleep with my little soccer playing friend, did you?"

"Yes, I did!" And Pamela hung up.

When Scott arrived at his office at ten that morning, his secretary informed him that Milton Schwartz had been trying urgently to reach him for the past hour. Pushing up with a forefinger the tortoiseshell glasses which had slipped down her nose, she handed Scott a stack of memos and telephone messages. Scott punched in Doctor Schwartz's extension.

"Good morning, Milton. Obviously you've got some

news on the blood samples. What's up?"

"Morning, Captain. The reason I was trying so hard to reach you is that I now know why you're so damn sick!"

Scott clenched his fist firmly around the receiver

"What is it, Milton? I need it straight."

"Sorry, Captain, but you've got the highest indexes of CMV I've ever seen in a living person. Your ratio is 3:166. Christ, you should be in a hospital! Has this got anything to do with the Berlinger tests and the test we ran last June? I recall a slight elevation in the CMV index then..."

Scott smelled a rat. Elation began a slow surge within him. The bad news was actually bringing relief.

"Milton, are you telling me that there's no sign whatsoever of HIV disease?"

"That's right. I'm happy to report that after two runs and screens of your blood that there's no sign of HIV. Unless the Berlinger lab put you in the CDC's complicating illnesses category!"

Scott could hear the slow sputtering draw of Milton's pipe.

"You'd better check back with Franklin and find out his prescription for your problem. Go home to bed, Scott, and call me if there's anything I can do."

Scott punched off the intercom and rifled through his messages and memos. Physically, he felt terrible. But his mind was simmering.

Pamela Kramer had called three times—Urgent!

Franklin Nelsen had telephoned—Please call back.

Cher had called—she had been asking for two months. Would Scott be the guest speaker at her forthcoming AIDS

Charity Dinner and rock concert next Tuesday night?

"Wizard" had telephoned—Need to speak to Scott about HIV!

Schwarzenegger had called—for tennis at his court in Malibu on Saturday morning. Please confirm today!

There were at least twenty similar messages. The memos were from department heads regarding the day's business schedules. Scott filed them all in a neat pile on his desk. His forehead was hot and he was sweating again. He suppressed a dry cough. Normally a workaholic, he knew he could not continue his regular business routine. He rang his secretary, Linda Powell.

"Yes, Mr. Reid?" Linda's calm voice always soothed him.

She was daily stability, his right hand. He depended on her. Yet the relationship had always been one of a professional nature.

"Linda, please organize the staff's interoffice meetings without me. And put Doctor Schwartz in charge of all medically related issues. I'll call Stan down in finance and he can handle any monetary details that might arise..."

The ticker tape was running rapidly across the bottom of the CNN News Channel on top of his desk and Scott saw that the symbol for Medical Reference Laboratories, MRL, was trading up almost three points for the day. The announcer said there was no news that MRL knew of for the rise in the corporation's stock. Scott continued.

"Linda, I'm feeling horrible and I just want to be alone for the day. I'm going to turn the car phone off. Tell anyone who calls that they can leave a message here or on my machine at home. Also, call Rosa and tell her to have a hot bath ready for me in thirty minutes. Bye, I'm out of here."

"I'll take care of everything, Mr. Reid. Feel better, we'll miss you around here."

Scott drove off, feeling grateful to have such an efficient, caring and devoted employee.

The Blaupunkt stereo in Scott's Porsche blared Pachelbel's "Canon" on the L.A. classical FM station. The violins and cellos soothed his throbbing headache, yet he wanted to cry every time he heard this piece. But even when he was abandoned to an orphanage as a little boy by his drunken mother, Scott *never* cried. Although he came close numerous times after he was told no one knew who his father was.

A quick gear change brought Scott to a smooth halt at a busy light at the intersection of Ventura Boulevard and Coldwater Canyon Drive. He closed his eyes and tilted his head back on the headrest listening to the music. A tattily dressed Rastafarian hitchhiker, with dirty dreadlocks hanging out from under a multicolored knit beret, banged on the driver's window.

"Spare change, mon?"

Scott jumped back to reality. He let the window down and handed the scruffy character a crisp ten dollar bill. A large, scabbed black hand snatched the money up like a sucking vacuum cleaner and then a voice whined sarcastically,

"Thanks a lot, mon. You cheap fucker. Got a fuckin' new Porsche and only give me a fuckin' tenner. Fuckin' capitalist pig!"

Scott drove off shaking his head in disbelief. He then keyed his private office telephone code on the car's digital dialer.

"Linda, call Cher and tell her I can't make her concert, but I'll forward a contribution and to keep up the good work. And call Arnold and cancel tennis for Saturday. Tell him I feel rotten and I couldn't carry him as usual in doubles, but tell him I'll take a raincheck." Scott chuckled into the phone, then continued. "I'll call Frank and Pamela myself if they happen to call back. Thanks, Linda. Bye for now."

Scott then yelled into the telephone before hanging up.

"Wait, Linda, I almost forgot! Tell Wizard I'll call him as soon as I have more news on the HIV thing."

Wizard Stone was a professional basketball star and a close personal friend. He had been diagnosed with HIV, which he got from his dentist. The dentist—a genuine sociopath—was AIDS-infected and had purposely given the disease to numerous people before he died. Wizard was a perennial all-star, arguably the greatest passer and three-point shooter the game had ever known. He was also the only white player to have won the slam-dunk competition in the NBA. When he announced his early retirement from basketball, it created worldwide publicity for HIV.

Scott's elation was short-lived and he just wanted to get home to a hot bath. He floored the Porsche into the sharp, twisting corners going up Mulholland Drive. The steep, treacherous ravines blurred as he sped by. Within minutes he was letting himself in through the electronic front gates. His pair of yellow labradors ran circles of delight around the car. As Scott parked, the male retriever, Hardy, lifted a leg and peed on one of the radial tires. Cloyed steam rose from the metal rim.

As he patted the drooling, jumping dogs and walked into the house, perspiration gathered on Scott's forehead. He felt really ill. The sweat had created dark wet spots under the arms of his blue silk shirt. With a look of motherly concern, Rosa welcomed him. Her cheeks were heavily rouged and her lips coated with bright red lipstick.

"Meester Scott, jour bano es ready. Jour favorite refried beans and flour tortillas es warm for jou when jou finish."

"Gracias, Rosa. You're the greatest."

She smiled proudly and turned crimson.

"Jou look seek. Go upstairs, pronto. Comprendo?"

"Si si."

And Scott lumbered up to his room. He was so exhausted he fell on the bed to relax for a few minutes before taking his bath and calling anyone. His mind slowly wandered to the core of his cerebral cortex and an evening the past summer when he talked about AIDS with Milton Schwartz.

... Doctor Schwartz had sat in the lab, puffing his curved white porcelain pipe while he explained to Scott the cause of cytomegalovirus. He had put two metal mugs of cold, leftover instant coffee on top of a makeshift stove—the Bunsen burner on his lab bench, then inadvertently blew a large breath of rum-scented tobacco into Scott's face.

"Captain, you have a slightly elevated CMV titer. Have

you been out of the country recently?"

"Milton, if you recall, I was down in Mexico City a few months ago for the annual immunodiagnostic convention."

"Well, there's always the chance you ate some food contaminated with human feces. Maybe some lettuce with crap in it was used as fertilizer. This could easily put a little cytomegalovirus into your system. Eat shit and you'll feel like it, I always say!"

Blowing more bluish smoke straight in the air, Milton choked a bit on his own humor, but continued.

"These symptoms should go away in a few weeks with lots of rest and fluids. Your immune system will suppress the CMV in time. The good thing is you don't have to worry about HIV, Captain. You don't have any sign of it."

Scott could recall the potent rush of relief he felt at the time.

"Thanks, Milton. In the back of my mind I was worried as hell about AIDS."

"Captain, as a normal living white heterosexual, what are you so worried about this overblown scare for? *Do you realize that hepatitis kills more people in one day than AIDS kills in a year?*"

"I'm not sure if that should be a relief or not. What if I come down with hepatitis?" Scott said, grinning.

Then came a flood of verbiage from the agitated doctor.

"Don't look so gleeful, Captain, and for a man in your position in life, don't be so damn naive! You're one of the brightest minds in the immunodiagnostic field, but as a businessman, not a medical man. For example, do you realize CMV is now included in the Centers for Disease Control's HIV and AIDS list of complicating illnesses?"

Scott curtly retorted, "No, I don't, nor do I know what the list of complicating illnesses is."

Milton sucked in a large breath of air and quickly continued.

"Well then, let me explain, Captain. AIDS has been declining annually in rate and mortality since 1989, so the Government has created convenient medical data by adding twenty-three viruses to HIV statistics and called them complicating illnesses. This year, to adjust for the declining rate of AIDS, they've retroactively added three more viruses. They include invasive cancer of the cervix, pulmonary tuberculosis and two or more episodes of bacterial pneumonia, so they can have a convenient doubling of AIDS by the end of 1994. Then when they go to lobby Congress regarding this man-made plague—voila, more funds! What unmitigated horseshit!"

Scott sat upright.

"Milton, shouldn't HIV and AIDS be categorized separately—not lumped in with a group of other diseases? And what do you mean by man-made? Are you sure you know what you're talking about?"

Before Schwartz could answer, the mugs of coffee foamed and boiled over onto the top of the lab benches leaving a streaked, chocolate-looking stain on the white surface. As he handed Scott a steaming mug, he yelled his reply.

"You're damn right, I do! What the government has failed to tell the general public is that AIDS *is man-made!*

And if you'll hold your horses, I'll explain who made it in a minute. But please understand, I'm aware AIDS is horrible for anyone who gets it. But it's almost completely controllable. It's the multi-billion dollar industry which is now out of control, not the disease!"

Milton paused, took in a large breath, blew some cool air into his mug and continued. "And the funds allocated are certainly not being spent in the best interest of the victims. In fact, some people in government and private industry are making the disease bigger in every way they can. And they've succeeded, because it's become the biggest medical scam ever perpetrated on the taxpaying public!"

Scott sat silent for a few moments absorbing these revelations. The Musak in the background droned an old Moody Blues song, "Nights in White Satin." It had been one of Rebecca's favorites.

"Why do you think that, Milton? I know we're working our butts off here at the lab to try and find some kind of solution for AIDS."

"We're different, Captain. We don't accept government funds for research. Again, the people that do accept funding, do it knowing full well they're never going to find a vaccine for the virus, which as you know, is almost next to impossible. There are 9,000 to the fourth power possible AIDS viruses and 9,000 base pairs on the genome. Shit, Captain, that means there are trillions of possible genetic combinations! No way in our lifetime is there ever going to be a vaccine developed for this disease."

Scott liked Milton Schwartz. He considered him one

of his closest friends. He thought the doctor might be gay but they had never broached the subject. Scott knew him to be a brilliant scientist and one who was seldom wrong in his grasp of the essentials of a medical debate, and he had listened attentively as Milton excitedly held forth to his audience of one.

"This disease, this supposed plague in America, has only killed on average, about eleven thousand people per annum over the past twelve years. Most of those deaths could be prevented even without a vaccine. AIDS may be lethal, but it's not a very infective agent. It doesn't travel easily from person to person, nor does it travel through the air."

Scott stiffened. "Come on, Milton, eleven thousand people dying a year may not be a plague but it's certainly one hell of a tragedy! Just ask those Oscar show participants wearing their red AIDS bows. They sure as hell know more than their fair share of victims."

"Good God, Captain, of course it's a tragedy! I mean *only* eleven thousand deaths in the statistical sense that we have auto accidents killing four times as many every year. And then there are a half million heart victims each year, one million cancer victims—smokers number five hundred thousand dead per annum. Or worse yet, think of all the abused women and children who die each year." Milton went to take a sip of the cooling coffee and burned his lips. The coffee spilled onto the lab counter.

"Shit—that hurts! I've got to invent something to keep this from always happening."

As he wiped his lips with the sleeve of his smock, a

few pens and pencils tumbled from his coat's upper pocket into the spilled coffee. He picked them up, wiped them on the other sleeve, stuck them back in the pocket and continued.

"Hell, booze kills four hundred thousand people every year and handguns kill more people on average. Yet percentage-wise, we're spending about ten times more on AIDS than all the others combined. Tell me, why is no one appointing a czar or yelling *plague* or *epidemic* about these other more lethal things?"

Scott had tried to say something, but Milton cut him off.

"Don't answer that, Captain, I'll tell you."

The physician smoothed his falling wisps of hair over the top of his gleaming dome.

"First of all, this is collective social guilt. No one person's at fault for creating this industry. We all fall into the trap and become part of the system and then it's an industry that grows out of hand, fed by hysteria. God knows we have enough misinformed, screaming celebrities in this town to instill the fear of plague into anyone. Why can't we have their wonderful intentions and energy put to good use instead of spreading propaganda?"

Scott had worked on charities with many of the people Milton was talking about and he nodded his head.

"It's hard to admit it if you're wrong in life, Milton. Especially when you've put your belief in the system and you've lost friends to these damn diseases, as they have and I have."

Milton pondered this for a moment, then spoke even more rapidly.

"That's exactly how they suck the public in. Phony statistics and pity! But you know, Captain, there's always been some disease or plague threatening to wipe out all of mankind. There was syphilis, malaria, polio, tuberculosis, smallpox, the bubonic plague and now potentially the Marburg and Ebola viruses. Never for centuries was there a vaccine or cure for any of these killers. Millions died. But man still prospered and procreated in numbers the pessimists thought were impossible. Hell, if you'd listened to the Government's statistics on herpes just fifteen years ago, you'd've thought mankind was soon to be annihilated, and now you never hear about it except in association with AIDS!"

A uniformed janitor wheeling a cleaning gurney by the door dropped a metal bucket and a mop with a loud crash. He poked his head in the door and grinned an apology. Then Scott said,

"That's true. But there must be some logical explanation."

Milton spat out his answer.

"You can bet your ass there is. Herpes was the CDC's and the government's disease of the 1970s. The last one to make big money on. But it wasn't a killer. It wasn't a polio. There was no pity factor, so they couldn't sell it to the public. It was just oozing sores on the lips or genitals so it had no long-term clout with moral do-gooders like AIDS does. It got chucked by the wayside the minute AIDS hit." Milton's face had turned purple with rage.

Scott asked, "So what happened to all the herpes in the states?"

"Captain, now most herpes viruses are on the Centers

for Disease Control's list of complicating illnesses!"

Scott had loosened his collar and belt during that tirade and bent to pull up his socks. Then he realized he wasn't wearing any—just his old leather docksiders.

"Milton, just out of curiosity, what are the other twenty-five complicating illnesses?"

The doctor inhaled deeply from his pipe.

"I'll leave a list on your desk in the morning. But, my uninformed friend, let me first educate you on how AIDS started and the cover-up that followed."

Milton exhaled a blast of aromatic smoke and continued.

"In the early 70s. the World Health Organization, in collaboration with the National Cancer Institute's laboratory in Fort Detrick, Maryland, started experimenting with retroviruses. They put a mad genius named Adolf Troutmann, a virologist, on a project to develop a vaccine against the outbreak of Ebola virus."

"You mean he worked on the Zaire and Reston viruses?"

"Different viruses, Captain, however, the same project. If you recall, this Troutmann monster disappeared in a military helicopter crash somewhere in central Africa, during a regional outbreak of Ebola back in '84."

"I remember reading about that. The press made a big deal out of Ebola's frightening possibilities at the time."

"They were investigating the wrong thing. They should have concentrated on Troutmann and a Doctor Zbrinski who disappeared along with him. But I'll explain that in a minute. Ironically, their demise happened the same year the government found out that Troutmann's retroviruses caused AIDS in all the people he and Zbrinski had injected during their experiments."

"What?" Scott was incredulous.

"That's right, Captain. This madman—and I know he was mad because he was working under me at NIH. The guy was seven foot tall and looked and acted like a geek. His assistants swore the guy was wacko, one even said he saw him eating flys."

"That's beyond wacko!"

"True, but I'll repeat, the guy was a damn genius. At that time he told me he was someday going to annihilate every "nigger and faggot" in the world with a retrovirus he was developing. He told me he had tried retrovirus experiments on a couple of human subjects way back in 1957 when he was a visiting resident in Tangier, Morocco. Naturally, I thought him more than weird and I recommended his termination from the Institute. He went from there to the National Cancer Institute. Once he got set as head of their research vaccine program, Troutmann developed two deadly retroviruses. He used them in an experiment during the Marburg and Ebola outbreak in central Africa during the 70s."

Stunned, Scott asked, "What the hell would he do that for?"

"Obviously, some form of experiment that he wanted to use human guinea pigs on. Remember, Captain, this is the same mentality that brought us Agent Orange during Viet Nam. But why, only Troutmann and God know. *The result was acquired immune deficiency. AIDS! The first human retrovirus known to man and it's 100 percent fatal.*"

Scott asked sceptically, "So how did he manage to inject the AIDS retrovirus into people?"

"Judas, you're my boss! The head of a major corporation and medically educated, but I would like to respectfully point out that you're one dumb shit when it comes to the biggest immunodiagnostic challenge and cover-up in our own industry."

Scott laughed heartily.

"I sure appreciate the respect, Milton, but just tell me about the cover-up."

"Captain, the WHO and NCI decided to let Troutmann use his Ebola vaccine as their inoculating vehicle in Africa during 1976. At the time the Marburg and Ebola virus looked like it had the potential to be the next black plague to strike the earth. They were in a panic for any kind of vaccine to help their cause."

"Milton, are you telling me that this scientist willingly mixed lethal retroviruses into Marburg and Ebola vaccine for some kind of medical experiment?"

"That's right, Buckaroo. Until recently, I never believed the crazy bastard would actually do what he had said. But remember, AIDS started showing up almost simultaneously in the United States and these other countries after he started his vaccination program. Now the infection rate is about ninety percent heterosexual worldwide and just the reverse—ninety percent homosexual in America and Europe.

"So why is AIDS heterosexual in the rest of the world and mostly homosexual in America?" Scott queried.

The janitor had finished mopping the hall floor and scooted by the open door, an arm locked protectively around his mop handle. Milton waved and rambled on.

"At that time Ebola or Marburg viruses were unknown, except by a select scientific community in America working with "hot viruses" and some doctors in Africa. So Troutmann decided to use Hepatitis B vaccine as his inoculator here. He had his former colleague, Zbrinski, who had become head of the New York City blood bank, do the dirty work. Troutmann convinced Zbrinski that he was on his way to a Nobel Prize with his work involving the Ebola vaccine and that his mixtures of retroviruses in Hepatitis B could lead Zbrinski to share any potential awards with him. Zbrinski was duped and set up his own clinical study. Only non-monogamous gays could participate. He then had them injected with the tainted vaccine and waited to see if it helped rid them of hepatitis."

"Hold on Milton, I've got to play devil's advocate for a minute. Why would he only allow sexually active gays to be inoculated?"

Schwartz looked up at the oval clock on the lab wall and watched the sweeping hand tick off a few seconds.

"I don't know. I sure as hell have my own theories, like a bigot like Troutmann being behind the study, but I always found it strange that they insisted all of the subjects be promiscuous, huh?"

"That certainly gives food for thought," said Scott.

"And armed with knowledge about the transient homosexual life style and their promiscuity back then, I'm certain Troutmann was aware how rapidly any disease they contracted would spread."

"What did the data on their experiments show?"

"The WHO reported that by 1981 around five percent

of all people injected had come down with AIDS. By '84 sixty percent of all inoculated had become full-blown. When the data was released, the CIA and the Justice Department immediately seized the reports and classified the material "National Security Risk." Shortly after that, Doctors Troutmann and Zbrinski conveniently disappeared in a helicopter accident."

"Holy balls!" snorted Scott.

Milton leaned over the counter, gripping his forgotten mug.

"Today, it's my guesstimate that one hundred percent of the hepatitis vaccine receivers are infected with AIDS! *So what do we get—a disease that the WHO and the CDC grab on to for new funding and a man-made epidemic in the gay community!* Think of all those poor innocent bastards in Africa and up in San Francisco. Is it any wonder they think the whole world's coming to an end and that they've got a rightful bitch?"

Scott sat forward. "Milton, if what you're telling me is true, why don't you publish your own findings or write a book?"

"Captain, even though all the facts are available to anyone who wants to contact the NCI, the CDC and the WHO and pass their own judgement, I don't think anyone could ever prove what happened. Myself, I don't need the aggravation. Hell, If I wrote a book on all this, some nut would probably shoot me for telling the truth."

The truth was, Milton Schwartz did not want his mother, Esther, now in her late seventies, to find out her son was homosexual. Publicity of that magnitude would expose him in the media in a very short time. That skeleton in his private closet kept him quiet.

Staggered by these revelations, Scott began educating himself in every way possible to become an expert on HIV and AIDS. He read the journals, searched the data bases, and visited numerous AIDS hospitals in California, where he grilled the specialists in charge of the dying patients.

It wasn't long before the realization clicked into place in his mind as simply as a shutter falls over the objective eye of a camera. Milton had been telling him the truth!

His mind reeling, Scott slowly got up from the bed. He decided to watch the televised proceedings of the Senate subcommittee meeting on further government funding for the AIDS problem. He walked into the bathroom, switched the television to C-Span, then climbed into the steaming tub.

Various medical experts and corporate executives, including Ralph Landen and Gino Rigitinni from Medical Reference Laboratories, had been summoned to Washington. Senator Richard Spout was in charge of the hearings. His voice was so resonant that a microphone was barely necessary when he spoke in the congressional chambers. The legislator had a thin mustache and mounds of wavy black hair. He also had a bulbous nose, which somehow failed to detract from his handsome appearance. He wore a bright red bow-tie and spent a fair amount of time pruning his mustache with a wetted finger. The eight-man committee he headed consisted of six Democrats and two Republicans. They were debating and conferring with government and business leaders on where to best spend the five and a half billion dollars of taxpayer monies appropriated for AIDS.

Senator Spout said sonorously, "Gentlemen, do we spend new funds for research for a vaccine or do we continue administering to the problem of spending the funds at hand for the people already infected?"

Rigitinni immediately voiced his opinion. "Mr. Chairman, I think it's obvious that more funds are needed to be spent by Medicare and the government for the blood testing of all citizens before this plague gets out of hand."

Ralph Landen concurred. "I agree, Mr. Chairman."

Senator Spout responded, "I, too, agree with you, gentlemen. I think quick action is necessary to prevent any further deleterious effect on society from this horrible disease."

In very short order, the Committee unanimously voted that a further half-billion dollars would be allotted to the blood testing of all Medicare patients before this "epidemic" got out of hand. MRL controlled one-third of that market.

Scott suddenly realized why MRL's stock was already up almost three points that morning before this news was announced. Insider information! He wondered just how much Senator Spout knew about the workings of Medical Reference Laboratories.

Original pilgrims, the Spout family resided in Oyster Bay, New York. The family tree dated back to the early seventeen hundreds in the New England area. The clan had made their fortune brewing beer and the Belgian-

American patriarch, now in his nineties but going strong, should have been dead long ago. He drank a bottle of Gordon's gin and smoked ten Cuban cigars a day. A good Catholic, he had sired one son and seven daughters.

Richard had recently been reelected to the U.S. Senate for his fifth consecutive term in a tainted election campaign. The taint being that most people thought the senator had somehow gotten away with doctoring the number of votes he needed to get elected. Yet when he was indicted on these charges, he was exonerated in the courts of his adopted home state of New Jersey. And there were rumors that Richard had ties to the underworld. A friend of his who was set to testify at an upcoming House Committee meeting on Mafia involvement in the U.S. medical industry, mysteriously disappeared before the trial. Rumors never proved, but true nonetheless. Only Richard's association with a top Eastern law firm, his family's fortune and his well-knotted ties to the underworld kept him in government.

Josh Kramer was a longtime acquaintance of the senator, for Richard was also on the Senate Committee for International Defense. And as much as Josh disliked the licentious politician, he had learned that legislative tenure, not political ability or integrity, is what counts most in Washington. And most of Josh's fortune had been made in the contracting of government defense projects around the world. Josh had sold eighteen percent of the original shares of Medical Reference Laboratories common stock to friends of Richard's when the senator assured him that he knew the foreign owners personally. He parted with these shares because he knew one day he would need Spout's support on the various health and defense committees the senator chaired.

Richard was twice divorced, or annulled—as the Cardinal from New York liked to call it. The senator was an inveterate womanizer. He loved cocaine, gambling and whores, in that order. He was a born puppet and sleazy to the bone, yet he maintained a facade of folksy respectability. Deep in his shallow heart he truly believed he was going to be elected president one day.

All seven of the Spout daughters were married and had children. Tons of children. Richard, ever the good uncle, played baseball and went sailing in the bay with them. He always made sure there were plenty of photographers around.

Scott was so sick after his bath that he sat on the floor of the bathroom. Rosa peeked in, then came and patted him down with a fluffy towel and told him to eat the hot food she had left beside his bed.

The odor of the food made him nauseous. He was sweating again and felt dizzy and his cough came in deep husky roars. He moved the food tray into the bathroom and then crawled into bed. The telephone rang and out of ingrained habit, he picked it up. Instantly he realized his mistake. When Pamela did not say, "Hello darling, it's me," he knew there was a problem.

"You lying son of a bitch! How could you give me AIDS? Have you forgotten just who I am? I believed you when you said you had some goddamn sighto-virus, or whatever you claim you had. But giving me AIDS and not telling me is inexcusable! What am I supposed to do now, you bastard?"

Scott stifled a groan. "Pamela, you don't have AIDS, so calm down. Where did you get this nonsense from, anyway?"

"I've got my sources!" she screamed. "And if I don't have AIDS, just what in hell have you given me? I know goddamn well that you tested positive for HIV!"

Scott coughed and tried explaining. "Look, I haven't given you anything, especially AIDS! I admit there's been a false diagnosis made by the Berlinger's lab. But it's a total mistake. Milton and I have run three different blood tests on me since that Berlinger test result and they've all been negative. Someone's made an egregious error! All I have is a nasty case of CMV."

His voice rose, rasping. "Now, I want to know who at Medical Reference Labs gave you confidential medical information on me? Did you contact Ralph Landen? Because whoever released this data is going to get their butt in a sling."

"Scott, do you think for one minute I'm going to buy that story? That I'm going to believe you and Milton over the top hospital and laboratory in the world? Bullshit!" Pamela hissed.

"I'm going right this minute to my doctor and have a blood test run on me. And you had damn well better hope for your own sake that it's negative!" There was a loud click as Pamela slammed the telephone down in Scott's ear.

The room seemed to be spinning and Scott coughed up green phlegm into a tissue as he lay back in bed. His chest ached. He thought back to when he had first started his affair with Pamela. Was it her cunning? Was it his grief? Loneliness? Sorrow, or maybe just a desire for companionship? Whatever it was, he now realized the old law of physics, that opposites attract, must have been the only way it was humanly possible for them ever to have gotten together.

...It was on Valentine's Day, 1989. He had been in Paris on a business trip and was staying at the Plaza Athenée. He enjoyed the hotel's central location. It allowed him to stroll down the Champs-Elysées and get lost among the throng of internationals who crowded that boulevard twenty-four hours a day. On one of his after-dinner treks, he wandered off the boulevard and slanted down Rue George V towards the River Seine, when he heard a shrill, two-fingered whistle. He turned around and saw Pamela in a long fur coat. Taking her high-heels in hand, she started running towards him. It was dry, but blustery and cold and she was puffing for breath as she reached him. She radiated excitement. Her cheeks shone with the dark-red tint of Bing cherries, her black eyes were gleaming and drops of dew stuck to her long eyelashes; her lips were deep mauve and her brown face glowed from under the hood of a white sable parka. Scott, no longer looking at her as a friend's wife, allowed himself to clearly see what he had known all along, that indeed, she was a beautiful woman!

"Scott, what are you doing in Paris on the most romantic day of the year? Looking for a red rose? Or maybe a Parisian Valentine?"

She knew full well what he was doing there. She had followed him after reading in a business column in the *New York Times* that he was in France for the entire month of February. She had been divorced from Josh for over a year. She was lonely and she was a woman who got what she wanted!

"Not to be too unromantic, Pamela, but the yellow rose is my favorite flower. Not the red. And I wasn't here looking for a Valentine. Just a routine business trip and going to my favorite restaurant, the Beauville. What are you doing over here this time of the year?"

Pamela gave Scott a coquettish smile and squeezed his hand.

"I came to find my Valentine! And I promise, I won't ever forget your attachment to yellow roses, but get just a little romantic, Scott. Come on with me and I'll give you your Valentine's Day present."

"Hm, maybe I should be wary of your motives," Scott said. "After all, Saint Valentine was beheaded in Rome under Emperor Claudius on this very day. Where's the romance in that?"

"Come on, you old know-it-all." Pamela took his arm and clasped it firmly to her side.

His curiosity aroused, Scott agreed to follow. They took a taxi to Sotheby's auction house, where an armed guard allowed Pamela entrance into a back room full of antiques and paintings. An obsequious salesman, who obviously knew Pamela, took them to a painting sitting on an easel that was draped in black velvet. Pamela told Scott to close his eyes and when he did she uncovered a Vincent van Gogh canvas—a scene of a brilliant yellow wheat field.

"Happy Valentine's Day, darling!"

Scott opened his eyes and was too stunned to speak. He had told Pamela some years back about his love of the Impressionists, especially van Gogh, but he would never have imagined her remembering such a conversation.

Pamela had tears in her eyes as she watched Scott gaze at the painting. Even the auctioneer stood transfixed by the moving scene between the two, although he was even more moved by the fact that he had sold the painting to Pamela for twelve million dollars. Huskily, Scott broke the silence in the dark room.

"This is beyond romantic. Notwithstanding my long-time attraction for you while you were married, I never realized you cared about me, Pamela."

Pamela put her arms around Scott and hugged him tightly. Deeply affected by the gift, Scott continued with a touching awkwardness, "I'm usually not a man at a loss for words. I don't have a present for you, so I can only thank you from the bottom of my heart. Now, in celebration, I know a restaurant up on the Mount that serves the best tortoni in the world. May I invite you to join me for dinner?"

Pamela once again put her hand in his and squeezed it hard.

"Let's walk up the hill. I'd like to stop at the Basilica on the Mount before we go to dinner. It's not that far from here."

As they walked slowly hand-in-hand, up the wind-blown streets toward the church, Scott stopped at a street vendor's small steam engine popcorn machine and bought two, large boxes of buttered popcorn. They laughed and spilled and pushed the salty popcorn into each other's mouths as they walked.

"Scott, how come we never got together sooner than this?" Pamela said. "I've always been attracted to you, too."

Popcorn forgotten, Scott replied, "Well, I've never gotten over Rebecca and I just always had too much respect for Josh. I never allowed myself to want you because I might hurt his feelings or damage our friendship."

"I certainly understand your loyalty to your former marriage, but Scott, darling, don't worry about Josh's feelings, unless you're doing a business deal with him. I know you're his best friend and he thinks of you as a son, but he's a big boy and our relationship was over long, long ago. From now on let's just talk about the future. Let's forget the past."

Scott put his arm around her and they leaned into the wind and the hill.

The steps up to the entrance of the Basilica were steep and challenging after their long walk. Pamela dipped her fingers in Holy water and crossed herself upon entering. Scott stood silently behind her. The church was dark and musty smelling. Candles were the only source of light in the huge, cavernous building. Construction drapes hung everywhere and Scott could see the building's interior was being renovated. Pamela took his hand in the darkness and led him down a long aisle, lit sparsely by a few candles hanging from the ceilings. Lonely-looking porcelain icons stood upright in their niches against the cold stone walls. They stared sadly as she led him into the shadows of a wooden pew, which was covered on top by a canvas cloth hanging from a scaffold. Pamela genuflected, then knelt down to pray in the tent-like setting and Scott settled back comfortably in the hard pew. It was cool and dark. She started giggling to herself and whispered,

"I'm so horny for you, I could die."

A brief concern about sacrilege crossed Scott's mind. But after all, he was in a house of worship, where people went to seek what they wanted, right?

Her silhouette flickered against the dim candlelight and he could see tears running down her cheeks while she laughed. She gently fondled him. He became erect. Silently, she unzipped his trousers, then turned deftly around on her knees, looking up at him with a radiant smile.

She reached inside his trousers.

"Scott! This is the best Valentine's present you could've ever given me." Her words dissolved into a greedy moan.

Her mouth on him was warm and wet and smooth.

Organ music, Haydn's Symphony No. 99 in E flat major, drifted softly down from the rafters of the church. Scott lay flat on his back in the pew and Pamela lifted her dress up under her fur parka and eased on top of him. She wore no panties. Their bodies were damp with excitement and they slid silently together like wet potter's clay. Their own organs moved in harmony with the organ being played and they joyfully climaxed along with the music.

Pamela whispered, "Habibi, I've always loved you."

Scott didn't think he loved her in the same way. There could never be another love like he felt for Rebecca. But he was somehow mesmerized by Pamela's charm. He did not want to tell her that, so he laughingly diverted her.

"I'm more than flattered, but what did you call me?"

"Habibi. It means my love, in Arabic. I have lots of romantic names to call you."

Scott joked, "It's the unromantic ones I'm worried about!"

Pamela then kissed his eyelids and softly said.

"Iyuni, means my eyes. Pronounce it after me, Eye-oo-nee! And hayite means my life. Hi-eh-tee! Don't ever forget I'm half Arab, so I know the original language of love."

Scott nuzzled her ear with his lips and pronounced the words perfectly. Pamela pulled him on top of her again, moaning,

"Hayite!"

Scott's aching body and his coughing pulled him back from Pamela, Paris and the memories. He was tired. Completely enervated, he fell asleep and slept for thirty hours straight. The blinds were drawn tight to keep out any light and block as much noise as possible. Even the raccoons' nightly raid on the rubbish did not wake him. Rosa checked in on him while he slept. He was sweating a great deal, tossing and turning and coughing a lot, but he did not wake up for a day and a half.

The green flashing 0:00 on the clock of Scott's VCR was the first thing he noticed when he finally stirred. He knew the electricity must have temporarily gone off during the night. That realization made him aware that his brain was now functioning and he buzzed for Rosa and asked her to bring up his breakfast. On top of his lamp table, he spotted the "Ross Perot for President" sticker that Milton had given him to paste on the El Camino. Scott laughed to himself. He felt better and would put the sticker on later. Rosa peeked in his door, grinning cheerfully, and proffered his breakfast tray and the *L.A. Times*.

The first thing Scott noticed was that he had slept through the last day of September. The paper's date was October 1, 1992. Normally, he headed straight for the financial section. But on this morning he decided to read the sports page first. As he thumbed his way through the paper, his eye caught a picture of himself and Pamela on the front page of the society section. He dropped the rest of the paper on the bed and started reading the article.

> "TELL ME IT CAN'T BE TRUE!"
>
> "Prominent Beverly Hills mega-millionaire, socialite Scott Reid, a regular feature in this column over the years, has been diagnosed as having tested POSITIVE for the VIRUS that causes AIDS. Yesterday this reporter spoke with Pamela Kramer, Mr. Reid's former companion and current business associate, regarding this tragedy. Ms. Kramer, who has tested NEGATIVE for the virus, appeared to be in a state of emotional shock as she spoke with me. She said we all had to do what we could to prevent this horrible epidemic from spreading further into society. She has donated ONE MILLION DOLLARS to Cher's upcoming AIDS charity dinner and rock concert, in the name of Mr. Scott Reid. WHAT A GAL! This reporter was not able to reach

Scott for his comments. His office and his home were not accepting calls. Understandable, you poor dear. GET WELL SOON, Scott!"

Mount St. Helen's was not much more explosive than the vitriol that now spewed from Scott. He knew he had to get to the bottom of this immediately. He needed a good cerebral enema in order to flush this sewage from his mind. A rational conversation would calm him down, so he dialed Franklin Nelsen at his private number at the Berlinger Clinic.

The phone rang and rang. Just as Scott was about to hang up, an out-of-breath voice bellowed into his ear.

"Hello, Nelsen, internal medicine."

"Frank, thank God for small favors." Scott said. "I thought maybe you'd already left for Kenya. I need to talk to you badly. Have you got five minutes?"

"Hey, buddy, I've always got five for you. But we gotta make it fast, Matty's all packed and dying to get going. And they're screaming for me up in Administration. Since I didn't get a fax from you yesterday about your own lab's test on you I figured you'd just taken my advice. Did you start the AZT program up in San Francisco?"

Agitated, Scott growled, "Frank, Milton Schwartz, my corporate physician, knows nothing about your laboratories' erroneous positive HIV test on me. But when he double checked my blood here at my lab, it was negative for HIV! I repeat, *NEGATIVE!* Only a horrible case of CMV. My ratio is 3:166. I felt like I was dead yesterday and slept the whole day. That's why you didn't hear from me."

Having run into his office to answer the telephone,

Nelsen had been standing while talking to Scott. He now sat down at his desk.

"Listen to me, Scott, and you listen carefully. I don't have much time and I want to get you back on your feet and as close to normal as an HIV patient can be. I mean no disrespect to Doctor Schwartz, but he's a lab physician, an academic scientist, and I'm sure a doggone good one. But he's not a doctor working daily with patients suffering from AIDS, or a professional lab tech trained to find these viruses. Maybe he didn't use the latest test kits like ours."

Scott spoke urgently into the phone.

"You're wrong, Frank. Someone's made a mistake back there, not Milton! For Chrissake, Pamela's already put it in the papers that I'm HIV positive. I've got to get this mess straightened out. You and Milton are the only ones I trust with this issue. I need your help, Buddy. Do you want me to forward you another sample so you can recheck it again at your lab?"

Franklin was irritated but continued, "Scott, I'm out of here in less than an hour, right after my last appointment. You can run all the tests you want anywhere you want. You'll find we're not wrong, my friend. We don't make those kind of mistakes. We have the best doctors and technicians in the world working for us. We double-check everything we do before making a judgement on a patient. I've personally checked with our Omaha lab on your blood test and you definitely have HIV."

His voice softened. "I'm sorry, Scott, but that's the way it is. I'll express-mail you some AZT to get you started on treatment and I'll forward a prescription. Then I want you to contact Doctor William Ryan up in San Francisco. He's a Stanford man and he's a specialist in HIV disease. He knows how to deal with the psychological impact of the illness and patient denial."

Scott pleaded, "Frank, this isn't the kind of help I need. I'm telling you there's been a mistake made and I can prove it. How did Pamela get the confidential information that your lab had tested me positive for HIV, if there's not something amiss here?"

Franklin sighed. "Scott, I've no idea how your rich girlfriend came to her conclusions. I've always told you that she had more money than brains. Knowing her, she probably made it all up. But I've heard all of your arguments before. The way to help yourself is to do what I'm telling you over the next couple of months while I'm going to be gone. Quit denying you have a problem—*you've got HIV!*"

Frustrated, Scott said, "That's absolute rubbish, Frank."

Franklin replied in a firm, but impatient tone. "Look, Bud. Your T-4 cell count is low, dangerously low, about four hundred. I promise you, the AZT will stabilize this and maybe bolster your immune system at that level or higher. I've talked to every medical expert at the CDC in Atlanta and they assure me you could potentially live a normal life with this virus for the next twenty years, if you take the proper precautions."

Through his receiver, Scott could hear the hospital pager echoing in the background. He recalled Milton telling him that AZT killed the majority of people who took it.

"Doctor Franklin Nelsen, Doctor Franklin Nelsen, you're wanted urgently in Administration."

But Franklin continued, "And remember, Buddy, our government is pouring billions of dollars into research for a vaccine for this disease. Be logical. I'm sure they're going to come up with a cure before that time and you'll live long enough to tell our grand-kids how we licked this problem. Now I've got to run, Bud. Do as I say. Call Billy Ryan up in Frisco, have a chat with him and get started on the AZT as soon as it arrives. Matty and I'll be thinking of you in our prayers. I'll be calling you and be back in November. Doggone that page! `Bye for now, Scott."

The dial tone buzzed in Scott's ear as he picked up his Earl Grey tea and took a sip. It was cold. He hung up and stared at his breakfast tray in frustration. He spooned the lemon yogurt on top of the peanut-buttered toast, ate it hungrily and drank the rest of the cold tea. Then he called Milton at IMA Laboratories.

Kiddingly, Scott said, "Doctor Schwartz, I presume!"

Milton was in his private office, puffing on his white porcelain "Woodie." He was smoking his favorite blend of Borkum Riff tobacco. Only his coworkers down the hall, who were always offended by his smoking, noticed the smell. But because Milton had already read the *Times* on Scott and Pamela, his thoughts were not on how much he enjoyed his favorite aroma, only on what he could do to help his friend.

"Good morning, Captain," he said. "I read the article already. What a cunt!"

"Which one, Pamela or the columnist?"

"Both!"

Scott could hear Milton blow smoke angrily into the mouthpiece. "Milton, I just talked to Frank, and he thinks we're the ones that are mistaken in our results. I don't mean to offend, but can you get a colleague you trust to run a few different types of tests on more of my blood? Then I'll take those negatives, along with yours, right to the head of their testing lab as soon as you can get them to me. I've got to get this ridiculous scenario cleared up fast. It's liable to ruin my sex life after I'm over CMV!"

"Glad to hear you're not losing your sense of humor, Captain. And no offense taken. I forgot more about medicine while I was taking a crap this morning than those little shit lab jockeys back there will ever know!"

Scott could not help but chuckle over Milton's pride and candor. He had not stopped talking.

"They're all part of the system that covers up for each other before they'll ever admit they're wrong. And as for your buddy Nelsen, he's one of those ivory tower clinical know-it-alls who spreads around medical bullshit! Like him and all the paid-off virologists in this country who have no scientific evidence that HIV causes AIDS, but by the process of simple correlation they're willing to say it does, or like his latest article that said you can't get AIDS from mosquitoes." Milton huffed his contempt. "He writes about it in all the medical periodicals and tells it to all his medicrat pals—these people all believe their own lies because they can legally create a bunch of phony data to verify 'em!"

Scott said defensively, "Milton, I'm sure Frank could substantiate his article."

"Wrong, Captain. In fact, he didn't run any tests on human subjects. Nobody has! I'll tell you what I'd like to do to all those uppity shits. I'd like to ask them to volunteer so I could put them all naked in a room full of mosquitoes infested with the AIDS virus for thirty days. After they'd all been bitten good by the mosquitoes, then tell them we'll gather data on them over the next ten years to see if they develop AIDS! I'll bet not one of those self-righteous know-it-alls would volunteer."

"Why not? It would certainly prove if they're right!"

"I'll tell you why not. The reason, Captain, is that the size of the AIDS virus is a hell of lot smaller than the malaria virus. And if you remember, the anopheles mosquito certainly infected and killed millions over the years by carrying that big old malaria virus around in her proboscis. Those doctors know that and that's why they wouldn't volunteer."

Scott laughed, but the sound was strained. "Milton, I'm sure glad you don't have an opinion on anything, but I still need to know if you can get somebody to do my blood this morning."

"Sure, sure, I'll get Doctor Graziano from our infectious disease department to come in," Milton said. "He can draw some from you when you get here. What time will you be in?"

Satisfied, Milton blew a thick ring of bluish smoke into the receiver.

"Milton, I know Nicki Graziano. We played golf together last summer. The ringer beat me out of two bucks on the back side of Riviera. Tell him I'll be there about noon."

Once out of bed, Scott dressed in a Prince of Wales gray checkered suit. He put on a blue French-cuffed shirt and twisted a dark red tie in a Windsor knot around his neck. Then he grabbed the Perot bumper sticker off the lamp table, got in the sparkling El Camino and headed for his office.

By the time Scott arrived at the laboratory, the gossip column had swept through the building like a runaway tornado. A cameraman for one of the networks stood in his parking space wielding a mini-cam, hoping for an interview. And a leggy, attractive female reporter pushed a microphone into Scott's face.

"Mr. Reid, was the article in this morning's *L.A. Times* correct regarding you testing positive for HIV?"

Annoyed, Scott looked towards the camera and said directly into the microphone, "It was absolutely false. And I would like it pointed out that my attorneys will be visiting Ms. Kramer and the columnist regarding a libel suit. I have nothing further to say at this time. Thank you."

A leper would have received a friendlier welcome than Scott did that morning from his employees. However, a few workers came out of their offices to say hello. They perched like buzzards at a safe distance.

Linda Powell was crying openly as he entered his private office. She had on a low-cut, red and white polka-dot dress and wore a single strand of greyish imitation pearls. As usual, her glasses were slipping down her nose.

"Why didn't you tell me, Mr. Reid? God, I knew you were sick, but I didn't think you were dying of AIDS. I work next to you everyday. Maybe you've given it to me? I'm sorry, I just don't know what to think. My mother called and said I should quit. I don't know what to do. I respected you so much."

Her tortoiseshell glasses had fogged up and she reached

in her purse for a tissue to clean them.

Scott could not help but notice that she was using the past tense.

"Linda, I respect you very much, too. I want you to understand that I am *not* positive for HIV. There's been a terrible mistake made and I'm trying to get it rectified as soon as I can. You don't have to worry about your own safety, nor should you feel you have to quit your job. I'll be having Doctor Graziano from the infectious disease lab come to my office shortly to take a blood sample, which will clear up all of this misunderstanding in a short time. Please let me know when he arrives. I won't be taking any outside calls."

As Linda put her clean glasses back on, she seemed pacified. She drew herself back up into a bright, professional stance and said, "Mr. Reid, you have stacks of calls, but the only one I think you'd better answer immediately is Mr. Kramer. He said it was urgent you contact him as soon as you came in."

It seemed to Scott that all of the people who had left telephone messages only wanted to verify that he had HIV. He decided to wait until after Nicki Graziano was finished taking the blood sample before he called Josh. There had been no call from Pamela. Scott now realized that he had been basically right about her—he did not understand her at all! The intercom buzzer brought him out of his thoughts. It was Doctor Graziano.

As they shook hands, Scott noticed that the doctor shook weakly with his fingers and they were damp and clammy.

"Good morning, Nicki, you old bandit. I haven't forgotten about the two bucks you conned me out of. No twenty-handicapper can birdie the eighteenth at Riviera! You've heard the grapevine that I've got one foot in the grave with AIDS?"

Nicki Graziano, perturbed that Scott had thought him a cheat, replied, "Yes, I heard the rumor mill this morning. But Milton tells me they're wrong, you've only got a terrible case of cytomegalovirus. If that's true, let's just take some blood and verify your negative status. I'll run a routine Western blot and an HIV antibody test."

Impatiently, Scott interrupted, "Nicki, Milton's already run those tests. Could you run anything else so we have positive proof that I'm clean?"

"Well, to make absolutely sure there's no further chance of a mistake, I'll also run the blood through the ELISA test kits. They can simultaneously detect antibodies to HIV-1 and 2. These kits are over 99% accurate and so sensitive they utilize higher serum volumes and detect both IgG and IgM antibodies. A negative ELISA will stow all the gossip in a hurry. Give me your best vein, will you, Scott?"

As Scott watched the young, curly-haired and slightly built physician draw blood from his right forearm, he was reminded of the great boxer of the same name, yet there was no physical similarity between the two. Although Nicki spoke with an Eastern-accented slur, almost like a punch-drunk fighter who had retired too late. Idly, Scott noticed that his shirt cuffs were monogrammed, *N.N.G,.* the same as the engraving on his gold cuff links.

Milton appeared at the door unannounced. His bouncing belly was impregnated with the morning's generous allotment of pastry. His pipe dangled from his mouth unlit, but one could still smell him coming from a distance away. Under his lab smock he wore his usual frayed-at-the-collar, button-down shirt, covered by a ragged V-necked pink sweater. With his left hand he smoothed some damp stands of hair over his bald dome.

"Aside from that monster needle in your arm and a giant dose of CMV, how you feeling, Captain?"

"Much better. Thanks, Milton." Scott said. "Most of my coughing has stopped today. Last night I slept like a baby and it did me a world of good. I feel like a new man. By the way, since I'm going to be besieged by every damn reporter in the city about my supposed HIV, I'm going to have to defend myself. Any more quick facts on the subject you can give me?"

"I could stuff your head until I was blue in the face with what I know, but first I want Nicki to pop an extra tube out of you for my own analysis down in R&D."

Reluctantly, Nicki Graziano handed Milton a small tube of Scott's blood and put the other small red cylinder into his own medical bag. As Nicki began to leave, he turned around and said, "I want to take about a week on this and run every test I can come up with. I'll write up a paper on the results, which you can be assured will be in absolute confidentiality, and you can take it along with Doctor Schwartz's old test—all the way to the Supreme Court if you like."

"Thanks, Nicki. I hope to see you on the golf course in a few weeks," Scott said.

No sooner had Graziano left the room, than Milton

started rambling with the pent-up verbal flood of a man who has just had his mouth unwired after a broken jaw.

"Captain, I want you to tell all of those hopeful Pulitzer winners that the HIV and AIDS diseases are a giant medical and bureaucratic scam!" He paced the room, agitated. "Yet it's a real paradox, because there's absolutely no scientific proof that HIV causes AIDS, just ask any virologist who makes that claim to use Koch's postulates to attempt to verify their belief."

Scott recalled vividly from his days in medical school. The standard measure used to determine whether a particular microorganism is the cause of a disease is a set of three laws known as Koch's postulates.

The first law says that the suspected microorganism has to be present in *all* cases of the disease. Scott knew that HIV is not. *Over twenty percent of all AIDS patients show no traces of HIV whatsoever, not even its antibodies.* The second law says that the microorganism must be able to be taken from a host, animal or human, and further spread in pure culture. *This cultivation can only be done in 50 percent of all AIDS patients.* The third law says that inoculations of pure cultures of the microorganisms into animals must produce in them the same disease. Scott also knew from his own lab's work, that *HIV has been injected into thousands of laboratory animals, and not one has ever developed AIDS.*

Milton hadn't missed a beat. "On the other hand, AIDS has the potential to be a serious epidemic if we don't take the measures necessary to control it. Remember, the AIDS virus is so potent that it can live for ten hours on a dry plate. And it mutates so damn fast that it scares me. Five times faster than influenza, ten times faster than most viruses and a million times faster than human cells. This syndrome is lethal, Captain. Yet on the other hand, AIDS is not an infectious disease. In fact, it's very controllable!"

Scott lamented, "Come on, Milton, those reporters are never going to buy that. Hell, the government is telling everyone that this thing is running rampant, and what you're telling me is certainly contrary to accepted medical opinion!"

"I know that," Milton retorted. "But they're the ones doing the cover-up. Ask the bastards if they've ever heard of 'Farr's Law.' Remember it? One of the best validated principles of epidemiology—an epidemic recedes at the same rate that it arose! And I'm telling you again, Captain, this disease peaked in 1989 and I can prove it. Hell, you can prove it yourself with the CDC's own statistics."

"I'll quote you on that," Scott said. "What else can I throw at them?"

"Here are a few you can toss around for debate. Up until April of 1992 there were approximately 215,000 cases of AIDS in eleven years of CDC documentation. Out of those, 140,000 died. Yet in Africa there have been arguably millions of cases of AIDS without the same results."

Convinced he had heard a flaw in Milton's reasoning, Scott took in a large breath and quickly cut in, "Right, I'll bet millions more have died!"

Milton brought a match to his unlit pipe and started to suck.

"Wrong! Only 200,000 have ever died of the disease in the last eleven years in all of Africa, and I think that figure's too high. So why the discrepancy here? Have any of those reporters questioned such a high mortality rate in America? Ask them if they've investigated if any other medical statistics have been switched over by government reporting agencies, like the CDC transferring numbers from another virus to AIDS to show a misleading number of cases or deaths?"

Shocked, Scott stared at his friend.

"What are you implying, Milton—that the government builds up false data to get funding?"

Milton whirled and shook his finger like an angry judge.

"*Yes, I am!* As I've told you before, they've helped make this disease an industry, and a damn profitable one. Soon, the tune's going to be nearly ten billion dollars a year. But what every average heterosexual, about 250 million in the United States, should be told is that there've only been 2,750 cases of heterosexual AIDS in America! And most of those poor people were hemophiliacs. Divide that by eleven years of data and you're averaging 240 cases of AIDS per year. On average, fifty percent a year died. That's only 120 heterosexuals dead of AIDS per annum! Shit, Captain, the average straight person has about the same chance of being killed by a grizzly bear."

Scott was flabbergasted. He rubbed his face, squinted his eyes and said, "I think you've given me more questions to ask them than they'll have to ask me."

"That may be true, but this is the big one. Why all this media and political hysteria for a disease that's avoidable by most of the small population it affects?" Milton puffed his pipe furiously.

"Milton, what about the minorities in America, don't

they number about sixty million?"

"True enough, and arguably there are about five million homosexuals that I include in that minority group. They, the prostitutes and the drug users are the ones most prone to AIDS. But with proper sexual and drug habits it's been proven they can control the spread."

Scott interrupted. "How about the discrepancy between blacks and whites?"

"Well, there are about thirty million blacks in the country." Milton slowly relit his pipe. "And they've got a higher infection rate than whites because drug use and prostitution are disproportionately higher in their population. The only problem we have is to control the spread of AIDS in the small segment of society that includes the homosexual community, prostitutes and drug users. But the government's intervention is making it worse."

"May I quote Doctor Milton Schwartz on this?" Scott asked wryly.

"You're damn right, you can. I can document anything I ever discuss about this subject! And I've got plenty of other scientists who agree with me. We're just in the minority at the moment." Milton glowered out the huge window behind Scott's desk at a smog-choked skyline.

"But how about all of the victims that don't fit into those groups?"

Milton's eyes lit up like two embers.

"I'm damn sorry for them, just as I'm damn sorry for any unfortunate who's got any kind of illness. Hell, that's why I became a doctor, Captain! I get so pissed off when I think of all the innocent victims of this AIDS tragedy to come. And right now, you're a good example. Some asshole has made a mistake in the system by saying you're infected when you're not, and you may suffer the consequences of that error for the rest of your life."

Scott bent his head toward the floor and spoke quietly.

"I hope not. But I'd sure like some answers and I'd just like to know what to say to all the questions that are going to be coming my way."

"Well listen, Captain. Be sure to tell whoever asks you that the tragedy is something the media, politicians, drug companies and the medical community have created and if they really want to stop the spread of this horrible disease, then damn it, *start taking the practical measures necessary to do so, instead of screaming for more government funding and protection of individual rights.*"

Milton was sweating and the wisps of hair he had draped across his head were now glued in place.

"There's lots more, Captain, but I think you'd better get some lunch and get back home to bed. Rest and plenty of liquids are the best things for you for the next few weeks. Don't worry about the gossip. We'll have you fit as a fiddle and out of this mess in no time. I'm off on vacation starting tomorrow until the fifteenth. Would you give me a call when you hear anything from Nicki?"

"Will do, Milton," Scott said, the fatigue coming through in his voice. "Thanks for the info. By the way, where are you going?"

"I'm taking Esther to the Catskills. She loves her Jewish comedians, so we'll be staying at Grossinger's. Take care, Captain."

Milton put the tube of Scott's blood and his pipe in his baggy white smock pocket and waddled out as quickly as he had come in.

Scott noticed that the leaves of the large hanging *Ficus pumila* in the corner of his office were drooping and needed water. He went into his bathroom, opened a lower cabinet, pulled out a small plastic bag of blue powdered fertilizer, mixed a teaspoon of it into a bronze long-necked watering can, filled the container until the water foamed and then carefully watered all the plants in his office. When finished, he picked up the telephone and punched in the code for Josh Kramer's telephone number.

...When Josh left Scotland for California in 1946, he took with him one hundred pounds, his Gaelic brogue, a change of clothing and a letter from his mother in his duffel bag.

Los Angeles and Josh fit together like a pair of well-made gloves. His good looks, foreign accent, charming smile and gift for banter made for easy introductions. His insatiable desire for wealth drove him to use his strong back relentlessly to accumulate funds. He washed cars, bused dishes, sold shoes in a department store, worked nights in a gas station, and picked citrus during the migrant season on weekends. Every two weeks he religiously forwarded half of his earnings to his parents back home.

A year quickly rolled by before Josh was able to secure a nine-to-five job. Hughes Aircraft hired him as an assembler of airplane parts. Bored to the point of desperation on the assembly line, he applied for a patent on a ratchet wrench he designed that allowed a man to work the line at ten times the normal pace of a worker using a manual spanner. It worked, and it got the attention of Howard Hughes. Hughes personally gave Josh a check for a million dollars and a ten percent royalty for the rights to the tool. The wrench was soon sold to nearly every defense contractor, mechanic and hardware store in the world, and Josh was on his way.

As Southern California grew like a mushroom, Josh branched out into multi-areas of investment, all the while enjoying the benefits of his ten-percent royalty from Hughes. He believed in land as a basis for investment, but also realized that people would always be going to war, getting sick, and dying. So he bought real estate, small defense-oriented companies, insurance companies, medical companies, and funeral homes.

As time went on, out of sheer lonesomeness he married a towering Bel Air socialite and sired a son. Marriage was not easy for him, for his businesses kept him isolated from a normal family life and his wife eventually took a lover. Tragically, one weekend in the '60s, on a trip with her gentleman friend and the child to the Grand Canyon, her private plane crashed, killing them all.

Although Josh suffered great anguish on losing his son, he bore it stoically. Marriage never crossed his mind again until one night in 1974, while he was out on the town with Scott.

They were celebrating that evening at a topless nightclub on Sunset Strip, when Josh saw the most beautiful woman he had ever seen. A dancer, named Pamela Al Saud.

She was twenty-two, yet in spite of the age difference, he fell head over heels for her. Her musical accent, large bare breasts and her audacity completely charmed Josh into an early proposal. He felt an immediate kinship. Pamela was just like he had been, when raw, bold and determined, he arrived in the States.

Against all logic, they married. Pamela learned and practiced every social grace required to entertain people and run Josh's estates. However, after some years together, her desire to have a child, and Josh's inability to grant her wishes, led her into having an extramarital affair. She became pregnant and gave birth to a baby girl, naming her Melissa.

Years before, Josh had a vasectomy out of a terror of ever losing another son. Pamela never knew about his decision and Josh never said a word to her about the baby's parentage. He treated Melissa as his own, often sending her on his private jet to his parents in Glasgow, but he abandoned all interest in Pamela. They shared no intellectual companionship or common interests and as time went on, Josh began to care only about his businesses.

Out of guilt, Pamela began drinking heavily and she, too, gradually drifted out of the relationship.

The marriage had been convenience and comfort for both of them, and despite the efforts they made, passion and love never flared between them. Josh made sure there was no legal trouble during their amicable divorce proceedings. He was a kind and generous man. He gave her Castle Rock, and one billion dollars in a trust fund for the child. Pamela was made executor and allowed the interest on the money until the child became twenty-one. Then all of the funds would revert to Melissa.

As soon as Scott heard Josh's thick Scottish brogue and raspy voice, he felt better.

"What's up, Scott?"

Though they had a mentor-protege relationship, Josh always felt as though Scott was his long-lost son. The little boy who was killed in the airplane crash with his first wife. His face had faded from Josh, but the hurt never did.

"I read the article in the *Times*. What in hell prompted Pamela to make such an announcement? Is it true?"

In all the years of Josh and Scott's relationship there had never been any duplicity between them. Nor were there any stagey Hollywood bearhugs, or other Southern California fakeries, only a direct look in the eye and a blacksmith-firm handshake each time they met. Josh never had any animosity towards either Scott or Pamela for their affair. He knew Scott needed someone after Rebecca, although he could never figure out how Scott had settled on Pamela. But Josh was now in his sixties and a realist; he was happy for both of them.

He knew he would get a straight answer and Scott replied. "What did the great bard say, 'Hell hath no fury like a woman scorned?' Josh, I have no idea what set Pamela off, other than her thinking I had maybe given her AIDS. But I assure you there's been a mistake. Ironically enough, at Medical Reference Labs. Somehow Pamela got hold of that erroneous information and spilled her guts to the reporters. I'm hoping maybe you can help me get to the bottom of this mess."

Sympathy came through the Scottish burr. Josh stretched his stiff, bowed-legs under the desk. His toes cracked. He stood up, stretching his thick, powerful body to it's full five feet eight inches. With a thump, he plopped back down in his chair.

"Scott, that's quite an accusation. You know I'll stick my neck out to the moon for you, but how could such a thing happen?"

"I just don't know at this point. But I do have something called CMV."

"What in hell's that, Scott?"

"Sorry, Josh. For the layman, it's called cytomegalovirus. It's a nasty little bug, but it'll go away with time and rest. If you'll recall, a few weeks ago I went up to see Frank Nelsen at the Berlinger Clinic."

"I remember."

"Well, they did my usual annual and ran a special blood test at Medical Reference because I've been feeling so punk. All of a sudden I get this message from Frank that I've tested positive for HIV. So I immediately had Milton Schwartz here at my lab run double-checks on my blood. They were all negative for HIV, Josh." Scott blew a soft puff of air between his lips and continued, "Then I called Frank with our results and he claimed he'd personally checked with the Medical Reference lab in Omaha and that there was no mix-up. I'd definitely tested positive for CMV and HIV!"

Perplexed, Josh asked. "Why don't you just send him some more blood, Scott?"

Scott sighed, but pressed on. Josh had always been the

anchor he could hold on to. His personal rock of Gibraltar.

"He's leaving for Kenya today and doesn't have time to rerun another test for me. So I had a different physician at my lab take some blood today. He's going to run every test known to man and he ought to get back to me within a week to verify my negative. The problem is, Pamela has spread this ridiculous story to the press and Medical Reference Labs will have to verify it if some reporter starts nosing around. And you know that's going to start happening today. Do you think you could give Ralph Landen a call so we could get to the bottom of this?"

Josh's reply was immediate.

"I'll ring him right this minute. I just talked to him a little while ago in D.C. to congratulate him—he just got that Senate committee to approve more mandatory testing for this damn thing. I'll get back to you as soon as I've talked it over with him. Don't you worry, Scott, we'll get this straightened out in no time."

Scott felt like a hermit. He did not want to go outside his private office and socialize with anyone, for any reason. To get his mind off it all, he picked up the paper and read up on what else was going on in the world. The upcoming Presidential election hogged the news. Ross Perot seemed to have lost his bid by dropping out and then deciding to come back in, George Bush seemed unelectable because of his broken "read my lips" promise. The pundits seemed to think Bill Clinton was going to be the next President. There were numerous articles on AIDS and campaign promises by the Democrats to spend even more on the search for a vaccine.

Scott moved to the financial section and checked on

IMA Laboratories, Inc. It was up half a point from the day before. He knew that once the gossip column on him was read by the institutional traders, the stock was going to go into a tailspin. After all, most of them bet on the jockey, not the horse. He was tempted to purchase a large block of IMA Laboratories when that happened, just to show them that once it was proved he did not have HIV, the stock would shoot right back up. Ruefully, he realized he was right back to his troubles.

White and red lights flashed constantly on Scott's digital telephone board. Red lights meant internal calls and white, outside calls. There were more white flashes than red. Physically, he felt quite good, yet he did not feel up to working and putting up with the telephone inquisition. He decided to ignore Milton's advice and go home and hit some tennis balls on his new ball machine. He buzzed Linda.

"If Josh Kramer calls, tell him I'll be at the house. I want no other calls forwarded. You can dial the emergency number at the house if you need me. I'm out of here—'bye for now."

By the time Josh reached Landen in Washington, D.C. at seven-thirty p.m., Medical Reference Laboratories in Nebraska was closed for the day.

"Landen, you old devil. Sorry to bother you twice in one day, but I've received some rather disturbing news from Scott Reid. Seems he's tested positive for HIV at MRL."

The sound of the board chairman's voice made preppy Ralph Landen fling his skinny legs off the hotel bed he was lying on. He sat hunched over in the heart-patterned underwear Joyce had given him for his birthday. In his high-pitched voice, he said,

"I know, Josh, I just talked to Omaha. I didn't realize your boy Reid was so popular with the press. The lab told me the news people were there all day long trying to confirm that MRL had tested him positive. And of course Joyce has called me three times about it. How in the world would anyone know unless he released the news himself?"

"Here's the problem, Ralph," Josh continued. "Pamela, in one of her fits, gave the news to a gossip ragger here in L.A. Scott and I want to know how she got hold of it from MRL. And if that leak isn't bad enough, Scott says he reran his blood through his own lab and came up negative for HIV! Can you trace down the leak? Is it possible we made a mistake of this magnitude at MRL?"

Landen, tall as a beanstalk, sat straight up on the bed, defiantly ready to defend his company.

"Josh, anything's possible. But it's damn unlikely. We've run millions of these tests over the past ten years and we haven't made a mistake yet. You know we have all the latest testing equipment and our patented kits. We've hired the best scientific advisors, physicians and technicians that money can buy. They adhere to the toughest safety and screening standards required by the FDA. But nonetheless, I'll check into the possibility that some error was made, first thing tomorrow morning. What concerns me more is the leak of our confidential records."

Although Landen could not see him, Josh nodded in agreement. Ralph piped on, "By the way, Josh—Richard, Gino and I are going bonefishing down in Curacao the day after tomorrow. Why don't you join us? We'll only be gone six days."

"The fishing idea's great," Josh said. "But first thing in the morning when you have an update on Scott, call me."

"Will do."

"And Ralph, I'd like to bring Scott along fishing, whether he's sick or not. I think it would do him a world of good to get away from all of this for a few days. It wouldn't bother any of you gentlemen, would it?"

Landen's mind whirred. It was one thing running a major blood-testing lab for HIV, however, it was another thing having to socialize with a client who had tested positive for the virus. Ralph knew Richard and Gino would not be for it. They didn't like Scott Reid without HIV! But this was Josh Kramer talking.

"Are you kidding, Josh? We'd be delighted to have him along."

"Great. We can take my Gulfstream. I'll talk Scott into it and arrange to pick up you three at Dulles. Whatever we discover about this problem, we can certainly sort it out during the flight and a week fishing. My secretary will call you on the times. Get back to me as soon as you can on what you find out about Scott's test."

Hector Gonzales, Rosa's boyfriend, who cleaned the pool twice weekly and did the gardening, was watching Scott hit tennis balls with the rotating ball machine. Hector was stoic and seldom talked to anyone. He had a Pancho Villa-styled mustache and straight black hair. Little India-ink tattoos of initials covered his hands and he had walked with a limp since he was hit in the leg in a drive-by shooting in East Los Angeles some years back. He was stocky, strong, and always wore a tight T-shirt to emphasize his build. Because Scott took a chance on hiring him when no one else would, he idolized his employer.

The ball machine made a strange popping sound every time it regurgitated a ball. Scott was slugging balls as if he were practicing for the pro tour, but he was gradually feeling sucked down again. Reluctantly, he realized Milton had been right. He should be getting plenty of rest and lots of liquids, not practicing tennis. The court seemed to be spinning and his nausea was returning. Scott felt drenched in perspiration, and he dropped to his knees to recover his equilibrium. Hector left his pruning shears hanging mid-cut in a hibiscus tree and quickly hobbled over to help him. He hauled Scott up under the arms and helped him upstairs into a cold shower. Rosa, concerned as usual, brought up a glass of fresh-squeezed grapefruit juice, and made him drink it.

"Meester Scott, usted mucho malo! Acostarse ahora!

She unplugged his telephone, put on the answering machine, and turned off his television. Shooing Ginger out the door, she tucked in the covers at his feet.

Shivering and clammy, Scott once again fell into a deep sleep. He woke at six a.m. and it was still dark outside, but he felt regenerated. Wobbly, he wandered to the bathroom, peeked into the mirror, then grabbed his razor from the soapstand. While he scraped stubble off his face, he looked furtively at his skin for any sign of HIV disease. He knew he was just being paranoid, but CMV is a powerful virus. And he had been feeling deathly sick. Finding nothing, he splashed a liberal dose of lime-scented after-shave on his chin.

At a few minutes after seven Scott turned on the stock market tape on CNN. Within thirty minutes the news came on. Trading in IMA Laboratories, Inc. stock on the NYSE had been halted with the stock down by four points—to twenty-four dollars. Reports had hit Wall Street that Scott Reid had tested positive for HIV and had a few months to live. Scott sat and stared at the screen.

What was happening to his life? Who had made this horrible error? Why did Pamela have to report this mistake to the press? Who told whom that he only had a few months to live? His mind was racing. He decided to take a pen and paper and write down an outline of a plan. To get it straight, and get it out there.

At ten o'clock Rosa arrived with his breakfast tray and a Federal Express package from Franklin Nelsen. The package contained a months supply of AZT, a renewal prescription for another month, Doctor William Ryan's telephone number in San Francisco and a short note. Scott started laughing.

They all really thought he was infected with HIV!

He plugged in the telephone and started retrieving his messages from the answering machine. Josh was the only one he cared to talk to.

Ralph Landen had already spoken that morning with the physician in charge of Medical Reference Laboratories' testing facilities. The doctor had verified, after checking every computer record once again and talking to every technician in both the upstairs and downstairs labs, that indeed, Scott Reid had tested positive for both CMV and HIV. It was impossible that there had been a mistake. He immediately faxed Landen in Washington, D.C. What the physician did not tell Landen was that he was enjoying an affair with Joyce, Landen's wife, and that *he* had told her about Scott's positive test. What he said was that it was possible that after someone had seen Scott's earlier symptoms with the CMV and HIV, they had mistakenly reported this to the press. He concluded that in fairness to Scott Reid, he felt the news release was done maliciously, not because of any insider information or corporate leak. Nonetheless, MRL had no alternative but to verify their findings to the press.

Landen immediately faxed this news to Josh.

"Morning, Josh. I feel like Chicken Little. The whole world is falling on my head this morning."

"Get a hold of yourself, Scott." Josh rumbled. "It's never as bad as it seems, but in your case—well, it may be. I have a fax from Landen in front of me that states emphatically that MRL has in no way made a mistake and you have definitely tested positive for HIV."

Scott fumed, "That's rubbish, Josh! I can prove it and I'll fax you over all the results from here. And I told you, I've got one more test coming at the end of next week that will use every available method known to medicine. That for sure will verify my not having HIV!" Scott's voice was rising. "I need to get out a press release immediately to clear my name."

"I repeat, get a hold of yourself, Scott!" Josh snapped. "Think about it for a minute. If you release a statement that your own lab tested you negative and the Berlinger Clinic and MRL tested you positive, who do you think the public's going to believe? Listen. Have your guy get your test verified by an outside laboratory next week and when you make your release questioning the original results at MRL, you'll have some substance behind it."

"That's a good idea, Josh." Hope crept into Scott's voice. "I'll call Nicki Graziano right now and have him do just that. But I'm also going to fax you over Milton's results on me so you don't think I've gone over the edge. By the way, who spilled the beans at MRL to Pamela?"

Josh replied disgustedly, "The head physician at MRL thinks Pamela probably just guessed you had HIV from your symptoms and reported it to the press out of malice. If I can read between the lines, this means he's sleeping with our friend, Joyce. She probably got it out of him and then told Pamela. That's just a theory between us, though, Scott. And you don't have to fax over your test results. You can bring them along when you meet me at the airport."

"What are you talking about?" Scott asked.

"We're going fishing! I've told Ralph that you and I would pick up him, Richard and Rigitinni in Washington tomorrow night for some bonefishing down in the Caribbean for six days. We're going to Curacao in the Netherlands Antilles. It'll do you good to get your butt away from all of this chaos."

Scott smiled into the phone. "You're a kind man, Josh Kramer. It won't be easy putting up with that pompous ass Richard and his natty little thug, but you're right, I need to get away from this mess. I need plenty of rest and liquids, just like Milton prescribed. What time is takeoff?"

"I'm happy to hear you'll enjoy the company. We leave at thirteen-hundred hours tomorrow from Gunnell Aviation over at the Santa Monica airport."

"I'll be there, Josh." Scott lay back on the bed. Sadly, he stared at the picture of Rebecca that was sitting on his nightstand. He thought she looked angelic. Picking up the photo, he touched the glass. Her memory haunted him.

REBECCA

Her family was in the wine business in Sonoma County and had California's largest vineyard and private label winery. Rebecca, as an only child, lacked for nothing material in her youth. She had been spoiled and sheltered all of her life by her parents and nannies, but as part of the sixties generation, she rebelled against her family and their pampered life style. At seventeen, she became pregnant and was sent off to Arkansas by her parents for the summer to get an abortion. The drunken country doctor botched her D & C and unknowning, she left his small clinic sterile.

When she went off to college that fall, she set out to divorce herself from her family and, like all budding flower children, was determined to bloom into a genesis of her own. She started by letting the hair under her arms and on her legs grow freely. Then she graduated to marches against the "evil" corporations in America. Yet she never lost her grip on the proceeds of the ample trust fund that her parents had provided for her. A trust fund fueled by some of the same companies that she was protesting against.

In 1964, her freshman year, she pledged to join Delta Kappa Gamma Society, a sorority on the Palo Alto campus. Much to her astonishment, she found her roommate was not white. She held out her hand and for the first time in her life was about to touch a black person.

"Hello, my name's Rebecca Platt. I'm your new roommate."

"Hi, Becky."

"It's Rebecca, if you please."

"Rebecca it is."

A firm, warm black hand, with fingers full of bright ruby nail polish, clutched hers. "Welcome and make yourself at home. My name's Matty Jones. You can put your things in the closet over there. Also, there's only one rule the house strictly enforces. No men in our room, darn it all." She winked broadly.

Matty was big-boned, but gorgeously trim and athletic-looking. She wore her straight, shiny hair in bangs and a page boy curled under at the bottom. She smiled and started whistling a new Beatles tune—*Sergeant Pepper's Lonely-Hearts Club Band.*

In her ignorance, Rebecca had only known blacks from a distance as field workers at the vineyard of her parents winery. She didn't know what to expect from Matty, so she started putting her clothes away and thought it best to make small talk.

"Thanks, Matty. As long as I can smoke, you won't hear a complaint from me. And, not to worry, men don't seem to like me. What year are you in?"

Matty was astounded by her new roommate. All of Rebecca's delicate features were classic. Her figure was lithe. Her fingers were lengthy and slim as expensive pens. She had aristocratic, high, protruding cheekbones. Her complexion was creamy and transparent as rice paper. Her nose was straight and the nostrils flared. She had cat-grey eyes and her brown, shoulder-length hair flowed like corn silk. She could have been on the cover of *Vogue*. It was obvious, only she did not know she was beautiful.

"I'm a sophomore and I'm engaged to a guy who's studying to be a doctor. His name's Franklin Nelsen and you'll probably be seeing a lot of him around campus. He thinks he's a big football hero. Myself, I'm majoring in opera and theater and I'm a cheerleader during football season. How about you?"

Rebecca was impressed. She lit up a cigarette and shyly replied, "I'm afraid you're stuck with a freshman. And I'm taking English lit. I'd like to be in music, but my parents didn't think I had enough talent."

"Parents can sure be a pain in the butt. I can see by the length of your fingers that you must have been a pianist."

Rebecca felt at ease with that remark. She wondered if Matty had already noticed that she didn't shave the hair under her arms. She was pleasantly surprised to discover her new roommate's kindness and intelligence. And the smoking didn't bother her!

"Yes, I was. I tried to please my folks, but they just wanted me in Carnegie Hall and I wasn't good enough. So now I just play for my own pleasure. Mostly Chopin. Do you like him?"

"He's my favorite classical composer, but I love jazz the best. You know, Monk, Parker, Coltrane, Montgomery—that type." Rebecca was embarrassed. She didn't recognize a single name. Fortunately, Matty continued, "And I *die* over Miles Davis. He's my all-time favorite. Maybe we can sneak up to San Francisco one weekend and hear him play?"

"Sure! I'd love that."

During their first semester living together, they played the piano in the dorm lounge and sang and talked every night for a long while before bed. Naive, sheltered Rebecca had been unaware that blacks had a middle class, let alone an upper, social and monetary class. She heard long and fascinating stories about Malcolm X, Martin Luther King, soul music, James Brown, Chuck Berry, drugs, peace marches, the Vietnam war, civil rights, the pill, women's rights and football. They giggled uncontrollably when they smoked their first pot together and as time went by they became fast friends.

The scholastic work came easily to Rebecca and she was on her way to becoming an honor student; yet, she still found time to join every radical group on campus in protest of whatever was the rage at the time.

Still, she found no solace in her adventures. Rebecca was a born follower. She had found no focus for her growing restlessness, until one Saturday morning Matty came running into the room yelling, "Come on and get dressed, Rebecca, we're getting your nose out of the books and going to the 'Big Game' this afternoon!"

"Matty, I've never been to a football game. I wouldn't know what to do. I'd rather sit here and read Eliot or cummings than watch all that violence."

"Come on, you'll love it! And besides, you'll finally get to meet Franklin."

"Oh, all right. But I'm coming straight home afterwards."

The autumn day was brisk, but sunny. The Stanford stadium was packed with seventy-five thousand screaming fans; Rebecca had never seen so many people together at one time in her life. All seemed to be dressed in either blue and gold for Cal or red and white for Stanford. Rebecca felt lucky that she had worn a bulky, red turtleneck sweater. Her hair was pulled back in a long braid with a red chiffon scarf tied at the end, and she had on white corduroy slacks and a pair of L.L. Bean duck boots.

A small, swirling wind made a mini-tornado of fallen elm leaves under one of the goalposts. A cannon, tilted upward on a two-wheeled chariot, was being fired indiscriminately into the air by the Stanford male cheerleaders and huge puffs of smoke belched from its barrel after each volley. Someone dressed as a large California golden bear was circling the field, egging on the blue and gold fans to heights of hysteria. Pom-pom girls waved bright, fluffy streamers on both sides of the stadium. Rebecca had a seat right behind the Stanford players' bench and she could see Matty on the field leading a cheer. With her legs scissoring high, Matty waved and then started belting out the school's fight song through a red and white megaphone. The fans in the stands all stood up and screams from the

Stanford half of the seventy-five thousand fans burst from their throats, as a hundred or so red-and-white-clad football players ran onto the field from the tunnel. The fans on the opposite side of the stadium hoisted placards in unison that said, "GO CAL!"

Two players, one the largest human being Rebecca had ever seen, and the other with his helmet off—the handsomest—moved apart from the other yelling players and strode to the center of the field. There they met with a number of men in black-and-white-striped shirts and two other blue-and-gold-clad Cal football players. Everyone watched anxiously as they flipped a coin in the middle of the field. A student band blared the Cal fight song from a section above her.

One man in a white hat and striped shirt touched the shoulders of the immense man in uniform number 65 and the handsome one wearing number 12, motioning for them to turn around with their backs to the south goalpost. The other two opposing players then stood and faced them and the man in the white-hat made a kicking motion toward the blue and gold players. A large cheer went up and the two Stanford players put their helmets on and ran toward their fellow players. Another huge yell went up from the crowd. The soft downy hair on Rebecca's arms stood on end. She had never felt such electricity. Like everyone else, she stood up and started jumping and screaming—for who knew what. She could hear the coaches yelling instructions to the players heading onto the field. Among them was the large man. Matty waved again and pointed to the big man. "That's Franklin," she mouthed, "number 65!"

Rebecca unwadded her damp football program, which had been squashed in her excitement. It read:

Franklin Nelsen. Senior. Major: pre-medicine. All American. Offensive guard, co-captain. Track and field. 6' 5", 270 lbs. Home town: Fort Worth, Texas.

His photo showed a gap-toothed Huckleberry Finn smile on a huge, Afro-curly head.

The other man, number 12, had his helmet off. He was squatting directly below Rebecca, one knee on the ground and one hand leaning on the helmet. His damp hair was dark brown and he ran his fingers through the sweat, pulling the hair straight back in the direction it grew. She was so curious about what was going on around her that she forgot to look up his name in the program. He appeared to be of normal height. His lean, muscled body emanated energy. His face was tanned and taut with anticipation. He knelt motionless, like a cheetah waiting to pounce on the first prey that moved. Rebecca recalled his graceful stride onto the field and his cocky grin. He seemed to have complete self-control, and the other players gravitated to him. Then, majestically, she thought, he stood up and started throwing a football back and forth with another player. The ball spiraled perfectly every time he threw it to the other gangly player. They were nervously joking about something when someone yelled, "Reid, get your butt warmed up!"

Rebecca thought that an odd request; however, number 12 yelled back confidently, "Don't worry, coach. The arm's warm."

She was also confused as to why all of these athletic young men kept patting each other on their rear ends.

A student in the crowd behind Rebecca was yelling down encouragement to number 12.

"Come on, Scott! These guys are a bunch of puss—let's score on the first drive!"

An older fan shouted, "Scott Reid, we love you! Go get 'em!"

Number 12 looked intently out to the field while all of the players lined up across from each other at mid-field, and he called to number 65, "Let's kick ass, Frank! If you guys don't run it back, get me good field position."

Rebecca had no idea what he or anyone else was talking about, but she got so carried away in the crowd's euphoria that she cupped her hands and screamed at the top of her lungs to the disappearing Franklin Nelsen, "Come on Franklin, let's kick some ass out there!"

Scott turned around at the sound of Rebecca's voice and smiled at her. His eyes were the deepest, most penetrating blue she had ever seen. He had a red bandanna wrapped around his sinewy, perspiring neck. His lips were full and his cheeks tan, but flushed with color. It seemed to her that he had hundreds of dazzling white teeth in his mouth. He winked and gave her a raised-fist salute.

Then, laser-like, his entire concentration locked on to the field as the crowd screamed and a little Cal player kicked the football to the far end of the field to a Stanford player. She grimaced as twenty-two bodies collided in full stride. Whistles blew over the pile of massive torsos and limbs on the forty yard line. A small group of players ran off the field and number 12 ran on. The coach patted him on the rear end as he left the sideline. The entire Stanford rooting section hollered, "COME ON, Scott!"

How gauche, she thought, as she yelled his name with the chorus. Why did she seem to be enjoying the physical violence of this autumnal male ritual? And why now did she feel the warm damp sensation between her legs?

Rebecca unwadded the crumpled football program again and moved her finger down to player number 12.

Scott Reid. Junior. Major: pre-medicine. Co-captain, Quarterback. 6' 1", 185 lbs. All Conference, Football. All American, tennis. Home town: Los Angeles, CA.

She tore out the grainy photo and slipped it into her pants pocket.

As Rebecca watched Scott lead his teammates time and time again to rally from behind, she saw the compelling confidence she was looking for. A person afraid of nothing, one who commanded instant respect from others. A winner. A human being who knew who he was and what he wanted and how to get it. Romantically, she wondered whether it was like this for Josephine when she saw her Napoleon storm into battle.

After the "Big Game" was won, the real crowd celebration started. They swarmed the field, pounding and patting the winning players all over; screaming their names and tearing down the goal posts. They then hoisted Scott on their shoulders and carried him across the field to the tunnel leading to the dressing room. When they put him down, he trotted over to number 65. Franklin, grinning his gap-toothed smile, picked him up with one arm and shook him like a rag doll. Matty was crying and ran over to Rebecca, dragging her into their circle of celebration. Scott looked down from Franklin's grasp and said to her.

"Hey, beautiful one, thanks for the support before the game. Join us for a beer over at the Rathskeller?"

It was as if Saint George had ridden up on his white stallion and slain all of the dragons she had feared in her life. With all that must have been going through his mind that afternoon, he actually remembered her cheering him!

She decided not to go straight home.

REALITY FACES RUMOR

The modified Pratt and Whitney turbine jet engines on the silver Gulfstream V were being warmed up on the tarmac in front of the terminal at the Santa Monica airport. They screamed their desire to be airborne. KRAMER was painted in black down the tail rudder of the plane. The aircraft had been customized to fly twelve people anywhere in the world in the utmost luxury. It had three bedrooms, a kitchen, a dining room, a private study for Josh, complete with devices that would communicate electronically anywhere on earth, and a large lounge with leather seats. There were two Korean stewards to accommodate the passengers.

While Scott buckled his seat belt, he handed Josh a file folder containing all of the test results Milton had taken on his blood over the past few months. Josh mulled over the papers in silence as they took off over a haze-streaked Los Angeles. He simply could not understand the discrepancy in the results. In less than an hour, the big jet was just another vapor trail in the western sky.

"Scott, is it possible MRL has some equipment available to detect HIV that you don't have at your lab?"

"I've thought about it, and I asked Milton," Scott said. "He says there's only a one-in-five million chance of that happening. There's a mutated HIV-2, which can't be detected a hundred percent with the old Western blot test. But, Josh, there are only about fifty thousand cases of this mutation worldwide, of which only about forty have ever been discovered in America. Highly unlikely I would be unlucky enough to have caught that. Anyway, the physician who's analyzing my latest sample will be using every test available on the market, so I can prove beyond a doubt by next week that I only have CMV. What you also fail to understand is the logistics of a person like you or me ever getting AIDS. It's almost next to impossible with our lifestyles."

"Speak for yourself, Scott. You're talking about me and I'm an old duffer now. I'm happy to get it up occasionally for Annie. But you, on the other hand—I keep reading that you're out putting your dick in every little Hollywood hopeful that hits town. I'd think you would be quite susceptible to any kind of V.D., and I'm certain that's what Pamela thought."

Scott inhaled the aroma from the leather seats, then coughed a throaty, dry cough. He felt drowsy. He put his hands behind his head and laughed at Josh.

"Hey, Josh, I had no idea you bought those grocery store

tabloids. If I got half the action I'm credited for, I'd have been dead long ago from overexertion, not AIDS. Why don't we just chuck this conversation until I get you the new test results?"

"Good idea. Have you ever been bonefishing before?"

Scott yawned rudely. "Nope. I've got no idea what a bonefish is, and I don't imagine Richard or Gino do either."

"Look, Scott, I know you don't like the Senator and his little mouthpiece, but they're some of those necessary evils. Don't let the pricks bother you like they did at the shareholder meeting."

"I won't," Scott assured him. "As long as they don't start bugging me about this HIV thing."

"I'll make sure we steer clear of that subject. Now, let me tell you about *Albula vulpes*, the bonefish. This little silver bastard will give you the best fight, pound for pound, of any game fish in the world. I've fished every warm-water shallow in the seas where they exist and I'm telling you, they give you sport like you've never had before. But I always throw the buggers back because they're no good to eat. We'll be going over to an outer island between Aruba and the coast of Venezuela. We have a cabin to stay in at night, we'll have a few drinks, relax, and go fishing all day. How's that sound to your aching body?"

There was no answer from Scott. Josh smiled like a proud parent, for Scott was already sound asleep.

About an hour before touchdown in Washington, D.C., one of the stewards woke Scott up. He left behind a tray, on which there was a chicken salad sandwich, a cup of mint tea and a hot, damp towel. Josh was in his private study, telephoning and faxing around the world to check on his business interests.

Even though the Gulfstream was thirty minutes ahead of schedule with a favorable tailwind, Ralph, Richard and Gino were already inebriated when the plane arrived. They greeted Josh noisily. Richard, with the foul mouth he was noted for, couldn't wait to tell Josh his latest insipid ethnic joke. He bellowed in his heartiest congressional chamber voice, "Josh, old buddy, do you know why Wop men want to grow moustaches?"

Josh did not bother to answer him. He just glared, so the senator pressed on with the punch line.

"So they can look like their mothers."

Richard slapped the Italian on the back in hilarity.

"Did you get it, Gino?"

The Sicilian attorney gave him a drunken, woeful grin. The Korean steward who had taken the senator's jacket, stoically grimaced. Josh did not laugh. Scott silently wondered to himself why he had ever come on this trip. He looked out the plane's window, hoping to get a glimpse of the multicolored autumn foliage. Burnt-red leaves of indigenous oaks or maybe the gold-and-silver tipped three-pronged maple leaves—but they were completely enveloped in darkness.

Gino carried on a large, bulging briefcase along with the senator's personal bag. With great reluctance he and Richard shook hands with Scott. As soon as they thought no one would notice, they stealthily went to the toilet and washed their hands.

The pilots filed their flight plan with the Dulles terminal tower for over Cuba and Haiti to Willemstad, the capitol of Curacao, and they were airborne. Josh and Scott chose to pass on the drinks that were offered, but the other three ordered double martinis. It did not take Richard and Gino long to say what was on their minds. But the attorney did the talking. For effect, he asked Scott in his roughest, back-alley Newark voice, "Say, Reid, are these rumors true about you dying of AIDS? Because if they are, don't you think you should be taking some precautions on our behalf? Like maybe staying at home?"

Grinning through his acne-scarred face, he winked at Richard and Ralph.

Scott was instantly hot.

"Look, you uninformed jerk, I was invited on this trip by Josh and I wasn't too thrilled to find out you were going to be here too. And I don't have AIDS!

Josh interceded with authority.

"Let's set some matters straight, gentlemen. First, Gino and Scott, why don't you let bygones be bygones over the last MRL meeting? Scott, you raised holy hell at that meeting because you thought MRL was not spending enough of their profits on R&D for AIDS. If you recall, I allowed your views to be heard by all of the shareholders present. Gino and his backers disagreed with you in favor of a stock split, hiring another lobbyist and raising salaries for officers and directors. You then sold all of your MRL holdings—which was your right—and at a *large* profit, I might add. So, why not let the issue drop there?" Everyone looked at one another sheepishly.

Josh's eyes narrowed. "And Gino, you're still a director of my corporation in good standing at this point in time. Don't push your luck by questioning why a personal friend of mine is a guest on my aircraft!"

Gino, who had a mouth like a lamprey, sucked in a gulp of air that moved all the way through his bobbing Adam's apple. Josh continued.

"Second, Scott has shown me documents from his own laboratory. Those results show him negative for HIV. Until we have a third opinion, which Scott has coming next week from another lab, don't you think it would be prudent to withhold final judgement? After all, mistakes happen. Let's all just relax and have a good time fishing. And when you boys are finished drinking, you take the bedrooms for some shut-eye. Scott and I slept on the way here. Now, if you'll excuse me, I'm going back to work in my study."

Nodding, with bloodshot eyes and far too drunk to debate anything rationally, Richard and Ralph agreed. Neither of them believed that Medical Reference Laboratory had made a mistake in their blood test on Scott, but Josh's word was law on this airplane. Gino was still attempting to catch his breath, but he did move his head up and down.

Other than the drone of the jet engines, there was silence in the cabin. Then there were some mandatory polite smiles and some thumbing through the magazines that were lying on the lounge tables. Landen yawned and in short order got up to go to bed, banging his head on the overhead bin. Ralph was six feet eight inches tall and gangly. When he was drinking he completely forgot about his height and often had a knot on his head in the morning. But he did not forget his token manners, and said in a slurred squeak, "Good night, all. See you in time for the fishing."

Richard, smoothing his thin mustache with a finger, soon followed. Although he was already drunk, Gino ordered another double Beefeater martini. He sat directly opposite Scott and stared at him belligerently. Scott admired the silver mane of hair Gino had blow-dried and coiffed straight back. After a brief period Gino removed his gaze and dialed the combination lock on his leather briefcase. Once that was done, he extracted a key from his waistcoat pocket to open the top lock. Scott could not help but notice what a huge production Gino was making over the contents of his briefcase. Must be something very important, he mused.

Gino leafed through papers for an hour, all the while downing more martinis. Scott adjusted his reclining seat to its lowest position and was almost lying down. But he was wide awake, watching the constellation Orion twinkle outside his oval window. He stretched his entire body like a cat, trying to find the brightness of Venus.

All of a sudden Gino slumped against the bulkhead of his seat with a solid thump. Vomit spilled down his silk shirt and tie. Lying in that seat was Gino's open briefcase. Papers were strewn over the seat and the floor from Gino's fall. The stewards had shut down most of the lights so Scott unbuckled his seat belt and leaned over the empty seat next to Gino to retrieve the falling papers. Staring up at Scott from the floor was a legal-looking document that said:

"MEMORANDUM OF WISHES, ZAFRA LIMITED."

Scott knew that Gino represented Zafra Limited on the Board of Directors of Medical Reference Laboratories, however, he did not know who the beneficial owner of Zafra

Limited was, nor did anyone else in America. He looked at Gino, slumped over, his head now propped against the window. Frothy drool bubbled from his mouth. He reeked sourly. Scott got on his knees and picked up the Memorandum of Wishes from the floor to put back in the briefcase. On the bottom line of the front page it read in capital letters that the beneficial owner of Zafra, Limited was RICHARD T. SPOUT.

Scott mumbled to himself, "I'll be a son of a bitch—Richard!"

That meant the senator was the sole owner of Zafra Limited, based in the Netherlands Antilles. This corporation was hidden in a secret bank account by what is called a *Memorandum of Wishes*—a document issued by a bank setting up a foreign corporation that wants to conceal the name of the beneficial owner of the said corporation. As the beneficial owner, Richard Spout had all the voting and controlling shares put in his name in the Memorandum of Wishes. He had been secreting funds offshore for years which he accumulated in different accounts and overseas locations. He never knew for sure when his father was going to die, or if he was ever going to be appointed trustee of the family fortune. Therefore, Richard took precautions for his own future.

He hid the Memorandum of Wishes in a safe-deposit box in another bank in the Netherlands Antilles and appointed nominee directors to his company, Zafra Limited. Those nominee directors, his bank, his stockbroker and his accountant had no power whatsoever to withdraw funds or to act in any way without his consent. They were effectively inert, except that they appeared to any outsider or tax-collector to make all the corporation's decisions. On paper, they appeared to be the owners of the corporation, but they were only trustees. Completely safe from anyone's prying eyes, Richard Spout owned and controlled eighteen percent of a fast-growing billion-dollar company, and slick-figuring Rigitinni made sure that nothing could tarnish this pot of gold.

Scott felt vindicated; his intuition had been right. The senator knew far too much about the business of Medical Reference Laboratories. Scott picked up the next stack of papers. It too contained a Memorandum of Wishes, only this time for a Hong Kong corporation, Malaysian Latex. The world's largest producer of rubber gloves for the medical industry. It had recently grown to over a billion dollars in annual revenue because of the AIDS scare. The beneficial owner of this corporation and two other Luxembourg corporations was also Richard T. Spout. Scott thought he could guess who Richard's partners were in these operations. As he went to put the papers back in the briefcase, Gino's hand shot out of the shadows, grabbing him by the wrist. His breath smelled like vomit and he growled, "You snoopy, AIDS-infected faggot. You'll pay for this!"

Scott, kneeling and caught off guard, had no time to react, or to say anything. Gino quickly snatched all of the papers from him and crammed them into the case. He lurched over the back of Scott's legs and staggered off into the senator's bedroom. Scott heard him wake Richard, then all he could hear were whispers.

Josh stuck his head out from his study.

"Hey, Scott, is everything quiet on the battlefront?"

Scott did not know what to say. He wanted to go tell

Josh what he had just discovered, but he wondered if it was possible that Josh was involved in some manner with Richard Spout. It was incomprehensible. But he would wait until he could think the whole situation out. After all, Josh had invited him on this trip to the tax haven Antilles with Richard and Gino. Two men Josh knew Scott despised.

He answered Josh, "Yup, the drinking brigade all went to bed."

The toilet was in the rear of the plane and Scott got up to walk back to it. As he tiptoed by Richard's bedroom the senator's deep-voiced whispers were mumbled. Scott could not make out the words, but they were loud and angry. Gino could hear them clearly, however.

"Gino, are you sure the bastard saw everything? How could you let something like this happen? Your orders were to never have those documents outside of the Antilles or Hong Kong. What the hell were they doing in your briefcase anyway?"

"Richard, for Chrissakes, you told me to bring them from the safe-box to you in the States, remember? I was the one who begged you to never take them out of the offshore banks. We were all drunk...maybe I nodded off for a while. How could I know this queer would get a case of the nosies?"

The senator's hair was matted down on one side from sleeping and he tried fluffing it out with his hand while he talked.

"Gino, just because the guy's got AIDS doesn't mean he sucks dick. After all, he's been hosing Kramer's ex-wife for a long time. You don't think he'll go running to Josh, do you?"

"There's no way he would go to Kramer. How does he know that Josh isn't in it with us? After all, we're the ones in business with Kramer, not him! Our problem is what in hell do we do about this?"

The senator was still fussing with his cowlicked hair.

"Do you think the bastard saw our Hong Kong operation?"

"Absolutely. He was sucking up that data like you suck up the President." Gino's air of confidence returned with his wit.

"You're not very damn funny, Gino." Richard snapped. "If you'd been more careful we wouldn't be in this predicament. But it's as simple as this—the prick's got to go. You know what I mean?"

"I read you, senator. If he's got AIDS, our problem is solved, if he doesn't, I've got plenty of acquaintances out in Los Angeles who could take care of this matter for us before it gets out of hand. Just let me handle it, OK?"

"Okay, Gino. But no slip-ups and we have to get it done as soon as possible. Understand? Now get out of here and go wash up. You smell like a stinking pig in puke."

The following morning the private jet, with full flaps on, landed on the short runway in Willemstad. The chargé d'affaires from the island's ministry of tourism was on hand to greet them. He was a short, robust mulatto, wearing a floral red shirt and rubber sandals. He was missing his two front teeth and he lisped to the arriving party.

"I apologize for my appearance, however, my dentist is very expensive and I have no funds to replace my teeth—they were gold ones!"

It was a photographic bonus that a U.S. Senator was

with Josh and the chargé d'affaires quickly sidled up between them so the local press could capture a few pictures of the visiting dignitaries.

It was quite a picture. From right to left stood tall, scrawny Ralph Landen, stocky Josh Kramer, red-nosed Senator Richard Spout, Scott Reid, sulking, hung-over Gino Rigitinni and the beaming and brightly-clad island official. After this brief ceremony, the diplomat piled them into a van and took them to the hotel for the night.

Curacao is relatively flat, but the many colorful, pastel-painted Dutch villages, clear water, swaying coconut trees, and flowering shrubs set off a scenic atoll. The water is so clear that submarine visibility sometimes exceeds two hundred feet, making for fantastic fishing and diving around the shallow reefs.

The Antilles are composed of two groups of small islands. The northern group of islands, southeast of Puerto Rico, are part French. The three southern islands, Curacao, Aruba and Bonaire, are located near the South American coastline. Although tourism, shipbuilding and oil refining from Venezuela's rich Orinoco fields are of prime importance to the economy, the islands are well-loved by tax experts around the world for their incorporation laws and strictly enforced banking secrecy. Over four hundred banks and thousands of world wide companies are incorporated there.

The hotel was located on a beautiful, wide white strand of beach that runs in an enlongated horseshoe for about three miles on the east side of Curacao.

A Norwegian cruise ship lay anchored outside the bay. Richard and Gino spotted it at the moment the van pulled up to the hotel's canopied front door. Neither of them realized that the liner was owned by Kramer Enterprises.

"Gino, look at the size of that boat!" The senator yelled. "Nothing but horny Scandahovians. Poo-den-dum and Poo-see. I don't care if they smell like kipper snacks. Let's get a dinghy out to that ship."

Embarrassed, the dignitary volunteered, with his tongue protruding between the gap in his front teeth, that one could rent a rubber raft with a motor on it at the beach.

Josh glared angrily at Richard.

"Senator, has it ever dawned on you that you're a paid representative of the United States government?"

The legislator adjusted his bow tie and retorted, "Josh, I just give the people what they want. Come on, let's hit the beach, Gino."

The hotel staff unloaded the new guests' fishing gear and baggage. The plan Ralph had made was for them to spend one night on Curacao and then helicopter over to the outer island in the morning for five days of fishing.

Scott felt the effects of the tropical heat and humidity. He did not think he was ill, all he wanted to do was lie down for a while. He also wanted some time alone to contemplate his previous night's discoveries. He left a note for everyone at the front desk telling them he would meet them for dinner at eight, then went to his room. Josh and Ralph decided on a round of golf at the small nine-hole course behind the hotel.

The overhead fan squeaked noisily and after a time it woke Scott from his slumber. He felt quite good as long as he was relaxing, but any form of physical effort seemed to drain his energy. He decided to resume his outline for the press. He took a pen and hotel stationery from the desk and started writing down his thoughts.

It was not the right time to file a libel suit against Pamela or the columnist. They could wait. It also seemed best to wait before saying anything to Josh about Spout's ownership of Zafra Limited—*and* his theory that Richard was involved with an underworld Hong Kong corporation that controlled most of the world's supply of rubber medical gloves. Scott could not believe Josh would in any way be involved with these people, but he also knew that business made strange bedfellows. There were too many unknowns in this mysterious equation.

Scott also had no idea that Gino, too drunk to stop him, had watched him out of the corner of his eye while Scott perused the Memorandum of Wishes. The telephone rang. It was the soprano voice of Ralph Landen.

"Scott, I hope I didn't wake you, but we've decided on an early dinner so we can get cracking first thing in the morning. Can you make it down in thirty minutes?"

Scott put on a blue blazer over a white cotton shirt and white slacks. He slipped docksiders over his bare feet and then took the elevator down to the restaurant.

At a corner booth he saw Josh waving for him to join them. Engrossed in the two dates they had found, Richard and Gino did not bother to welcome Scott. A pair of ultra-blond Swedish girls from the cruise ship, dressed in nothing but fluorescent-colored string bikinis. During the afternoon they had all snorted cocaine in Gino's room and they were now laughing in stoned humor.

The island has a large sea turtle farm, so the restaurant's

turtle soup and turtle steaks had been ordered for all.

While noisily chewing the leathery meat, Richard was telling the captive blond audience whom he and Gino had trapped in the corner, all about his knowledge of turtles. Ralph and Josh told Scott about the golf course they had just played on.

The cruise ship's whistle blasted an ear-shattering call for all passengers. The girls excused themselves. Bouncing breasts and firm glutei brushed against Richard and Gino as the young ladies crawled out around the table heading for their floating home. But that was as close as those two men got to their intended prey, for the girls never came back to the booth.

Apart from the thunderous clatter of the rotors, the helicopter ride over to the outer island in the morning was deathly quiet. One could make out the coastline of Venezuela through the plexiglass. Richard and Gino were sullenly silent—they were both still angry at what Scott had seen on the plane. But their mood changed once the helicopter landed. They ensconced themselves in the cabin, had a drink and yelled profanities at the crew of the dingy fishing trawler waiting to take them to sea.

The fishing was spectacular. Josh had not understated the bonefish's desire to fight. They were not large—about twenty to thirty pounds, but the fish split the water like exploding mortar shells every time someone got a strike. The water was a crystal clear aquamarine, the sea flat, the sun baking hot. Scott could feel the infection in his body subsiding. Aside from the unshaven and ragged crew, there were no other people around, just peace and quiet.

They fished, played cards and backgammon and drank beer and rum for three days. Aside from their own voices, the only sounds were the waves lapping the shore and the abundance of multicolored island birds singing. On the fourth day, Gino came down sick and they had to radio for the helicopter to pick him up for a ride to see a doctor in Willemstad. The others stayed to enjoy the last day of fishing and solitude.

Gino was malingering. He was not in the least sick. He had private telephone calls to make to Los Angeles. He went to a public telephone booth armed with a handful of coins. His first call was to IMA Laboratories and his nephew, Doctor Nicki Graziano.

"Nicki, Uncle Gino here. I need a favor. Or to put it another way, *we* need a favor. Know what I mean, Kid?"

The young doctor, physically slight, but mentally competent, was one of those people who are born with a chip on their shoulder. He adjusted an engraved gold cuff-link that was protruding through his monogrammed French cuff.

"Gino, you're talking to one of the Family. You don't have to explain. How can I help?"

"Your boss." Gino rasped. "Scott Reid is having some of his blood tested for HIV at your lab. Then he said he's sending it out to another lab for a second opinion so he can make a news release when he gets back, saying he doesn't have HIV. I need to know who's doing the testing and if you can find out the results for me. No questions asked."

Nicki leaned forward in his lab chair, his interest

piqued. He needed to do a few favors for the Family so he would get some notice.

"This must be fate, Gino. I took Scott's blood right before he left and I've already run his tests. He's a lucky man, he doesn't have HIV, only a bad cytomegalovirus infection. But Gino, I didn't forward his blood to another lab for further testing yet because I know my tests are one hundred percent accurate."

There was a long silent pause and sputtering static on the telephone, although Nicki could hear someone breathing hard.

"Gino, you still there?"

"Yeah, kid, I'm here. Listen, have you told anyone? Anyone at all, about Reid's blood test that you took?"

"No, Gino, not a soul. Why?"

"I warned you, Nicki, no questions. I need your help and I need it as soon as Reid gets back in town. Right now you have to tell anybody that asks that Reid tested *positive* for CMV and HIV. Including Reid, if he calls. Do you understand?"

Nicki stood up with his telephone and was pacing his office floor. His starched shirt cuffs had crawled up his lab coat sleeves. He craned his neck to see if the lab's door was shut tight.

"I don't understand, Gino, but you know I'll do it for you. Can't you give me a few more details?"

"Because you're Family, I'll give it to you straight, Kid. If Reid doesn't die quickly of the AIDS everyone thinks he's got, then there's going to be a contract on him. Now you reading me?"

Doctor Graziano ran his hand through his damp, curly

hair. He knew the code. Family came before any other relationship.

"So you want me to take care of this matter in a medical way?"

"You got the gist of it now, Kid. As I said, everyone already thinks Reid's got AIDS. All he needs is to actually have it. It's simple. Once he's got it, he's gone and out of our way. How long do you think something like that would take to finish the job?"

A chill ran down Nicki's spine. "Probably around three months at the earliest if he was really infected," He said. He felt numbly calm.

Rigitinni whispered into the mouthpiece, "You mean you'll be able to do it?"

Nicki knew this was his litmus test with the Family. If he turned it down or failed to do it, he would probably not get another opportunity to prove himself or his loyalty. He replied matter-of-factly, "It won't be a pleasure, but leave it up to me. I'll get it done and call you to confirm when the job's completed."

Ecstatically, Gino said, "That's my boy! And look, Kid, we need this taken care of as soon as Reid gets back to town. Also, whenever you call me, make damn sure it's only on my cellular telephone line. All my calls at home in New York are taped for my protection. I want it that way. So no personal business on that line, capiche?"

His voice hardened. "And remember, Kid, no fuckups!"

As dusk set in and red hues gleamed though wisps of feathery cirrus clouds, Scott, Josh, Ralph and the Senator quit fishing for the day. They retreated back to shore and the comfort of the cabin. Josh and Ralph decided to take a walk on the rocky beach before dinner.

Clad in an unbuttoned army fatigue jacket and his bathing suit, Richard made a rum and coke and sat drinking it in the bungalow. His fair skin was very sunburned. Scott, evenly tanned in jeans and a striped blue and white shirt, was sitting at the table working on his press release. Richard got up, spilling some of his drink down his bare belly, and walked over to the table, pulled out a chair and sat down with Scott.

"Look, Reid, I know there seem to be some bad feelings between you and Gino, but don't mind him. He doesn't mean any harm. He just thinks he's protecting Josh's interests at MRL, that's all."

The senator emitted a rancid rum belch and continued.

"I'm sure you're aware I'm heading the Senate subcommittee on AIDS funding. I think I might be able to help with your HIV problem. I've met every top doctor in the world who knows anything at all about the subject."

Scott dropped the pen he was writing with and said abruptly,

"I appreciate your concern, Richard, but I don't have an HIV problem and I'm extremely tired of your attitude. As Josh told you earlier, I was misdiagnosed by MRL and I'm in the process of getting it straightened out. I'm working on my press release right now. An outside lab is doing an analysis to confirm that the story on me being positive was all a mistake."

Richard, his nose now a deep purple, took a long sip of his rum and coke.

"Well, that's a relief to hear. I was telling Gino, what an irony it would be if you gave five million bucks to some nigger AIDS charity when you sold your stock in MRL and then you get the goddamn disease!"

Scott's voice was steel. "I'll repeat it for the last time. I do *not* have HIV. And the next time you see Mike Tyson, why don't you try calling him a nigger to his face."

Richard snorted, "Gino's right, you are a touchy bastard."

"You're both right," Scott said. "I am a bastard and I'm damn touchy about bigots. Especially political bigots!"

The senator stiffened. He hoped that Gino would soon have Scott out of the way, but being a coward, he did not push the present issue. He took a long swig of his drink.

"I'm no racist, hell, I've got lots of colored friends. Look, Reid, I'm truly happy you think you don't have AIDS, but calm down and tell me, what were your views that made Gino and the stockholders so mad at that meeting? Josh said you knew what you were talking about and that I might learn something." The senator gave Scott a sly grin, winked and continued, "Who knows, even though I'm not in the White House yet, I might be able to use a little of my influence up on the Hill, if you've got something to say."

Scott was repulsed by the man's audacity, but tried being polite. "Thanks, Richard. What I'd like to know is if you've any idea the heights of malfeasance and fraud being perpetrated about AIDS in medicine, law and the legislatures? The lies and deception are beyond comprehension."

The senator got up, went over to the cooler and made

himself another rum and coke. Then he sat back down.

"Like—what kind of lies and deception?"

"For example, how often has the public heard that there's a vaccine just around the corner?"

Richard hiccuped and quickly replied, "I'm sure there is. We're spending billions to make sure that happens."

Scott was disgusted.

"Well, let me tell you as a man who has spent his life in the medical business, there *can't* be a vaccine for this virus. It's mathematically impossible. And as to your supposed billions spent—around six billion last fiscal year, I believe. Why is it that over ninety percent goes to attorneys, advertisers, administrators, government grant holders and so forth and less than ten percent of the funds actually go to patient care or any kind of research?"

Richard puffed up and put on his legislative voice.

"Reid, my boy, that's hardly fair. After all someone's got to be compensated for taking care of this problem."

"Then why not just compensate the infected directly?" Scott asked. "It would be more efficient and helpful. People want their daily needs cared for. They don't want government manipulation and funding for medicines that don't work! Jesus Christ, Richard, can't you understand that incompetent management of public funds by government is hardly taking care of the AIDS problem in America!"

Scott shoved his chair back from the table and glared at Richard, who replied silkily, "Right, let's just give the goddamn fags some cash. Come on, Reid, just tell me what in hell was on your mind at that meeting?"

"Look. What I was trying to tell those people at the shareholder meeting was that self-interest groups and the government are promoting AIDS in order to build a multi-billion-dollar industry. I don't believe the average citizen or shareholder wants to be part of that. Why should they get stuck with taxes for the billions of mismanaged funds you politicos allocate to these self-interest groups?"

Richard waved his hand in dismissal. "Sorry to interrupt, Reid, but we're only talking about six to ten billion dollars. We've got a multi-trillion dollar economy here."

Caustically, Scott replied, "As Senator Everett Dirksen once said, 'a billion here and a billion there and pretty soon we're starting to talk about real money!' Try to understand, Richard, the average guy, the taxpayer who's footing the bill, just wants to do whatever it takes to solve the AIDS problem. So I stood up and told people that it was outrageous for Medical Reference Laboratories to have six paid lobbyists in Washington working on more funding from the government for AIDS *testing*, when MRL ought to be investing those funds in AIDS *research*. That's it."

Idly brushing some sand from his matted hair, Richard said,

"Reid, I think you should take a look at how much help those lobbyists have been in getting the government involved with medicine over the years. They do a damn good job."

"Senator, why don't *you* take a good look at what our government and these lobbyists have done for us in medicine over the past thirty years?"

Scott's voice rose. "In 1962, when there was no Medicare and almost no other form of government involvement in medicine, the United States was number one in the world in every form of health care. It also had the most inexpensive medicine in the world. Today the U.S. is number twelve in the industrialized world in health care—and it is by far the most expensive country in the world for medical care. That's why you politicians and the lobbyists should *not* be trying to solve the AIDS problem! Your bungling interference has created a tragedy all over the map. Whether it's about AIDS or any other type of national health care."

A bright red and green plumed parrot squawked noisily in a palm tree outside the small cabin window. The legislator gave the bird an angry scowl, then turned and watched the sun starting to set for a brief moment. The parrot was busy pruning its tail feathers.

"Scott, I'm sure we could have been more efficient in our spending over the years, but how about the innocent victims of this tragedy?"

"Sadly, Richard, too many of them have become a vociferous minority who are more interested in protecting their privacy and freedom to infect others with this disease, than they are in protecting public health!"

Indignant, the senator asked, "Are you suggesting that we politicians take a stand against the queers, the druggies and the other AIDS-infected people of this country to protect public health? That's political suicide!"

Scott's voice was relentless. "So what? That's your duty. To protect the majority of your fellow citizens, not to pander to minority groups. Remember, senator, although this is a highly communicable disease, it's also a very controllable one. And it's about time you politicians told people it's a man-made one."

The legislator banged his glass on the table. Little pearly

beads of perspiration dotted his thin mustache.

"Bullshit, this ain't no man-made disease! I've been told by medical authorities that the green monkey in Africa and a fruitcake steward for Air Canada started spreading AIDS around the world years ago."

Scott spat his words in disgust. "Richard, do you mean to tell me you believe that crap? You make it sound like the monkey and the airline steward were bonking each other. Don't be so stupid. And let me remind you—there isn't a shred of scientific evidence that AIDS ever existed in America before '78!"

Like a doomed pawn thinking somehow he is still going to capture the queen, Richard said, "How about all of these articles I've read where they've dug up bodies from the 1950s and through DNA tests they found AIDS?"

Scott rejected this argument flatly. "Those are completely false and unsubstantiated rumors. I'm going to send over to your office all the data on how AIDS got started in the world and then maybe you won't come off as such an ignoramus. But I'll tell you, senator, homosexuals in this country were picked out as a group and infected with this disease in a way that borders on a Nazi mentality. And now they and every other innocent infected with this disease have to live up to their moral responsibility not to spread it any further. They have this human obligation just as they have the right to expect help in some fashion."

Richard's deep voice boomed, "We're adopting legislation every day to help these people, but we can't stop faggots from butt-holing one another, or sticking gerbils up their asses, or the goddamn dopers from shooting up and sharing dirty needles, or women from turning tricks." Sanctimoniously, he added, "They have to accept the fruits of their perversions."

Scott calmly replied, "I agree that people have to be held accountable for their lifestyles. But you politicians operate under the guise of protective legislation, good intentions, and individual rights. And yet you allow taxpayer monies to keep funding government laboratories that are still inventing retroviruses like AIDS. Richard, who knows what the next test tube might contain—it could be another AIDS—or worse! So why don't you get your fellow legislators to stop the testing of retroviruses instead of being so damn concerned about other people's private lives?"

The senator pleaded, "We can't stop research and development just because there's been a mistake or two in our programs. After all, we're doing everything we can to eradicate this disease."

Scott was so angry that he began crumpling the press release he had been working on into a tight ball in his fist.

"Senator, that's ludicrous and you know it. The American government doesn't tell people the truth about the transmission of this disease. When have you seen a government report that tells people that they can get AIDS from oral sex, by coughing or sneezing, by the public blood supply, by your infected doctor or dentist or from food handlers or other restaurant workers? You haven't and you won't because I believe that government doesn't want to stop this disease. In fact, you're trying to avoid doing what's necessary to control the spread!"

Richard quickly butted in. "Nonsense, Reid. We're spending a fortune and we're going to spend more to help control the spread of this."

"You just don't get it, do you. In a recent *London Sunday Times*, they scream about the fact that the AIDS epidemic has leveled off. They're suggesting cuts in government spending for AIDS in the U.K., Richard! But here in America it's just the opposite. Spend, spend, spend. With no results."

On his way to his third rum and coke, Richard said angrily,

"What do you want us to do, quit funding AIDS and put this nation into full-scale panic?"

"I think you've already put the nation in unnecessary panic, senator!" Scott retorted. "But I'd like you to do what's right—not what's politically convenient. For example, I know you've been told that one of the biggest problems associated with full blown AIDS is dementia. You've got thousands of cases of innocent people *purposely* being infected by mentally deranged people with AIDS. There are cases of prostitutes, doctors, dentists and jealous lovers with AIDS maliciously giving people their disease. Just imagine for a moment what a demented air traffic controller could do to you and hundreds of others on the next commercial plane you're on."

That got the senator's attention. He itched to interrupt, and pointed a finger at Scott, but Scott pressed on.

"You've heard these stories time and again in your senate committee meetings, yet you keep allowing infected people to intermingle with the rest of society. Even now you're trying to bring HIV-and-AIDS-infected immigrants into this country. What's the matter with you people, have you lost all common sense?"

Richard stood and gulped the last of his drink. As he started walking back to his chair, he tripped over the broken rubber thong hanging from the middle of one of his zorries, threw them both off, sat down and sarcastically replied, "And what's this magic cure-all you're talking about?"

Scott pointed his finger at the senator. "To start with, do the same as most of the countries of Europe do, where by the way, they have almost no incident rate of AIDS. That is the mandatory testing of all workers, then mandatory isolation from the workplace of the infected individuals!"

"Are you nuts, Reid? For sure I'd never get reelected!"

"We're not talking about your reelection, asshole, we're talking about survival! I realize it's not politically popular to protect the public health in this fashion with AIDS patients. But we do it with leprosy, cholera, measles, hepatitis and any other potential threat to public health!"

Richard sat with the back of his chair tilted away from Scott. He put his hands behind his head and said, "Come on, Reid. This's different."

"No Senator, it's not. And answer this question for me. Why should we as private citizens be forced by the government to interact with the AIDS-infected?"

Before Richard could reply, the door of the cabin burst open and Josh and Ralph came in, each holding a squirming rock lobster. Josh said, "Boil some water and let's eat!"

❧

Due to heavy fog the Gulfstream was not allowed to land at the Santa Monica airport. Instead, the seaside tower vectored the plane to the Burbank terminal in the valley. Gino had decided to return to Los Angeles with Josh and Scott. As the aircraft taxied to its mooring, Gino pointed out an oval window and said, "Welcome back to the real world, boys. Here come the reporters looking for a story."

Scott, who had been feeling physically decent for the first time in weeks, fought back a surge of queasiness.

"Josh, how did they manage to be here when we were supposed to be landing in Santa Monica?"

"That's their job. Wouldn't you call the air traffic controller to see where they were rerouting the planes? Relax, Scott. Gino and I can get off first. You stay on the plane for about thirty minutes. We'll tell them we dropped you off in Washington with Richard. That'll get them speculating. It's been a great trip. Call me when you get home."

Once the door of the plane opened, the reporters, like starving anteaters breaking up an earthen hill, stuck long, tongue-like microphones into any opening they could find. Not finding their prey, they dispersed within fifteen minutes.

Scott strolled out into the late afternoon sun with his carry-on bag and casually made his way to the terminal. He put a dollar's worth of coins into a big red Coke machine. The can dropped with a clunk into the bin. Sipping the cold drink, Scott hailed a cab and told the driver to drop him off at IMA Laboratories in Encino.

Paternally, Josh had not allowed Scott to call the laboratory or Doctor Graziano from the plane. He wanted Scott to forget all of his problems for six days. Scott had been grateful, but now he was eager both to clear his name and to start on some kind of medication for the CMV so that he might again savor his usual limitless energy.

The taxi driver babbled all the way to the laboratory, but Scott paid no heed. He tipped the cabbie an extra ten dollars and told him how much he enjoyed his conversation.

It was Monday, the ninth. Superstitious, Scott quickly figured that the upcoming Friday would be the thirteenth. Excited to be back, he wandered the halls of the lab. There were few people around, only the security guards and the janitorial staff, so he walked up to his office. His digital desk clock greeted him, blinking the time and date. Whistling, he circled the thirty-first on his desk calendar pad. Halloween. One of his favorite celebrations, and it was just a few weeks away. Most of his CMV symptoms would surely be gone by then and he could throw his annual costume party at the house. He hoped for a clear night and a full orange moon.

Scott was starting to perspire heavily again and felt slightly dizzy. It was only the traveling, he assumed. He called down to Milton Schwartz's office. No one answered; then he remembered that Milton was on vacation until the following Monday. He punched Nicki Graziano's office number into the intercom. Surprisingly, the physician answered himself.

"Infectious disease, Graziano."

Nicki had been working late because he did not want

what he was working on detected by anyone. He had saved a liter of blood from a patient who had recently died of AIDS brought on by *Pneumocystis carinii* pneumonia. The patient also had the rare infection, HIV-2.

One does not die from AIDS itself, one dies from the various opportunistic infections which correlate with AIDS. This patient had died because an invasion of the fungi, *Cryptococcus neoformans,* had caused a pulmonary infection so severe that the pneumonia took his life.

Nicki had been working on the project since the day he received Gino Rigitinni's telephone call from Curacao. He had just finished putting some of the AIDS-infected liquid into a twenty cc syringe. Just as he put the syringe into his small, padlocked office refrigerator, the intercom went off. His heart started thumping when he heard Scott's voice. He could hear its beat echo in his head.

"Nicki, you old golf ringer. Glad to know somebody's working around here. Do you have time to come up and have a chat with me before you go home?"

"Scott, welcome back. I was just thinking about you. I've got good news and not-so-good news. First of all, I can't find any trace of HIV in your blood. Only a lot of cytomegalovirus. But I didn't take enough blood last time to send out a sample to another lab so we could have them do a specific HIV-2 test. So, the bad news is that I'll have to draw some more blood when you feel up to it and then send it out for the final analysis. I could have that result next week."

Eyes shut, the physician gripped the phone and waited for Scott's response. This could be his chance to inject the lethal dose of tainted blood.

Scott said, "Nicki, come on up with your tools and get your blood right now if you've got the time. I just want this albatross off my neck as soon as possible. And by the way, do you have anything you could give me to pep me up? My trip was invigorating, but the flight back seemed to drain all of my energy."

Nicki's mind was racing, but he quickly grasped that he had been handed the perfect opportunity to implement his plan.

"I could come up and give you an IV of cortic steroids and a giant blast of B-12. It'll take about thirty minutes. This won't take away your CMV, it'll only mask the symptoms, but you'll have some real energy to burn. Then we can put you on an oral diet of a steroid called Decadron for a few weeks to make sure that energy doesn't go away. I'll take some more blood, but we'll have to wait until next Monday before I get your results back from the other lab."

Nicki figured that if he was able to inject his solution of steroids and tainted blood into him immediately, by the following Monday Scott would possibly test positive for HIV when they took his blood sample and no one would be the wiser. If not, the AIDS would certainly show up in the next four weeks as Scott started to feel the effects of the disease.

"Come on up whenever you're ready, Nicki. I'm just going to be here catching up on my mail."

It is not easy to kill a man in cold blood, especially under the guise of friendship. And as a doctor, Nicki had seen firsthand the horror of dying of AIDS.

The infected individual becomes progressively sick

with a variety of maladies. The symptoms are insidious, beginning with several weeks of fever, weight loss, malaise and night sweats. Debilitating drugs like trimethoprim/sulfa-methoxazole are forced intravenously into the body, causing more adverse reactions. Headaches, cramping abdominal diarrhea, altered mentation and meningismus often occur. Eventually a prolonged, febrile, wasting illness sets in and victims die a slow, painful, and too often—lonely death.

Nicki's rubber-gloved hands were shaking as he filled the syringe and squirted the AIDS-tainted fluid into the IV bottle of corticosteroids. When that vial was full, he put the half-empty liter bottle of infected blood into a sealed plastic pouch and returned it to the back of his office refrigerator. That accomplished, he loaded an intramuscular syringe with the reddish B-12 fluid. He put everything in his black medical bag, discarded the gloves, removed his lab coat, pulled his cuffs down through his tweed jacket sleeves and started upstairs to Scott's office, rolling an IV stand ahead of him.

It was peaceful in Scott's office. He had put on an old recording of Ravel's *Bolero* and was reclining in his high-backed brown leather chair, watching the lights of the valley sparkle below the office. Pamela's van Gogh hung on the wall, a shining field of swaying yellow wheat in its security-lit frame. Scott felt content. He was about to be exonerated.

Nicki rapped on the door. "Hi, Scott, nice to see you back. How was the trip?"

The curly-haired doctor started removing the gold-engraved cuff links from the cuffs of his starched shirt. As he started rolling up his sleeves, Scott said, "Great fishing. Have you ever gone after bonefish? They're one fine sport, I'll tell you that."

As the doctor was unpacking his medical paraphernalia, Scott noticed that Nicki's hands were shaking as he pulled on a fresh pair of thin, white rubber gloves. He wondered if things were all right in Nicki's personal life. Out of politeness, he said nothing.

The young doctor replied, "I'm not much of a fisherman, I'm afraid. But from your tan, the weather must have been nice. Now, take off your shirt. I'll draw a little blood and then stick a butterfly needle into your forearm to get this IV started. I can zap you anywhere later with the B-12."

Nicki drew the small tube of blood, put it into his medical bag and then inserted the small drip needle into the large blue vein in Scott's forearm. The needle was connected to a long translucent plastic tube which curled in Nicki's hand. He connected it to the vial containing the AIDS-contaminated steroids. He then hung the bottle upside down on the arm of the IV pole, letting the fluid drain into Scott's body.

They both watched as the first drops of the deadly concoction started dripping down the clear tube.

Scott had a habit of putting records or CDs on repeat and *Bolero* kept playing its monotonous melody softly in the background. Nicki walked around Scott's outstretched left arm and injected the B-12 into his other shoulder, then gave him a quick pat on the back.

"I hope I didn't hurt you with this horse needle. We

use it for liquids like B-12 and gamma globulin, since the mixture is kind of viscous and anything smaller would clog up. Say, you don't mind if I leave you alone here for a few minutes while that IV finishes dripping, do you? I've got to lock up down in the lab."

Nicki's voice was cracking. Scott figured he was just tired from working so late.

"Not at all, Nicki. I'm starting to feel better already."

As silently as he could, Nicki ran all the way down stairs to his laboratory office. He barely made the bathroom before vomit spewed up from his guts. He retched until he got the dry heaves. Then he carefully took off the latex gloves, took a few minutes to run some water through his curly hair and to wash his face, and walked back upstairs into Scott's office. He cleaned up the medical mess, disconnected Scott from the tubing and rolled the IV stand to the door.

"All done, Scott. You should feel like a million bucks by morning. But listen, don't overdo it. Even though your index on the CMV is sinking rapidly, your ratio is still pretty high. I don't want you to start having a relapse. Take it easy and get plenty of rest and drink lots of juices. I'll be at my place all weekend if you need me. See you next Monday if I don't hear from you."

The physician picked up the tubing and empty half-liter bottle of venom. As he started carrying them out the door, Scott said, "I can't thank you enough, Nicki. And leave all that crap here. Maintenance can clean it up tomorrow. I'm sure you've saved my life, you old bandit. Good night."

They shook hands. Nicki's handshake was limp and he could not look Scott in the eye. He turned and quickly disappeared through the door. Scott fell asleep in his chair, listening to the music.

There is a public telephone booth in front of the Safeway store at the corner of Ventura and Sepulveda Boulevards. Nicki did not want anyone tracing his call, so he went in the store and got twenty dollars worth of quarters. He then dialed Gino's Park Avenue apartment in New York City. A recording answered.

"There is no response at the number you are calling. If you will wait a moment this call will be transferred to the customer's mobile cellular telephone."

Numerous electronic beeps sounded for about thirty seconds and then a ringing started. Gino answered. He was sitting at an outside table in a sidewalk restaurant, talking to three haute-coutured Iranian women whom he had boldly joined for coffee.

"Rigitinni."

"Uncle Gino. Mission accomplished. When can I talk to you privately to discuss some details?"

Gino, mindful that others were present, replied, "I'm not sure I know what you're talking about. He's only been back in town for a few hours. I flew back with him and I'm here in L.A. Where are you calling from?"

"I'm in the valley. Where are you?"

"Nicki, I'm at a restaurant over on Canon Drive in Beverly Hills. If you can come over right now, you could join me and some friends for dinner and we could discuss this matter further."

"You're really here in L.A.?"

"Yeah, Kid. It's a place called Cafe Roma."

"I can't believe you're here," Nicki said shakily. "I know the place, they make the best clam linguine in town. I'll be there in half an hour."

SCOTT'S MARRIAGE

By the spring of 1965, the university paper, *The Cardinal*, printed in its gossip section that Scott Reid and Rebecca Platt were an item. They certainly were in Scott's mind. Rebecca was the most beautiful and fascinating woman he had ever been with. She was also the most intelligent, well-bred person he had encountered in his young life. He had spent his childhood in various Catholic orphanages around the Los Angeles area and his upbringing was one of strict regimental discipline. And even though the catechism classes had turned him into a complete agnostic, he drew the best he could from the experience.

Although they had never slept with one another, they soon became inseparable. Away from Rebecca, Scott could not sleep. He kept Franklin awake nights moaning as if he were Romeo, he ate poorly and his studies suffered; he could not even concentrate on spring football. Rebecca stopped playing the piano with Matty in the evenings and sat moping by herself.

Scott thought of how much he missed Rebecca's strange health-diet. She was a strict vegetarian, yet she chain-smoked. She smoked skinny Chesterfields in a long, solid silver cigarette holder, then flicked the smoked nub out with her thumbnail when she was finished. He missed her habit of drinking a flute of champagne and putting it on top of the piano while she played Chopin for him. Her silly rhymes in his ear when they necked. The warmth of their shared affection for Franklin and Matty. Her hilarious attempts to join him in his shitkicker dancing on Friday nights at the "Palomino Bar." Her hippie ways and her constant penchant for joining every protest organization on campus and their ensuing arguments over the cause of the week. Her touching maternal habit of reading aloud to him from sections of classic novels on their picnics.

And he missed touching her—the downy feel of her soft skin next to his. He admired her shyness and gentleness to all creatures. He had never needed, or wanted, anyone in his life before. It hurt too much. He knew that every time he befriended someone as a child they mysteriously disappeared, or he was transferred to another foster home.

He was sexually experienced, but before Rebecca, he had never felt anything but lust; except for Sister Mary at the orphanage when he was twelve. She used to let him sleep with her and occasionally, on top of her. He thought he loved her, but even she was transferred from his life when Father Donahue came upon them one morning in the same bed. Now it hurt too much to be apart from Rebecca.

Rebecca thought of how much she missed Scott's strange ability to flatulate on command. He would always ask for a big hug, and when she squeezed him, he would belt out a loud blast of air. She would always say, gleefully, "You're disgusting, Reid! You're nothing but an old fart."

And he would always reply. "You're jealous because you grew up with such a tight sphincter. Besides you love my musical ability and my bouquet."

She dwelled on the lack of security she felt when she was away from Scott. He made her feel loved and wanted. He loved what she was, not what someone else wanted her to be. Not like her parents. They had met Scott and took an instant dislike to his confident ways. They thought him arrogant and crass and beneath their social sphere. Naturally, the more they did to dissuade Rebecca from seeing him, the closer she clung.

Every second they were apart, Rebecca missed Scott's whiskers when he forgot to shave; his tight muscles and fabulous ass. She missed the hillbilly music he liked to listen to, and his teasing her because she could never duplicate it on the keyboard. She missed his curiosity and openness to learning. His insatiable desire to improve himself. His ability to teach her new things, even the margaritas and pot they shared together. His unlimited optimism and confidence. His kindness to everyone. His gregariousness—people followed him as if he were the Pied Piper; even homeless dogs had followed him home. His horrible habit of making greasy hamburgers in her kitchen and devouring them like a ravenous carnivore. But most of all, she missed him hugging her and saying,

"Rebecca, I love you and I've never loved anyone before and I'll never love anyone else but you. I want us to have lots of babies together one day. I want us to have a son, too, and start a whole line of Reids."

God, she lived to hear that. And she could not wait to bear those babies. More urgently, she could not wait to have sex with him.

Just before the start of Scott's senior year that fall and on his twenty-first birthday, Rebecca took all of her savings from the bank and purchased the brand-new, red Chevy El Camino, half-car, half-truck hybrid that Scott had been admiring. She and Matty drove it over to Scott and Franklin's apartment as a surprise.

Franklin had graduated the past June and was now enrolled in medical school. Scott was helping him memorize *Gray's Anatomy*, when the girls started honking the El Camino's horn down below. Scott looked down from the balcony window and Rebecca yelled, "Happy Birthday, you old fart!"

Matty was crying as Scott ran down and swept Rebecca up in his arms. In a choked voice, he said, "Will you marry me?"

"In a minute, my darling."

"We'll have babies together."

"Tons of them, my love!"

Franklin had ambled down and draped his arms around Matty while they watched the proposal.

"You guys are going to make me sick if you get any mushier," he pronounced. "Let's go eat somewhere, have a beer, and celebrate Scott's birthday."

The four of them somehow piled in the front seat. Scott had to shift gears between Rebecca's legs, not that he minded the silky feel of her thighs, and Matty had to sit on Franklin's lap with her head bent over, not that Franklin minded that either. They drove off laughing to find a restaurant.

After an hour on the freeway, Franklin said, "Where the heck are you going, Bud?"

"To Reno. We're going to get married and you're going to be best man and Matty's the bridesmaid."

Rebecca had her arm around Scott's neck and nearly throttled him.

Matty squealed, "I love it! How romantic!"

Franklin blurted, "I've always said you were crazy, Reid!"

Hours later, the cramped foursome finally stopped to eat in Reno, Nevada. Franklin ordered champagne and went and purchased a Monte Cristo cigar as a present for Scott, not knowing he would be lighting up a lifelong habit for his friend. Scott took the cigar band off and put it on Rebecca's ring finger, and said, "That's the best I can do for now. But I give you my word, I'll shower you with diamonds and furs."

"All I'll ever want is your love, Scott."

Franklin grunted, "Man, it's gettin' deep in here!"

Matty dove in her capacious bag for a tissue.

Scott Reid and Rebecca Platt were married by a lay

preacher, in a white chapel, in a simple roadside ceremony that evening in Reno. Franklin and Matty were their witnesses.

Scott put Franklin and Matty on a bus home and then drove Rebecca up the Sierra Nevada mountains, through Donner Pass into a small town called Truckee, California. There, they spent their first night as man and wife in a cheap, run-down motel which had a purple neon sign hanging over the front door. The sign said, "BILLY & MAE'S HONEYMOON INN." The "&" was burned out and the sign blinked monotonously. They asked for the honeymoon suite and the skinny innkeeper spewed a dinner breath answer.

"Hey, folks, the rooms are all the same" A blast of garlic overwhelmed them, as he boomed, "ROMANTIC!"

Nonetheless, Scott swept Rebecca off her feet and carried her over the dingy threshold. Bullfrogs croaked passionate cries of love in the pond nearby. A huge, circular white moon shone brightly. Crickets chirped from beneath the window sills and the wind whistled softly through the needles of the pines and firs.

Nature could not have made two bodies more perfectly fitted. Once in bed they discovered lips, tongues, hands, genitals—every curve and gradient of their bodies melded together. They explored and delighted in one another and made love numerous times during the night. Rebecca finally had her security.

Pleasantly exhausted, Scott woke to the face of a sleeping angel. In the luster of the early morning, while the yellow and violet water lilies on the pond were opening their petals for the sun, he whispered, "I love you, Rebecca. There will never be another woman for me."

Rebecca crooned to him, "Let's have a son—right away."

Scott was beyond happiness. He finally had a family.

After Rebecca notified her parents of her marriage, she dropped out of school. All she wanted to do was get pregnant and give Scott the son he wanted. Scott graduated after leading Stanford to the Rose Bowl his senior year. He would have liked to have given pro football a shot, especially to get a signing bonus so that he could give Rebecca all the things she deserved. However, no professional team drafted him. Even though he had always won from grade school on through college, they said he could not throw the long ball. But, with his good grades and Rebecca's ample trust fund he swallowed that pill manfully, and enrolled in medical school that fall.

As time went on and they did not conceive the son Rebecca wanted so desperately to give her husband, she tried every remedy she read about to induce a pregnancy. Scott would tease her and tell her it was fun practicing and he didn't care if they had a dozen girls first. Finally she got an appointment with a school gynecologist to find out if there was something physically wrong with either one of them. He referred her to an L.A. infertility specialist, who shattered her hopes. She was sterile. Not Scott, but her! She was devastated. How could their love come to this?

She did not tell Scott and started smoking a great deal of pot and drinking more margaritas than was healthy.

Then Franklin and Matty got married and Matty was joyfully pregnant within three months. When the baby boy was born and at the christening, Franklin announced, "We have named our son Scott, in honor of my best friend."

Everyone toasted the child and Franklin continued, "But we all understand we're saving the complete name, Scott Ian Reid, for Rebecca's son." Cheers went up and everyone drank another toast.

The following day, Rebecca added Valium to her routine to calm her nerves.

Never one to worry about the intricacies of birth control, Scott assumed that Rebecca was quietly taking birth control pills, avoiding pregnancy on purpose until he finished med school. He was proud of her maturity, as it would allow him to later support his family in the manner she knew he believed in when he became a doctor. He was so grateful for her generosity and her constant love. It filled the empty void that had lingered for so long in the hollow of his life. He could not wait to finish medical school so he could repay her for all of her kindness. He yearned to lavish every material dream upon her and his children.

During Scott's second year of medical school, he developed a diagnostic testing kit, using a radial-immuno-diffusion method to speed up the testing of blood that physicians took from patients to be diagnosed in a laboratory. The kit worked so well that numerous physicians at the medical center started using it and asking where they could buy more.

Scott realized that if he could talk someone into manufacturing the product for him, he could potentially save countless lives over the lifetime of the product. He could benefit medicine and mankind more with this product than he ever could be by being just one more ordinary physician. All he needed was a reputable scientist to write a paper on the clinical findings about the kit. He contacted Milton Schwartz in Los Angeles and was gratified by his response. Doctor Schwartz not only wrote the paper, but did the clinical trials. He convinced Scott to drop out of medical school and join him in Southern California to start a manufacturing company.

Rebecca was then twenty-two and had free access to the principal of her trust fund. They drove the El Camino south, past Carmel and Big Sur on Highway 1, through Santa Barbara and into Los Angeles. She bought them a small, one-story, wood and brick ranch house that sat on one acre in the San Fernando valley, and financed the initial prototypes. They formed IMA Laboratories and hired Milton Schwartz to direct the scientific operations. Scott oversaw manufacturing and quality control. When they had a finished product, Scott took it and sold a contract for five hundred thousand dollars worth of test kits to the National Aviation and Space Administration (NASA). They wanted to use the compact kit for blood-testing the astronauts. From there, the trickle of sales soon became a torrent.

IMA Laboratories took on two hundred new employees and grew with amazing speed. Finally, Scott made a common stock offering to the investing public. The proceeds from the sale of that offering made him the fortune he had been dreaming of.

As prosperity came and the years sped by, Scott realized Rebecca was unable to have children. Helplessly worried, he tried appeasing her sorrow with gifts. A car, a house, a 5-carat, pear-shaped diamond wedding ring, mink shawls and coats, numerous pets, and a condo in Aspen. He even offered to adopt a child, which she turned down in a rage of tears. All she wanted was to have babies with the man she loved. And the accumulating presence of Scott's gifts only upset her more, for she never wanted to lead a life as shallow as her parents' had been.

But, still lacking a solid sense of self, Rebecca secretly turned to a foolish and nefarious solution. Qualudes at night and amphetamines in the morning. Amylnitrate poppers for a quick start during the day when Scott needed her or they would be socializing with Josh and Pamela Kramer—although Pamela would have nothing to do with Rebecca unless the men were around.

Occasionally, Franklin and Matty flew out to California with the children, which only made Rebecca feel more insecure. Scott would take her back to the woods of Wisconsin once a year to see their friends. Rebecca loved to go fishing with Scott and sit on the bottom of the boat, listening to the chilling call of loons on the lake. He would sit in the back of the boat on the upper seat and braid her hair in the fashion she had worn it on the very first day he had seen her at the Stanford—Cal football game.

Over the years, Rebecca wrote to Matty and often talked with her on the telephone; however, even this warm echo of her closest friendship only temporarily improved her outlook. Rebecca often thought of suicide. She was naturally shy and had never made friends easily. She always had her fantasies, piano, poetry, music, literature and Scott to keep her happy. With Scott more and more busy tending to his success, she drifted into deep depression. He was such an optimist and so busy, at first he didn't notice the subtle change's in her behavior.

Rebecca started visiting psychiatrists. They tried every antidepressant known to medicine, all to no avail. One night she tried swallowing a full bottle of sleeping pills, but she vomited them up in horror. It seemed to her that even death did not want her. A month later, she turned to heroin. Although the sweet oblivion made her forget wanting a baby, it also gnawed like an evil rodent at the remnants of her personality. She began lying to Scott. Then to Josh, who admired her immensely, and to Milton, who adored her—he was the only person who had ever gotten away with calling her "Becky." Over time, she stopped writing to Matty and quit caring about her appearance. She lost weight, her skin became infested with scabby sores and she had no appetite. She cried all of the time.

Reluctantly, in 1977, Scott forced himself out of denial and put her in a drug rehabilitation center. Without his permission, a therapist used electroshock treatment, which put Rebecca into screaming nightmares. She tried escaping and begged to call Scott. The doctors would not allow it. They put her in solitary confinement and then increased the voltage in her ECT treatments. She couldn't take the pain and one night crawled out through a window and stole a car in the parking lot. She just wanted to be back home with Scott.

The car was a tan 1967 Plymouth with a gold-flecked stripe running down its long, high tail fin. It had a 327 cubic inch, 350 horsepower engine and it could go from zero to sixty in about six seconds. As the owner ran yelling from the building, waving his arms to head her off, she panicked and her foot lodged between the accelerator and the brake. She lost control of the car and hit her pursuer, killing him instantly. Then as the car sped out of control, it hit an oak tree head-on. It all took less than ten seconds. The police guessed she hit at about seventy miles per hour.

Rebecca lived—catatonic and crippled—almost beyond recognition.

A state court found her guilty of premeditated, negligent manslaughter and sentenced her to twenty years in the state women's correctional center for the mentally and physically disabled.

Scott was beyond grief. He lost interest in life and all but a few people. He reverted to isolation. He visited Rebecca every week, but as time went on, it dwindled to once a month. Then once a quarter. Finally, twice a year. It was too hard on him to see what was left of his once pristine Rebecca. He had to wheel her around the compound in a wheelchair, avoiding all of the other raving mentally ill and pitifully disabled women in the institution. Tenderly, he would wrap a woolen Stanford red-and-white blanket around her, but she never seemed to recognize him or anyone else. Josh stopped visiting her after his third trip to the state facility. Milton faithfully brought her gifts and sent notes of encouragement every month. Matty wrote every week. But she never received a reply and Franklin would not let her go to see Rebecca. He thought it would do no good.

Rebecca's entire body had been disfigured. Her golden

corn-silk hair now lay plastered with perspiration to the sides of her head, her alabaster skin sagged under its own weight and the scars from the stitched facial wounds made her look like a grotesque old woman. She would sit hunched over and stare into space, drooling; her pianist's hands were gnarled and she kept them twisted together in her lap. Scott always kissed her on the head when he left and told her he loved her. She never responded.

A CURIOUS SIGHTING

Doctor Milton Schwartz's house was on Sweetzer Avenue in the middle of the Jewish district of West Hollywood. He bought in that area so his mother would always be able to walk safely to Temple. The front exterior was painted a gaudy pink and the facade was trimmed with wooden gingerbread. A gay friend of Milton's had done the architectural work free of charge. There was the usual manicured postage stamp front lawn and a small garden in the rear of the house where Milton's mother, Esther, planted vegetables and flowers.

Esther was from the old country. She dressed in tiny floral-patterned outfits that looked like they were made from old flour sacks. She constantly wore a ragged pink apron around the house. She combed and braided her hair every morning and coiled the braids into a bun on the back of her head, sticking a wooden hairpin through the round, mounded hair. Milton was always apologizing to everyone for her appearance, saying she looked just like a Russian peasant.

Other than Milton's smoke-infested room, the interior of the Schwartz home was filled with Esther's old fashion Germanic furniture. Lined up in rows in silver frames were numerous black and white pictures of relatives. They graced the top of every flat object in every room. Milton always found it troublesome to invite anyone over to visit, as Esther always greeted everyone in the same fashion.

"So you're Miltie's friend. I've heard so much about you! So ven are you leaving?"

Milton had cut his vacation short and come home a week early so his mother could visit her rabbi at the synagogue that Saturday. Milton was dying for a smoke, but Esther had him sitting in the living room where he was not allowed to smoke, listening to Beethoven and reminiscing about their trip to the Catskills.

Milton thought Esther might have a mild case of Alzheimers', as she repeated everything. He had heard the same story numerous times on the plane trip back home. She spoke through her broken dentures.

"Miltie. I vant to go back. Didn't ve have a good time? I'll never forget, I can't vait til I tell your Uncle Hymie, ven that fat comedian I liked told that joke about the ninety-year old couple who decided to get a divorce? Remember, Miltie?"

"Momma, for the hundreth time, I remember!"

Esther was laughing to herself.

"They vent to a judge and asked if they could get a divorce. And the judge ..."

Milton could take no more of his mother for the evening. He wanted a good cigar or his pipe. Even though she had not finished the joke, tears were streaming down her face, she laughed so hard. He interrupted. "Momma, I'm going down to the tobacco shop. Finish listening to your music and turn off the record player before you go to bed."

"Miltie, so you're leaving? Bring your Momma some bagels for breakfast. Shame on you, Miltie, you're just like your Papa. Oy, I'm all alone by myself."

Thirty years earlier, Esther's husband "Izzy" had left one night to take out the garbage and had never returned.

"Miltie, already you'll stop at Nate and Al's. They're open for sure and you can get some lox and cream cheese, too."

Due to the strict antismoking laws in California, people form private smoking clubs to enjoy their habit. Scott and Milton belonged to a cigar club called Naz's in Beverly Hills. Naz also had a retail tobacco shop next door to the club. It was where most of the people in the entertainment industry bought their smoking paraphernalia. Men stopped by for a brandy, backgammon, good conversation, a smoke and most of all for their privacy. The club and tobacco shop were located in the atrium of a group of shops on Canon Drive. Within the atrium there was Charlie's small place for shoe repair, Rosanna's silver shop for trinkets, George's chic French boutique, a T-shirt shop, a Lebanese optometrist, Giuseppe Franco's hair salon where Scott had his hair cut every month, and the Cafe Roma.

Scott was a friend to all of the proprietors, whereas Milton only inhabited the area now and then to have a smoke at the club and an espresso at the cafe.

Scott often took Milton to lunch at the Cafe Roma, which sat across the archway from the cigar club. There they could sit at an outside table after a meal and enjoy a good cigar, or Milton his pipe.

Milton parked his mint-condition white 1959 Cadillac in the parking lot behind the shops. He backed into a space so no one could accidentally clip the huge bug-eyed tail-fins.

From the parking lot and alley there are two archway entrances to the shops. The one on the right goes past the shoe, silver and optometrist shops and George's boutique to the Cafe Roma. The one to the left, to Naz's cigar club and the hair saloon. In the center of the atrium, around a dry cement fountain, were the cafe's outside tables. The tables were covered with red and white cloths and each had a vase of fresh-cut flowers. Milton went in the left archway to the cigar club, looking over the diners as he walked. He noticed Gino Rigitinni, Nicki Graziano and three well-dressed middle-eastern women dining at a table behind the fountain. Milton took a quick look, but they did not see him. He chose not to go over and say hello, in case they might want him to stay for dinner and make up a third couple. Instead, he sneaked into the sales office of the tobacco shop next to the cigar club and bought Scott a box of Number 4 Monte Cristos, picked up a carton of slim Chesterfields that he thought he would take out to the hospital for Rebecca, even though she had not smoked for years, and got himself a large Churchill in a silver tube.

Milton then walked over to the delicatessen and picked up lox, cream cheese and a sackful of hot bagels for his mother. On the way back to his car, he took out his cigar and licked saliva all around it. He got in his parked car and took a little guillotine cigar-cutter to the end of his Churchill and chopped it off. He took a match and lit the cedarwood wrapping from inside the tube, then lit his cigar with it. As he blew a large plume of smoke out the window, he reached inside the sack of warm bagels, took one out and started munching. The Thrifty drug store was open all night at the end of the alley. Milton sat in the dark, smoking and watching people walk through the alley behind the shops. Most of them were going to the pharmacy.

Milton was a loner.

After finishing their fresh whipped cream-filled napoleons, Gino's three Iranian companions excused themselves and departed. Nicki hunched over and told him in hushed detail what had transpired at IMA Laboratories earlier that evening when Scott unexpectedly returned.

Gino was ecstatic.

"Nicki, this calls for a celebration! Waiter, a bottle of Dom Perignon, please."

Nicki was not as enthusiastic. However, he knew he was now on his Family's favored list. Gino continued, "I thought I was going to have to stay in L. A. for at least a few weeks to get this problem solved. I really appreciate your quick work, Nicki. We won't forget this. About how long before you think the project will be completed?"

The Family code did not specify that one had to murder in order to advance in the hierarchy or be looked upon favorably. The act, if called upon, was one of duty and loyalty to the group. Nicki felt guilty for betraying Scott and at the same time he felt a strange thin surge of pride. He had finally advanced beyond puberty with his peers. Somewhat remorsefully, he tugged the cuffs out from the sleeves of his tweed jacket and replied, "Around the first of the year is the medical estimate. I'll keep you up to date. How long you going to be in town?"

Gino tilted his chair back on two legs and ran both hands through his blow-dried silver hair.

"Now that we've had this meeting, I can return to New York tomorrow. I won't be back here again until the funeral. Come on, let's finish this bottle of bubbly and then hit the sack. I'd like to get out of here on an early flight. I taxied over here, Nicki. Can you give me a lift over to the Four Seasons?"

They touched their glasses together and tossed down the last of the champagne. Gino affectionately patted Nicki's face and then put his arm around his shoulder. Nicki smiled and did the same to Gino. They walked with their arms around one another through the archways back into the public parking garage where Nicki was parked.

In the darkness, they did not notice Milton sitting in his Cadillac watching them. He was finished with his cigar, but now on his third bagel, which was covered with lox and cream cheese.

He wondered what the two men were celebrating.

THE LIE

After the Caribbean trip, Scott decided to follow Milton's advice and stayed home for the week. Franklin called from Kenya on Scott's second day home. The line was full of static and Scott could barely make out Franklin's voice.

"Hi, Bud. How you feeling? Matt..."

"I can't hear you too well, Frank," Scott cut in. "But I'm fine. I still haven't heard back on the blood test. Some weird lab problem. Don't worry, though."

"Bud, I can barely make you out. Did you go to see Billy Ryan yet?"

"No, not yet. Everything's okay. Did you get to ride an elephant?"

Franklin was screaming to be heard. He bellowed, "I went to the AIDS center. I'm disappointed. I'll tell you about it later. We're leaving today on safari. We just wanted to see if you were okay before we left and were out of contact with civilization awhile..."

The line started to break up and Scott yelled, "All okay. Have a great time. Say hello to Matty for me."

Scott contacted no one else during the week, although Josh had left three messages.

Scott relaxed by gardening, reading and writing what he now thought of as his exoneration speech. By Saturday afternoon on the fourteenth, jet lag from the trip had worn off, the steroids and B-12 had absorbed into his system and Scott felt so good that he called up his tennis pals, Joe, Harold, and Irving and invited them over for their normal Sunday game of doubles.

The steroids gave him a sense of euphoria. He had his old pep and did not ache all over as he had for the past couple of months, although he had a strange dizzy sensation and a small loss of equilibrium. He spent the day in the garden with Hector Gonzales. They pruned the rose bushes for the spring and trimmed the red bottlebrush plants that lined the driveway. They worked with their shirts off and the hot sun beat down on their backs. It soon took its toll on Scott, so he went inside to enjoy Rosa's fresh, iced chamomile sun tea.

HIV-2 is asymptomatic. Therefore, Scott had no idea what was going on inside his body. Usually it can be anywhere from two to six weeks after the primary infection before the infected individual comes down with the telltale symptoms. CMV or mononucleosis-like-illness, fever, myalgia, headaches, diarrhea, sore throat and macular rashes. Scott had already experienced most of these symptoms with his cytomegalovirus infection, so when Nicki cloaked the symptoms with B-12 and glucocorticoids, Scott was sure he was well on his way to recovery.

At dusk he put on a frilly, brown suede Western jacket, a blue and white checkered shirt, a pair of Levis and his handmade snakeskin cowboy boots. He went in the closet and loaded his Smith-Wesson .357 magnum revolver with five hollow points and stuck it in a holster to put under the seat of the car.

Los Angeles had become a dangerous city. He was not about to take any chances. He drove his Porsche down the hill to the California Pizza Kitchen on Beverly Drive and had his favorite barbecued chicken pizza and goat's cheese salad. He still did not feel up to socializing and explaining the mistaken HIV test to anyone. He decided to drive over to the Comedy Store on Melrose Avenue, sit in the dark and listen to the new comedians. On the way he punched in Josh Kramer's private telephone number. Josh answered.

"Hi, Scott. Where've you been hiding?"

"Sorry I haven't returned your calls, Josh. I just needed to be alone for a few days."

"No problem, Scott, I'm happy to hear your voice. Looks like you escaped from the press intact last week. How are you feeling? Did you get your test result back yet?"

"Josh, I'm feeling great. One of my lab physician's gave me a booster shot of steroids and B-12 on the night we got back and it's worked wonders. But it's going to be another week before he clears my blood with the outside test results. I thought I'd just hide out by myself at the Comedy Store tonight. If you care to come and join me, I'll make it an early night," Scott said.

"No thanks, Scott. I'm watching a rerun of the Rangers game in the cup finals on the satellite. Do you think those steroids are going to help your golf game? Because if they do, I'm free to play tomorrow and take some of your money."

"I've got the boys coming for doubles in the morning. If I'm up to it after that marathon, I'll give you a call. Bye."

A long-haired biker on a Harley chopper belched a roar of noise and exhaust smoke as he cut in front of Scott trying to pass a convertible full of young girls. Scott swerved and honked. The biker, who wore a Nazi helmet, flipped him the finger. Scott reciprocated and then slowed, looking for a side street where he could park. He found a spot and backed in. An instrumental version of "Do You Remember" was playing from the car radio and Scott sat and listened to the tune. Smiling, he remembered the first time he had met Josh Kramer.

...Scott had just formed IMA Laboratories in the basement of their first house in San Fernando valley. He was in the process of raising money for IMA by taking it public when his stockbroker invited him to play tennis at Josh's house. The broker had hoped Josh would be impressed by Scott's tennis game and that he would somehow get involved with Scott's new medical corporation.

Although Josh was a two-handicap golfer, almost a pro,

he was not a good tennis player. He desperately wanted to be. He hired the top pros in Los Angeles to teach him and on this particular day he invited a pro over to be his doubles partner against Scott and the broker. Josh and the pro lost love and love. The pro offered every excuse in the world. Scott responded angrily.

"Look, Buster, why don't you just give my partner some credit. He played great. You lost because neither of you know's how to play doubles. You're the pro, you shouldn't be playing singles in a doubles game. Mr. Kramer, I hope you're not paying him to teach you this crap!"

"I like your tennis and your candor, Scott. Please call me Josh."

"Okay, Josh. But, I want you to know that I've got a book on doubles at home which you can borrow that will improve your game by ninety percent. Your strokes aren't bad, but your doubles strategy is all wrong."

"Scott, if I can play like you, I'll read anything you've got."

The pro left in a huff.

Josh liked winners. He called Scott during that week for another game of tennis on the coming weekend. He also did some due diligence on IMA Laboratories, Incorporated. He liked what he saw. He was even more impressed when Scott showed up for the tennis game with the book on doubles he had promised. When he found out Scott was a struggling entrepreneur, who had invented a lifesaving medical product, he knew he was going to do something to help him get started.

After the match he asked Scott, "I'd like the opportunity to participate in the original equity offering of IMA Laboratories if I could. Who's doing the underwriting?"

"Josh, I'm more than honored, but I came over here to play tennis. Not to solicit you. You can purchase my stock on the open market like any other investor, as long as you know the speculative risks of such an investment. But I'll tell you this. If you've got the guts to buy stock in my company, I'm not going to fail!"

The next trading day, unbeknownst to Scott, Josh, using one of his offshore trading companies, became the second largest shareholder next to Scott Reid in IMA Laboratories, Incorporated. As this was a fledgling company and Scott was only twenty-four, Josh also purchased one hundred percent of IMA Class B cumulative voting stock which, by converting it to common stock, would allow him control of the company one day if he needed it.

Their friendship blossomed, even after Josh married Pamela. For some hidden feminine reason Pamela would have nothing to do with Rebecca, but Josh introduced Scott and Rebecca to the right people in Los Angeles. He taught Scott golf and got him into the best country clubs and the private financial circles of California. They went to football games together, to golf and tennis matches. They dined regularly in each other's homes and even went on vacations with one another. They had shared time together in some manner every week for the past twenty-three years.

After holding his IMA Laboratories common stock for fifteen years, Josh sold the shares for a twenty-five million dollar profit. But he never told Scott that he was the beneficial owner of the offshore company that owned the second largest position in IMA, because that offshore company still controlled one hundred percent of the IMA class B stock. Josh wanted Scott to run the company with no outside interference.

By the time Scott got home from the Comedy Store, it was one a.m. The steroids were in full effect. He could not sleep. He sat at his desk and picked up the outline of his news release. If Nicki had the negative blood test results back on Monday, he could make his announcement in time for the coming weekend edition. Although Scott had turned down a request to be interviewed two weeks earlier, he decided to let Barbara Walters do a television interview with him regarding his own experience and his views on HIV and AIDS. He was going to demand a printed apology for the slander from all parties involved.

On Monday, October 16, Scott bounded into the IMA Laboratory offices ready to put the whole HIV fiasco behind him. Pleasantly exhausted from a Sunday of tennis and golf, he spent the morning getting caught up on two weeks of desk work. Among his messages and files, he found two old telephone memos to call Pamela and one to call the gossip column reporter who had quoted her. They wanted to speak to him before he began any legal action against them. There was also a memo from Nicki stating that the blood he sent over to the outside lab was insufficient for the test they needed. He would have to come up today and draw some more blood. What really had happened was that in his nervousness, Nicki had accidently broken the other tube of Scott's blood that he had drawn the week before. Scott was momentarily upset—now he would have to wait an extra few days to get his negative result. But the next item on his desk cheered him up again.

Under the pile of papers on his desk was a brown and yellow box of Monte Cristo Number Fours. Scott took out a note from the little white envelope taped onto the cigar box.

"Dear Captain, Welcome back. Your ass-kissing Head of R & D!"

Scott laughed to himself, but felt remiss for not bringing Milton a gift from the Caribbean. He fingered a solid shape in his inside jacket pocket, and smiled.

Milton had always coveted the solid gold lighter that a Sheik from Saudi Arabia had given Scott during a dinner with Pamela. Scott wrapped it in some white stationery, put scotch tape around it, packed it in his old leather monogrammed satchel, then had a messenger pick it up and deliver it to Milton's office with a note:

"Good smoking, my ass-kissing friend. Just remember, the bag is mine. The Captain!"

Scott buzzed his chief financial officer and told him to file a 10K form with the Securities and Exchange Commission, which would allow Scott to purchase more IMA Laboratories common stock on the open market that week. Scott instructed him to purchase one hundred thousand shares at the market price in Scott's personal account. He was prepared to show the gnomes of Wall Street that he planned in complete faith to run IMA Laboratories for a long time to come.

Scott noticed that his annoying cough had disappeared. Although the perspiring and slight dizziness were still there, he felt full of energy. He rang Linda Powell's extension.

"Linda, could you please arrange for Doctor Graziano to come up to my office so he can draw some blood for his outside testing?"

Outfitted in a spaghetti-strapped navy blue dress that gave new meaning to décolletage, Ms. Powell adjusted her glasses and ushered Nicki into Scott's office. As usual, she stopped by the van Gogh painting of the yellow wheat field. She stood transfixed for a few moments, gazing at it.

"I know you two won't believe me and it's not that the painting is worth millions, but that's the most beautiful object I've ever seen. I'd die for that!"

She blushed. A deep red crept up her neck and face, like mercury in a thermometer dipped in hot water.

"Oh, I'm so sorry, Mr. Reid. Please excuse me."

She spun around on her backless high heels and left the room.

The young physician was perspiring more than Scott. "How are you feeling after our experiment?" he queried.

"I had my first normal-feeling weekend in about three months," Scott said. "I don't know how to thank you enough. Let's get my blood over to the other lab this afternoon so I can have their analysis back as soon as possible. By the way, I took four bucks off Josh Kramer over the weekend at Bel Air. That stuff you gave me works miracles! He's always getting into my wallet on the golf course. You'd better watch out or I'll be getting my money back from you." He grinned warmly at the young physician.

Nicki gave a nervous laugh, then drew the blood and departed as rapidly as he had come.

Scott punched Schwartz's office number on his intercom.

"Milton, thanks for the stogies and welcome back from the Catskills. Was it as exciting as my fishing expedition?"

"Hi, Captain. You're welcome for the smokes, but you really didn't have to give me that lighter. If you can believe it, I'm speechless."

"You're right, I can't believe it. So how was the vacation?"

"About as exciting as watching flies crawl up a drape. Esther drove me nuts. She did ask about your health, though. How *are* you feeling, Captain?"

"Milton, I feel fantastic! Nicki gave me some steroids and a B-12 shot the day I got back and I had a weekend like nothing was wrong with me. I even played golf and tennis on Sunday. I think I'm over the worst of this damn CMV. I had him take some more blood this morning for an outside lab to finish off all the tests. They're going to run a particular HIV-2 test that will clear me of any possibility of having the virus."

The smoke from Milton's pipe plumed upwards like miniature cumulonimbus storm clouds. He jotted a note on his pad to have a frank talk with Graziano over in Infectious Disease before the week was out. A look of concern etched his face as he puffed on his pipe before replying, "Look, Captain. Nicki's a fine young doctor, but he's an inexperienced kid when it comes to patient treatment. And you know, we shouldn't be doing that as lab physician's anyway."

Scott thought he detected a little envy, but let Milton continue.

"Let me warn you, Captain. That treatment only masks your CMV problem. I know it makes you feel better and you've been sick for a long time, but you've finally got your titer count down to a livable level and you'll only stay on the road to recovery by getting plenty of rest and fluids. Nothing else. There's no vaccine. The only cure for CMV is your own immune system. Give it a chance. If you go on screwing around like you're still not sick, you're going to have a serious relapse. Now, take my advice and get your ass out of this office every day by noon and go home and relax in your garden."

"You do have a way of putting things plainly, Milton. I know you're right, but God, it felt good to just get out and do something physical for a change! I'll cool it for the week, or at least until Nicki gets my test results back. Though I might ask you to do a little celebrating with me when I get out my release on this whole mess."

Scott was speaking more and more quickly in his excitement. "I'll send it down to you so you can read it. By the way, I'm going to throw my annual Halloween bash. Do you think you could come in that same stupid Pillsbury Doughboy costume that cracks everybody up?"

"Captain, I promise to wear my costume if you promise to take it easy between now and Halloween," Milton said. "And consider yourself now on Esther's shit list. She made that costume as a Ku Klux Klan outfit. She figured that way I wouldn't go into any dangerous black neighborhoods. Wait until I tell her everyone thinks her son is the flaming Pillsbury Doughboy! You may be banned forever from trick or treating on Sweetzer Avenue."

Scott smiled and hung up. He finished his business for the day and drove home to follow Milton's sage advice.

On the afternoon of Thursday the 19th of October, Nicki Graziano telephoned Scott's house.

"Scott, we've got a small emergency. I need to come over and talk to you immediately. Are you available?"

Scott had been in the garden with Hector, rigging up a wire fence to keep the raccoons out at night. Scott was still feeling physically good and had been on the oral steroids for the past few days, but he could tell from Nicki's tone of voice that it had something to do with the test results.

"Come on over, Nicki. Was the result not what I was hoping for?"

"Let's talk about it when I get there. Do you want me to bring you anything on the way?"

"Well, if it's bad news that might reflect on Milton's earlier tests, you might bring him along."

Nicki had told no one what news he was about to deliver to Scott. Doctor Milton Schwartz was the last man he wanted along. He lied, "I thought of that already and was hoping he could make it, but I checked with his secretary and he's tied up in a meeting. I can be over in less than an hour."

Scott left Hector to his own devices to deal with the wildlife and went in the house to shower.

Standing naked in front of his bathroom mirror, Scott noticed some bluish blotches on his toes, right under the nails. Fear began to crawl under his skin. He had experienced many strange bodily sensations over the past few days and his mind never seemed a hundred percent clear, but he had attributed this to the injections. He tried to keep his apprehension under control, but the question rolled over and over in his brain: had Milton Schwartz been wrong all along and Franklin Nelsen right?

Scott showered and put on a silk Sulka smoking jacket and his black, royal-crested King Edward slippers. He thought he might as well be comfortable. He heard Rosa shout on the intercom, "Meester Scott! Doctora Graziano he es here."

Scott lit up a Monte Cristo and walked out into the moss-filled cobblestone driveway to meet him.

The yellow labradors sat on their haunches, their ears pinned back, teeth bared and growling as Nicki approached. Scott had never seen them behave like that as long as he had had them. He had to hold them back with a firm grip on the scruff's of their necks. As a hunter, Scott should have realized that animals can smell fear and sense danger, but his own mounting fear dampened the instinct. Nicki held out a clammy hand.

"Nice of you to come, Nicki." Scott said. "I was planning a slow walk through the gardens but something's upsetting the dogs, so we'd better go up to my study."

The youthful physician seemed to have regained his composure since the last time Scott had seen him. He had a file folder under his arm that he handed over before he took his seat.

"Scott, I hate to rain on your parade, but there's something in your blood that needs further testing over the next few weeks. Ah... it won't allow you to make your news release."

Scott had begun reading the data in the folder. He was calm on the surface, but tension coiled within him.

"Are you saying I'm HIV positive?"

Nicki quickly blurted, "It's hard to believe, but it looks like HIV-2."

"What!" Scott's composure dropped away and his breathing quickened.

"I know it must be a shock, but if I'm going to help you I need to know a few things about your past medical and travel history," Graziano said in his professional voice. "Have you had any blood transfusions in the last ten years and have you been to Latin America or Africa during the same period of time?"

Scott was engrossed in the other lab's test results and he answered Nicki abruptly, "Yes, I've had a blood transfusion and I've been to both places in the last ten years, if that's the answer you're looking for."

The reply seemed to please Nicki. Habitually, he reached for his shirt sleeves, then stopped and took out a small note pad from the inner pocket of his jacket. He punched the end of a ball-point pen with his thumb.

"Did you have sex when you were overseas? Sorry to be so nosy, Scott, but I think you know what I'm driving at. If you've had blood transfusions from an infected donor or sexual relations with an infected individual, we could at least pinpoint where you might have contracted this virus."

Irritably, Scott said, "Nicki, I got the blood transfusion from a local hospital and the blood came from the Red

Cross. I've had a very prolific and wonderful sex life wherever I've traveled. I've also enjoyed anal sex, but not homosexually. I'm not circumcised. And no, I didn't use condoms. I suppose now I'm a cynic and in the high risk category for HIV."

"That you are, Scott!" And Nicki jotted down a few notes.

"That may be, but I don't see enough in this test to make me feel Milton's been wrong in his analysis."

Defensively, Nicki explained. "Scott, I appreciate and respect your faith in Doctor Schwartz, but I would like to point out that the envelope glycoproteins of HIV-2 differ from those of HIV-1 and the serologic assays he used at IMA to test for HIV-1 antibody do not always detect a person's infection with HIV-2. You must take into account that HIV-2 causes a syndrome indistinguishable from AIDS."

"I'd like to check with Milton again to see exactly what tests he ran before I accept this result," Scott said.

"Please understand, the other lab has not completely confirmed that you're HIV-2 positive." Nicki said. "But there's enough evidence in your blood to suggest that you are, so we have to send them more of your samples over the next few weeks. Also, Scott, I'm a lab physician specializing in infectious diseases. I don't think I'm qualified to treat you further with what might be a severe medical problem. But I know plenty of specialists in this area that you could go to in absolute confidence."

Scott looked at him directly. He was slightly pale but his voice was even.

"Thanks, Nicki. I'm eternally grateful for the help

you've been to me. I'll talk to Milton and if necessary, we'll contact one of these AIDS specialists and get to the bottom of this thing. I won't be in the office tomorrow, I'm going out of town. So I'll see you on Monday. Rosa will show you the way out. Thanks for coming over."

Nicki stuffed the notepad and pen in his pocket and left relieved. The matter was now completely out of his hands. Scott would get other medical help, who would assume that he had become infected because of his blood transfusion, travel or life-style. They would treat him in the same ineffective fashion they did all other AIDS patients. The disease would then run its course in a very short period of time, leaving the patient dead. And in this case, no one would ever think anything was amiss.

Scott walked the garden with the dogs, who were once again behaving normally. He pondered his situation. Anything was possible. Eight years earlier he had a pint of blood transfused during an operation to stitch up an artery in his left arm that had been sliced open in an auto accident. And he certainly had never taken precautions regarding any kind of venereal disease over the years. But *HIV-2*! It just did not add up.

Scott felt almost as close to Milton Schwartz as to Josh Kramer and Franklin Nelsen. Milton was a real professional in his work. People thought him eccentric, but he was seldom wrong about medicine. Scott found it hard to believe that Milton had made a mistake *twice* in his testing. Yet from Nicki's explanation of how hard HIV-2 was to detect and how similar it was to AIDS, maybe Milton had not had the proper equipment?

Scott walked up to his study, scolded the dogs for jumping on the sliding glass doors, then went in and keyed Milton's coded home number on the telephone. Esther answered.

"Scotty, so nice to hear your voice. So ven are you coming to see your step-momma?" She always considered Scott her second son.

"Soon, Esther, real soon. Say, is Milton in? I need to speak with him—it's urgent."

With her mouth still on the receiver, she shouted at the top of her voice. Scott held the telephone at arm's length.

"MILTIE, YOU BETTER ANSWER QUICKLY IN YOUR ROOM. IT'S THE MAN WHO SIGNS YOUR CHECKS!"

Milton was busy with his new word processor, installing a modem so he could have a direct link to the laboratories' medical files. He put down his screwdriver and answered, "Hi, Captain. What's up?"

Scott started to speak but Milton cut him off. "Momma, get off the goddamn phone."

"Oy, now my son is svearing at his momma." There was a click on the line.

"Milton, sorry you were tied up with your staff meeting and couldn't come over earlier with Nicki, but I did ask him to bring you along."

"What?" blurted Milton.

Ignoring the outburst, Scott continued, "And I've got to tell you, I don't quite know what to make of the other findings he brought over. I can't believe you could overlook *twice* what they claim to have found."

"Hold on a minute, Captain! First of all, I didn't have

any staff meeting today. And second, I didn't know you had a meeting today with Nicki, nor do I know anything about the blood analysis that Nicki had done at the other lab. He hasn't spoken to me about it yet. What did he say they found?"

"HIV-2!"

"That's bullshit! That's impossible! Christ, you'd have to go to Uganda and fuck a whole tribe of infected Africans to get that mutated virus. It hardly exists in America."

Somewhat agitated, Scott asked, "All of what you're saying may be true, but in the meantime the Berlinger, MRL's lab and now an independent lab are telling me I have some kind of HIV. What am I supposed to think? Is it possible you made a mistake, Milton? Or is it possible you didn't use test kits that were specific enough to identify the HIV-2 in my system?"

The smoke in Milton's room was suffocating. He was sucking furiously on his pipe.

"Captain, I'm telling you as a physician and as a friend—you don't have HIV-2! I ran enough tests to know that. You know as well as I do that the enzyme-linked immunosorbent assay that I used is 99% accurate for detecting HIV-2. I didn't make any mistakes. I can do those goddamn tests in my sleep. There's something fishy going on here and I'm going to get to the bottom of it!"

Milton took a deep drag from his pipe and then continued, "I've still got a tube of your blood in my lab fridge that Nicki drew from you before you went to the Caribbean. I'm going over to the lab right now and run another ELISA. I'm even going to try isolating the virus or detecting the provirus DNA by polymerase chain reaction. I know they didn't try that! If this is all negative, which I'll bet you anything it is, I'm going to fire that asshole Graziano for putting you through this mess. I'll call you later, Captain."

It was obvious to Scott that Doctor Milton Schwartz did not care for Doctor Nicki Graziano.

The dogs sat obediently outside of the glass doors of Scott's study. The female, Laurely, gave him one of those dog smiles and whined a little. He opened the door and let them both in. Tails wagging and tongues licking his hands, they plopped at his feet with sighs of contentment. He pushed the buttons for Linda Powell's home telephone number.

His secretary was getting ready for a date. She was sitting at her dressing table, clad only in her black panty hose. Although her glasses had slipped down her nose, she could see her perfectly formed breasts reflected in the mirror. Her nipples were large and dark brown, and stuck straight out like the ends of bullets. Her hair was in curlers and she was trying her fourth color of lipstick to coordinate with the new green, low-cut dress she had just bought at Guess.

"Oh Mr. Reid, I'm glad you can't see me now."

It was a lie. She had wanted Scott Reid to see her naked for a long time.

"Linda, I hope you'll forgive me for bothering you at the house when it's not an emergency, but I'm not going to be in the office tomorrow and I'd like you to get started on the mailing list for my Halloween party. The invites are on the top of my desk. You'll see it's most of the same people as last year. I'd appreciate if you could ask everyone to fax or telephone whether or not they're going to be coming."

"I'll take care of it first thing, Mr. Reid. Good night."

It was four a.m. when Milton finished with his test results from the tube of Scott's blood. They were all negative for any form of HIV-1 or 2! There was something drastically wrong. Milton stuck a white gum med label on the half-full tube of blood and wrote on it, "Scott's blood, drawn day before Caribbean trip—*NEGATIVE HIV!*" He stuck it in his lab refrigerator.

As much as Milton wanted to pick up the telephone and wake Nicki to get an explanation, he felt since they had not spoken, he should give him the benefit of the doubt until morning as a professional courtesy. But why did the young physician tell Scott that he had been in a staff meeting that day? And he desperately wanted to see the test results from the other lab Nicki had received. Just what kind of tests they had used to detect HIV-2 in Scott?

Milton knew all of these questions could be addressed face-to-face in a few hours. He wandered over to the hard couch in the corner of his office and lay down. Although his head was bent at a sharp angle on the armrest, within seconds he was snoring.

At eight-thirty a.m. his secretary, Myra, banged into a file cabinet with a hot cup of coffee which she was carrying in to surprise him. It was not the first time she had found him in that position. She let out a yelp and Milton jumped up. His clothes were rumpled. He rubbed the sleep from the corners of his eyes and said, "Thanks, Myra. If you would, I'll have another cup of coffee, A.S.A.P. And ring up Doctor Graziano over in infectious disease and see if he's in yet. If he's not, have him come to my office as soon as he arrives."

In a few minutes, Myra safely delivered Milton a scalding cup of black coffee, along with a sweet roll filled with custard.

"Doctor Graziano's not in yet," she said. "But I left your message. Are you going home to clean up?"

Milton slurped the hot liquid. He spat it out and yelled, "When the hell is somebody going to invent coffee that doesn't burn your goddamn mouth!"

He then proceeded to eat the roll and light his pipe, scattering crumbs and ashes down his front. It never occurred to him to clean up and change clothes.

No sooner had Milton switched on his computer than he spotted Nicki walking down the corridor some distance away. It was too far to yell for his attention, so he got up and started following him.

Nicki turned the corner and entered his private office. Before Milton knocked, Nicki knew he was there. He could smell him. Although Milton had thrown on a clean white lab coat, he reeked of stale tobacco. He had a deep frown on his face and growled, "Nicki, what's this bullshit you're giving Scott about testing positive for HIV-2? I want some answers, my young friend, and I want them this morning."

With a deep swallow and a none-too-steady voice, Nicki started in on his defense.

"Doctor Schwartz, if you recall, Scott asked me to send his blood to an outside laboratory for another opinion. I did that and they came back with this test result. As you can see, it differs slightly from your analysis."

He handed Milton a file folder marked, "CONFIDENTIAL!" Milton quickly scanned the material. He did not want to believe what he read.

"This is full of shit and you know it! Scott couldn't have tested positive for this virus. This lab has only used the Western blot to check his blood. I did that already. How on earth have they come up with this?"

Defiantly, Nicki shot back, "Now, hold on a second, Doctor Schwartz. You can insult them, but not me. I didn't want to tell anyone my results on testing Scott's blood, but remember the blood I took from Scott before he left for Curacao? Well, it tested the same as this laboratory's. Positive HIV-2! So we both can't be wrong."

Milton stood frozen in his footsteps. He had spent the entire night checking the exact blood that Nicki had taken from Scott before the trip. It was negative for any traces of HIV! Nicki had obviously forgotten about the tube of Scott's blood he had given him the day Scott left for the Antilles. Why was Nicki lying? And how had the outside lab now tested Scott positive for HIV-2? He had only been gone on his trip six days and Milton *knew* Scott's blood was negative before he left.

Milton stood staring at the doctor for a long time, until Nicki asked, "Are you all right, Doctor Schwartz?"

"Yes, yes. I'm just a little stunned by the news, and the difference in the results, that's all. Have you got any suggestions on what we should do for Scott?"

Milton took a plastic pouch of tobacco out of his inner jacket pocket and started stuffing his unlit pipe. He knew he was on to something. He noticed that Nicki's telephone board was lit up like a switchboard, but that he had not tried to answer any of the flashing lights.

Milton decided to stay awhile.

"Mind if I sit down and have a smoke?"

"No, not at all. You're the boss." Nicki said. "Look, Doctor Schwartz, I like Scott and I'd like to help him, but I told him yesterday that I just didn't feel qualified. After all, I'm just a lab physician, I'm not practicing in infectious disease. I feel the best thing that I could do as a doctor and his friend is to see that he gets to the right AIDS specialist."

Milton thought he would try and get to the heart of the matter. "Nicki, why did you tell Scott I was in a staff meeting yesterday, when you know damn well I wasn't?"

The curly-haired doctor started tugging at his nose, ran his slender fingers quickly through his hair, then habitually pulled at his starched shirt cuffs. Nicki was clearly nervous, and he stuttered, but he continued.

"I...I didn't mean to be deceptive, but when I called Scott, he said he wanted to speak to me alone about the test results. I...I guess he thought it would be embarrassing enough with me there, much less bringing anyone else along."

Another lie. Scott had distinctly told Milton that he had asked Nicki to bring him to the house. Milton knew he had better take it slowly in order to find the truth. Scott could be in real trouble. The fact was that an outside laboratory had now tested his friend HIV-2 positive! How did Scott's blood get contaminated between the Caribbean fishing trip and the day Nicki drew blood for the outside tests?

Milton finally lit his packed pipe and took a deep drag from it. The pungent rum-laced aroma filled the sterile room.

"I'm sure you're right, Nicki. Listen, I'm going to get started on a plan to help Scott and find out if he's really infected with this virus. Do you still have him on oral steroids?"

Nicki relaxed somewhat. It seemed as though Milton was off the track.

"Yes. I've got him on a declining dose of Decadron for another few days."

No longer trusting Nicki, but needing to play it out as far as it went, Milton said, "We're both aware that he still has a good amount of CMV in his system. But he says he feels physically fit since you put him on this medication, so I'll continue a similar treatment. And I agree with you, you shouldn't treat him any longer. I'll send a sample of his blood over to another lab in two weeks, see how he feels in the meantime. And if the next test verifies he's HIV-2 positive, I'll get him to a specialist."

Nicki was relieved.

"I'm glad you agree with me, Doctor Schwartz, and I hope for Scott's sake that this will all be taken care of somehow."

A very attractive red-haired secretary poked her head through the door.

"I'm terribly sorry to bother you, Doctor Graziano, but a gentleman named Mr. Rigitinni has been holding on the line for over ten minutes. He says it's urgent."

"Thanks, Brenda. Tell him I'll call him back in five minutes." Nicki smiled and winked at her as she ducked out the door, then said to Milton, "Isn't that funny. Getting a call from my uncle Gino. He's a director with MRL, you know. I haven't heard from the guy in over two years. I wonder what he wants?" Milton's control evaporated in a lungful of pipe smoke he inadvertently inhaled. He could not get his breath, and started to choke. He had just seen them together. Arm in arm, no less. His temper surfaced abruptly and he blurted it out.

"What the hell are you lying to me for, Nicki? Scott told me he asked you to bring me to his house yesterday. You just lied about that. Then you told me your blood test on Scott was positive for HIV-2 *before* he left for the Caribbean. You seem to forget that I also took a tube of his blood that day, and goddamn it, I spent all of last night right here in the laboratory checking that blood for HIV-2. There was none, Nicki! I'll spell it for you, *N-O-N-E!* Are you listening to me?"

Nicki stammered, but Milton raged on.

"And then you tell me you haven't seen your uncle in two years? I saw you with him the other night at the Cafe Roma over in Beverly Hills! What the hell is going on?"

Nicki tried to answer, "You're mista...," but Milton cut him off.

"You'd better come up to my office this afternoon and give me some straight answers or I'll call in the authorities at the American Medical Association and fire your ass so damn fast you won't know what hit you!"

Finally, Nicki grasped at a last-ditch stratagem.

"You're mistaken, Doctor Schwartz. That was Roberto,

my Uncle Gino's twin brother, you must have seen me with."

Milton wanted to get out of Nicki's office and telephone Scott. He spun his belly around, the rest of his body followed and he duck-footed it down the hallway like an angry goose.

Nicki did not completely lose his composure, but he was shaken to his very foundation. He had to speak with Gino before he met again with Milton Schwartz. If he left the office immediately, he would have the entire weekend to work out a plan with Gino. He would know what had to be done.

Nicki was not by nature a liar, but he was a glib conversationalist, so he never imagined there would be a slipup of this magnitude. How could he have forgotten the tube of Scott's blood that he had given to Milton Schwartz? And who could have imagined someone would have seen him together with Gino in Los Angeles?

Nicki could not call Rigitinni from his office, so he rang the new red-haired secretary.

"Brenda, please take all my messages for the day. I need you to buzz Doctor Schwartz's office at exactly four o'clock and tell him I went home sick. I'm feeling terrible, think I've got the flu. Tell him I'm sure I'll be fine by Monday morning. I'll ring you later from my house."

He then left by the back door into the parking lot. He drove over to a Denny's restaurant, where he was friendly with the manager, and got twenty dollars worth of quarters to call New York.

Milton was exhausted. There was a definite trace of HIV-2 in Scott's blood in the test results from the outside lab. There was also something happening that he could not comprehend. He tried to recount to himself everything that had transpired since Scott first came to him that past June complaining of being sick, but nothing added up to Scott getting AIDS. Scott had tested positive for cytomegalovirus and had all the symptoms of that disease. It had never made any sense that the Berlinger Clinic tested him positive for HIV. Somehow this had to be a mistake made by the MRL people, the same as when Pamela told her gossipy story to the newspapers. But how could another laboratory now test Scott's blood positive for HIV-2?

Milton had run every medical diagnostic test known for HIV on Scott's blood. It made no sense! It also made no sense that his fellow physician, Nicki Graziano, was now lying to him about Scott. Milton decided to work backwards, starting with when Scott arrived back from the Caribbean. He needed to verify everything with Scott and tell him what was going on. He punched Scott's office number. "Mr. Reid's office, Ms. Powell speaking."

"Linda, Milton Schwartz. Is the Captain around? Tell him I need to speak to him urgently."

"I'm afraid Mr. Reid is out for the day, Doctor Schwartz. Is there anything I can help you with?"

"No, not a thing. Do you know where I can reach him? This is an emergency!"

With one hand, Linda tugged the low neckline of her dress up above a round brown nipple that was about to peep over the edge and continued, "I have no idea where he is. You might try him at home. Do you want me to give him a message if he calls in?"

"Please tell him to call me immediately. Either at my office or my house. Also, write this down. Have him start on twenty milligrams of prednisone three times a day. I'll send the pills up to his office later. And tell him I want to give him a booster of gamma globulin over the weekend."

Milton hung up, wondered if Scott was having an affair with the sexy Ms. Powell. He wouldn't put it past him. Despite his worry, he grinned to himself and pushed the telephone buttons for Scott's home number.

The answering machine picked up the call. Milton left a message.

"Captain, it's urgent I speak with you. Call me whenever you get this message. All I can say now is do not trust anyone but me regarding your latest test result. I repeat, *do not* speak to, or trust in anything that Nicki Graziano might try to tell you."

Milton was so tired from lack of sleep that he returned to his couch in the corner of his office and fell into a deep slumber.

Scott had booked a commuter flight that morning for the hour-long trip to San Francisco after phoning Nelsen's friend, the AIDS specialist William Ryan. Scott had told Ryan he thought he was HIV-2 positive and he wanted to be tested to confirm that diagnosis. Scott also told him that his name was Milton Schwartz.

After the quick flight, the taxi ride through the drizzle

and fog from San Francisco International to the city center took about thirty minutes. Scott got out at Market and Jackson. He ran over and boarded a cable car to take him up and over the hill to the physician's office.

The fog felt like wet velvet draped across his perspiring forehead. Scott could see the base of the Oakland Bay bridge and the collapsed section of freeway from the 1989 earthquake lying beneath it. In the distance he could make out Nob Hill and, very faintly, Twin Peaks to the North. Alcatraz Island sat empty and silent among the blasts of the fog horns in the bay. The cable car driver clanked his bell and pulled dual levers to stop the car at Jackson and Castro Streets. Scott paid the attendant a dollar and hopped off.

The doctor's office was on Castro Street and Scott walked up the stairs to his third-floor clinic. Doctor William Ryan had sandy hair and brown liver spots on his face and hands. There were a score of medical diplomas and certifications hanging in black wooden frames on the wall behind his cluttered desk. He was a blunt individual who greeted Scott heartily.

"You don't look like a Milton Schwartz to me, you look like a fellow Irishman. Strip down to your shorts, please. On the phone you said you're a friend of Frank Nelsen's and you've tested positive for HIV-2. Even in San Francisco that strain of virus is most unusual. Who did your previous diagnosis—Frank?"

As Scott was undressing he stipulated, "If you don't mind, Doctor Ryan, until I get a positive verification of what I think is a mistake on my previous test for HIV-2, I would rather not say who did the test. But you have my word that you'll get a complete explanation from Frank."

Apprehensively, the Irish doctor exclaimed, "Well, let's give him a call now!"

"Frank's in Kenya right now, but I'll have him call you as soon as he returns." Scott assured him. "In the meantime, I'd rather not explain anything. After you've done my physical, would you just be so kind as to take a blood test for HIV and then call me with the results next week at this number in L. A?"

"I'll be happy to run a test for you," Ryan said, reaching into a drawer. "I'm sure you realize you have to sign a consent form for having your blood drawn for an HIV test."

Scott was appalled.

"Are you serious? I signed all kinds of forms before when I got tested, but I didn't realize one of them was because a doctor can't run a blood test for HIV without a patient's consent?"

"I'm afraid that's correct. We don't need the patient's permission to draw blood for any other type of infectious disease, but it seems the government has decided to make HIV a political disease. Physicians are the least protected people in the world when it comes to the risk's of unknown exposure to this killer."

Scott signed the consent form as Milton Schwartz and then gave the physician Milton's private IMA Laboratory telephone number. Doctor Ryan smiled warmly and did as Scott requested. He had heard every excuse and story in the world about AIDS. He was a tolerant and compassionate individual who genuinely wanted to help his fellow man.

Physically, Scott still felt well; however, the strange sensations of dizziness and loss of balance would not go away. Doctor Ryan had pointed out the blotches on Scott's toes. They were more pronounced. There was even a subcutaneous bluish-red spot on his right forearm. Scott was perspiring heavily and decided to spend the night at the Fairmont Hotel up on Nob Hill. This time he took a taxi.

Milton's secretary shook him by his lab coat lapels as hard as she could. He finally woke up. He sat up and said, "My God, Myra, what time is it? I'm waiting for Graziano to show up and a call from the boss."

"Doctor Schwartz, it's time for all good secretaries to go home. It's after five-thirty. I haven't heard anything from Mr. Reid and Doctor Graziano's secretary called up earlier. She said he was going home ill for the day and he'd talk to you on Monday. I think I'll be doing the same. Your messages are on my desk and the coffee's on the hotplate. Have a nice weekend, Doctor."

Not having eaten all day, Milton finished off the stale box of donuts and sweet rolls the staff had left behind. The hot coffee revived him and he drifted back to the puzzle that was surrounding Scott—and threatening to engulf him. There were so many questions he needed to ask. He lit his pipe and contemplated. Did Scott have any enemies who might want to kill him? After all, Scott was a wealthy and powerful man. Did Scott have any kind of sex in the Netherlands Antilles? Any recent blood transfusions? Any IV type of drug use?

Like a firecracker going off, a wild thought suddenly exploded in Milton's head. Was it possible that Nicki

Graziano gave Scott an IV of steroids that were tainted with infected blood and not just oral steroids as he had assumed? Why? Milton could not answer that. He knew there were rumors that Gino Rigitinni had ties to the underworld. And Nicki had lied to him. If this wild hunch were true, would Nicki be so foolish as to have left any evidence behind? Why not? He had forgotten about the tube of Scott's blood that he had given Milton before leaving for the Caribbean.

Security had shut off most of the fire doors in the laboratory, so Milton had to call a guard to open the hallways in order to get into Graziano's office.

Letting himself in with his master keys, bypassing the security card system, Milton could not help but notice the cleanliness of Doctor Graziano's outer office. He had not been aware of it earlier. It was too neat. It did not look like anyone had ever worked there. When he entered Nicki's private office, it was even cleaner. Milton then realized that maintenance had already cleaned up for the weekend. He searched the room with a flashlight, looking for clues. Anything would do. All he could find were neat piles of medical periodicals, published articles on infectious diseases and personal memorabilia. One misplaced magazine was lying under the table. Milton bent down to pick it up, and with a dull thud his empty pipe dropped on the floor, leaving a small pile of half-burnt cinders on the carpet. As at home, or in his own office, Milton did not notice the cinders. But he did pick up the pipe.

Just as he was about to leave, the beam of his flashlight caught the glint of a polished metal padlock on Doctor Graziano's small white office refrigerator. Why would Nicki keep this appliance locked?

Curiosity got the better of him. He returned to his office and got a packet of mechanical tools. He ambled back to the young doctor's office and decided to figure a way to open the refrigerator so that no one would know he had been in it.

The padlock was on a simple hasp. All he had to do was remove three Phillips screws from the front of the refrigerator and the door came open when he pulled on the handle.

Milton shined the flashlight inside the small cold box. There was an assortment of labeled medicine bottles, contrast media and vials of various IV steroids. Oddly, because Nicki knew what the refrigerator contained, there were also a few open fruit juice bottles. Hidden behind the bottles and vials was an unlabeled liter bottle of fluid that had been hermetically sealed in a plastic casing. It was half full and had no label. Milton took it out and shined the light on the bottle through the plastic. It appeared to be blood. He put it in his tool packet and then replaced the screws on the front of the refrigerator door. He wiped down the entire appliance with his handkerchief and, after looking around with the flashlight, felt sure that he had left the office exactly as he had entered it.

Once back in his laboratory, Milton put the half-filled bottle on an instrument-cluttered counter. With surgical scissors, he carefully cut the bottle free of its plastic casing. He pulled on a pair of thin, white rubber medical gloves. They had been powdered by the manufacturer, Malaysian Latex, Ltd. The box they came in said they were distributed by a Hong Kong corporation.

He extracted fluid from the bottle with a long syringe. After two hours of various tests, Milton verified beyond a doubt that the fluid was blood. And it was HIV-2 positive! He said out loud, "Judas Priest! They've killed the Captain."

Tears welled up in his eyes. Milton knew there was no saving his friend if Scott had been injected with this fluid. He had to find out if Nicki Graziano had given Scott an IV of steroids the night Scott had come back from the Caribbean. Milton kept asking himself, why? It was no use calling the police. His story would be too preposterous. He had to talk to Scott first and show him the evidence and find out if his theory were true. Together, they would figure out what to do.

Milton put the incriminating bottle of material in his bottom desk drawer, under his cans of pipe tobacco. No one would ever look there. He pulled off his rubber gloves, put them in the disposal and then punched Scott's home telephone number.

The answering machine picked up once again. Milton pleaded with it.

"Please, Captain, your life's in danger, call me at my house or the laboratory as soon as you get in."

Milton thought of driving up the treacherous Mulholland Drive and Coldwater Canyon route on his way home, but realized that if Scott had been home he would have called him back right away. So he got in his old Cadillac and drove slowly the long way through the flat valley. He decided to make a stop at the Woman's State Institutional Hospital off Ventura Boulevard and leave the carton of Chesterfields he had bought for Rebecca. They had been lying on the front seat for some time now, with a red-and-white bow around them and a card addressed to "My Becky." He left them with a night watch nurse and asked that she have them delivered to Rebecca in the morning. He then cut over Laurel Canyon Drive down to his house in the Fairfax district.

Nicki answered the operator's request and deposited six dollars worth of quarters in the telephone coin box. The call, as usual, was forwarded to Gino Rigitinni's cellular mobile phone. Gino was sitting by himself with a large white towel wrapped over his head at the side of an indoor tennis court on Long Island. He was sweating from the early evening match he had just finished.

"Rigitinni."

"Uncle Gino, can you talk? I think I've got some problems on the project out here."

Gino ran the dry towel through his damp hair and said, "Yeah, I can talk. But I got some problems with the project back here, too. I called you because I heard through the grapevine that our boy Reid was out playing tennis and golf all weekend like nothing was the matter with him. The people upstairs want to know what's going on, Nicki. I told them the problem was taken care of. Now what's the problem you think you got?"

"Look, Gino, Scott was out playing all weekend because I gave him enough medication to boost his energy for a couple of weeks. His other lab test came back positive for HIV-2, so you can be assured I did what I had to do. He won't survive through the spring with this virus in his system. But my problem is Milton Schwartz."

Gino had been rubbing his hair furiously with one hand with the towel and it stood straight up.

"You mean that fat pipe-smoking yid who looks like Pigpen?"

"For Chrissake, Gino, he's the head of R & D here at IMA."

"So what, Nicki, how in hell is he a problem?"

"Because he's a smart clinical scientist and doctor, that's why. He had some old blood of Scott's stored in his laboratory and he reran tests on it. Of course it didn't contain any HIV-2 before Scott left for his fishing vacation with you. So he thinks something's not kosher. He caught me in a slipup on the facts...."

Gino screamed, "You mean he caught you in a lie! Nicki, I warned you, no fuck-ups!"

Nicki panted into the phone, "Don't worry, I think I fooled him, because when he told me he saw the two of us here in Beverly Hills the other night I told him that was your twin brother Roberto, not you. Quick thinking, right, Gino?"

"It's stupid, kid. You know I don't have a twin brother! What happens if he checks that out with Reid, huh? How do you know he hasn't already done that?"

"Because Scott's out of town today, that's why," Nicki said. His palms were slippery with sweat. "But I'm calling you because Schwartz's threatened to fire me and go to the authorities if I don't give him all the answers he's looking for. I skipped out of work to call you and I can put him off until Monday or Tuesday by saying I'm sick. But I don't know what the hell we're going to have to do with him."

Gino's voice was cold and businesslike.

"I can take care of that problem for you by next week. Get me the guy's license plate number and tell me what kind of car he drives."

Eagerly, Nicki responded, "That's easy, Gino. He's got an old, white '59 Cadillac and it's got one of those personalized plates on it that says MILTON'S."

"Okay, Nicki. I'll handle the Schwartz problem before the week's out. Don't you worry about him. Have you made sure you haven't left around any incriminating evidence that could trace you to Reid's infection? Think, and make damn sure you're clean!"

Gino cut off three thousand miles with the click of his index finger. He pushed down the antenna of the mobile phone, folded it together, finished toweling off his head and walked to the showers.

Nicki drove home to Hermosa Beach and sat outside his house watching the sunset, waiting for darkness so he could return to IMA Laboratories when everyone had left for the weekend. He cooked hot dogs and beans and watched the news on television. He thought maybe he should call up his new secretary, the freckled redhead, Brenda, and take her out dancing later that night. He could tell her he was feeling better. But since it was possible he would not be returning to work before Tuesday, he decided against it and switched the television to Friday night baseball. The ball game lasted eleven innings and ran until midnight. This was a good time to go to the lab and remove the only trace of evidence.

The same security guard who had let Milton through

the fire gates unlocked them for Nicki when he got to the laboratory. Nicki then walked unescorted to his office and turned on all of the lights. He could see that maintenance had cleaned, yet he instinctively shuffled his medical articles on the table into neater rows. He took out his security card and entered his private office section. Walking directly over to the padlocked refrigerator, he reached into his pocket and extracted a small key. The gold engraved cufflinks he was wearing peeked out from under his tweed jacket sleeves and sparkled against the overhead lights of the laboratory office. He moved the juice bottles and labeled vials of medicine around. Then panic coursed through his body. The half-liter of infected blood he had hidden in the refrigerator was not there! He checked the padlock. It had not been tampered with. He wiggled the hinges on the doors. They were firm. Desperately, he reshuffled the contents of the refrigerator and put them on the floor. The infected blood was gone.

As Nicki moved to put back the bottles and vials, he saw a small pile of grey and brown cinders lying next to the side of the refrigerator. He picked it up. It was not all burned. What didn't fall through his fingers was cut in chunky strands. He smelled it. Pipe tobacco. Milton Schwartz!

Nicki realized that since maintenance had already been through the office vacuuming that night, Milton must have been there right before him. Angry and frightened, he still had the presence of mind to put the items back in the refrigerator and lock up his office and leave. He walked calmly to his BMW in the parking lot, then drove over to the same public telephone booth he had used earlier in the day. He had plenty of spare quarters lying in the glove box. Once again he dialed Gino's New York number.

Sound asleep, Gino answered roughly, "Yeah, Rigitinni!"

"Uncle Gino, you said you were going to take care of my problem out here some time next week, didn't you?"

Gino was furious and tired and he was not thinking of doing business on his personal, tape-monitored line when he shouted into the telephone, "What the fuck's the matter with you, Nicki, calling me up in the middle of the night to verify my word! I told you I'd take care of Milton Schwartz and I will. You just make goddamn sure you've taken care of Reid with that injection you gave him!"

Nicki replied before Gino could hang up, "I have an emergency with Schwartz. He broke into my office and took something that could implicate *us* in this thing. I need to have you take care of this problem immediately. Can you do it?"

"What the hell do you mean, implicate *us?*"

"Well, I'd saved some extra infected blood in my office refrigerator in case I had to redo Scott if I hadn't given him enough HIV to infect him. I mean, that was smart, wasn't it, Gino? And Schwartz snuck into my office tonight and stole it."

Gino was now wide awake.

"Nicki, listen to me. Don't worry any more about it. He'll be taken care of before the weekend is out. Okay?"

"Okay, Gino."

"Nicki, I don't want you to talk to anybody until you hear from me again. Do you hear?"

"Yeah, I hear you, Gino."

"And don't worry, we'll take care of you. You helped us out and we're going to help you out. Go to bed, kid. And stay home by yourself for the weekend."

The next morning, Gino's secretary removed the monitored conversation from the recording machine. She dated and labeled the tape "Personal Calls" and filed it with the other legal recordings hidden in his study closet. She then put a new tape in the machine.

On Saturday morning, a beam of bright sun peeked through a crack in the drapes of Scott's room on Nob Hill. It shone directly into his eyes. He sat up and stretched. He felt refreshed again. The clock on the bedside table said twelve o'clock. Noon. He got up and opened the drapes to see the Golden Gate bridge spanning the bay before him. The day was crystal clear. Sailboats laden with multicolored spinnakers flocked in a circular pattern between the bridge and Sausalito. A large passenger ferry pushed white-capped waves in its wake as it headed for Tiburon.

Scott pushed the telephone's button for room service.

"This is Mr. Reid in room 2001. May I have a pot of Earl Grey tea, two croissants with raspberry jam, a natural yogurt and this morning's *Chronicle*, please."

Scott shaved and showered before room service arrived. When the waiter brought the food, he took two Decadron 0.75 milligram steroid tablets with the breakfast. He read the paper and was enjoying being content and lazy, away from the problems of Los Angeles. After deciphering the news, he decided to check out, go down to Fisherman's

Wharf for the afternoon and then fly back down south in the early evening.

For the first time in years, Milton went to temple with his mother. They walked hand-in-hand over to the synagogue on Santa Monica Boulevard. The rabbi's voice had a soothing effect on Milton, but he could not help thinking of Scott and wondering where his friend was. He left Esther at the synagogue and went for a walk by himself to ponder Scott's fate. After a short time he turned around and walked past the temple to find his mother walking with a group of people. They were headed toward Milton's house so he followed them. In the distance, he noticed two young men in a black pickup truck stopped in front of his house, looking over his Cadillac parked outside by the curb. After a cursory inspection, they quickly drove off. Milton smiled to himself. He knew his mint-condition Cadillac was admired by every car aficionado in town.

Milton avoided his mother's cronies and waited for them to depart before he entered the house. He tried Scott's home number. "Captain. You must get hold of me immediately! It's Saturday afternoon. I'll be here at my house or over at the lab."

The last shuttle flight left San Francisco at eight p.m. and Scott was on it. He was at his house before ten o'clock. The dogs greeted him, but Rosa was in her room with Hector watching Saturday night wrestling and did not notice his arrival. He quietly slipped in the back entrance to his study. He had planned on showering and crawling into bed to watch television, but the flashing red light on the answering machine caught his attention as he walked through the dark study. He switched on a desk lamp, grabbed a pen from its holder and sat on the edge of the chair to jot down his messages. The first two calls were from Milton. When Scott heard that his own life was in danger, he forgot the rest of the messages and pushed Milton's home telephone number.

Milton had answered every call at his house for the past twelve hours. He grabbed the telephone on the first ring.

"Captain, I've been trying to reach you since yesterday! We've got to meet and talk right now."

Scott was exhausted from his day in Northern California. "Milton, I went up to San Francisco. Using your name as an alias, I might add. But I'll explain that to you later. Right now, I'm beat. I need some rest. What's this that my life's in danger? Christ, I'm just starting to feel normal for the first time in months."

Esther was going to be angry in the morning. Milton lit his pipe in the living room.

"I can't discuss much on the phone because it's too complicated. But I've got to know, Captain, did Nicki give you an IV of steroids the night you came back from the Caribbean Islands?"

"Yes, he did." Scott said. "But I told you that before, Milton."

The pipe smoke was streaking through the pristine air

of the living room as Milton said cynically, "Yes, you told me he gave you steroids. But no, you didn't tell me he gave them to you with an IV Also, did you know he was Gino Rigitinni's nephew?"

"Milton, you're not making any sense. I have no idea if Gino is Nicki's uncle. But what are you getting at? Your first message said I'm not supposed to trust Nicki anymore. Yet, I've felt super every since he gave me the B-12 shot and the steroids. Is there a little professional jealousy involved here?"

Stung, Milton shouted, "Listen to me, Captain, there's something beyond belief going on here. *I think Nicki has injected you with HIV-2 tainted blood!"*

"Milton, that's crazy! Where the hell did you even get such an idea? Why would Nicki want to do such a thing?"

"I don't *know* why. And I don't have the time for any petty bullshit, nor do you. So please, just answer my questions. Have you noticed any blotches anywhere on your body lately, or have you suffered any dizziness or loss of balance or any nausea?"

"I've had all of those symptoms. But you don't really think I've got AIDS now, do you?"

Milton had hoped not to hear it.

"Yes I do, Captain! But we're wasting valuable time. Please wait up for me. I have to go over to the lab and pick up some blood to show you. After I've explained what I've found out we can decide what to do. I'll be at your place a little after midnight."

Milton hung up before Scott could debate the issue.

Scott's mind whirled. What's happening? Do I have

AIDS? Why would Nicki Graziano want to harm me? What blood? And was what Milton said at all remotely possible? He was confused and on fire with apprehension.

He went into his bedroom and turned on the television, then went into the bathroom for a steam before Milton arrived.

When Milton picked up the half-liter of infected blood from his desk drawer at the laboratory, he put a gum med label on the bottle—"Tainted blood—found in Graziano's fridge!" He then went to his lab refrigerator and took the tube of blood labeled "Scott's blood, drawn day before Caribbean trip—*NEGATIVE-HIV.*" He carefully wrapped the two pieces of incriminating evidence in plastic bubble wrap and put them into a padded envelope. From his medical cabinet he grabbed a vial of gamma globulin and a syringe for Scott and stuffed them and the padded envelope into Scott's monogrammed leather satchel. He checked out with the security guards and went to the parking lot.

On this night Milton knew he had to take the shortcut up Mulholland Drive, then over to Coldwater Canyon Drive to Scott's house. He would save at least forty-five minutes. As he got in his car, he noticed a high-wheeled black pickup parked outside the company's parking lot. This truck had a thick, large wooden board for a front bumper. He wondered where kids today got the money to buy such expensive machinery and to do such strange modifications to a perfectly good factory design. It seemed that all of them had altered Jeeps, convertibles or pickups, just like the two admiring his Caddy that morning.

Milton packed his pipe, lit it, took a deep drag and headed up the hill toward the short cut to Scott's. He did not notice that the pickup pulled a U-turn and followed him.

Under the best of circumstances, Milton Schwartz was not a good driver. The winding route of Mulholland Drive was to him a dangerous piece of road that he normally avoided.

The huge Cadillac plowed into the corners going up the hill. Its original shock absorbers were well beyond their prime and the car wallowed like a rudderless river barge. Milton wound through the twists and turns as fast as he could. He was in a hurry to see Scott and to get to the bottom of the mystery lying in the medical bag beside him.

There was a set of headlights behind him and Milton noticed that the lights were at a higher level than the trunk of the Cadillac. Like the lights of a raised pickup truck. But he was in a hurry and paid no further heed.

Milton gassed the car up the steepest grade of the hill. He could see pin-dots of light twinkling in the houses a thousand feet down below in the valley. As he reached the apex of the small mountain, it seemed to him the hill had gone on forever. He did not notice when the lights on the vehicle behind him went out.

Milton pointed the chrome Cadillac hood emblem straight down the precipitous incline. As the speedometer hit fifty miles per hour, he realized he had gained too much speed. He knew there was a ninety-degree hairpin turn at the base of the incline, which went around the steepest cliff on the road. In his headlights he could see the flickering of the fluorescent yellow warning tape on the low guard railing around the turn.

He touched his brakes and looked in the rear view mirror. In the red glare of the Cadillac's bug-eyed tail-fins, a pickup truck's wooden bumper came straight at him. He heard the tinkling of broken glass and the crunch of his trunk crumpling as the pickup smashed into the Caddy's tail-fins and pushed him ahead. The speedometer leapt to over sixty miles per hour. Milton tried desperately steering the wheel in every direction, but the car lunged straight ahead.

The metal barrier on the hairpin corner was no match for the weight and velocity of the bulky Cadillac. The huge car burst headlong through the guardrail. The face of the cliff was five hundred feet straight down, and no governor was going to be able to give Milton a last-minute reprieve.

Milton's headbeams lurched into space and the car was airborne. He was frantically puffing his pipe and slamming his foot on the brakes, as though they might act like flaps on an airplane and set him down to a soft landing. But the law of gravity prevailed and the white Cadillac flipped over in mid-air. The passenger door was flung open and Scott's satchel floated out into the blackness as the car came crashing to earth about halfway down the cliff.

Before the sparks from his pipe ignited the fiery explosion, Milton thought it sad. He had never taken the time to tell his best friend, Scott Reid, just how much he had loved him.

There were no cries of pain or suffering. The immense impact of the crash created forces of devastation similar to a bomb blast. Milton's neck snapped like a dry matchstick and he died instantly.

Up on the road above the fireball of wreckage, the pickup skidded to a stop. Two men jumped out of the cab and scurried around to the rear bin. They pulled the two side pins and dropped the tailgate. With great effort, they pulled a large black plastic garbage sack onto the ground, which thudded as it hit the pavement. One of the men untied the rope binding the top of the sack and the other reached inside and started pulling out a body by its arms. It was a curly-haired man dressed in a jacket and tie.

The two men picked up the pliant corpse up by the feet and under the shoulders. As the jacket sleeves crawled up the limply hanging arms, they could see two engraved gold cuff links sticking through the starched, monogrammed French cuffs of his shirt. One of the killers briefly thought of pocketing them, but the distant whine of a siren below kept his mind on his mission.

They clumsily carried the body as fast as they could over to where the Cadillac had broken through the guard barrier. They heaved the body in the air. It fell like a boulder and bounced twice off the side of the cliff before landing to be engulfed in the burning wreckage.

The blizzard of white-dotted static on Scott's five-foot television screen hissed at him as he woke with a start. He had fallen asleep waiting for Milton. The digital clock flashed 2:30 A.M. in bright green. Where was Milton? He had said he would be at the house around midnight.

After his steam bath Scott had been lying on the bed with a robe on and he got up and went to the bathroom and splashed water on his face. He was perspiring heavily again, and felt very tired and dizzy. He walked downstairs and took two steroid tablets with some milk and cookies. Oreos. Like a child he split them in half and licked the white filling off one half before eating the other. He then picked up the kitchen telephone and punched in a number.

"IMA Laboratories, Security speaking. How can we help you?"

"Yes, my card code is number one. Scott Reid. I need to know if Doctor Schwartz is still in the lab?"

"No, sir. Doctor Schwartz checked out with main security at exactly 11:30 p.m."

"Are you positive of that? This is an emergency!"

"It's not only right here logged on the computer, but I personally seen him drive away in his big old car. I'm more than positive, sir."

What the guard failed to mention was that earlier he had jotted down the partial number of a mud-splattered license plate on a black pickup truck that had been parked outside of the laboratory for some time that evening.

Something wasn't right. Scott decided to try Milton's home. Nervously, he pushed the buttons of the telephone. It rang numerous times, finally he heard a faint voice.

"Miltie, vere are you, your momma's all alone?"

"Esther, wake up. It's Scott. I need to know what time Milton left your house. I can't find him."

"Scotty, so nice to hear your voice, so ven is Miltie coming home? Too late he's vorking. I vaited up so long already the TV vent off. I'm sleeping in his chair."

Scott realized the conversation could go on all night without him garnering any information other than that Milton was not there.

"Esther. Don't worry, I'll go over to the lab and find

Milton and have him home in no time. Go back to sleep."

It was now three a.m. and Scott was more than concerned. He picked up the telephone book and looked in the front emergency numbers for the Highway Patrol. He dialed it quickly. A woman's voice answered, "C.H.P. How can we help you?"

"My name is Scott Reid and I'm trying to find out if there've been any car accidents reported involving a Doctor Milton Schwartz? He would've been driving from the valley to Beverly Hills. Probably by way of Mulholland and Coldwater."

"How do you spell Schwartz, sir?"

"That's with an H. S.C.H.W.A.R.T.Z."

Scott could hear the officer key the information into a computer. The policewoman instantly replied, "I'm sorry, sir, but there's no information on any accident involving a Doctor Milton Schwartz. There's been one major accident on Mulholland Drive at about midnight, though. A single car accident. Automobile unidentified as yet. The license plates are being run through Sacramento now. Two fatalities. Individuals unidentified. I'm sorry, that's all the help I can be."

"Madam, did you say two fatalities in one car?"

"Yes, sir, that's correct."

"Thanks. That couldn't have been who I was looking for. He was alone. Good night."

Scott shed his robe, went into his closet and dressed in jeans and a sweater. He put on a leather jacket, his snakeskin cowboy boots and a N.Y. Yankee baseball cap. He found the keys to the Porsche and headed for the garage.

As exhaust exploded from the tailpipes, the dogs barked and Rosa switched on the exterior house lights. Scott did not stop to explain where he was going. He roared out of the electronic gates up Coldwater Canyon Drive towards Mulholland Drive.

It was about one mile to the crest of the hill and it did not take long to reach it. As he came to the signal light at Mulholland and Coldwater, he saw that he could not turn left onto Mulholland Drive. The police had it barricaded. Numerous fire trucks, with their lights and sirens off, were coming back through the wooden roadblocks. Scott pulled up to a Highway Patrol car and asked the officer what the barricade was for.

"A car went over the cliff about two miles up the road and it started a brush fire when they hit. We just now got the blaze under control and you'll be able to pass through in about thirty minutes." "Any idea what kind of car it was? I'm missing a friend tonight."

"No sir, I don't. I drove by the scene and the fire appeared to have destroyed most of it, from what I could see. Have you called our emergency number about your friend?"

"Yes, I have. Thanks, Officer."

Scott pulled out and drove down the hill toward the valley on Coldwater Canyon Drive. He found an all-night Stop and Shop and bought a large bottle of Coke and a bag of rippled potato chips. He walked back in the parking lot and sat in the car with the stereo on. It was four a.m.

He was worried. It was not like Milton to be late. What did he mean by all of his warnings? What blood was he going to get at the laboratory? Who cared if Nicki Graziano was Gino Rigitinni's nephew and what connection did this have with Scott's problems? What did he mean that he thought Nicki had injected him with infected blood? Whose blood? And most of all, what gnawed at Scott was that Milton said he thought Scott now had AIDS!

A huge red-cabbed tow truck, one used for hauling large trucks or for towing cars stuck in inaccessible places, pulled up at the stop light in front of where Scott was parked. Dangling from its locked hook in the rear was a burnt, crushed shell of a car. The crumpled bug-eye tailfins gave it away. It was a 1959 Cadillac. Still impressed on the burnt license plates was—"MILTON'S."

Sickened, Scott pushed the digits on his mobile telephone and asked the information operator for the number and address of the county morgue. He knew it would be quicker to go in person, rather than try to get any information on the telephone from the morgue. He put the car in gear and burned rubber leaving the parking lot.

The administrator at the morgue, a ghoulish-looking individual with two large brown warts in the middle of his forehead, greeted Scott as though he were lonesome for companionship. It was five a.m.

"Mr. Reid, I'm afraid the remains of the two victims aren't identifiable. They were burnt beyond recognition. From the license plates, we know the car was registered to a Doctor Milton Schwartz here in Los Angeles, but nonetheless, the remains will have to be identified and confirmed by dental records. We'll have that done Monday. Usually concerned relatives contact us right away and then we pretty much know who they are. There were only three personal items found in the wreckage. A stem of a porcelain pipe, a solid gold cigarette lighter and two gold cufflinks. The fire must have been devastating."

The administrator put the items on the counter in a translucent plastic bag. Scott could see the cuff links engraved with, "N.N.G." and Milton's favorite white porcelain "Woodie" and the gold lighter he had given him.

Nicki N. Graziano and Milton Schwartz, dead in an auto crash together! It made no sense. Why were these two together after what Milton had told him on the telephone? What was going on?

Sadly, Scott said, "I know who these items belong to. They were employees and friends of mine. I've been out looking for them most of the night. Where do we go from here?"

"I'm afraid, Mr. Reid, there's nothing any of us can do until Monday. But why don't you contact the next-of-kin and they can call us tomorrow and get us started with the identification. You know, maybe their dentist's and doctor's addresses, and so on. But, I think the best thing you can do now is to go home and get some sleep. You look exhausted."

Scott was not aware he was perspiring until it started dripping down his forehead. His hair was damp. His mouth felt like dry cotton. He took a handkerchief from his jacket pocket and wiped off his brow.

"Thanks for your help. I'll do just that."

On Sunday the television stations reported the accident, sans names of the victims until relatives were notified. But on Monday the names of the deceased and a description of the accident was in the newspapers.

TWO LOS ANGELES PHYSICIANS
PERISH IN FIERY CRASH!

> In a spectacular middle-of-the-night accident, two local scientists died when the car they were driving Saturday evening missed a corner and plunged over a five-hundred-foot cliff on Mulholland Drive. Doctors Milton Schwartz and Nicholas Graziano were burned beyond recognition. Their remains were identified by dental records. Dr. Schwartz was driving and Dr. Graziano was apparently thrown from the car as it went over the embankment. The scientists worked for IMA Laboratories, Inc. in Encino, and had been working late on the night of the accident. Police investigating the accident said there were no witnesses and no alcohol was involved. Excessive speeding was cited as the cause of the crash.

Separate services were arranged for the two men. Esther's rabbi said shivah at the synagogue on Wednesday morning and Nicki Graziano's family held a Catholic service and wake for him that same afternoon.

Few paid their respects to Milton Schwartz. There were no tears, except Esther's. Milton was remembered only by a few silent, gaudily-dressed gay friends who stopped by Esther's house later in the day. Milton's secretary, Myra, his Uncle Hymie and Scott were the only others in attendance.

Scott had Hector and Rosa take Esther home with them

and install her in the guest house on Coldwater Canyon Drive.

Nicki Graziano's wake boiled over with hundreds of shocked friends and family. No one could believe a tragedy like this could have struck down such a promising young physician. Gino Rigitinni gave a moving speech in his honor. Everyone wept but Scott.

Scott was more than perplexed now that he knew that Milton was correct. Gino was Nicki's uncle! What did this connection mean? And what had become of the tainted blood—the proof that Milton had been talking about?

It must have been burned in the fire.

SICKNESS AND THE TRUTH

After Josh divorced Pamela he moved into a pent house condominium in Century City. He never wanted to see a regular house again; nor did he ever want to have a constant parade of guests occupying his home. His unit was two rooftop condominiums made into one giant twelve-thousand-square-foot home. The immense, beamed ceilings were cathedral-peaked and twenty-five feet high. Light flowed in like Jacob's ladders from the skylights.

Josh had the condo decorated in a South American motif. All the works of art hanging on the walls were from either the American west or Latin America. Few were by known artists. The paintings were colors and patterns and settings that Josh had found to his liking over the years. Multicolored woven Mexican Indian baskets, hand-loomed tapestries and Mayan and Aztec sculptures were strewn everywhere. There was an immense library wing, and a large section of the condo was partitioned off for his personal office. Facing west, the condo had a panoramic view of the Pacific Ocean, and looking south from its private pool, one could see downtown Los Angeles.

The condominium complex had every possible amenity. There were tennis courts, putting greens, swimming pools, a community center and an indoor gym. The communal gardens and lakes, linked together by arched wooden bridges, looked more like a Hawaiian Island than California.

It was common gossip that Josh's secretary, Annie Bhalla, slept with him, notwithstanding his horrendous snoring, and spent most of the work week in the condo. She was a thirty-year-old, multilingual Pakistani from Karachi. A Punjabi and a Moslem. She had a white smile that lit up a room and black eyes that looked as if they could see in the dark. When she turned sixteen, her parents, by custom, married her off to a military man. He was killed during a border clash with India when she was twenty-two. She believed this was her *jinn*.

Her father had been head of the Air Force and in her youthful travels she became fluent in five different languages. She was of medium height and build, but always concerned about being underweight. She was not, and she amply filled the western-style clothes that Josh picked out for her, yet she never became completely Westernized. She wore a rouged henna *tikka* on her forehead, just between her eyes. She still loved to lounge around the condo in flowing saris and her black, straight hair usually contained a colorful madras bow.

Josh had met her at a business conference in Pakistan the summer of his divorce and offered her a full-time job in Los Angeles. Annie had not hesitated and flew back with him on his Gulfstream. He was never sure if he hired her because she was a better tennis player than he was, or for her efficient work habits.

Although Kramer Industries had their corporate headquarters in downtown Los Angeles, Josh traveled constantly and seldom went into the offices. His worldwide business interests kept him occupied all over the planet. His latest acquisition had him in Hong Kong for two days during the funerals for Milton and Nicki. The purpose of Josh's trek was to purchase the largest supplier of rubber gloves to the medical industry. The company supplied every U.S. government hospital and military medical base in the world. Richard Spout had told him the company was a steal for one hundred million dollars.

Annie often accompanied Josh in his travels. With dignity, she kept up the guise of the efficient secretary. She even caddied for him on the golf course. But what Josh now loved best was to stay home in Los Angeles, do his business at the condo and play a little tennis and lots of golf. He was a generous philanthropist, but he was not a man interested in the cultural or society sets. His only social joys were visiting his parents and sisters in Glasgow, being with Scott, Annie, his adopted daughter Melissa, and collecting his odd assortment of art.

There was nothing on earth Josh would not do for Scott.

As a layman, Josh found it more than possible that Scott could have contracted HIV. He had known Scott to have been with numerous female companions of less than social registry caliber before his recent two-and-a-half year affair with Pamela. Josh knew from some past private detective work during his marriage to her that Pamela had some strange sexual inclinations of her own. Such as having numerous unknown male partners.

Scott's Halloween party invitation sat on Annie's desk. On the day after the funerals, she had asked Josh in her Pakistani-English lilt, "I say, do you want me to ring Scott's secretary and find out if the party is still on in light of the past week's events?"

Josh was more concerned as to why Scott had not called and told him the results of the outside blood test.

"No, I'll call him myself. I need to talk to him anyway."

Josh shut his library door. Jet lag weighed heavily on him. He was clad in a Scotch plaid bathrobe and shuffled around his mahogany desk with one leather slipper falling off, and plopped down in his office chair to telephone Scott.

Esther Schwartz was sitting by the pool petting the dogs. She was grateful for Scott's hospitality, but her sad heart ached to go back to her house and cook him his favorite deep-fried blintzes. Just as she had done for years for him and Milton.

Scott was sitting upstairs in his study reading the paper. He stared at an article in the financial section. Kramer Industries had purchased Malaysian Latex, Limited for cash this past week. Dismayed and confused, he let the paper fall. He knew in his heart that Josh could not be in business with Richard and Gino, but he could not help feeling leery of the recent coincidences that seemed to link them.

Scott watched Esther slip the yellow labradors scraps of food from the serving tray on which Rosa had brought her breakfast. The dogs drooled and wagged their tails for more. Idly, Scott wondered what it would have been like to have known his own mother. When the telephone rang, he was thinking of what Milton had said the night of his death. Scott had been haunted by it since then.

"I think Nicki has injected you with HIV-2 tainted blood!"

Now Milton and Nicki were both dead. What was going on? Why were Nicki and Milton together on Saturday night? Was it possible Milton had found Nicki at the lab that night and brought him along to expose him? Or was somebody else behind their deaths? Why did Milton want to know if Nicki was related to Rigitinni? Was it in the realm of reality that Milton had been wrong in his testing right from the start? And why were Scott's symptoms getting worse? Was Milton right, that Scott already had AIDS? Scott knew that he had to contact Doctor Ryan in San Francisco to get the results of his blood test. Scott was so absorbed in his thoughts that the answering machine picked up the incoming call. He heard Josh's voice and cut in.

"Hold on, Josh, I'm here."

When the answering machine's recorded voice finished, Josh boomed, "Hey Scott, I'm sure sorry to hear about the tragedy with your friends. I had to be overseas for a couple of days after I heard about it and I didn't want to call and be a bother, but I did have Annie send flowers to the families. Do you have any idea how it happened?"

"It appears it was just one of those unfortunate accidents, Josh," Scott said. "Milton was one of the world's worst drivers and the police told me he was speeding on a dangerous section of road and lost control. He was a hell of a good friend and besides missing him, I've no idea how I'll ever replace him at the lab."

Josh reached down under his desk and pulled his slipper back onto his foot.

"I know Milton was a real pal of yours, Scott. I'm damn sorry. But how about this Doctor Graziano? Wasn't he the one taking your blood to an outside lab for conformation on the HIV?"

Scott decided to stall Josh on this issue.

"Yes, he was the doctor. I've been so tied up with the funeral arrangements and everything, that I forgot to find out where he sent my blood sample so I can get my press release out before the Halloween party."

"I kind of thought maybe that's why you hadn't called me with the results. So you're still having the Halloween bash! That's good, Scott. It'll be a diversion from what's been going on in your life lately. How're you feeling, anyway?"

Scott had doubled the dose of steroids that Milton had left for him and on Tuesday he had a lab physician give him an injection of B-12 and gamma globulin. Scott's blotches were spreading and his dizziness was still there, but he felt energetic. And he was suffering no more weight loss or nausea.

"I'm up to golf and taking your money on Sunday, if that's what you're getting at. I think I'm just about over this CMV bug and I'll be happy to just get my life back to normal," Scott joked weakly.

"By the way, Josh, I saw in the paper this morning that you bought Malaysian Latex. Did Richard or Gino have anything to do with that deal?"

Josh did not like discussing his private business with anyone, but from Scott's tone of voice he felt he should answer him.

"They sure did. Richard recommended the company. You know he has access to every government deal around—and Gino put the legal package together with the principals in Hong Kong. Why do you ask?"

"I just want to know if you're in business in any way with those two, that's all."

"Listen, Scott," Josh rumbled. "I wouldn't ever be in business with either one of those two! And after the Caribbean trip, I'd sure as hell never socialize with them again. I made a mistake letting Rigitinni on the Board of Directors of MRL some years ago. I'll admit he's never done anything other than make the right corporate decisions and profits for the shareholders, but he's from the gutter and I think he may have ties to the underworld. To me, now, he's like stink on shit. I can't get rid of it. And the other one—Richard—speaks for himself. He's just an obnoxious, know-it-all asshole. He's given me good business tips, but I have to accept the fact that the voting public keeps putting jerks like that in office and I have to work with them to get my government deals put together."

Scott had heard exactly what he had hoped for. He interrupted, "Say no more. I just thought you were getting a bit too cozy with those two pricks. I'll tell you more about what's on my mind after I trace down my blood test. Tell Annie to come early on Saturday night. Rosa wants her to make that potent Pakistani cider again this year. See you about eight."

"And Josh, one other thing. Don't come as Cyrano de Bergerac again. After all these years, everybody knows it's you behind that long nose and those bowlegs."

"Okay, Scott, I'm going to surprise you!"

Scott hung up laughing, but immediately punched in the San Francisco number of Doctor William Ryan.

Doctor Ryan's secretary had a nasty head cold. She had a fever and a runny nose and the constant fog that had been hanging over the city the past month did nothing to make her feel better. In a phlegm-choked voice she said to the doctor, "I called your patient, Milton Schwartz, at the Los Angeles number you gave me and they said he was deceased. Apparently he was killed in a car crash this past weekend. By the way, Doctor Ryan, did you know he was a physician?"

The cold bug being a communicable creature, Ryan blew his red nose into a tissue.

"What do you mean—he was a physician?"

"The woman who answered the phone this morning said, 'Doctor Schwartz's office.' So I asked her what kind of doctor he was. She said he was a laboratory physician in charge of IMA Labs' research and development. I guess with his blood test result it was just a matter of time anyway, huh?"

The secretary took a seat in one of Doctor Ryan's desk chairs and he leaned back in his office chair.

"You're right, the poor man didn't have long to live. With the amount of virus I found in his blood, I'd like to do a little more investigative work on this case. In all my years of dealing with AIDS I've never run across a positive HIV-2 patient before. I'm curious as to where he picked this up. All we need in San Francisco is a new mutated virus spreading. Could you call L. A. again and find out if he'd ever been to Africa? As soon as you're finished with that, I'm going over to O'Leary's for some lunch. Want to join me?"

As the secretary got up from her chair to leave, she smoothed out the wrinkles from her white uniform. Then the telephone rang. Ryan said, "Take it in here and then we'll go out the back stairs."

The secretary smiled and reached over the cluttered desk and pushed a flashing red button.

"Doctor Ryan's office. May I help you?"

"Yes, you could. My name is Milton Schwartz and I was in to see Doctor Ryan last week. I need to speak to him personally. Is he available?"

The secretary's nose dripped unnoticed. Her mouth hung open and she sputtered, "Yes..., yes he is, Doctor Schwartz. Just a minute."

She pushed the hold button on the telephone and turned to Doctor Ryan and blurted, "You're not going to believe this. But this's somebody saying they're Milton Schwartz."

Doctor Ryan blew his nose again and said in a hoarse voice,

"I'd better take this in private. Thanks."

He pushed the flashing red button.

"Bill Ryan here. Is this Milton Schwartz?"

"Doctor Ryan. Nice to hear your voice again. Yes, this's Milton Schwartz and no, it's not. I think I owe you an apology and an explanation so we can get on with whatever my problem is. The real Milton Schwartz died this past weekend. He was a physician who worked for me and a personal friend. My name is Scott Reid. I'm Chairman of IMA Laboratories down in Encino."

William Ryan was more than familiar with IMA Laboratories. He was a shareholder in the company's common stock, which he had purchased on the recommendation of Franklin Nelsen as a close friend of the owner, Scott Reid. Ryan listened intently as Scott continued, "I'm sorry to have deceived you, but I thought it necessary at the time. You see, I run an immunodiagnostic lab..."

Doctor Ryan could not keep himself from interrupting. Although he was more curious than angry, he said testily, "Mr. Reid, this is a real mystery to me. My secretary telephoned your offices this morning and found out Milton Schwartz has died. And I know all about your company from annual reports and from Frank Nelsen. So I'm curious. Why did you have to come all the way to San Francisco to get a second opinion on your blood and to use an alias if you're a friend of Frank Nelsen's? Why didn't you use your own diagnostic lab?"

Scott took a sip of the iced tea Rosa had put on his desk.

"It's a complicated story, but I'll try and make it brief. Last June I got sick with flu-like symptoms that kept lingering. I had Doctor Schwartz run a blood test on me, including a Western blot. All he found was an index rise of cytomegalovirus. No sign of HIV. He prescribed rest and fluids. I didn't follow his advice to begin with and I got worse. In September I was feeling so bad that I decided to go back to the Berlinger Clinic and see Frank. I'm forty-eight anyway, and I thought I might as well get a thorough going-over. I had no sex life during the time of Milton's test and my visit to the Berlinger, so you can imagine my surprise when Frank calls back and tells me I tested positive for HIV!"

Doctor Ryan wanted to interrupt again and tell Scott that he had found worse, but instead he decided to listen. Most AIDS patients needed to talk out their frustration and denial. He could hear ice cubes tinkle and Scott take a gulp.

"So I had Milton run another HIV antibody check at my lab, using the ELISA kits. *Nothing!* I was completely negative, except for a huge rise in my CMV ratio. Which, ironically, Frank's lab also found. I told Frank about the negative HIV Milton found and he said Milton had made a mistake."

Scott paused for a moment. Through the receiver, he could hear a trolley car clanging its warning bell in the background. The doctor didn't say anything, so Scott continued, "Then a few weeks ago, toward the beginning of October, I brought in another physician from my lab, Nicki Graziano, who gave me an IV of cortic steroids and a B-12 shot. I had him take some blood of mine to another lab outside IMA. That lab came back with a slightly positive HIV-2 result. As did Doctor Graziano in a test he ran here at IMA with the same blood. I've felt physically good, although some what dizzy and feverish, ever since he gave me the injections of steroids and the vitamin B-12 shot."

Ryan was still confused.

"So why did you come up here to see me? It appears that your Doctor Milton Schwartz just made a mistake."

Defending Milton, Scott shot back.

"Logically, it would seem so, but Milton Schwartz was not a man to make mistakes, or to make up stories. Besides, he was a close personal friend of mine. So when I confronted him with Doctor Graziano's and the outside lab's results of HIV-2, he said that was impossible from the batch of blood I had given them, because he had checked the very same blood and found it negative. He told me he even went so far as to try and isolate the virus by polymerase chain reaction with that blood sample. Neither Nicki or the other lab did that. They did just standard ELISA tests on my blood."

Scott paused to catch his breath and take another swig of tea.

Ryan said, "Please, go on."

"I was really at a loss for what to do, so I remembered your name from Frank and I flew up to see if I could find out the truth. Then the day after I was up in San Francisco, Milton called me and said he thought that I had been injected with tainted HIV-2 blood in the steroid IV that Nicki Graziano had given me. He said he had the proof and he was going to bring it over to my house and show me. He was killed a few hours later. Doctor Graziano was killed with him. You must understand, it was Graziano who had injected me with the IV steroids!"

For the first time in his narrative, Scott's voice cracked a little. The physician drummed his fingers on his desk. Then pulled a handkerchief from his lab coat pocket.

"Doctor Ryan, I have no idea what Milton was talking about or what's going on. I need to know exactly what you found in your test results of my blood."

There was a long pause. Scott could hear the doctor blow his nose. William Ryan also inhaled a deep breath and said in a raspy voice, "Mr. Reid, I don't want to say disparaging things about your Doctor Schwartz who just died. However, doesn't it appear to you that he was trying to cover up the original mistake in his diagnosis? I mean, his story about you being injected with infected blood sounds like a plot from a bad Agatha Christie novel. After all, three other medical sources have tested you positive for HIV. And I'm very sorry to have to confirm their results. You definitely tested positive for HIV-2 here at my laboratory."

Scott's jaw tightened as Ryan finished what he had to say.

"I think you'd better face up to the situation and either come up here for treatment. Or I can recommend someone in L.A. for you to see."

In Scott's stunned mind there was no thought of who was right or wrong, or what Nicki might have done.

"Are you telling me I have AIDS?"

The physician paused before he spoke. He looked up at the collection of antique airplane photos that lined his wall. It was so silent in his office, he could hear the air conditioner humming.

"I'm sorry, Mr. Reid, I am. Your CD4 cell count is only about two hundred and fifty per milliliter. That's less than twenty percent of the total lymphocyte population in your body. I'm afraid that's full-blown AIDS. I can only recommend immediate primary prophylaxis."

The ice cubes in the tea had melted and Scott shook the dregs of the leaves to the bottom of the glass, then drained it in one gulp. Only a tri-leafed piece of mint and some undissolved sugar crystals remained. It suddenly did not seem to matter that the dew on the bottom of the glass had made a white, circular watermark on his marquetry teak desk.

Scott was well-versed in medicine. He knew there was no cure for this disease. Only a miracle could save him. It no longer seemed to make any difference how he was infected, because he had just been handed his death sentence.

"Doctor Ryan, I have no desire to see another physician in L.A. Frank'll be back at the end of November and between the two of you I'm sure I'll have all the competent medical help I'll need. How bad's it going to get, and how long do you think I've got?"

"Let's take one thing at a time. First, if I'm going to try and help you, please call me Bill."

"That's a deal, Bill. My friends call me Scott. Where do we start?"

"I'd like to start you on pyrimethamine/sulfadoxine and zidovudine to reduce the incidence of opportunistic infection. I can call it down to your pharmacist. I'd then like you to come back up here on next Monday, the first, for further examinations, and we can follow up with your blood on a weekly basis. Outside of God's intervention, Scott, we're looking at a few months at best. It's possible that by the end of November you're going to be quite ill. Is there any way you can contact Frank earlier?"

Scott sat up straight, and his voice came out level and even.

"Thanks for your candor, Bill. I have no idea how to get a hold of Frank, but I'll try. You can call the medicine down to Thrifty Drug on Canon Drive in Beverly Hills. I know the pharmacist. I'll be up Monday and we can discuss my future. Is it all right to continue the steroids? Because I feel pretty decent. I also took an I.M. of gamma globulin and some more B-12."

"Scott, none of those will hurt you. You could continue the gamma globulin treatment through the weekend, but the steroids could mask the nitroblue-tetrazolium tests for bacterial infections that I'll be running on you, so you'd better knock them off. By the way, for my information, have you been to Africa during the past ten years, and was Milton Schwartz a homosexual?"

Scott thought, here it comes, all of the personal questions on how he got the disease. Including his sexual preferences.

"Yes, I have. And I had sex while I was over there. But the woman is still alive and healthy! And yes, I think Milton was gay. But to save you time, I'm not homosexual and I know of no one whom I've had sex with that has AIDS."

William Ryan did not like this part of being a doctor. He replied dejectedly, "It's nothing personal, Scott. I just need to know in order to track down where you got infected. Plus, as you know, this virus has a long incubation period, so it's hard to trace where one has picked up the disease."

Scott felt bad about being so cynical. "You're right, sorry, Bill."

With compassion, Ryan replied, "I understand. I look forward to seeing you on Monday. If there's anything you need, call this number and it'll be transferred to wherever I am."

Scott lowered the telephone receiver as if it were fragile as a tiny baby, and softly set it in its cradle. He then turned in his swivel chair to look out at the pool and his flower garden.

The Coral Dawn, Scott's climbing hybrid roses, blossomed and drooped lavishly above the guest house door. Their satin petals glistened bright pink in the sun. In the shade below, colorful butterflies fluttered from plant to plant. White perennial irises and blue delphinium spouted in full bloom, their green foliage filling the base of the rock chimney and the brick flower boxes around the small log house. The citrus trees were bulging with lemon, lime and orange fruits. His favorite yellow roses were bursting open, their fallen petals covering the ground like snow. Wild poppies in red and amber blanketed the hills and oak-filled canyons behind the main house. A group of furry gray squirrels, tails twitching in the air, scampered up the trunk of a giant acorn tree. A midnight-black crow screeched at them for climbing into his territory and a keen-eyed hawk floated on outstretched wings in the hot air currents above the arroyos. Ginger lay sleeping upside down in the corner of the study. She was purring. And Big Bird sat in his cage, whistling flirtatiously.

Scott's eyes moistened, but he did not weep. He simply felt a wave of gratitude. He was alive.

Esther and the dogs had fallen asleep in the hot sun. The dogs were in the shade under her chaise lounge. Her mouth was wide open and she was snoring loudly. Her dress had edged up and Scott could see she had on a pair of pink woolen snuggies. He chuckled to himself. Such friends.

Scott made a decision that he was not going to suffer during his last days. He would do whatever it took to alleviate the pain. He was going to live out whatever time he had to the fullest. He went to his dresser drawer and took out his stash of cannabis and rolled a joint Cheech and Chong would have admired. Scott felt oddly content under the circumstances, but he was also drenched in smelly perspiration and his hands were shaky, cold and clammy. As he inhaled a huge drag of smoke, he realized that there were some loose ends that he would have to tie up to make for a smooth transition after he was dead. He took a notepad from his desk and jotted down the items that he would have to attend to in his will:

Rebecca.

Company.

Estate.

Material possessions.

Friends.

Dogs. Ginger. Big Bird.

Scott found it sad that there was not more to his life, or to anyone's life. Yet he also felt that if one had family, friends, trust, love and loyalty, that was about as rich as one could get. All of his money was not going to buy him out of the coming meeting with the Grim Reaper. He took another hit of grass and punched Linda Powell's private office number on the telephone.

"Linda. Would you be so kind as to call all of the directors and tell them we're having an emergency meeting tomorrow afternoon at four o'clock. Everyone must attend! Then put out a press notice both interoffice and to the newspapers that due to my friends' deaths, I'll be taking a three-month leave of absence from IMA."

"Mr. Reid, do you also want me to release to the press the copy you wrote last week to go with your negative HIV report? And are you going to do that TV interview? Ms. Walters' agent has called several times for an appointment."

From deep in his lungs, Scott exhaled a thick cloud of smoke.

"No to both. Put those projects on hold. The blood test hasn't come back yet, so I can't release anything to the press and I don't want to give an interview to anyone. But tell everyone who calls that the Halloween party is still on. I'll meet you at two tomorrow. 'Bye for now."

Linda hung up. With one finger, she pushed her glasses back into place. She stood up and paused, wondering what Scott Reid's three-month leave of absence really meant.

A fly had flown into Esther's open mouth and she woke up yelling and spitting.

"Vat is this? A bug on my person and I'm only just sleeping."

Her dentures had almost come out and she forced them

back in her mouth. The dogs had run from under the chaise lounge when she screamed. They found calmer shelter in the garage.

The thought of the filthy fly triggered in Scott an instinctive need not to take any chance of infecting anyone else with his disease. He recalled from his reading on AIDS that chlorine killed the virus. He rang Rosa on the intercom.

"Hola, Meester Scott. What jou want?"

"Hola, guapa. I want you to have Hector drive down to the hardware and get five gallons of chlorine disinfectant. Then I want you to wash and wipe down the entire house with it. Tell Hector to do the inside of my car too. From now on, I want you to use that in every room each day. Comprendo, Rosa?"

"Si, si Meester Scott. Jou want Rosa to poot stinky cloro all ober jour habitacion. Si?"

Rosa laughed to herself. Her employer was always coming up with something different. But she felt lucky working for him over the years. He had always treated her as a friend and an equal. She made more money than any of her friends and Scott paid for her and her family to go on holiday each year to Mexico. She went on decorating and getting the house ready for the Halloween party.

The pot had an instant effect on Scott. In spite of the devastating news, physically he felt great. He decided to shower and drive the Porsche down to Rodeo Drive and buy the dark grey suit he had been admiring in the window of Bijan's. He had not purchased it before because it was priced, with black mink overcoat, at thirty-nine thousand dollars. With a macabre chuckle, he said to himself,

"What the hell, Reid my boy, you only live once!"

At Castle Rock, Hubert was obsequiously serving dinner in Pamela's bedroom suite. Joyce Landen was visiting from Omaha and staying for the week. The week before she and Pamela had been to a health spa in Ojai for three days trying to lose some weight. Joyce had not been successful. Of course it did not help that she had secretly driven every night to the Baskin-Robbins in town for a double hot fudge-banana split. Pamela, who worked out daily, did not need to lose any weight. She was just lonesome since she had broken off her relationship with Scott and went along to the spa out of boredom.

The telephone on Pamela's desk started ringing. It was a private line to Pamela's bedroom suite that only Josh and Scott had the number to. Pamela glanced over at Joyce and barked, "Get out, Joyce. And take Hubert with you. That's a private call."

Joyce looked hurt, and with a pouting frown and sticking out her tongue, she departed for the guest room.

"You're cruder than any man I've ever met!"

Pamela's heart was beating rapidly and her mind was racing. What if it were Scott? What was she going to say? The telephone kept ringing and she picked it up. There was a great deal of static on the line and a voice sounded like an echo. It was from a mobile phone. Then the line cleared and she recognized Scott's baritone voice in mid-sentence.

"...thought I had lied to you, but I didn't. I'd like the chance to explain..."

Pamela cut him off because she had not heard the beginning of the conversation. With her mercurial ability to change personalities to suit the situation, she said wistfully, "Habibi, it's me. I couldn't hear you earlier. Are you in your car? Because you're still not coming through clearly."

"Yes. I'm down on Wilshire Boulevard. There's always a dead zone here because of the high-rises. I'm on my way to the house. I'll call you right back. This mink coat I've got is hotter than hell!"

Pamela thought he was talking about a gift for her. Scott could not hear her clearly, but she shouted, "Hayite, I adore you!"

By the time Scott returned to the house, Hector had already returned from the hardware store with the chlorine and was busy with Rosa scrubbing the kitchen. Scott smiled to himself as he noticed that Hector had on more of Rosa's bright red lipstick than she did. Rosa saw Scott looking and flushed a deep brick shade. Scott winked at her and walked upstairs to telephone in his study. Pamela started talking before he had a chance to say anything.

"Iyuni. Is it really you?"

"Pamela, I called to apologize..."

She cut Scott off before he could continue.

"No, my darling, please forgive me. I acted like a vindictive child. It's the Arab in me. I thought you had lied to me about having tested positive for HIV. And I thought you were out with other women again and ignoring me. I just wanted to get even with you."

Scott now cut her off.

"Please, Pamela, let me speak for a moment. We have to talk about this HIV problem..."

Laughing, Pamela interrupted.

"I know all about it..."

Scott was wondering how she had found out so soon. Did she even have a connection with Ryan? Or was she having him followed? And why was she so happy if she knew he now had HIV-2? Pamela had continued talking.

"...Joyce is here in town staying with me and she told me that you have proof that you don't have HIV. I'm so happy. I don't even care if you try and sue me. I was so wrong. I'm just a stupid woman in love. Scott, when you make your announcement saying I was wrong about you being infected with HIV, I promise I'm going to publicly make an apology. I'll beg your forgiveness on my hands and knees at your Halloween party if you'll let me come. Will you, habibi?"

Scott was dumbfounded. He felt this was not the time to break the truth to her. He quickly decided that he would tell both Pamela and Josh face-to-face at the party.

"Sure, you can come. Bring Joyce if you like."

"I heard it's on Saturday. That's a long way off. I'm so horny for you I could die! Couldn't we meet later on to-night?"

"Pamela, the party is less than forty-eight hours from now. I'd give anything to be in bed with you right now. But I can't. We've got so much to talk about. And I still have Milton Schwartz's mother staying with me and a board meeting tomorrow I need to get prepared for. So bear with me, my dear."

Pamela chortled, "I will. But do I get my new coat at the party?"

"I'm not sure I know what you're talking about."

"Habibi, you're such a mystery man. I'll see you at the

party. I hope you recognize me in my costume."

Pamela hung up and telephoned her florist with an order to deliver twenty-four long-stemmed yellow roses to Scott Reid's home.

On Friday morning, the 29th of October, Scott's house was inundated with workers getting the property ready for the Halloween party.

At noon Scott dressed in his new grey Bijon suit. He then drove over to the laboratory and met with Linda Powell and his interoffice staff. Pending board approval, Scott appointed his president the new CEO, and he appointed the financial officer the acting president of IMA Laboratories in his absence.

After this was completed, Scott went to his office. On his intercom he called the lab physician who had given him the gamma globulin shot earlier in the week. Scott asked him to bring more gamma globulin and one hundred cc's of morphine and a box full of syringes up to his office. The doctor complied. He gave Scott a shot of gamma globulin and left the syringes and vials of morphine on Scott's desk.

Scott then held his last Board of Directors meeting. Since he had made no public announcement denying that he was sick, they all assumed he was taking the leave of absence because his HIV infection was getting worse, not because he had lost two friends. Of course no one said what they were really thinking. But it was discussed what effect Scott's absence would have on the price of the corporate stock. Scott had told them that no matter what the stock did, they should buy it. He then adjourned the meeting. Only one board member shook hands with Scott in parting. The rest waved from the other side of the room.

Linda had acted as the corporate secretary during the meeting. She wore a fluorescent pink dress with her usual plunging neckline and a chain of imitation white pearls. Her long nails were colored pink, she had on a pink headband and pink shoes. She had drenched herself in the fragrance, "Pink Bunny." Not once during the meeting did she have to push up her glasses. Scott noticed that she had switched to contact lenses.

After the meeting Linda followed Scott into his private office. As usual, she stood staring for a few moments at the yellow wheat field painting of van Gogh's hanging on the wall. Then she said to Scott as she handed him the minutes meeting to sign, "Mr. Reid, I know I'm being awfully pushy, but I think I know why you're taking a leave of absence. I just want you to know that nobody is going to talk me out of leaving my job because of your health. I'll be here when you get back and if there's anything I can do for you personally, would you please call me at home?"

Scott held out his hand for her to shake.

"Thanks, Linda. You're a very beautiful and perceptive young woman. I'll miss you very much while I'm gone. Good-bye for now."

Linda came up to him, but she did not proffer her hand. Instead she hugged him and began to cry.

"I'll miss you too, sir."

Scott put the syringes and vials of morphine into his brief case and drove home.

Saturday morning brought a dry, warm, sunny day. The

security police were the first to arrive at the Reid residence. Scott's annual Halloween party had become one of Los Angeles' fall society events and everyone who made the business, political, sporting, television, film and entertainment world go around would be there. About five hundred guests in all. Then came the caterers, the decorators, the electricians, the carpenters, the servants, the parking attendants, the country and western band, the jugglers, the liquor truck and the newspaper reporters. Naturally, Esther told each of them how to do their jobs.

The decorators and electricians had taken down the net on the tennis court and laid out a grass matting over the clay surface. The carpenters had set up a stage at one end of the court and the decorators strung orange and black crepe throughout the wire siding of the tennis court. They hung jack-o-lanterns, white skeleton bones, and flying black papier mâché witches; on the grass matting they set out giant orange pumpkins with carved faces, piles of hay, corn shucks and barrels full of water and shiny red apples for bobbing. The tennis court opened on to the swimming pool area and the guest house. There was about an acre of space that they decorated in the same fashion for the guests to wander through. All of the trees on the property were strung with tiny, sparkling white Tivoli lights.

Scott always had a midwestern theme to the party. Everyone came in costume and prizes were given for the most original. There was a fiddler and a caller for square dancing. They would serve Annie's homemade Pakistani cider in clay jugs, Hector's smoked pork rib barbecue, and Rosa's hot pecan pie for dessert.

Scott was in his bedroom most of the day. He smoked some pot and watched sports on television. Rosa brought him the mail and he read a postcard stamped from Kenya, which had a picture of a large black gorilla on the front. It was from Franklin.

"Dear Bud,

Hope all is well. We're having a great time. Going to visit the African AIDS Center today. Hang in there until I return. Matty says a prayer every night for you.

Your pal, Frank.

P.S. I thought this photo looked a bit like you!"

Scott did not feel well and could not eat. He was nauseated and his dizziness was more pronounced. He ignored Doctor Ryan's advice, took a triple dose of prednisone and a cold shower. While toweling off, he thought that the reddish-blue blotches had spread on his feet. He noticed two small, dark purple lesions on the left big toe. Then he took a short nap, but woke up soaking in perspiration.

At dusk people started arriving by the bus-load, dressed in every conceivable Halloween costume that Hollywood imaginations could concoct. Scott had rented a vacant lot two blocks up Coldwater Canyon Drive for his guests to park in. They were then bussed to the house, where security guards checked them in. There were numerous hired greeters to welcome and serve everyone as the festivities started.

Scott stayed upstairs in his room for two hours. He

still did not feel like socializing and dreaded the need to expose his disease to his friends and the public. Who was ever going to believe that Milton had tested him negative all this time? And who was going to believe that he was possibly murdered?

Scott washed himself with chlorine, then had a steam bath and lit another joint. When he heard the country and western band start playing outside, he decided to go downstairs and join the party. He could hear the square dance caller yelling and clapping.

"Swing your partners to and fro, now do the do-si-do."

Scott put on a green surgical gown, cap, latex gloves, paper foot covers, a face mask and hung a stethoscope around his neck. He was paranoid about spreading his virus and he was going as safely as he thought possible.

Shining through the bedroom window was a huge, round, orange harvest moon. Ursa Major, the Big Dipper, hung tilted as if to pour the other twinkling stars onto the party.

As Scott walked down his carpeted wooden staircase, he was stunned to see the majority of the guests had little red AIDS bows displayed on the front of their costumes. As the crowd saw him coming down the stairs they started applauding his presence. Everyone knew it was Scott Reid behind the surgical mask. They started touching him, patting him on the back and uttering words of praise and condolence. He stiffened. The last thing he wanted was anyone's pity. A sycophantish starlet, made up to look like Scarlett O'Hara, arm-in-arm with a film producer dressed as Rhett Butler, pinned a red bow on Scott's surgical gown.

"God bless, Scott. I want you to know, both you and the Wizard are in our prayers. If there's anything we can do to help, please call us."

She blew Scott a kiss from the palm of her hand. Although the producer could see Scott had on thin white rubber gloves, he only grinned in embarrassment. He did not shake hands with Scott.

In frustration, Scott said, "There is something you could do for me and Wizard. Instead of acting like a sheep following this well-intentioned, but naive Hollywood cult crowd all wearing their red ribbons to social events, you could start pinning these little bows on all the innocent people blasted with hand guns. I've heard the total killed and maimed each year in this country far exceeds the number of HIV and AIDS-infected!"

In non sequitur, the starlet added, "I didn't know that! Oh, by the way. I noticed that your canary is sitting in his cage singing away, uncovered. You have to put a cloth over him at night. He'll die if you leave him like that!"

"Lady," Scott snapped. "I've had that bird for almost fifteen years. Never once has he been covered at night. And I might add, when is the last time you were in the forest and saw a canary sleeping under a cloth?"

Before she could answer, Scott turned around and walked away. He tore the red bow off and put it in his pocket.

Since his physical problems started, Scott had completely avoided society. He had no idea of the magnitude of the rumors and gossip that had circulated about him.

Scott never read the tabloids or periodicals as Pamela did. He had talked to no one socially about whether he had or did not have HIV. He suddenly felt like a pariah. He yearned for the safety of his bedroom.

Scott did not recognize Josh anywhere, but Pamela and Joyce stood out like sore thumbs. They were dressed as hookers. Both in black and chrome S & M outfits. With spike heels, fishnet stockings, miniskirts, black leather hoods for masks and chrome studs for belts, and they both carried leather whips. Pamela was about six foot four with her heels on and Joyce was about five foot three. Seeing Scott's discomfort, Pamela walked over to the crowd surrounding him.

"Iyuni, did I surprise you?"

"Somehow, Pamela, I knew it was you and Joyce. Have you seen Josh anywhere? I need to speak to all of you in private as soon as we have the opportunity."

"No, I haven't seen him anywhere, but I was only looking for you. Do you want us to say something to everyone when you make your announcement?"

"What announcement?"

"About you being negative for HIV, silly!"

"Well, that's what I want to talk to you about."

A very tall man in a long black suit, with two red AIDS bows pinned on its lapels and a black stovepipe hat on top of his Abraham Lincoln rubber face, interrupted Scott and said in a muffled voice, "Hi, Scott, it's Wizard! I left messages at your office when I heard you tested positive. I'm sorry. But isn't it weird being treated like this because we both got this virus? I know you're not planning on checking out any more than I am, man. I'm planning on playing ball next year and I hope you're gonna be down at your courtside seat."

Scott held up his rubber surgical gloved right hand for a high-five hand shake. Wizard slapped Scott's hand hard. The noise made a cracking sound. Scott laughed.

"Wizard, I'll do my best to be there. I'm sorry for not returning your calls. But I thought I wasn't infected and I didn't want you to think I was misleading you. How about some golf next week? I'll fill you in on all the details then."

"No problem, Scott. I had a hard time admitting it to myself, much less the public! Call me on the golf, I'd like to get out and play. Right now, I've got to get out and dance with my wife. Great party, Scott, catch you later."

Pamela was now joined by Joyce and they both came up and linked themselves arm-in-arm with Scott. He said to them.

"Could you please go upstairs in my study? I need to talk to you both privately. I'll be up in five."

The two skimpily-clad women paraded up the wooden staircase like they were working Forty-second street.

Everyone at the party but Josh, Annie, Pamela, Joyce, Rosa, Hector and Esther thought Scott was infected with HIV.

And they were right!

Scott knew that he had procrastinated long enough to his friends. He had to find Josh and set the matter straight. He asked Rosa to get Hector and Esther and go up in his study and wait for him. He then walked out to the tennis court where the square dancing was. He saw neither Josh nor Annie. A bent over, hunchbacked Quasimodo, dressed in rags and with one eye bulging, tugged on Scott's arm.

"Bon Jour, Scott, which way is Notre Dame?"

"Josh, by God you did surprise me!"

"I told you I would. But when are you going to surprise all of these people with your announcement? I can't wait to see their faces."

Scott said, "I can't right now. I need to..."

Josh cut him off.

"Come on, Scott, why don't you get up on stage after this next number and do it now? Christ, Scott, they all think you've got it. You should have taken care of this before the party."

"Listen, Josh, I need to talk to you and Annie upstairs in my study about that. Would you meet me up there in five minutes?"

Annie, dressed as Guinevere, in a long blonde, peruke wig, gave Josh a puzzled look and then took him by the hand. They left the dance to go up to the study.

It was close to midnight and the master of ceremonies was telling everyone they would then unmask for the prize for best costume. The fiddler, stomping his leg up and down to the beat, was in the last stanza of Flight of the Bumblebee when Scott wandered through the boisterous crowd bidding everyone to enjoy themselves. Then he made his way up the stairway.

Josh was playing with the dogs in the study when Scott arrived. Annie was sitting on the floor beside him. Pamela and Joyce were whispering something in each others' ears, and Hector, Rosa and Esther were chatting on the couch.

As Scott entered the room, Josh said to him, "I've never had a pet in my life, Scott. Seems they never liked me or I never had time for them. But these two hounds of yours follow me around every time I come over here like I'm their sire."

Pamela glared at Annie, then looked at Joyce and said, "He does like to keep company with animals, haven't you noticed? If it were a mongoose with a little red dot on its forehead, he'd probably be the father."

Before Annie or Josh could defend themselves, Scott shouted,

"Shut up, Pamela! Your prejudice won't be tolerated in my house."

Pamela, Joyce in hand, started for the door. Scott quickly continued, "Before you leave, Pamela, there's another matter I need to discuss. I asked you all to come up here to listen to what I have to say and pass your own judgement's on what I tell you."

Hector, Rosa and Esther sat up straight on the couch to listen. Josh and Annie got up from the floor and sat in a chair next to the teak desk, Annie on Josh's lap. Pamela leaned against the wall, pouting. Joyce looked curiously at Scott. The gathering of costumed party-goers and workers looked more like a roomful of circus performers than a gathering of friends. Scott continued, "I guess I owe you all an apology. It seems that ever since Pamela made the announcement that I was HIV positive, I've inadvertently lied to all of you."

Josh interrupted brashly, "What do you mean, Scott? I thought you brought us up here to tell us about the negative test results you had from the outside lab!"

Joyce and Pamela spoke at almost the same time. Joyce kept going in her squeaky soprano, "Scott, Ralph told me you had proof already that you weren't infected with HIV."

Then Pamela quickly added, "Hayite, I'll apologize to everybody right now. I'm sorry I've been such a bitch. I didn't mean to put Scott through all of this gossip and embarrassment!"

Scott was having no success trying to speak through all of the chaos and Esther, who had not put on a costume for the party, though many people thought she was dressed as Golda Meir, said, "Oy, veh! Be quiet already. Scotty vants something to say!"

Scott continued calmly, "What I need to tell you is that I thought I was negative for HIV from Milton Schwartz's tests at my laboratory, but I received news only yesterday that Milton was wrong. I flew to San Francisco for an independent test of my blood and their result confirms that I'm HIV-2 infected. It appears I have AIDS."

As Scott paused, one could have heard the proverbial pin drop in the small room. In a moment, Hector put his arm around Rosa as she started to sob. Esther's eyes were watering. Pamela was glaring at Joyce. Annie, still sitting on Josh's lap, hugged him closely as he bowed his masked, grotesque head.

Scott quickly continued, "I assure all of you, I didn't do this on purpose. I believed that Milton's tests were correct and that a mistake had originally been made in testing my blood at the Berlinger Clinic."

Pamela shrieked, "Scott Reid, you're nothing but a liar. And to think I wasted the last three years of my life giving you my love! And you, Josh Kramer, you should be ashamed of yourself, shacking up with that darkie Wog. It's her people, the monkeys, and the niggers, that spread this damn disease in the first place! Joyce, I've had enough of these hypocrites. Let's get out of here."

Joyce gave Scott an evil look through her black leather hood, then stuck out her tongue. Pamela grabbed her hand and they hurried through the door.

Annie wanted to cry or to speak, but chose not to dignify Pamela's remarks with a response. Josh yelled, "Pamela, who the hell do you think you're talking to? In the future stay as far away from me and Annie as you ..."

Josh stopped. As Pamela and Joyce hastily departed they had left the door open and the noise of the party drowned out any chance they would hear him. Hector closed the door.

Scott knew it was useless to attempt an explanation, but he tried anyway.

"I'm sorry, Annie. I'll never forgive her for saying that to you, but I suppose I can't blame her for hating me for what's happened. Is there anyone else who feels the same way about me? If so, please leave and there'll be no hard feelings. Otherwise I'd like to explain what I plan to do."

Josh moved Annie off of his lap and stood up so forcefully that his action snapped the wire holding the plastic hump; it fell to the small of his muscled back. He tore off his Quasimodo mask and looked around the room. He could see from their expressions that they were all supportive of Scott. Then Josh stared directly at Scott, saying in a deep, paternal voice,

"Scott, we'll have no more of that kind of talk between us. We're going to lick this thing together, whatever it takes. Now, tell us all what happened."

For the first time since Doctor Ryan had given him the

news, Scott sensed the reality of what was happening. In silence he stared at his small group of friends. They sincerely cared. He also felt violent cramps and nausea. Before he could reply, he dashed out of the room into the bathroom of the main bedroom. He fell on his knees over the toilet bowl and regurgitated, then doubled over with cramps and fell face forward onto the tile floor.

Esther was the first one to reach Scott. She sat on the floor and cradled his head in her lap.

"Scotty, Scotty. Don't vorry. Your step-momma vill take care of you. Tomorrow I make you chicken soup."

Esther kissed him on the forehead. Scott's surgical gown was drenched in perspiration. He was cold and clammy and he had the shakes. Josh bent down and picked him up in his arms. His bowed legs wobbled, but he carried Scott to the circular bed. Hector limped behind, offering to help.

The master of ceremonies was announcing the winner of the costume prize on the stage below the bedroom window. He bellowed, "Come on up, Quasimodo. We all want to know who you really are. Has anybody seen the winner, Quasimodo?"

None of the people in Scott's bedroom paid any attention to the announcement or to the party that was raging on. Annie went over and closed the wooden shutters of the window, blocking out most of the noise from below. Rosa, whose sobbing was now under control, gently placed a cold washcloth on Scott's face. He opened his eyes and said, smiling, "I wasn't trying to get out of telling you all what happened, nor was I trying to get out of our golf game tomorrow, Josh, but right now I think we should continue this discussion in the morning."

"It's all right, Scott. I'll take care of the party and get them out of here as soon as possible. Do you need a doctor?"

"Hell, no! That's the last thing I need. I've got plenty of medicine and once I get some sleep, I'll be fine in the morning. But listen, all of you. I don't know how contagious this disease is. I don't want to infect anyone with what I've got. I..."

"Don't talk nonsense Scott. Annie and I'll come back about eleven tomorrow morning. Now just get some sleep."

As soon as everyone had left, Scott shakily got out of bed and went to the bathroom. He decided not to take the medication that Doctor Ryan had called down to the pharmacy and took two aspirin instead. Scott put the bottle in his medicine drawer alongside the vials of morphine.

The dogs barking at his bedroom door woke Scott. Ginger hopped off the bed and scurried down to the kitchen. The room was pitch black. Hector had come in during the night and closed all of the shutters and drawn the drapes. Scott thought he must have dozed off for a few hours after taking the morphine and the aspirin, but when he switched on the bedside lamp he saw the clock blinking, 10:30 A.M.

Scott stretched and felt good again. No aches, no nausea, no headache, no sweating. The dogs kept barking and clawing on the glass sliding doors. He got up to scold them and when he opened the curtains, there was a small fat, black-masked baby raccoon stuck between the two sliding doors. The kit was shivering and whining and reached out a paw against the glass towards Scott. Scott slid open the inner glass door and the raccoon scampered under his bed in fright, his fluffy ringed tail hanging out from under the comforter. The dogs saw that and jumped high against the outer glass door, howling in vain. Scott put his robe on and went out and took them to their kennels.

The cleanup crew had arrived early and Hector was showing them where to finish. As Scott walked by the open kitchen window, he could smell the bacon and huevos rancheros that Rosa was cooking for breakfast. He walked into the kitchen and saw a white stack of steaming flour tortillas sitting on the counter.

"Buenos dias, guapa. It smells delicious. What time do we eat? Do I have time to shave and shower?"

"Buenos dias, Meester Scott. Si! Meester Josh and Senorita Annie come en media y hora. Senora Esther es coming now. Comprendo?"

"Claro!" Scott answered.

Then he took a seat in the booth next to the stove.

"Rosa, I need you and Hector to know that I'll understand if you want to seek other employment under the circumstances I told you about last night. I'll compensate you both for a year and buy you a house somewhere that you can choose. I'm sure one of my friends would hire you both in a minute."

Rosa had a deep frown on her face. She licked the red lipstick on her teeth with her tongue. Then she waggled her spatula in Scott's face and said firmly, "Meester Scott. Hector and me, we talk mucho en noche. We not leave jou. Jou not be seek long. We make jou better. OK? Now jou go upstairs an shower. We eat soon."

Josh, Annie and Esther were seated at the table eating

by the time Scott arrived back downstairs. Josh greeted him heartily.

"Good morning, Scott. You sure as hell gave us a scare last night. How're you feeling today?"

"Morning, everyone. As usual, after a bout of feeling horrible, I feel fine the next day. Let's eat and forget about that and then maybe Josh and I can get in at least nine holes today."

Esther asked, "Scotty, you mean you vant already you play golf today after last night?"

"Yes, my concerned little momma, for two reasons. One, just to get out and enjoy the world and two, I'd like to speak to Josh confidentially. After that all of us can discuss what's to be done."

Josh said, "I'll call Bel Air and get a tee time. Finish your breakfast, Scott."

As Josh got up to use the telephone, a dark furry little animal with a long tail ran between his feet, scurrying out the kitchen door.

Annie yelled, "I say, Scott, what was that?"

Scott smiled.

"Just a buddy of mine I'd forgotten about."

Scott put his golf clubs in the trunk of Josh's heavily armored Rolls Royce Phantom VI and they drove off to the country club. Scott fiddled with the stereo and the mobile phone. Josh soon became impatient in the silence.

"Come on, Scott. Tell me what in hell's happened. It sounds as if you could use all the help you can get."

Scott had his raspy cough back. He hacked into his fist.

"First of all I have to apologize for not having complete faith in you. I didn't come to you right away because I thought you were in business with Gino and Richard."

"What do you mean, Scott?" Josh stared at him. Scott's next statement came out in a rush.

"I mean, Gino is on the board of MRL and you were so damn excited about Landen getting Richard's committee's approval for more funding of HIV tests, which benefits your corporation, that I thought you were in business with them. Then you invite me to the Netherlands Antilles with those two and right after that you purchase Malaysian Latex."

"What the hell does this have to do with you having AIDS?"

"Josh, I'm not sure. Please hear me out. What I'm going to tell you borders on the unbelievable."

As Josh stopped at the red light of the Sunset Boulevard and the west entrance gate of Bel Air, a young man wearing a blue L.A. Dodgers baseball cap, pushed a pamphlet towards Josh's window.

"Hey mister, only twenty bucks for a map to the stars' homes."

"Scott, now that borders on the unbelievable. Twenty bucks! They should let you screw a celebrity for that price."

Josh accelerated through the white marble arched gate and turned up Stone Canyon Road towards the country club. He continued where he had left off.

"Josh, listen to me. I think I've been murdered. I..."

"What the hell are you talking about, Scott? Are you telling me one of those little starlets you used to boff gave you AIDS on purpose?"

Josh pulled the car into the entrance of the Bel Air

Country Club.

"No, it's not like that at all. Let's stop for a beer at the Men's Club so I can sit down and tell you my theory without you interrupting me every two seconds."

The valet gave Josh a paper stub and took the Rolls to the parking lot and the caddy master.

The mens' bar was empty and Scott and Josh took a table in the darkest corner of the room. They ordered German beers. Scott took out a cigar from its tube and cut off the end. Josh said, "Well, let's hear it, Scott. You've certainly aroused my curiosity."

Scott took a deep drink from the mug of frothy beer, which left a small white mustache on his upper lip. He wiped it off and lit up his cigar.

"There were two reasons I didn't come to you sooner and that I seemed to be deceiving everyone. First, I know business makes strange bedfellows and I couldn't comprehend why you invited me on the trip with Richard and Gino, unless you were doing business with them in some kind of offshore operation."

Offended, Josh quickly said, "I just wanted to take you fishing, Scott. To get you away from all the crap you were going through. Nothing else! I've told you. I'd never be in business with those two butts."

"I know that now, Josh, but please let me finish. I found out some things on that trip that I think you need to be aware of and that I think may have cost me my life. Again, I didn't come to you right away because I had no idea at that time if you were involved. When you purchased Malaysian Latex, I was in even more of a quandary. I..."

Josh had finished his beer. He interrupted again and at the same time ordered two more.

"I'm sorry, Scott, you've got me so damn confused. Stop before you go any further. What's my business with MRL or the purchase of Malaysian Latex got to do with your problem?"

Scott blew out a large breath of uninhaled cigar smoke.

"I'll tell you in a minute if you'd just let me finish. I have to preface all of what I say with the fact that I took Milton Schwartz at his word and medical abilities. I believed that he had tested me negative for HIV from the beginning. He wasn't a man to make mistakes and besides, he was one damn close personal friend. The night he died, or was killed, he phoned me and said that I had been negative for HIV all along, but now I was positive because I had been injected with HIV-2 infected blood by Doctor Graziano. He said that he was going to the lab and getting me the proof. A blood sample of some kind, so I would know what he was talking about. He told me in no way to get near Nicki or believe anything that he might try and tell me. He asked me if I knew that Gino Rigitinni was Nicki's uncle."

Scott drained his beer and continued. "Josh, Milton wasn't speaking to Nicki, he thought that Nicki had murdered me, yet within two hours they were both dead. Killed in the same car crash together. So I've been asking myself ever since, how could that've happened?"

The whistling barman, with a yellow pencil behind his ear, brought over the two fresh beers and set them on the table. When Scott went to sip the froth from the top of the mug, Josh said, "Scott, this's sounding a little melodramatic. Are you sure there wasn't a little professional jealousy here? After all, one doctor is telling another that he's made a mistake. Then the other doctor makes up some absurd story about you being murdered instead of facing up to it. Unfortunately, it sounds like human nature to me."

Scott took a gulp of cold beer. He coughed a raspy cough.

"I've thought all of that out. It just isn't true. Milton wasn't that kind of man. Plus which, I'm sure everything I found out on the Caribbean trip ties in somehow to what's happened. You said yourself that Gino was from the gutter and might have ties to the underworld, right?"

"True, Scott, but I still don't get the connection."

"If you'll recall, on the way down to the Caribbean Gino got pissed. He was so drunk that he vomited all over himself and passed out. When he did, all of the papers he was working on spilled out of his briefcase onto the floor. I went to pick them up and put them back for him. When I did that I saw that the top paper was a Memorandum of Wishes for Zafra Limited. You know—legal proof of ownership of a corporation offshore. I couldn't help but notice that the beneficial owner of Zafra Limited was none other than Senator Richard Spout."

Josh exploded. "What!"

"Josh, that's not all." Scott said. "When I saw that, I shuffled through the papers and saw that the honorable legislator was also one of the beneficial owners of Malaysian Latex. Along with two other Luxembourg corporations."

"I'll be a son of a bitch!"

"Then Gino woke up. He caught me off guard and grabbed the papers from me and said I'd pay for what I'd seen."

"Jesus Christ, Scott, why on earth haven't you told me this before?"

"Josh, that's what I've been apologizing for. You're the closest thing I've had to a father. You've also been as good a friend as I've ever had. But you're tough, Josh, and you're one private bastard most of the time. Hell, I didn't know what to think. You seemed in such cahoots with those two assholes that I didn't know if you were in business with them or not. And I didn't want to get you in hot water with the authorities if you were. So I decided to wait and see what happened. It appears I waited too long. I hope you can forgive me for thinking such crap."

Josh drained his beer mug slowly. His eyes were moist, but he looked at Scott directly.

"Scott, you don't owe me an apology. I owe you one. You could only come to the same conclusion about me that anyone else would've under the circumstances. I've created such a facade, such a shield of protection for myself over the years, that it's carried over into all of my relationships. I was even blind to what a shit Pamela really is. But, Scott, other than my old man, you're the only friend I've ever had. It's true, I've always thought of you like a son, but it's my friendship with you that I treasure. And I'm sorry my habits made you think something else of me."

Josh paused and took a deep breath, but continued.

"Now, neither you or I know yet what's fact or fiction

about outside involvement in your getting AIDS, but you tell me that for sure you know you have it. Who told you that?"

Scott watched Josh position his arm across the table as though he wanted to arm wrestle. Josh held his powerful hand open. Scott put his hand into it. They sat there silent for a moment, eye to eye, elbow to elbow, hand in hand, looking like combatants. This was as close as the two of them had ever come to an embrace. Scott then answered, "Before Milton died, I went up to see a medical pal of Frank Nelsen's in San Francisco. A doctor named Bill Ryan. This may sound funny, but originally I went as Milton Schwartz."

"Why?"

"Because Milton had tested me negative for HIV and was having a dispute with Nicki, the Berlinger Clinic and MRL over it. I thought that if Milton had another negative test to back up his work, we could get to the bottom of who was right and who was wrong. Under the circumstances, I didn't want any blood test of mine coming to the lab under my own name, so I told them I was Milton Schwartz." Josh removed his hand from Scott's. "Still seems odd to me that you'd go as Schwartz."

"Goddamnit, Josh, let me finish. Before I got the test back, Milton was killed. I called Doctor Ryan right away because Milton had called me and said I was HIV positive. I told Ryan everything I've told you except the business part. He told me that I had a very rare form of AIDS. HIV-2! And that it's bad and that I'd be getting sick very soon. He called down medication for me to take and he wants me in San Francisco tomorrow for more evaluation and tests."

Josh suddenly started devouring the peanuts and pretzels that were sitting in bowls on the table. He took a swig of beer and mumbled, "I'll fly you up there, Scott. I want to go with you and get to the bottom of this thing. I've read that with proper treatment you can live out your life with this HIV. Hell, I'm sure there's a vaccine just around the corner. So let's go get you the help you need."

"Josh, I appreciate it. But I've got to be straight with you. I've been in the medical business all of my life and I've seen these test results. There's no cure or vaccine for this. I'm going to die. And I'm going to die soon. I want to live out the rest of my time in dignity and happiness. I'll do anything it takes to do that. I don't want to go waste away in some hospital, blasted full of experimental drugs that haven't worked on anybody so far. If there's anything you can do for me, besides being my friend, it would be to trace down the connection between Gino and Richard and what's happened."

Josh was furious and he blurted, "That's a bunch of bullshit, Scott! I don't want to hear any more of that kind of talk. Don't be such a pessimist! I'm going to see that everything humanly possible is available so you can live out the rest of your life, whether you're HIV-infected or not. But I think your pal Schwartz made a mistake and he was trying to cover it up with this ridiculous story. I don't think there's any connection between Richard and Gino and your HIV-2."

Josh kept talking, but took a napkin and wiped the

dew off the bottom of his mug. "But I'll tell you this, Scott, those sneaky bastards are finished with MRL as soon as I can get proof to back up your findings. And I'm going to have a private talk with Richard about his political future. Now, if you feel up to it, lets go play the back nine and go home and get ready to go to San Francisco tomorrow."

The two men touched glasses, drained their beer mugs and went to the golf course.

William Ryan's concern went beyond Scott Reid. He was worried that a new strain of HIV had entered Northern California. He called the Centers for Disease Control in Atlanta for information on how many cases of HIV-2 had been isolated in the States and the exact location of the discoveries. What he found out was puzzling. Only forty-one cases of HIV-2 had been reported in all of the United States. And each one had a direct link to an African contact. One had even died of the dreaded Ebola Zaire virus. Either the person had visited one of the infected areas, or was an immigrant, or had a sexual encounter with an infected individual in Western Europe or Africa. But there was no record of anyone that could *not* trace where the HIV-2 came from. There were eight cases in Los Angeles. One individual had recently died. The others were terminally ill.

A liter of blood from the deceased victim had been sent to IMA Laboratories in Encino, California, for further analysis. They had verified that he had died of AIDS brought on by the complicating symptoms of HIV-2 and *Pneumocystis carinii*. Ryan did *not* find it odd that Scott's own laboratory, IMA, had tested the HIV-2 victim's blood. However, he did wonder if there was any way Scott could have been exposed to the blood sample. He jotted down a note to ask Scott if he had ever personally worked with the blood at IMA Laboratories. But Ryan held no credence in the wild story that Milton Schwartz had told Scott before his death. The murder idea had to be a total fabrication.

On Monday, November 1, 1992 the stock of IMA Laboratories, Incorporated had another delayed opening. The board of directors had announced over the weekend that as of their last meeting, Scott Reid, chairman and CEO, was taking a three-month leave of absence due to the tragic death of two of his employees and personal friends.

Wall Street did not buy the story any more than the board of directors did. IMA common stock opened after two hours of specialists' sorting out sell orders, at nineteen dollars a share. Down five dollars a share.

As Scott and Josh sat in the waiting room of Doctor Ryan's office in San Francisco, Scott turned to Josh and said, "You know, my stock is worth fifty dollars a share and these sheep will drive it down to fifteen before I'm out of here. You might jump in there and take it over, Josh. We're a much better company than MRL. Even though you never had any faith in me when I got started, why don't you take a look and see what I've accomplished over the years?"

Josh felt it was time to tell Scott about his controlling shares of Class B stock of IMA. Even more, he wanted to tell Scott of his original faith in the young entrepreneur. After all, under the right set of circumstances, including Scott's death, Josh's Class B shares could allow Josh to appoint the chairman of the board, CEO and president of IMA Laboratories. Until this point Josh had always let the auditors vote his offshore-held stock in perpetuity and in favor of Scott Reid. So Josh said, "Look, Scott, there's something you should know about me and IMA..."

A white-uniformed nurse interrupted the confession.

"Mr. Reid, this way, please. Doctor Ryan is ready to see you now."

The AIDS specialist stood up from behind his desk and welcomed Scott and Josh.

"Good morning, gentlemen."

Scott said, "Nice to see you again, Bill. This is my friend Josh Kramer. He's been kind enough to fly me up here and offer his services for whatever future help I'm going to need. I hope you won't mind him being part of our discussion?"

Ryan immediately recognized Josh. It is hard to hide when you are one of America's richest men.

"I'm happy to make your acquaintance, Mr. Kramer. Scott, I don't mind his participation at all. You're going to need all the support you can get as this thing progresses."

Josh said quickly, "Doctor Ryan, Scott's told me that he has HIV-2, but could you bring me up to date on how bad his condition is? He seems pretty damn pessimistic to me."

The internist smiled gently.

"First of all, I need to run a few more routine tests and take some more blood. This is just so we know how to treat any opportunistic infections that might be lingering in the body. We routinely do a skin test for tuberculosis, a syphilis serologic test and a sputum smear. From my tests and the previous HIV positive tests on Scott we're quite certain of the progress of the disease in his system."

Impatiently, Josh asked, "And how far is that?"

Doctor Ryan looked over at Scott and Scott nodded his head. The physician then stated, "In all candor, Mr. Kramer, Scott has at best a few months to live."

Josh turned ashen. He had not expected such direct openness between patient and doctor. He turned to Scott, helplessly. The doctor continued, "I guess I wouldn't be too much of an optimist, either. But Scott has enough medical knowledge to know what he has to do to prolong his life and alleviate the suffering that goes with the later stages of the disease. He also knows when he's going to die. Ironically, in time, most of my patients tell me they find that comforting."

With a sad, pained expression, Josh said, "Are you telling me that there's no hope whatsoever? That with all of the advances of modern medicine we can't keep Scott alive for another twenty years or so?"

"I'm afraid not."

Josh pleaded, "Doctor Ryan, I've read that HIV patients can practically live out their life span if they'd take the proper precautions. What's so different about what Scott's got?"

Scott felt uncomfortable. He knew that Josh was used to getting his way and hearing what he wanted to hear.

Doctor Ryan also noticed it.

"Mr. Kramer, I'm sorry that you have to hear the brutal truth, but Scott and I have previously discussed what's happened with the disease in his system. Unfortunately, in life there comes a time when the body can't win every battle and we die, and Scott has reached that stage with this horrible disease."

Josh was not about to give up.

"But there must be something!"

"As I told Scott—only a miracle." Ryan said. "But I haven't seen one happen yet with someone with AIDS. By the way, Scott. I checked with the CDC and your own laboratory has analyzed HIV-2 positive blood in the past. Is there any chance that you were in direct contact with any of your clinical testing?"

Other than Milton's statement about Nicki injecting him with HIV-2 blood, this was the first time Scott was aware IMA Laboratories was involved with testing the rare disease.

"None. I haven't been involved with laboratory work in some time. More than fifteen years, to be exact."

"And you're one hundred percent sure that no one you've ever been sexually exposed to was HIV-infected?"

"Positive!"

Josh commented brashly, "How can you be so positive, Scott? I'll bet you don't even know if three-quarters of the women you've slept with are still alive, much less HIV-positive!"

"Josh, no one I slept with has AIDS! Don't you think someone would tell me if they had it?"

"You mean like all of the people you've called?"

The doctor interceded.

"Now, hold on a minute, we're just trying to get Scott the help he needs. Scott, I want you to think about what Mr. Kramer's saying. How can you be sure of all of your ex-partners? You've admitted that you've been very promiscuous over the years."

Scott answered, "Josh, I haven't called anyone because I believe I was given this disease on purpose and I haven't had any sex since that happened. And Bill, as promiscuous as I was years ago, I live in a small social world. I'd know if anyone had AIDS!"

Ryan quickly rebuffed him. Like a machine gun, the physician shot off his thoughts, counting on all ten fingers.

"Number one...it's not just the promiscuity, Scott, didn't you tell me you've been to Africa and that you'd had sex there? Number two...you've had a blood transfusion and you didn't know the donor. Number three...you told me you've never used condoms! Number four...you're not circumcised. Number five...you told me you've engaged in anal sex with women."

The doctor's knuckles cracked as he rapidly switched hands to keep counting. He started again before Scott could interrupt, bending the little finger of the left hand. "Number six...you also told me you had numerous gay friends. Number seven...were they just social friends or sexual partners? Number eight...and you've told me you used drugs. Number nine...how far did you go in using drugs? And number ten, did you ever use someone else's needle and shoot up crack cocaine, for example?"

Scott's color rose. This is not what he came to see the physician about. He spat his words.

"Wait a second, Bill! I've always been a heterosexual. Yes, I said I smoked pot. But you know as a doctor, only the Feds think that's a drug! I never said I used any drugs other than alcohol and nicotine. But even those I've used in moderation. The rest of what you say is true. I realize I may sound like the perfect candidate for AIDS, but I'm telling you both, I believe what Milton Schwartz told me. I think that I've somehow been murdered."

Ryan drew a deep breath. He looked over at Josh and frowned.

"Scott, would you remove your shirt? We'll get on with the tests I need to run on you. We can discuss your murder theory later. Are you aware that you've lost twelve pounds since I last saw you?"

"Yes, but that's to be expected, I guess."

"By the way, were you able to get ahold of Frank Nelsen? I'd like to speak to him about your prognosis."

"No, I didn't, right now he's in the middle of Kenya on a safari. I think it might be impossible to reach him."

The waiting room of the internist's office was packed with patients. When Doctor Ryan and his nurse had finished with the brief tests on Scott, the physician said to Josh, "Mr. Kramer, we're through for the day. I'll run these and have the results by Friday. Scott can stay on the medication I started him on and I'll need to see him on a weekly basis. He's going to be able to resume most of his normal activities, but as time goes on he'll start deteriorating. He'll need your help and support. I want to be able to call you at your home and for you to be able to reach me at my home in case of an emergency. So please exchange numbers with my secretary on the way out."

He extended his hand to both men. "Mr. Kramer, it was a pleasure to meet you. Good day."

Ryan made a mental note to be sure and talk to Scott about Milton Schwartz's murder theory at next week's appointment.

There was a great deal of small talk between the two men on the way to the San Francisco airport. The grim reality of the situation and the meeting with Ryan had left Josh groping for answers. Scott was perspiring heavily and for the first time, Josh noticed the unpleasant odor. As the limo passed Candlestick Park, Josh said, "Scott, I don't really know what to do, but I've got to start somewhere. I'd like to send the plane over to Kenya and pick up Frank Nelsen. He's not only your friend, but you told me he's one of the best in the world on HIV and AIDS. What do you think, could we track him down?"

"It'd take a bit of doing, but anything's possible," Scott said. "He visited the African AIDS Center in Nairobi before he left on safari. Maybe he's got some good news for me."

"I'll have the pilots arrange to leave tomorrow. Where can I get the details on where Nelsen was staying and who he's on safari with?"

"My secretary has his itinerary. But you must realize that Frank doesn't know that I've got AIDS. When he left, the test results he took showed I was HIV-positive and that I could probably have a pretty good twenty years or so with the proper medication. His tests didn't show HIV-2. So when he gets here, I'm going to keep reminding you that I've been murdered!"

It was Josh's turn to be angry. He retorted, "Why don't you knock off that conspiracy and murder crap, Scott! Can't you see that some rational friends are just trying to help you, or are you too far gone?"

On the flight back to Los Angeles, Josh stayed in his study in the aircraft, faxing and telephoning around the world in search of Nelsen. He wanted him back to the United States as soon as possible. Scott had started feeling nauseous and dizzy. His cough worsened in the air-conditioned cabin. He downed more steroids and fell asleep. By the time the plane landed at the Santa Monica airport, Josh had arranged for Franklin Nelsen to be in Los Angeles by Wednesday, November 3rd. The day of the presidential election.

Annie, ensconced in a comfortable, canvas-backed chair on the terrace of the penthouse, was watching the sun set over the small mountain range surrounding Malibu. She could see the dark yellow ball of sun waver in the haze of the city. Red geraniums with lush green leaves popped into view from the flower beds on the edge of the terrace as the sun began its descent for the night.

As her man walked onto the terrace, Annie knew from the look on Josh's face that the meeting with the doctor in San Francisco had not gone well. But she asked anyway,

"Sweetheart, how did it go?"

Josh looked haggard. He had aged with the news that his only friend was going to die. His huge shoulders sagged and his arms hung limp. He looked up at her and said sadly, "There's no hope, Annie. He's going to die in a few months at best. The tough bastard is taking it better than me. I don't know what the hell to do. It just seems so impossible. He and the doctor kept talking like it was just a case of measles. And then Scott has this weird theory that he's been murdered. I can't figure out why he's trying to defend this guy Schwartz. It seems to me that if Scott had come to us earlier and not put all his faith in that old pipe-smoking eccentric, then we might've been able to help him."

Annie stood up. Her radiant smile had disappeared, and tears were streaming down her face.

"Josh, Scott's not a person to be making up stories. He'd defend you to his death, too. Maybe you should call this doctor back in San Francisco and talk to him privately about what he thinks. I know how much you love Scott and I do, too..."

Annie's voice trailed off into sobs and she ran crying into Josh's arms. He squeezed her so hard in his frustration that she let out a cry of pain. For a few lonely moments, they stood holding one another tightly. The sun disappeared under the mountain range and a reddish dusk glowed over Los Angeles. Josh released Annie.

"You're right, Annie. Maybe the guy figured he couldn't say everything in front of Scott."

Josh went into his study and dialed the home telephone

number of Doctor Ryan in Hillsborough. The maid put the doctor on the line.

"Mr. Kramer, I had a feeling I'd be hearing from you soon. How can I be of help?"

"Doctor Ryan..."

The physician cut Josh off and said politely,

"Mr. Kramer, please call me Bill. I have a feeling we're going to be doing a lot of talking about your friend Scott Reid."

"Thanks, Bill. And my friends call me Josh. I apologize for disturbing you at home like this, but I was in such a state of shock this morning after what you told me, that I'm afraid I left some questions unanswered."

The physician put down his cup of coffee and sat down in an easy chair in his living room.

"No need for an apology, Josh. I was going to telephone you at the end of the week when I get Scott's test results back. I don't think they'll show anything different, but I'm concerned about his preposterous story about murder. Has he told you what this fellow Schwartz told him before Schwartz died?"

"Yes, Scott told me everything. This was why I was phoning you tonight. I want your opinion. Scott's not a storyteller. But I think he may be overly loyal to the memory of his pal Schwartz."

Bill Ryan took a long drink of the tepid coffee.

"Josh, there are many strange manifestations that happen to AIDS-infected individuals. One of them is dementia. They can do the most irrational things and make up the most believable stories. I've had patients purposely infect others just to get even with life. I've had them get violent and vindictive toward society at large. If you'll recall, Scott originally came to my office under an alias, and then told me a story that a doctor friend and employee of his had injected him with HIV-2 tainted blood."

"I know that," Josh said. "But Scott's not a liar. He didn't want the test result to be forwarded to his lab under his own name."

"Now, Josh, I'm sure from what I see and from what I've read about Scott, that he's an honorable fellow. However, as a physician I've got to deal with the facts. And those facts, which I pointed out for you in the office this morning, are so compelling that if one were to draw up a chart for the perfect AIDS candidate, Scott Reid would be at the head of the list!"

"So you think Scott's just covering for Milton now that Milton's dead?"

"Yes, I do. So I'd like to have a psychological evaluation done on Scott when he comes up next week. You might come along again. Another of the problems with the AIDS-infected is a neurologic syndrome. The most common being encephalitis. This usually begins early in the course of AIDS or AIDS-related complex and progresses from subtle cognitive impairment to severe dementia. But if we catch neurological disorders in time we can treat them with primary prophylaxis."

"Doc, in English, does that mean you're going to put Scott on medication that will make a zombie out of him? Because Scott won't take it, I assure you."

"Sorry to be so technical, Josh. But we usually use

sulfadiazine, pyrimethamine and leucovorin for two to four weeks and notice marked improvement in most patients. And yes, it does drastically alter their physiology. Yet I think I can talk Scott into doing this for his own good."

"Hold on, Bill," Josh said. "I can barely pronounce aspirin, much less understand all you're trying to say to me. But I've got good news. I'm having Frank Nelsen flown over here from Africa on Wednesday and he can come up on Monday with us to decipher it all. I just want to find something that's going to prolong Scott's life."

"We're going to do all we can to help Scott. And that's wonderful news about Nelsen. Frank's one of the best. I'm sure it'll do Scott a world of good to have a medical pal at his side. I'll look forward to seeing you again next Monday."

"Good night, Josh."

Josh realized that without any evidence there was nothing he could legally do to Senator Richard Spout and Gino Rigitinni over their suspected involvement with Medical Reference Laboratories, Inc. He also knew there was nothing he could say to either one of them until he had that evidence. All he could do was to try and buy them out in some underhanded way. Therefore, Josh's next call was to a private detective, Todd Butler. Josh had him leave for the Netherlands Antilles immediately to see if he could uncover anything incriminating on Zafra Limited and its beneficial owner. Although it was now midnight in New York, Josh decided to telephone Richard Spout at his home. The line was busy.

In Oyster Bay, New York, the barometer was falling. A

storm lashed rain onto the picture window of Richard Spout's oceanfront home. The blustery wind buffeted the two-story Colonial house and the large pane of glass in the living room. The force was so strong that Richard was worried the window would break. He could see huge whitecaps exploding over the rock foundation of the jetty at the end of his property. The white foam crashed high in the air, lighting up the pitch-black sky.

Richard was well-fortified by a bottle of Chivas Regal sitting on the end table. He picked up the telephone and listened for the dial tone. He pushed some numbers, hoping the lines had not been knocked down in Manhattan in the earlier lightning storm. The telephone rang only once and then it was automatically switched to the cellular mobile connection.

"Rigitinni here."

"Gino, it's Richard. Did you see the plunge in IMA stock today?"

"Yeah, I did. I got to thinking that maybe we should start buying the stock through the Zafra Limited account. At nineteen bucks that stock is selling for less than half of what it's worth. What do you think?"

"What do I think? Buy it, of course! I'm sure the news means Scott Reid only has a short time to live, having AIDS and all." The senator snickered.

Gino moved his cellular telephone to his left hand and ran the other hand through his thick silver hair. Then he said, "I'll start tomorrow. I think we could pick up a hefty piece of the company with the cash from the Malaysian Latex deal. When dickhead Reid croaks that stock'll dive some more and we can buy the rest of what we want then."

A screen door knocked loose in the wind was banging hard against the side of the house. Richard took the bottle of whiskey and filled his shot glass.

"Gino, I really called to tell you what a wonderful job you did on the Reid situation. That son-of-a-bitch not only knew too much about our business, he also knew too much about the profit potential of keeping this AIDS business going. About how much longer do you think we've got to wait?"

"Before Nicki was so tragically killed, he said Reid had a few months at best!" Gino's voice had an edge.

"Gino, I'm truly sorry about your nephew Graziano." Richard said smoothly. "What the hell was he doing driving with that fat Jew in the middle of the night, anyway? It must have been a real blow to the rest of the family. Nicki being so young and all."

Gino said piously, "Senator, it hurts to lose one of your own." Then he dropped the charade. "But I'm sure we'll be amply compensated for our loss."

Richard undid the floral bow tie from around his collar. He laid it on the couch and took a swig of the straight Scotch.

"You old silver fox. I was thinking the same thing. I want to cut you in on ten percent of the Malaysian Latex deal. Take the money and buy some IMA stock for yourself when you purchase stock for the Zafra account. Okay, Gino?"

"It's no wonder you always get reelected. You're a fair man, Richard Spout!"

"Night, Gino. And again, my condolences to the Family."

No sooner had the senator put down the telephone than it started ringing. There was no staff on duty and Richard was expecting no calls. He let it ring. He took another slug of Scotch in one gulp, thinking about going to bed. The telephone drilled on. Angrily, he picked it up. He answered in his deepest congressional chamber voice, "Senator Spout's residence. How may I help you?"

"Richard, I'd recognize your voice anywhere. This's Josh Kramer calling."

"Well, Jesus H. Christ! Sorry to be so goddamn grouchy answering the phone, Josh. The staff is off and I wasn't expecting any calls."

"No problem. I'm sorry to bother you so late at night. But I have some urgent business I needed to run by you."

The senator perked up. Maybe Josh had another moneymaking scheme.

"Sure, Josh. Go ahead!"

"Richard, I've had some business associates contact me about your friend's eighteen percent ownership in Medical Reference Laboratories. They'd like to buy them out at a hefty profit. Do you think there's any chance you could get them to sell their stock to my business associates off the market?"

The senator was so excited he almost gave away that he was the owner of Zafra Limited. His bulbous nose was purple. He sipped more whiskey.

"Josh, Rigitinni's in charge of the Zafra Limited people who control the MRL stock. I don't want to reveal anything confidential about his business or who's behind that corporation, but I know his friends in Luxembourg and I could have a private word with them, if you know what I mean."

At the mention of Luxembourg, Josh recalled Scott telling him that on the Hong Kong Memorandum of Wishes for Malaysian Latex Limited, there were two Luxembourg corporations. Josh coolly said in soft Scots... "Yes, I know what ye mean. Do you think you could do that and have Rigitinni get back to me as soon as possible?"

"Will do, Josh. Thanks for calling. I'll have Gino call you in the next week or so."

On Wednesday, November 3, 1992, Scott pasted the Ross Perot for President sticker on the bumper of his El Camino and drove down to the fire station on Coldwater Canyon Drive. He stood in line for a few minutes gossiping with his neighbors over the success of the Halloween party, then went in and voted. Scott made the assumption that this was the last time he would ever vote. He wanted to make a small statement.

By ten p.m. California time it was obvious from the exit polls that the Democratic ticket of William Clinton and Albert Gore was going to be elected President and Vice-President of the United States of America.

Scott was lying in bed watching the festivities on television. He had read Clinton and Gore's jointly-written book that had been published prior to the election. He listened as both verified what they had written. They were speaking at the Little Rock celebration about how much more federal funding they were going to allocate for the AIDS problem. How they would appoint an AIDS czar. How they were going to let gays into the military and allow HIV and AIDS-infected Haitians into America.

As Scott lit up a joint and inhaled the sweet tasting smoke, he laughed to himself. How could any adult say they smoked pot and never inhaled it? He guessed it would be the same denial mentality that was buying the AIDS scam. The gullibility of the voting public was beyond him. Scott turned off the television, butted the joint and fell asleep.

The ringing telephone woke him. It was 8:00 a.m. He sleepily answered to a familiar voice.

"You better wake up, Bud. The early bird gets the worm."

"Hey, Frank! When did you get in?"

"I got in late last night, but I didn't want to wake you. How you feeling this morning?"

"I'm much better now I know you're here. Have you talked to Bill Ryan yet?"

"Unfortunately, Bud, I have. But you should know I'm going to stay right here with you and we're going to get you the best treatment in the world. Josh said not to spare any expense. So I won't!"

Nelsen let out a nervous laugh. And Scott said, "I feel great in the mornings. Where did Josh put you up?"

"I'm right down the street at the Beverly Hills Hotel in a bungalow."

"Is Matty with you?"

"No, Josh was kind enough to have the plane take her

back to Wisconsin to be with the kids. She sends her love, though."

"Frank, I'll get ready and meet you at nine. We can have breakfast in the Polo Lounge—guaranteed the best eggs Benedict you've ever had!"

Scott showered and then drove down to meet his friend.

Nelsen was already sitting in a tree-shaded booth when Scott arrived in the Polo Lounge. He was a gentle bear, but one could tell by the bulging, knotted muscles in his forearms that he was still a powerful man. Scott could also see that his friend had gained weight. Franklin must have scaled at least three hundred pounds. He had also finished off the entire basket of fresh blueberry muffins, along with the tray of butter. When he saw Scott he stood up with a smile on his face and his hand outstretched. Nelsen's enormous body dwarfed the booth and everything around him. With kindness, he said, "You look great, Bud. I was worried that you'd wasted away after listening to Josh and Bill Ryan. How you feeling?"

Scott did not want to get into a philosophical or medical conversation with Nelsen, but he did want to get directly to the point of what he had decided. Scott shook hands and sat down.

"Frank, I feel amazingly good even though I know I'm going to die. I've thought out exactly what I'm going to do with the rest of my life and I'm hoping you'll go along with my wishes."

Franklin could never confront an issue openly the way Scott could, and he replied, "You know I'm here to help in any way I can. But can't we start with those eggs Benedict you bragged about?"

They called the waiter and ordered. Scott continued, "I've decided to live whatever time I have left without the normal medical treatment that you or Bill Ryan are doing for AIDS victims. I mean no offense either to you or to medicine, but no one has beaten the disease yet with the treatment available."

"Bud, come on, you can't just give up. That was never like you in your life! Heck, you're the biggest winner I ever knew."

"Thanks, Frank. We did win some pretty big games together, didn't we? But I mean quite the opposite of what you think. I'm not giving up at all. I'm facing reality..."

There was a doctor's look of disapproval on Nelsen's face and he interrupted, "Like the reality of believing someone murdered you, instead of facing up to the fact that your life-style got you AIDS! Come on, Bud. I didn't come here to have you talk nonsense to me. I came here to get together with Billy Ryan and find out the best treatment possible for you."

The tux-clad waiter, towel draped over his arm, set down the two steaming plates of eggs. He poured Scott his tea and left another basket of blueberry muffins. Franklin grabbed two for his plate.

While he was buttering one of them, Scott said, "Obviously, you've had some long talks with Josh and Bill. I've told you from the beginning that there was something strange about everything that's happened. Remember back when I asked you how Pamela got the test results at MRL? Somebody at MRL told her. Josh knows that. And you know damn well the rare form of HIV-2 I've got never showed up on your tests! So how come I've got it? Milton couldn't have made the mistakes you people are telling me he did. I believe what he told me!"

With a mouth full of blueberry muffin, Nelsen mumbled, "You can believe what you want, Bud. But the fact is that four people tested you positive for HIV. There was MRL, your own lab physician, Nicki Graziano, an outside laboratory he went to and Billy Ryan. Everyone of them found some form of HIV! And you know it wouldn't be unusual for us to miss HIV-2 because maybe we didn't use the same testing procedures as the other labs. Yet, I repeat, we all found some kind of HIV! But only Milton continually tested you negative. How come? Because he tried to cover up his original mistake, that's why. So stop this nonsense. You sound demented with talk like this!"

"Frank, I assure you, I'm not suffering dementia yet. That's a subject I've bitched about before. I'm well aware that AIDS victims can suffer from it, but I've never been more rational in my life. By the way, what did you find out at the African AIDS Center? They've been sending me literature that says they're having success with multivitamin programs and irradiating the blood with ultraviolet rays. Do you think that might be of some help to me?"

"You know, Bud, I don't want to hurt your feelings, but I think the money you donated for that hospital was wasted. They're just a bunch of quacks. They don't seem to want to listen to what we're doing over here with modern medicine."

Scott finished his bacon and put his silverware down. Angrily he replied, "Frank, the whole world is listening to what we're doing in America, and that's nothing. Not a goddamn thing except forming more government agencies, creating false statistics to get more funding and ripping off the public in the process. Just remember, my friend, if you get AIDS here, you die. No matter how doctors treat the patient with your modern medicine."

Scott was so frustrated that he knocked his knife and fork to the floor. As he bent to pick them up, the tux-clad waiter beat him to it.

"So understand, Frank, the whole idea of mine for donating the money and developing that hospital was exactly what you're against here in America. When I went over there I stipulated that no government physician or medicines that had already been tried would be used in my hospital. I set it up strictly for research *outside* the confines of normal medicine. And I've been told they're doing an excellent job and getting good results."

Although Nelsen had seen some remarkably effective treatment of full-blown AIDS using the very methods Scott had described during his visit to the African AIDS Center, he knew the FDA did not find this a therapy of choice and he was not about to buck the system. Not even with his best friend's life on the line.

He sarcastically retorted, "Well, you got your wish, Bud. They're into some pretty weird stuff, but I don't know about any good results that might benefit your situation. Now, are you going to see Billy Ryan on Monday so we can use some medical reason on you? We can straighten out then what we're going to do for you with good ol' proven American medicine!"

It was as if Franklin had not even heard him. Scott had no intention of listening to their version of medical reason. He wanted to go to San Francisco again and see if Ryan or Nelsen might have something outside the normal confines of AIDS treatment. If not, he would straighten out everyone on what his plans were.

"Frank, I'm looking forward to having you and Josh go up there with me Monday, but on my terms. In the meantime let's get out of here and see if you can still drive a golf ball three hundred yards."

Rosa, Hector and Esther spent the weekend spoiling Scott. No matter how hard he tried to tell them that he was capable of doing things for himself, they had everything done in advance. Without meaning to, they made him feel like an invalid. Frank, Josh and Wizard made up a foursome with Scott at the Riviera Country Club on both Saturday and Sunday. On Sunday evening Annie made a barbecue for everyone on the terrace of the Century City penthouse.

Scott was noticing some very strange sensations in his body. He had to steam bathe or shower three or four times a day because of his body odor. He still used the chlorine everywhere in the house. He had an abnormal amount of stomach cramps and diarrhea. His cough had returned with a vengeance. His balance seemed to be adversely affected. The blotches on his body were spreading. However, most of the time, with rest and steroids, he felt well enough to continue most of his daily activities. He tried to act as if nothing were wrong. But his clothes now hung loosely on his bony frame and everyone could see something drastic was happening to Scott Reid.

William Ryan greeted Franklin Nelsen with fondness and respect. The two of them side by side made a stark contrast. Ryan stuck out his hand and one small white hand was engulfed in a huge black fist. Bill Ryan, the small, sandy-haired Irishman, with a shock of hair always drooping in his face, normally had a mischievous smile for everyone. But due to the seriousness of the occasion, the soft-hearted doctor said sadly, "Welcome to San Francisco, Frank. I'm just so very sorry that it has to be because of such unfortunate circumstances. How was Africa? Did you find any help for AIDS at the disease center in Nairobi?"

Scott and Josh sat down in the leather chairs around the doctor's desk. There were piles of manuals and papers stacked at each end of the desk, but a clearing had been made between them so they could talk to the doctor. After shaking hands with Ryan, Nelsen went to take a seat alongside Josh and Scott. He replied, "Thanks, Billy. Do you realize we haven't seen each other since the reunion down in Palo Alto? Where does the time go?"

Franklin did not expect a reply, so he continued, "I guess we're all just getting busier and older. Billy, Africa's a mess. Politically and socially. Chaos everywhere. The AIDS thing seems to be out of hand in most countries and I'm going to be doing an article about my trip for the *New England Journal of Medicine*. I can't say I saw anything at the Disease Center that would help anyone in the States. They seem to have some strange ideas on fighting AIDS."

Scott could keep quiet no longer. He blurted, "No stranger than our ideas here! I haven't heard of anyone being saved by America's medical experts."

Josh then said, "Scott, we're all up here to get you the best treatment possible and to see if there's any way to stop or prolong this disease in your system. Bill, what've you come up with?"

The doctor scratched his head and shuffled through the papers on the top of his desk. He took out a manila file folder and handed it to Franklin.

Then Ryan replied, "Gentlemen, I've discussed with Frank on the telephone all of what's happened so far. As he can see from the recent lab results, some complicating illnesses are starting to show up in Scott's system. He was negative for any T.B. or syphilis, but his sputum smear showed signs of *Pneumocystis carinni* pneumonia. So I'd like to start by putting Scott in San Francisco General and doing a bronchoscopy, a bronchoalveolar lavage and I think a transbroncheal biopsy is warranted. Don't you agree, Frank?"

"I couldn't agree with you more, Billy. The sooner the better."

Scott was fuming. Distressed, he looked at the two doctors, who were nodding their heads in agreement.

"You're both mistaken if you think this's what I came up to San Francisco for," he said heatedly. "I came because I thought between the four of us we could come up with either a radical form of treatment that I might not know about, or an alternative plan to extend the limited amount of time I have left to live. Unfortunately, I don't hear that. All I hear is the same old medical dogma that's been used unsuccessfully on all the AIDS patients both of you've treated."

Josh could not believe what he was hearing. Scott did

not appear to want anyone's help. He said staunchly to Scott, "Wait just a minute, Scott. We're only here to help you in any way we can. You've told me yourself that Frank and Bill are two of the best medical men in the world for AIDS treatment."

The two physicians sat listening. Scott was sweating profusely. He wiped the perspiration back through his hair.

"Josh, I don't want to get into a deep discussion on what I said to you about AIDS. These two men are as brilliant as anyone in the field, but neither they nor anyone else has a clue how to cure AIDS. I won't spend the rest of my time wallowing in hospitals as a guinea pig for medicine and surrounded by unpleasantness and sorrow. I've made a decision on what I'm going to do. And the only way you can change it is to prove to me that there's a vaccine for this virus."

Franklin shifted his bulk nervously and asked, "What better idea do you have than the one Billy suggested?"

"My friends, it's called quality of life. I want to die with the least amount of pain and suffering possible. And with the most amount of dignity I can muster under the circumstances. What I plan on doing, is to treat only the opportunistic infections with normal medication to prevent them from spreading too fast. I'm going to treat myself with morphine, marijuana and steroids for the duration of this illness!"

Josh was incredulous.

"What?"

Scott tried to clarify his feelings.

"You heard me correctly. All I want to do is enjoy the few simple things I have left in life. My pursuit of knowledge, my sports activities, my business and most of all my friends. Let's face it. It's not like the world is losing another Albert Einstein. I'm just a lucky guy that had his fifteen minutes of glory on earth. I can't remember who said th..."

Franklin butted in.

"Bud, that sounds like a pretty drastic plan. Wouldn't you let us run a psychological evaluation first? From what you're saying, it sounds to me like there's already some symptomatic neurologic disease in progress. First your denial, then your murder theory and now you want to treat yourself with some homemade hogwash!"

Josh moved to the edge of his chair and looked Scott in the eye. He pleaded, "Come on, Scott. Give us a chance!"

Bill Ryan had seen and heard every type of discussion before in his practice of helping the AIDS-stricken. He listened with interest but said nothing.

Scott replied, "I'm sorry to appear ungrateful. I'm humbled by the concern and thoughtfulness you all have shown. I can assure you my mind is functioning perfectly. I'm hoping as time goes on that Frank and Bill will help me out in getting any further medication and the drugs I've chosen for my treatment. I can only thank you all for what you've tried to do for me, but all I want to do now is go back to my home in Los Angeles and get started with the rest of my life."

Scott stood up.

"Thanks again, Bill. I'll stay in touch."

Doctor Ryan extended his hand. Once again he had the impish smile back on his face.

"I admire your independence and I'll do everything in

my legal power as a physician to help you in the future. God bless you, Scott."

Realizing that Scott was going to stand firm in his decision, Franklin decided to return to Wochester, Wisconsin. He planned on returning to visit Scott on Thanksgiving with Matty and their children. He also thought that by that time he could possibly talk Scott into coming back to the Berlinger Clinic with him for treatment.

Josh and Scott returned to Los Angeles in silence.

The next day Scott knew that he had to go see Rebecca one last time. He did not know when the worst of the disease was going to hit him and he wanted to have a clear mind when he visited her.

He had Hector vacuum and polish the El Camino and shine the tires with Armor All. Scott piled the dogs in the back and drove over the mountain to the valley and the state hospital.

A white-coated, surly nurse wheeled Rebecca out into the sun. Scott grabbed the wheelchair by the two rubber handlegrips in the rear and pushed her out into the park-like grounds. He picked a bench near the wire mesh fence so she could see the dogs in the back of the car. Then he sat down and started talking to her.

"Well, my darling. I've got bad news. It seems that I'm leaving this old planet before you. I had always hoped to be here for you in case you ever needed me. But if this isn't a bitch, I've been murdered. It seems old smart-ass Reid knows too much. Don't laugh, it's true! And don't feel bad about it, because nobody else believes me either."

Rebecca had not moved. Yet he was certain she had

smiled. She had drool running down her chin and began slouching over. Scott wiped her face and kissed her on the mouth. The dogs noticed and started barking in the bin of the El Camino. Then he stood up.

"I know I'm talking to myself, but God, girl, I loved you so much. We had everything. How the hell did this ever happen to us? By the way, my darling, I've left the El Camino to Frank and Matty. Maybe they'll leave it to "Little Scott" when they pass on. You know, kind of a living memorial to all of us."

Scott looked at Rebecca for acknowledgment, but she did not move. He kicked the ground in frustration.

"Oh hell, what's the use. I've got to say good-bye now, Rebecca, but I'm sure we'll meet again."

He wheeled her back to the nurse's station and thanked the staff for their assistance. As he went to touch Rebecca's pianist hands one last time, to his amazement, she grunted. It was the first sound anyone had heard her make in over twelve years. She opened a gnarled fist and a wadded piece of paper fell out. She pushed it over to Scott. He put it in his shirt pocket and the nurse wheeled her inside the barred building. Sadly, Scott walked out to the El Camino parked outside the fence.

As he sat in the front seat, one hand reaching out the window behind him, petting the dogs, he reached in his shirt pocket with the other and took out the paper Rebecca had given him. It was a large, crumpled piece of note paper. As he unfolded it, small scraps fell into his lap. They were a brown-and-white Monte Cristo cigar band, and a cracked photo of him torn from a Stanford football program. Written on the piece of carefully folded paper was a poem, penned in black ink. It was dated, "1965, Our Honeymoon." It read:

NIGHTSCAPE

If we could capture the fire that is our love,
And while gathering it, compress it,
Grip it until in its concentrated form
It glows and grows so hot that
We can no longer hold it,

We then must fling it high and
Watch it soar in power ever higher,
Pure spirit, free unchained from time and
Space, a world unto itself,
Growing brighter like a star...

At night I look to heaven and see our love,
Hanging fixed above us in eternity,
I know you see it too
And that makes me smile. We share
A beacon in the night, a starry tribute.

Rebecca must have known and been aware of her surroundings all of these years. There was no other way she could ever share with him what these words expressed. He was certain she just wanted to be alone in her misery. He thought of going back in the hospital to tell her that he understood her wishes, but he just could not do it. He could no more change her fate than he could his own.

Scott sat in the front seat of the El Camino and cried for the first time in his life.

The sweltering, muggy autumn hung in the air during November. Los Angeles and Southern California had never known such a hot year. The beaches were packed and because of a storm a thousand miles out at sea, giant waves came crashing to shore. Environmental groups crowed that they were right about the ozone layer being depleted. There were theories about a new earthquake coming because of the heat. The farmers complained of the lack of water and drought conditions. The smog was horrendous. The murder and suicide rate climbed, and politicians begged for money to study the issues. But the surfers had never been so happy.

As the end of November neared and Thanksgiving was but a few days off, Scott's physical condition had deteriorated rapidly. He had lost another ten pounds. The red and blue blotches on his arms had become noticeable. His stomach cramps were debilitating enough that he was up to 15 cc's of morphine each night. His sweats were drenching. Rosa often had to change his sheets three times a night. Neither she, nor Scott, ever complained. Esther had moved fulltime into the main house in the bedroom next to Scott and was supplying him with limitless chicken soup and blintzes. Scott still found the strength to play golf every other day with Josh. Four times a week he, Annie and Josh went to a new movie, play or restaurant in town. Tennis was too exhausting, but Scott's pals came over and he watched them play doubles every weekend.

After his tennis pals had left on the Sunday before Thanksgiving, Scott telephoned Franklin.

"Hi, big fella. I got your letter about me coming back with you after the holidays when you're out here. And I thank you for the kind offer, but I'm staying here in the sun and earthquake country. I'm really excited to see Matty and the kids. Especially, Little Scott."

Franklin was disappointed. He had hoped with all his generous and loving heart that Scott would listen to reason. He knew it would be the last time Matty and his children would ever see Scott alive. Franklin also knew he would probably be with Scott when he died and he would have to bury his friend. Yet he said cheerfully,

"You're in for a surprise, Little Scott isn't so little! He's eating me out of house and home. He's excited about seeing his uncle Scott, too. How you feeling? Is there anything I can do for you from here?"

"No, nothing at all." Scott said. "Get my handicap back below ten would be my request, but that isn't going to happen. I'm afraid I've gotten an incurable duck hook."

The fax machine sitting next to Scott's desk started spewing out documents from his attorney. Scott said quickly,

"Look, Frank, I've got to run. I'll have Hector pick you up at LAX on Friday. 'Bye for now."

The document was a codicil to the will Scott had made out the week before. Scott's attorney wanted to make certain there would be no problems in a probate court; therefore, he was getting everything prepared in advance of Scott's demise.

Scott looked at the paper and laughed. It was a supplement to make sure that Josh would inherit Scott's two dogs.

Laurely and Hardy! The attorney had added into the modification of the will, a caveat, that in case the beneficiary could not afford the upkeep of the dogs, the humane society would then be held responsible for the animals. Scott had a feeling that the dogs would be soon living a life most humans would envy. The rest of the will was exactly as he had ordered:

Rosa and Hector would get one-fourth of the total of the estate. They would also receive the house on Coldwater Canyon Drive. Ginger and Big Bird would go with the house.

Esther would get one-fourth of the estate.

Doctor Franklin D. Nelsen, his wife Matty, and their children would get one-fourth of the estate and the 1966 Chevy El Camino.

Annie Bhalla would administer the remaining one-fourth of the estate by forming a charity for poets in the name of, The Rebecca Platt-Reid Trust Foundation, which would also support Rebecca in any manner she needed.

Linda Powell would receive the van Gogh painting of the yellow wheat field that hung in his office.

After taxes, Scott Reid's estate, including the stock in IMA Laboratories, Inc., was estimated at one hundred and ten million dollars.

❧

Two days before Thanksgiving, Josh received a telephone call from New York City.

"Josh, Gino Rigitinni here. I'm calling you back in regard to the MRL deal you spoke with Richard about. My clients are wondering how much your parties' offer for their stock would be?"

The traffic on Pico Boulevard below Josh's penthouse apartment was at a rush-hour roar. Sirens and horns blared. He motioned for Annie to shut the open study windows. She did so and the room was silent. Josh then said, "Thanks for responding so soon, Gino. As you know from the Malaysian Latex deal, I, or any of my associates, deal directly in cash. My party wants the Zafra Limited stock your clients own sold offshore to a Swiss-based group. They're willing to pay two-hundred and fifty million dollars for all eighteen percent of the Medical Reference Laboratories stock your clients own. The offer is only good for the next forty-eight hours!"

Gino swallowed hard. He looked up at the ceiling in his office as though it was the Sistine Chapel. A huge smile was on his face. He ran a hand through his silver mane.

"Josh, I can give you my word without discussing this any further with my clients that your people have a deal. When can we meet and finalize the arrangements?"

"I'll have my pilots privately deliver all the documents today and the cash will be transferred from Switzerland to the Netherlands Antilles upon notarized signatures from your clients or nominee directors. One other item, Gino. My associates want you to resign from the Board of Directors as part of the deal. I'm sure you can understand they want their own legal representation on the new board."

Gino was so excited that he was madly signalling his secretary to dial Richard's private line in Washington. He then answered Josh, "I understand completely. You can be assured that I will use my usual discretion in getting this deal put together immediately. I'll use only private couriers if I need anything more."

As soon as Josh had hung up, Gino's secretary put Mr. Rigitinni through to Senator Richard Spout. In glee, Gino said, "Richard, your worries are over! You don't ever have to worry about when your old man's going to die. You may now have more money than that ancient bastard does."

The senator had just arrived home and was pouring himself a drink. The legislator was in his apartment on Capitol Hill. He loosened his bright green bow tie and took a sip of whiskey. A few drops stuck to his thin mustache and he licked them off. His deep voice rumbled, "What the hell are you talking about, Gino?"

"Josh Kramer just called, and associates of his offered us two hundred and fifty million dollars for our Zafra Limited stock in MRL. All cash from a Swiss bank. No IRS, no taxes, no hassle! A done deal in forty-eight hours. Needless to say, without your approval, I accepted."

Richard knocked over his drink.

"Holy shit, Gino! You did the right thing. I'd have cut your balls off if you turned that offer down! There're no strings attached, are there?"

Nervously, Gino picked at an old pockmark on his face.

"None that I can see. They want me to resign from the Board of Directors. But that's normal. They'll put their own mouthpiece in my place."

Richard took a packet of cocaine from his desk drawer. He took a pinch and shoved a bit of white powder in each flared nostril. After a deep snort, he said ecstatically, "Listen to me, Gino. I've got a plan that I've been thinking about, but until now I didn't know how to implement it. You remember I wanted us to buy the IMA Laboratory stock of Scott Reid's company?"

"Yeah, I started buying the stock in the Zafra account last week like you said."

"I know you did, Gino, but here are my thoughts. With the new administration coming in, Congress will be doubling their funding for AIDS blood testing. I'm in charge of the committee where most of those funds go. Probably up to ten billion or more by the time Clinton and Gore get finished with their terms. So if there was some way for Zafra to get hold of the majority interest in IMA Laboratory after Reid's dead, then we could switch it from its primary business of immunodiagnostics to blood testing."

"I fuckin' love it!" squealed Gino.

On a roll, Richard continued, "I could put Landen in charge of the new IMA. He could bring over the majority of the Medical Reference clients in less than a year, and I could direct the bulk of the government and insurance contracts to IMA. Hell, Gino, we'll have the largest blood testing corporation in the world in less than five years! And best of all, we'd fuck Kramer!"

"Richard, that's the smartest idea I've ever heard you

come up with. What've you been sticking up your nose, smart pills?"

The senator was having wonderful delusions of grandeur. He took another pinch of cocaine and carried on.

"Gino, we could take the rest of the Malaysian Latex money and combine it with this two-hundred and fifty mil and get majority control of IMA Laboratories. Can you handle that?"

"It's a little complicated because Zafra's an offshore company," Gino said. "And I'll have to register the purchased IMA stock with the Securities and Exchange because IMA's a publicly-listed company. But approval should be no problem with your connections, Senator."

"As I recall my SEC law, Gino, one only has to register stock purchases over five percent of any company's outstanding stock with the SEC. So why don't you form a dozen or so new offshore companies, which will be owned by Zafra Limited? And then buy only 4.9 percent of IMA stock in each of those companies until we quietly have control. That way we bypass SEC registration. But damnit, don't run the price of the stock up too far or too fast!"

The attorney knew he was going to get at least ten percent of this transaction and he replied quickly, "Richard, sometimes you amaze me. I'll be on the deal as soon as the cash arrives."

The senator hung up laughing. He sat back with a satisfied smirk on his face.

A giant papier mâché cornucopia filled with fruits and grains was used as a decorative centerpiece on Scott's

Thanksgiving day table. Hector had spread dried Indian corn in its husks around the rest of the table. The cobs were dotted with multicolored rows of kernels. Wonderful aromas coming from the kitchen filled the house.

Matty had roasted and basted a thirty pound turkey, which she stuffed with bread and prune dressing. Esther had made mashed potatoes and giblet gravy. Annie contributed a fruit salad with fresh whipped cream, and Wizard's wife, Jennifer, had baked chestnut and raisin bread. Rosa had made her outstanding pumpkin pies, which were cooling on the open window sills. The five Nelsen children were eyeing the steaming pies with visions of large slices heaped with vanilla ice cream. Little Scott could stand the temptation only so long and he dipped his fingers in the hot pumpkin mush. Rosa proceeded to give him a whack across the hand with her plastic spatula. Giggling, the children ran for cover behind the guest house.

The men were playing golf. When they arrived home, Scott looked terrible. His coughing had doubled him over in pain. His hands were shaking, he was sweating and he had stomach cramps. His eyes were bloodshot and sunk deep in their sockets, and puffy purple bags hung beneath them. He had lost more weight and even more energy. He was now under one hundred and fifty pounds. He could not play the entire eighteen holes and had asked to go home for some medicine. Morphine was now his constant companion. Once he took it, along with huge doses of steroids, he felt good. But he was stubborn and had been trying to get along without it. He no longer could.

Josh followed Scott up to his bedroom, then closed

the door. Scott hurried into the bathroom and gave himself a subcutaneous injection of morphine. Within minutes he felt the relief. Josh smiled at him.

"Scott, you're one stubborn shit. Don't you think Frank could be of some help back at the Berlinger?"

"Naw," Scott said. "I sit here each day reading every published medical article on the treatment of AIDS. I assure you, Josh, there isn't anything out there on the horizon that can help me. Why don't we talk about something else. I feel pretty good right now."

"Sorry to be such a nag, Scott. Listen, I haven't told you yet that I got rid of Rigitinni on the board of MRL and I got Zafra Limited out as shareholders. I sent a private investigator down to the Netherlands Antilles, but he couldn't find any connection with Richard and Gino's involvement with Zafra. In any case, those two bastards won't be making any more shady deals with me, I'll tell you that!"

Scott said cheerfully, "Other than the birdie I got on that par three, that's the first good news I've had today! Josh, have you given any more thought to purchasing IMA stock? I can't tell you what a bargain you'd be getting."

"I'm sure you're right, Scott, but under the circumstances, I've felt it wouldn't be right for me to be buying openly into your corporation."

Josh took a deep breath and continued.

"Scott, I think it's time we had a talk regarding my involvement with IMA stock..."

The intercom blared.

"Meester Scott and Senor Josh, comida es ready. Jou get down here right now!"

Scott slapped Josh on the back.

"Come on, let's eat. We can talk business another time."

Everyone was seated and laughing as Scott and Josh went to sit at the table. Little Scott, his face still covered with crusty orange pie filling, looked up at Scott.

"Uncle Scott. How come you look like a scarecrow, are you sick?"

All of the adults went silent. The children shrieked with delight and chanted in musical unison, "Uncle Scott is a scarecrow, Uncle Scott is a scarecrow."

Franklin and Matty started admonishing the children, but Scott broke in and said, "Hey, Little Scott, I'm not sick. I'm just not very good-looking. But at least I don't have pumpkin pie all over my face like you do."

Little Scott laughed and wiped off the dried pie filling from his face. Franklin then stood up.

"As a Christian, on this Thanksgiving I'd like to say a small prayer of thanks for this wonderful gathering. Children, bow your heads."

The children put their heads down and their hands together in prayer and the adults glowed up at the towering presence of Franklin Delano Nelsen. With his chin up and his eyes closed, he spoke.

"Dear Lord, we thank you for this bountiful meal. We thank you for our friends and children and we thank you for our time here on earth. May you bless each and every one on this happy Thanksgiving day. And would you always look over our missed and beloved Rebecca. Amen."

Franklin's voice trailed off to a whisper. There was silence, everyone smiled, but looked sadly at one another.

Then Scott said quietly, "Thanks, Frank, those were beautiful thoughts. Let's all eat now. Happy Thanksgiving, everyone."

Two weeks before Christmas, on Friday, December 11, 1992, Scott's physical condition had deteriorated so badly that he had no areas of his body that were not bruised from the constant morphine injections he had given himself. He weighed one hundred and thirty-five pounds. Doctor Ryan had kept his word and supplied Scott with all the drug he needed. He knew the disease was taking its final toll and that the morphine kept Scott from suffering.

It was difficult for Hector, Rosa or Esther to be of any help to Scott. They tried in every manner, but he refused to be waited on. He did not have the strength to play golf, nor could his failing eyesight follow the ball any longer. He wandered the house like a sick, caged animal. On Chanukah, he drove Esther to temple. Then he put on his rubber surgical gloves and spent the day cooking for her.

Franklin and Matty called routinely. Wizard and Jennifer never quit cheering Scott on, although Scott knew it must have been frightening for Wizard to see what was happening to him. Josh and Annie were Scott's constant companions. They found it strange that as the end came near for Scott, fewer and fewer of all the hundreds of people Scott knew showed any compassion for his dying.

Scott's daily joy became smoking some pot, listening to classical music, watching sports and the stock market on television and rereading various novels that he had not picked up since his university days. The Russians interested him the most and he devoured the complete works of Tolstoy, Pushkin, Dostoyevsky and Chekhov.

It was becoming more difficult for Scott to get out of bed. He often lay all day in sheets soaked in perspiration, for he did not want to worry Rosa and Esther. Although blood poured from his bowels when he used the toilet and the blotches, which he now kept bandaged, oozed with infection, he adamantly refused to have a doctor see him or to go into the hospital. He knew he did not have much time left, however, he kept the worst of his condition to himself. He increased the dosage of morphine and steroids.

Forgiveness was part of Scott's soul. He did not want to leave behind any grievances and he decided to telephone Pamela and say good-bye. He pushed the buttons for Castle Rock's private line to her bedroom.

Pamela had not taken a new man in her life, for she still loved Scott. She had heard all of the rumors about Scott's deteriorating health, yet she could not find it in her personality to go see him unless he contacted her first. She knew the call was either bad news from Josh or a personal call from Scott. She also wondered why Scott had never given her the mink coat he had talked about on the car telephone some weeks past. Nervously, she answered, "Hello, Castle Rock."

Scott's voice was weak and he whispered.

"It's me. I don't think I'm going to be able to make our annual Valentine's Day celebration in Paris this year. So I thought I'd call and say, no hard feelings. I didn't want to leave it the way we parted on Halloween. I only want to remember the good times and the affection we shared."

"Hayite!"

And Pamela started crying. She sobbed into the telephone, "Do you want me to come and see you? I could call my doctor and see if he thinks it's okay."

Right to the end, Pamela was going to think of herself first and foremost. Scott decided to make it brief.

"No. I don't want that. I just wanted to let you know before it's too late, that I did truly care for you. God only knows why, but I did! I wish you well, Pamela. Goodbye."

Scott hung up and Pamela realized she was never going to see the man she loved again.

On the 20th of December Hector bought a giant, long-needled blue spruce for the Christmas holidays. He built a stand and set the tree in the living room. Scott forced himself out of bed. He looked terrible. He had not had the strength to shave for days. His hair was greasy and matted. He smelled. But he took a small shot of morphine and walked down the staircase to help Rosa, Esther, Josh and Annie decorate the room and the tree. Scott hung red and white stockings for everyone over the fireplace. He then lit a fire. The weather had turned cold for Los Angeles and the nights had dropped to almost freezing. After they had finished with the decorations, Annie made brandy and eggnog for everyone. Josh popped some popcorn on the open hearth. As they sat and reminisced about the past year, none of them realized the agony Scott was going through. He had them all believing he might live for another few months.

On the 24th of December, Christmas Eve, Scott was so ill he could not get out of bed. His body had wasted away so rapidly that moving in any manner drained all of his strength and energy. Only his indomitable will to live and the morphine and steroids kept him going. His friends had come over early to celebrate the evening and open presents. They brought them up to his bedroom where Scott was lying. Scott smiled and asked.

"Is it all right if I open my presents in the morning? I still believe in Santa Claus."

Everyone could see Scott was too sick to participate in any festivities. So they piled their gifts at the end of the bed. Hector, Rosa and Esther then brought up the many other brightly wrapped gifts from well-wishers for Scott that had been under the Christmas tree. Soon the bed was surrounded with colored boxes tied with bows. Then Josh said, "Scott, you're obviously not going to be able to join us tonight singing Christmas carols, so we'll have a quick drink and go home. Sleep well, Scott, and see you first thing in the morning."

Annie came over and kissed Scott on the forehead. He squeezed her hand gently and whispered, "Thanks. Josh would never stand still for this, but tomorrow, tell the old fart I love him."

Two hours later a neighborhood choral group started singing "Silent Night" outside of Scott's front entry gate. He could hear the words faintly in the distance.

Scott struggled out of bed to the bathroom. He could barely walk. He knew it was the end. His body had rotted from the unrelenting disease. He gave himself the largest injection of morphine that his body could tolerate. He sat on the toilet until the drug worked its miracle. Then he showered and shaved and put on his favorite Lagerfeld aftershave and talcum. He went into his clothes closet and put on a starched white shirt, a black bow tie, a tuxedo, complete with red cummerbund and a flowing white silk scarf. He slipped on his monogrammed black King Edward slippers and walked slowly over to the sound system in the bedroom. He had to grab furniture to keep from losing his balance. He turned on the stereo and pushed the repeat switch on, then put on a compact disk of the Montreal Philharmonic Orchestra accompanying Pavarotti as he sang, "Ave Maria."

The telephone rang and Scott shuffled over beside his bed and picked it up. In a hoarse voice he said, "Merry Christmas."

"Merry Christmas to you too, Bud. I'm sorry to call you so late but I had to help out in emergency surgery. How you doing? It sounds as if I woke you up."

Scott could barely keep talking, but in a frail voice he uttered, "Frank, you may find this hard to believe, but I've never been better. Wish Matty and the kids a happy Christmas for me will you? This looks like the last Christmas we'll share together, so I want to thank you for all you've been to me as a friend over the ye..."

Scott started coughing in deep, gut-wracking hacks. Sputum and blood came up on his white shirt. Franklin asked, "Are you sure you're okay, Bud?"

Scott wheezed, "I told you, Big Fella, I've never been better. I've got to go, though. Good-bye, my friend. I'll miss you."

Nelsen sat and listened to the dial tone after Scott hung

up. He was worried about his friend, but he would call him back on Christmas Day.

When Scott hung up he arranged the framed pictures of his friends around the end table of his bed.

He picked each up slowly and squinted at them. He could barely see. The disease had drastically affected his vision. Himself and Rebecca on the day of their marriage with "BILLY & MAE'S HONEYMOON INN" in the background. Standing beside Franklin in Stanford football uniforms during their collegiate days. Horsing around with Little Scott. With Wizard, standing courtside at a basketball game. Between Josh and Annie standing next to the Gulfstream in Karachi. With Josh on the first tee of the Riviera Country Club. Himself and Pamela in Paris with the Eiffel Tower in the background. With Milton and Esther in front of IMA Laboratories. Out in the garden, with Hector, with Rosa waving out of the kitchen window at the camera. With Laurely and Hardy, duck hunting. And the last one Scott picked up was a solo photo of Rebecca from her university days; her hair was braided in a ponytail and he thought she looked like an angel.

Scott set the photograph down and opened the end-table drawer. He took out a bottle of Courvoisier, poured himself a snifter and picked out a fresh Monte Cristo number 4 cigar from its box. He put the cigar in his mouth, but did not light it. He could taste the sweet tobacco. He sucked on it and then drank down the cognac in one gulp. Then he took out a copy of his will and stuck it under the picture of himself and Josh on the golf course.

Scott turned up the stereo with the remote control and slowly lay down on his bed.

The digital clock flashed 12:01. Christmas Day, 1992.

Scott put his head on his satin pillow. The morphine gave him euphoria and colorful, distorted visions. As he looked up at the ceiling, everything became hazy, dreamlike and soft. He felt no pain. With his cigar still in his fingers, he folded Rebecca's poem in his hands across his chest, then closed his eyes and listened to the music. Quietly, he accepted the unknown. Tears began to roll down his cheeks. Ginger delicately settled herself next to his feet.

The soul of Scott Reid did not stop functioning, but his other cells did. The complications from AIDS had drained the life from his body.

Scott died during the night.

JOSH AND TODD'S DISCOVERY

The burial of Scott Reid was to be in Hollywood at Forest Lawn cemetery on Thursday, December 31, 1992. On the previous Monday, the 28th, the stock in his former corporation, IMA Laboratories, had a delayed opening on the news of his death. The equities opened down three points a share, at fifteen and a half dollars on the New York Stock Exchange.

After making the funeral arrangements, Josh Kramer decided to get drunk. He cracked open a quart of twelve-year-old Black Label, poured himself a double scotch and soda, then sat in front of his television watching the trading activities on the business channel. As the stock symbols flashed across the bottom of the screen, Josh suddenly noticed some very strong activity in IMA stock. The pattern was straight up. Someone appeared to be purchasing huge blocks. By the end of the day the stock was the most active issue on the exchange. It had traded over two million shares and regained all of its opening losses. IMA Laboratories closed the day at eighteen dollars and fifty cents a share.

Josh realized that this was not an unusual trading pattern when there was drastic news that affected the management of the company. He also knew that whoever was purchasing the stock was ultimately going to have to answer to him once he converted his Class B stock to common stock; he would then be the majority stockholder in IMA.

Josh decided to continue his bender, and poured himself a triple scotch. This time, no soda. There was to be no more aging for this bottle of whisky.

On Tuesday and Wednesday the trading volume in IMA shares increased. It was the volume leader on the exchange each day and the stock rose in price to twenty-four dollars. Josh had not drawn a sober breath during that time. He just sat in a chair in his study and wondered if it were really possible that Scott was murdered? Could it have been true Scott had been purposely injected with some blood tainted with AIDS as he claimed? If that were so, he had to find the killer.

Josh gulped down the scotch and kept numbly quizzing himself. Why had he never told Scott about his initial involvement in IMA stock? Why couldn't he say to the man he considered a son, I love you? And why hadn't he spent more time with him? If he had it to do all over again, things would have been different.

On the day of Scott's funeral, New Year's Eve, the stock

market was only open a half day for trading. IMA Laboratories set a yearly high, with an opening block trade of two million shares at twenty-nine dollars a share. Josh had sobered up during the night, but the funeral was in the morning so he did not see the trading.

Throngs of people crowded the cemetery to pay their last respects to Scott Reid. There were at least five hundred friends and acquaintances and at least again that many curiosity seekers, who came to gawk at the celebrities among the mourners.

Josh was wound tight with misery. He had to have a cigarette. Quietly, he left the services and walked between the tombstones and manicured green grass. Finally, he sat on a flat stone slab behind a big, white marble mausoleum. In the serene silence, he lit up a cigarette and inhaled deeply. A few minutes later, after he ground it out, he heard muffled voices talking on the other side of the shrine. He recognized the deep voice of senator Richard Spout. He was talking to Rigitinni.

He had on a black suit, white shirt, dark tie and was adjusting the black handkerchief in his jacket pocket.

"I thought I told you not to run up the price of the stock so fast!" Richard said. "The damn thing was up to twenty-five bucks yesterday!"

Gino's silver blow-dried hair was low on hairspray and the wind had blown strands of it upright. He smoothed it straight back with both hands.

"Not to worry, Senator. I put in for our final block this morning. The damn thing may hit thirty bucks a share, but who cares? It's going to be worth a fortune now that we have majority control of the common stock."

Richard glanced around nervously, tugging at his bright paisley bow tie.

"Nobody can trace your purchases, can they?"

"I can assure you—no one can trace the individual purchasers. I've got complete bank secrecy outside the country. I'll consolidate the holdings into one parent company after the first of the year. Then register that stock with the SEC. A piece of cake."

To clarify matters, the legislator asked, "You mean you got the whole three hundred and fifty mil already spent?"

"Yup," peeped Gino.

"The stock funds from Medical Reference Labs and the Malaysian money, too?"

Josh crept behind a marble pillar. He had a horrible hangover and his thoughts were hazy. He wondered what stock they were talking about. Could it be IMA? Gino then answered Richard, his voice high and tight.

"I spent it all, just as instructed. You don't think I'm out here for this asshole's funeral, do you? I just used it as an excuse to see the Rose Bowl game tomorrow."

It took every bit of willpower Josh had not to leap around the pillar and pummel Rigitinni. But he stayed still and listened. Richard rubbed his booze-reddened nose, then spoke.

"Good job, Gino. I saw Ralph and Joyce sucking up to Kramer earlier. Why don't you go tell Ralph he doesn't have to kiss that billionaire's fat ass any more, because very soon he's going to work for you. Gino, you're going to be chairman of the board and Ralph will be the CEO. How does that sound for a reward?"

Gino had a crooked smile on his face as he said, "I love the chairman bit, but I was thinking under the circumstances that maybe ten percent of the deal was coming *our* way."

It puzzled Josh that the attorney seemed to be talking about someone other than himself involved in the deal. His hangover was such that he let it slide.

The senator put his arm around Gino's shoulder.

"You old silver fox. You're a hard-driving wop. You've got a deal. Ten percent. But I call all the shots, okay?"

They shook hands and started walking back to the graveside service.

When Josh returned, a minister was eulogizing Scott Ian Reid with a poem from Tennyson.

"Tears, idle tears, I know not what they mean,
Tears from the depth of some divine despair
Rise in the heart and gather to the eyes,
In looking on the happy autumn fields,
And thinking of the days that are no more."

So many people had shed tears for Scott during his illness that few friends had any left. Most of the gathering stood in respectful silence. Cameras flashed rudely as the inevitable ghouls caught a glimpse of a famous face.

Josh acted as one of the pallbearers. They laid Scott to rest and each threw a shovelful of dirt into the open grave. The pebbles echoed in the gaping hole as they bounced on the wooden casket.

By his request, Scott was buried on a hillside under a shady oak tree. The grave faced west towards the setting sun and the Pacific Ocean. His epitaph, Rebecca's poem, was carved in script on a speckled, red granite tombstone, and a plot for her lay waiting beside him.

Two weeks later in Omaha, Nebraska, Joyce Landen was excitedly preparing her family's move to California. This relocation meant social prominence! New California bachelors. And the best part was that she would be able to spend most days with Pamela at Castle Rock.

As Joyce packed, a wedding party drove by, noisily honking their horns. It was a typical country wedding. Tin cans and streamers trailed from the car's bumpers and several were decorated with fluffy colored crepe paper. One of the cars had—Just Married!—painted on the trunk.

Kim Yew and Ron Lee had been quietly married that day in St. Luke's Catholic church. They knew the celebration afterwards was a little noisy, but who could be harmed by their happiness?

On the same day in Los Angeles, California, the weather had turned warm. Josh was not sober, but he took Annie to the beach with the dogs to watch the sunset. Wizard and Jennifer were in their back yard shooting practice baskets. At Scott's old house on Coldwater Canyon Drive, Rosa had let his former pals in for an afternoon of tennis. Hector and Rosa had driven over and picked up Esther, then they were all going to the cemetery to visit Scott.

Linda Powell was kneeling at Scott's gravesite in Forest Lawn. She was dressed in a floral, low-cut summer frock. She had a grateful smile on her face. Waiting some distance away in the shadows of a large white mausoleum was a haggard-looking Pamela. She was dressed in black and had a black gauze, sequined veil thrown back over her head.

She was holding a bouquet of yellow roses.

By mid-January of 1993, the collegiate football games were finished for the year. The insatiable television-watching public then tuned to the professional playoffs and waited to see which teams would be in the Super Bowl.

The average American citizen also awaited the arrival of a new Congress and a new President of the United States in January. People wanted change.

Josh also wanted change, although he knew he was not going to have it. For Josh wanted Scott back. It had been almost three weeks since Scott's funeral and Josh still did not feel like returning to the living. Most days, he drank and watched the financial markets around the world. Nothing interested or motivated him. His confident stride disappeared and he moped around the penthouse, playing with Laurely and Hardy. He had moved them into a bedroom of their own, just down the hall from his. The loss of Scott had bent Josh's physique like a big tree that had been blown over in a storm. Rage filled his mind and his face became drawn and taut. His eyes became dull and lifeless. He wanted vengeance.

Josh was in his study when Annie brought up the *Wall Street Journal*. Josh poured himself a double Scotch whiskey and glanced at the headlines. Staring up at him was an article stating that Zafra Limited, a Netherlands Antilles corporation, had purchased controlling interest in IMA Laboratories, Inc. of Encino, California. Zafra Limited had appointed a new board of directors and management. The new chairman of the board of IMA Laboratories was Gino Rigitinni. He was to be representing Zafra's stock interests in IMA. The article went on to say that Ralph Landen, the president of Medical Reference Laboratories, Inc., in Omaha, Nebraska, was the leading candidate for the position of CEO of IMA Laboratories.

Josh jumped up and flung his drink across the room. It hit the wall near the ceiling and shattered into slivers. Brown whiskey stained in streaks as it ran down the wall.

Josh Kramer was ready to do battle. Just how naive he could have been? Why had he not cared when he heard at the funeral that Landen might be leaving MRL for another company? What did Rigitinni mean by ten percent of the deal coming *our* way, not my way? How could four different sources have tested Scott positive for HIV and Milton constantly tested Scott negative? Was this a weird coincidence or a series of planned calculations and strange mistakes? How come Pamela, who was Scott's lover, had not come down with AIDS? Was it possible that Milton had not made up the story about the AIDS injection? After all, Milton had told Scott that he was bringing him the evidence. If so, where was the evidence—the infected blood? Why wasn't some trace of it found in the car? And why was Nicki Graziano with Milton Schwartz on the night of the accident? Was it also possible Scott, Milton *and* Nicki had been murdered?

Josh, wondered suddenly how he could have doubted

Scott's word so easily. He yelled out the door to Annie, "Those bastards! They think they've got Scott's company. Well, they better think again!"

"Sweetheart, welcome back to the world. But what on earth are you talking about?"

"I'll explain it all to you later. Right now, get dressed. We're going out for a drive with the dogs."

Josh wheeled his dark green Range Rover up Coldwater Canyon Drive onto Mulholland Drive. Annie was in the back seat holding the dogs by their leashes as they bayed to get out of the truck. They stretched on their haunches and stuck their noses through small cracks in the rear windows into the gushing air.

When Josh arrived at the corner of Mulholland Drive where Milton's Cadillac had broken through the barrier, he found little trace of an accident. There were no skid marks and the broken guard rail had been replaced. The bush below was still blackened from the fire, but had grown considerably since the time of the crash. There were small amounts of broken tail-light and some amber-colored plastic pieces of turn signal lens scattered on the steep hillside.

Josh stirred the broken bits with his foot. How could the tail light have broken if the car had crashed through the barrier and had become immediately airborne? The tail lights should not have broken until the car crashed at the bottom of the ravine! And a 1959 Cadillac did not have amber plastic turn signal lenses. He picked up some red glass and yellow plastic and put it in his jacket pocket.

Annie had let the dogs loose from their leashes and

they ran down the side of the mountain, instinctively searching the terrain for game. Their noses barely left the ground in their circular wanderings. Every now and then they gave a bark or howl of delight.

Josh sat down on the steel railing, deep in thought. He stared down into the hazy valley below. He wondered if it would be possible to take a series of rope loops and rappel down the side of the canyon to snoop around the crash site. He decided to check it out with an ex-paratrooper buddy of his before trying it on his own. Scott haunted him. Josh's eyes became teary and he said, "This smog sure irritates my eyes!"

Annie imagined what he was thinking and started rubbing his shoulders from behind. Josh sat motionless while she massaged his back. A soft wind blew gently through the canyon.

The yellow labradors were running back up the hill. Hardy was chasing Laurely, who had something dangling from her jaws. Josh whistled for them to come. They both came sprinting towards their new keeper. Their wagging tails verified that they were both proud of the findings. Hardy was whining sadly.

Josh got up from the guard rail and went to pet them and Laurely dropped the parcel she was carrying. It was a scruffy, partially-burned leather satchel with the initials "S. R." embossed on its side. Annie picked it up and handed it to Josh.

"I say, what's this? It looks like a doctor's bag!"

Josh was in such a hurry to see what was inside the satchel that he did not answer. He tore at the rusted metal hinges and the bag opened. Inside was a large envelope which felt like it held a bottle that had been specially wrapped to prevent breakage. There were other medical paraphernalia. Needles and gamma globulin vials were scattered around the bottom of the bag. Josh took it over to the Range Rover and emptied it on the rear seat. Annie tore open the Styrofoam envelope.

"Sweetheart, there's a half-filled bottle of fluid in here that's labeled: Tainted blood—found in Graziano's fridge! And a small glass tube that says, Scott's blood, drawn day before Caribbean trip-*NEGATIVE-HIV!* What do you think we've found?"

Josh grinned from ear to ear. "Maybe Scott's murderers!"

"What do you mean?"

"My love, I can't explain it all now, but I won't rest until I've vindicated Scott. Let's go home."

He patted the dogs again and said, "You two didn't forget the smell of your old master, did you?"

The dogs, tongues hanging out, looked up, grinning proudly.

On the ride back to the penthouse Josh said to Annie, "As soon as we get home, call the pilots. I want them to fly Todd Butler down to Curacao and then over to Luxembourg."

Surprised, Annie asked, "You mean the private eye?"

"Yes, and I want them to leave today!"

As soon as they arrived home Josh went into his study and called the detective.

"Todd, I know we missed something before in our search for a connection between Senator Spout and Gino

Rigitinni regarding Zafra Limited and Malaysian Latex Limited. But now we might be talking about murder."

The private eye pushed the cap back on his head and blew air out his mouth. It whistled through his teeth. Josh continued.

"There's got to be a clue somewhere. You know—a paper trail, or memo pad or a tape recording made that someone's forgotten about. I want you and your men to trace every move, plane trip, telephone call, affair or crap that Milton Schwartz, Nicki Graziano, Gino Rigitinni and Richard Spout made during the last four months of Scott Reid's life."

"Mr. Kramer, if it's out there, I'll find it," Butler said. "How much time have I got and how many men do you want me to put on the case?"

"I want you to stay either in Curacao or Luxembourg until you find some connection. Then, recheck everything here in the States. I'm giving you an unlimited expense account and an unlimited amount of time. Put as many people on the case as you think are necessary to get it solved. But I don't want you to come back until you've got proof of their involvement."

Like a hungry dog snooping for a bone, Butler asked, "Have you got anything at all for me to go on?"

"Yes, I do. I'll fax you all of the trades of a stock called IMA Laboratories that've taken place in the last month and a half. I think you can find a broker or a banker who'll know who made those trades, then go from there. If you find a connection, you've got both Spout's and Rigitinni's east coast addresses. Keep on going with your investigation. I've got a limo picking you up in two hours. Call me as soon as you've got anything."

Josh hung up and pushed the private number of Landen's office at Medical Reference Laboratories in Omaha. Ralph had discussed all of the particulars of moving to IMA with Rigitinni and he had read this morning's *Journal*. He was expecting Josh's call. He braced himself. Then, realizing he was alone in his office, he drew his tall, lanky frame up in his chair and answered in a squeaky voice, "Landen, how can I help you?"

"Ralph, this is Josh Kramer. I'm not going to beat around the bush. Is there any truth to the rumor in the *Wall Street Journal* that you might be quitting MRL and going over to run IMA Labs for Gino?"

Ralph's voice rose a pitch higher than normal. He slumped in his chair and peeped, "Well, to be honest with you, Josh, I've held discussions with the new directors of IMA and they've offered me a package that I find difficult to turn down. I was about to call you and give you thirty days to find a replacement for me, if that'll give you enough time."

"Ralph, I've always liked you, but loyalty is number one in my book. You should've come to me first. So listen to me carefully. I don't need thirty minutes to replace a man like you, much less thirty days. I'm going to call Security and have you removed immediately. So start packing your things the moment I hang up and there'll be no problems. Best of luck in your new position, Ralph. I have a feeling you're going to need it!"

Josh slammed the telephone down and lit up a cigarette. Annie knocked on the door and said, "The plane is ready any time you want it."

Josh was irate, but he was whistling a happy tune. He said, "Tell the pilots they leave in two hours. I'll be shaving and showering if you need me for anything."

Annie's smile lit up the room. Her man was back.

Todd Butler was a bulldog, both in physical appearance and tenacity. He cracked his knuckles when speaking to strangers, or when nervous, and it wasn't beneath him to occasionally pick his nose in public. Those repulsive habits, coupled with the black hair that grew like wild fescue on his body, his fire-hydrant build and slobbish desire to wear baseball caps and T-shirts on all occasions, led people to underestimate his intelligence. That was a mistake, because he usually got his man. Yet, it was not often that he was involved in a potential murder case, and he decided to make sure that nothing was overlooked in his search for clues. He began by assigning one man to each individual whom Josh thought might shed a clue on the matter. Todd then left for Europe.

He achieved nothing in Luxembourg and flew on to the Netherlands Antilles. Armed with Josh's stock data, he found his first clue. A secretary vividly remembered a Mr. Gino Rigitinni. She found him a repulsive, foul mouthed, silver-haired little bore who would not leave her alone. After a dinner date he had tried, unsuccessfully, to rape her.

The private eye bought her lunch and agreed with her

assessment of Gino. She was more than happy to supply Todd with all of the incriminating brokerage records he was looking for. Including violating her bank, and her country's secrecy laws by providing a photocopy of Zafra Limited's Memorandum of Wishes, which proved Senator Richard Spout was the beneficial owner of said corporation. In the meantime, stateside, one of his men had gone to IMA Laboratories. He had gotten a partial license number of a black pickup truck that had been parked in front of the lab the night Milton Schwartz died. Fortunately, a company security guard had recorded and entered the truck's number into a computer. The partial number was decoded and traced to a distant relative of Gino Rigitinni's who lived in southern California. When Butler received the news, he immediately flew from Willemstad to New York.

The inauguration ceremonies in Washington, D.C. for President Clinton aroused the nation. The parade and his trek from Charlottesville, Virginia, to the Capitol were watched by millions around the world. Moving speeches were made by the newly elected officials in the House and the Senate. They spoke about the economy, the budget, the deficit, social security, the environment, the military, the forgotten middle class, health care and AIDS.

Congress returned to session on Monday, January 25. One of the first items on their agenda was a Senate subcommittee meeting, chaired by Senator Richard Spout, regarding the allocation of new funding for HIV testing and AIDS research. This meeting was to take place on Friday the 29th.

Numerous businessmen, American Medical Association leaders, physician's and infected patients had been called to testify on behalf of the AIDS problem confronting America.

Franklin, representing the Berlinger Clinic, and Gino Rigitinni and Ralph Landen, the new management of IMA Laboratories, were among the invited guests and speakers.

Ironically, Josh, the owner of the largest blood testing laboratory in the world, Medical Reference Laboratory, had not been invited to Washington, D.C. He sat at home in front of the television with Annie, watching the proceedings.

Almost three billion dollars was to be spent fighting AIDS in the coming budget for which this committee was in charge. They listened attentively to the various stories from patients. They heard the AMA leaders tell everyone that the disease had the potential to bankrupt the nation's health system. They heard from business people who talked about lost productivity from the youth who were victims of the disease. They listened to the physician who treated the infected. The last to speak before the subcommittee voted on specific allocation of funds was Franklin.

As chairman of the subcommittee, Richard Spout banged his gavel for silence.

The floor of the Senate chambers became quiet as Nelsen rose to speak. Franklin's enormous body dominated the room. He cleared his throat.

"Ladies and gentlemen, and honorable members of this committee. First of all I want to thank you for the interest you are showing as concerned citizens towards this horrible epidemic called AIDS that is running rampant throughout our society. I can not only attest to the horror of this disease as a physician, but also on a human level. I want you to know that I just buried my best friend."

Franklin paused. In a voice choked with emotion, he continued. "His name was Scott Reid. Scott died of the complications of AIDS. He was successful, he was healthy, he was a productive American, he was a man every young person looked up to. My son is named after him, I loved him and he was my frie..."

The massive shoulders of Franklin shook with giant sobs, and tears streamed down his face. He trembled and could speak no more. Rigitinni stood up and handed Franklin a handkerchief. Franklin buried his face in it for a moment. Most of the session's participants were crying. The members of the committee, including Richard, hung their heads.

Annie had tears in her eyes and she hugged Josh. He stared furiously at the screen. They could hear the beeping of horns in the morning rush hour traffic from down below.

Franklin threw his shoulders back and, in a broken voice, continued.

"Please excuse me, but Scott Reid was my friend and he shouldn't have died from this deadly disease. Somehow, as a society, we let him down. So I come before you today to plead that we don't let any more Scott Reids die of AIDS. Our society cannot afford the loss of such people. Therefore I beg you to allocate more government funds for the testing of this killer. I apologize, I can't say any more at this time. Thank you."

Everyone applauded and Nelsen sat down to wipe away his tears. The committee chairman felt that after this emotional plea a lunch break was in order. He banged his gavel and recessed the meeting for two hours.

Josh did not feel Annie's sense of compassion, except for the loss of Scott. He was full of hate and revenge while watching the televised proceedings. The telephone in the study started ringing and he ran in to answer it.

"Mr. Kramer, it's Todd Butler. Hang on to your hat, I've got the murderers red-handed!"

"Are you serious?" screamed Josh.

The private eye could see the blinking lights of the Empire State building from his hotel rooms window. "Yep, I'm in The Big Apple right this minute waiting for a taxi to take me to Kennedy so I can get you this data immediately."

Impatient, Josh butted in. "Well, what have you got, Todd?"

"A photocopy of a document incriminating Senator Spout in illegal offshore activities and a tape of the killers that I'll play for you right this minute."

Butler chuckled and wiped his dripping nose on his sleeve. He was satisfied with himself. He turned his tape recorder on and inserted a cassette that he and his associate had recently purloined, and copied, from the closet of Rigitinni's uptown Manhattan apartment.

"Listen carefully, Mr. Kramer." The detective pushed the play button on the recorder, Gino's sleepy voice said, "Yeah, Rigitinni!" followed by Nicki's voice, "Uncle Gino, you said you were going to take care of my problem out here some time next week, didn't you?" Josh could hear that Gino was furious and shouting, "What the fuck's the matter with you, Nicki, calling me up in the middle of the night to verify my word! I told you I'd take care of Milton Schwartz and I will. You just make goddamn sure you've taken care of Reid with that injection you gave him!"

Josh was so ecstatic that he jumped out of his slippers. He yelled into the phone, "We've got those bastards, Todd. Goddamn it, we've got em!" He lit up a cigarette and sucked in a deep drag of thick smoke.

Butler sipped on a diet Coke, chewed on some ice and said, "Hold on, Mr. Kramer, there's lots more."

Nicki was talking again. "I have an emergency with Schwartz. He broke into my office and took something that could implicate *us* in this thing. I need to have you take care of this problem immediately. Can you do it?" The tape crackled a little, but Josh could hear Gino's response clearly. "What the hell do you mean, implicate *us*?" Nicki replied, "Well, I'd saved some extra infected blood in my office refrigerator in case I had to redo Scott if I hadn't given him enough HIV to infect him. I mean, that was smart, wasn't it, Gino? And Schwartz snuck in my office tonight and stole it."

Josh put his hand to his face in horror. His other hand gripped the receiver so hard his knuckles were turning white. Scott had been right and he had failed to heed his warning. His ears hummed hatred as Gino continued.

"Nicki, listen to me. Don't worry any more about it. He'll be taken care of before the weekend is out. Okay?" Nicki whined, "Okay, Gino." Another small blip was heard on the tape before Gino replied. "Nicki, I don't want you to talk to anybody until you hear from me again. Do you hear?"

"Yeah, I hear you, Gino."

"And don't worry, we'll take care of you. You helped us out and we're going to help you out. Go to bed, kid. And stay home by yourself for the weekend."

There was a snap in Josh's ear as Butler punched off the recorder and said, "I'm sorry about Mr. Reid, but they sure took care of Nicki, alright. Can you meet me when I get in, Mr. Kramer? I'll call and give you my arrival time in an hour."

Josh relaxed for the first time in weeks. The icy glint that had been in his eyes dissolved into a glow of satisfaction, the stiffened spine softened and he drew a deep breath.

"Todd, I'll be there with champagne. What a great job you've done. I want to hear all of the details. Get here as soon as you can and we'll pay a little visit to the D.A.'s office in the morning. 'Bye for now."

Butler pushed the sweat-drenched cap back on his head, put his feet on the coffee table and when he blew his breath out, enjoyed the sibilant whistle of air through his front teeth.

Later that afternoon, Josh and Annie watched as the members of the senate subcommittee, refreshed from a leisurely lunch, voted a further two billion dollars for blood testing of American citizens for HIV. Senator Spout, clad in a dark blue pin-striped suit and bright blue bow tie, had an enormous smile on his face as he banged his gavel down to verify the ruling. He beamed out into the audience and straight at Rigitinni.

Josh smiled contentedly. He knew in his gut Scott and Milton had been right and that the good intentions of the social legislators and the Franklin Nelsens of the world were wrong. He was also now certain who was behind Scott's death. He could not wait to prove it. In a new voice he said to Annie,

"I'm going to expose this whole AIDS scam and I'll have those two bastards in jail before they know what hit them!"

Enthusiastically, Annie grinned, "That's the spirit, Josh. What do you plan to do?"

"First, I'm turning all of Todd's evidence over to the police. Then we're taking a trip. I've contacted Dr. LeRoy Dutton, the Nobel Prize winning virologist over at UCLA, who happens to share Milton and Scott's HIV theories, and asked him to leave with us tomorrow for Nairobi. He'll visit Scott's AIDS hospital and we'll start our search for the truth. Arguably, this man's the worlds foremost authority on HIV and AIDS."

Annie nodded and nervously adjusted the madras bow on the back of her hair. She was excited by the importance of this mission. Josh continued. "You and I are going to explore the epicenter of this supposed epidemic even if we have to do it by foot. Once we have our information, we'll take it to the Senate committee on AIDS funding, or the press if that's what it takes. This, coupled with the illegal activities Todd's uncovered against Senator Spout and Rigitinni, should put them away forever and vindicate Scott's theories."

The Kramer Gulfstream landed in Kenya three days later. Dr. Dutton had spent the bulk of the flight educating Josh and Annie on his beliefs regarding the HIV/AIDS coverup. It definitely matched what Milton and Scott had told them. Dutton couldn't wait to work with the scientists at the Nairobi AIDS hospital. Josh had a limo drive them to a hotel and drop Dr. Dutton at the hospital. The beat-up, old black Lincoln had no air conditioning and the humidity was stifling in the horn-honking, bumper to bumper traffic. Josh's instructions were for Dr. Dutton to garner all the information he could in his four weeks at the hospital and they would be back to pick him up at that time to compare notes.

Ensconced at the Nairobi Hilton, Josh set out to hire a group of natives for a safari into the interior of Zaire. Within two days they had translators, gun toters and carriers ready for the journey. Josh leased an antiquated DC-3 to transport everyone on their circuitous trek. His plan was to start at the epicenter of the AIDS area near Lake Victoria and visit every doctor, hospital and government official who would give them information. Their first stop would be the city of Kisumu on the northeast shore of the lake, on to Mwanza, Tanzania on the south shore, up to Kisangani, Zaire on the Congo River and on the epicenter of the "AIDS highway." The plane would fly ahead to Kinshasa and wait for them as they drove for three weeks along the infamous highway east and explored the small inland jungle villages for AIDS data.

Once in Kisangani, Annie heard bizarre reports from the locals of British scientists taking care of infected natives in the deepest heart of the Congo, up near Bumba and Yambuku on the Ebola River. This was hundreds of miles away and not on their itinerary, however, Josh was driven and curious. His first week was spent in frustration over governmental red tape. He had seen thousands of poverty stricken children and sick people, but no sign of AIDS in the numbers he had been led to believe existed there. He was feeling ill, but decided to take a river boat with a handful of the armed guides and head up the Congo. He wired Dr. Dutton that they were taking an extra two weeks to trace down rumors of AIDS scientists in the middle of the jungle.

The steady thumping of the boat's diesel engine and the constant rolling of the small craft on the rippling currents of the river did nothing to help Josh's nausea. The overwhelming heat drained whatever reserves he had stored up for this expedition. He developed a fever and sought refuge in Annie's arms under a canvas canopy. The natives hummed a monotonous drone, sweating mangrove trees drooped lazily on the dense green banks of the river and the jungle foliage screamed its orchestra of cacophony at the drifting intruders. Josh got sicker as the day progressed.

After a feverish night, Josh tried to eat a light breakfast of poached fish. He vomited. As the hot sun brought steam up from the quiet river, he shivered under a wool blanket. Annie wiped his forehead with a wet towel. By the third afternoon on the river, he was delirious; ranting and cursing to no one in particular. The natives started avoiding him and Annie became fearful. She tried forcing down an herbal mixture the natives made for him, but Josh just brought it right back up. His pupils became dilated and his eyes glazed. But there was no turning back. They were half way to nowhere—Bumba—the deepest, darkest part of the veiled jungle that now surrounded them. Josh fell into a stupor. His chest grasped for air in heaving jerks. Annie held him tightly and cried.

At dusk, the heat was shimmering like dangling puppet strings over the still river water. Suddenly a burst of machine gun fire raked the air and raised white welts in the black water alongside the boat. On shore, a few hundred heavily armed antigovernment rebels waved for them to land on a sandy cove nearby. The lightly armed hired guards laid down their old weapons, knowing they were no match for the insurgents and quickly headed for shore.

The guerrilla commander dressed in military fatigues was quite polite for such a raucous introduction and said, "I am Colonel Tubutu. I represent Prime Minister Mulumba and the revolutionary people of Zaire. Welcome and where are you going?"

Annie replied, "We're looking for the British doctor who cares for the sick in the jungle. Can you help us?"

"Maybe. What is wrong with this man?"

"I'm afraid he's very sick. He needs medical attention immediately."

The Colonel bellowed something in his tribal language and the hired guards on the boat cowered with fear. The rebels raised their Uzi's and pointed them at their captors, then waved for Annie alone to step down from the boat. The commander barked another order and four husky men grabbed a blanket and boarded the small river craft. The diesel engine chugged unevenly. They gently placed Josh in the blanket and carried him to shore. They motioned for Annie to follow them. She did and they disappeared into the thick underbrush. Twenty minutes later, Colonel Tubutu slapped his thigh and the commandos opened fire on the guards and carriers Josh had hired. They kept firing until the boat sank.

Annie and the troops carrying Josh walked for about three hours before stopping to camp for the night. Monkeys screamed from the roof of the jungle. Insects crawled and buzzed in multitudes. Hot, oppressive dankness rose from the soggy soil. Annie was terrified, yet even more worried for Josh. He was covered with rancid sweat and muttering her name. Colonel Tubutu arrived with his other soldiers. Congenially, he said.

"We have a two day walk from this camp to our headquarters. Please have some food and get some rest. You are safe with us. While you eat you can tell me who you are and why you are in my country?"

Annie could hear the sound of drums coming from the pitch blackness. Numbly, she stared at the crackling red and yellow fire at the campsite. Her head was spinning for answers. Who were these people? What were they going to do with her and Josh? How could she help Josh medically? Where were they? How could she get a message to anyone? In hopes of getting help, she decided to tell Colonel Tubutu the truth and spent the next two hours explaining to him the story of Scott Reid, Milton Schwartz and their AIDS theories.

The Colonel listened patiently, chain smoking foul smelling cigarettes. His eyes devoured every portion of Annie's anatomy. He liked what he saw. When she was finished talking, he smiled and bid her good night. Exhausted, Annie fell asleep beside Josh.

After two more torturous days of following jungle paths, wading through muddy streams, climbing mountains and fighting back tears, Annie and the rebels walked into a flat clearing. They had reached the Colonel's headquarters. Well concealed grass-roofed huts were scattered in a small circular village. A large hut, with a walk around wooden veranda seemed to be the village center and the troops motioned for Annie to follow them to the buildings entrance. They led her there and deposited Josh on a clean bed.

Colonel Tubutu entered and said, "Your friend is safe now. You are tired. I told my wives to make room for you in my home until your friend recovers, so please come with me. We will make your friend well in a few days."

Annie was worn out and grateful. She followed Colonel Tubutu to his home and fell asleep. Josh rolled in his bed grumbling, "Got to find answers for Scott...AIDS ...man-made...murdered. He told me so...got to find answers out here somewhere." He screamed this over and over again in his fevered state.

In the morning, only women were to be found. None of them spoke English. Annie walked over to the main village hut where they had put Josh. Someone had obviously taken good care of him. His clothes had been removed. He had been bathed and cleaned up. She was relieved. He also had been medicated and mumbled incoherently while he slept. That afternoon she saw a nun dressed in a flowing, black habit steal around the hut where Josh was lodged. Annie yelled, but the nun disappeared without a word. How odd.

A week passed by, she was well treated by the laughing, bare-breasted native women. But no men showed up. Nor did she see the nun again. The village women fed her, gave her a beer like drink, took care of Josh and giggling, pointed out that she now had the main bedroom in Colonel Tubutu's home.

Late that night Josh became delirious again. Annie thought she heard him scream, but silence followed and the jungle noises resumed. She fell back asleep in the comfort of the Colonel's bed. In the main hut the nun sat next to Josh listening to him mumble, "AIDS...man-made...Monster...killed Scott...got to find answers." The nun looked over at the man sitting on a high stool next to Josh's bed; he had been there every night for the past week. He felt Josh's pulse and said.

"This man's going to die if I don't help him. Get me a 50cc syringe of morphine."

The nun thought to herself how that was more than

enough to kill a man, but followed orders. She brought back the loaded syringe and handed it to the man, who was still sitting beside the bed. Josh was on his side moaning when the man stuck the syringe in Josh's buttock and slowly injected the fluid. He waited five minutes. The nun watched silently. She saw a bearded white face peek around the corner of the door. She frowned at him. The face vanished. Josh's agony stopped. He was barely breathing. His eyes fluttered shut and his chest collapsed. The man sitting on the stool nodded his head at the nun and she slipped from the room.

It was muggy in the cramped hut. The man took off his thick yellow glasses and wiped them off. He bent the pliable metal rims around his ears, grinned a bucktoothed smile through his bearded face and stood up to stretch his gangly, seven foot body.

THE END

CREDITS

I wish to thank my pal, Peter Viertel, for his endless years of patience with me and for understanding my desire to write. I am forever grateful to Burt and Jane Boyar for believing in my work and abilities. The kindness of Alfred S. Regnery will never be forgotten. I am indebted to Brewster Blackmer, Lorraine Powell, Sonja Casero, Bill and Sylvia Gensky, Stuart and Gabby Chase, John Lodge, Mike and Merlyn England, Jilly Newsom, David and Judy Christian, Larry Barnett, Derwood and Johanna Chase, Mary Fisk, "Toby" Hogan, Philip Savage, "Sandy" Simon, Loretta Small and Sandra Hensley for their helpful suggestions during the writing of my novel.

But for the loving presence of Daphne, there would have been no poetry in my novel, or my life.

A lifetime association with the Kallestad family has shown me what the vicissitudes of life have to offer. Thanks, Jimmer, for always being you.

My computer guru in Spain, Paul Sedkowski, opened a whole new world for me. I thank him for this and his companionship.

I received inspiration and guidance from the written works of Nobel Prize winning virologist, Doctor Peter Duesburg. His tireless efforts to bring truth to the public, instead of misinformation regarding HIV and AIDS, have been understood and appreciated by many. I thank Neville Hodgkinson, science correspondent for the *London Sunday Times*, for his fortitude in exposing, "The Plague That Never Was," in Africa. I owe special thanks to doctors Mark Allen in Kansas and John Nelsen in Michigan for helping me with medical data. Everyone interested in the subject of HIV/AIDS should read Michael Fumento's, *The Myth of Heterosexual AIDS*. My racing companion and dentist, Dr. Rolf Versen, was of invaluable assistance. University of Virginia physicist, John Ruvalds, and Dutch biochemist, Albert Coenders, were more than helpful in their critique. And I thank, Doctor James Makumbi, minister of health, Uganda, for his hospitality and informative data during my trip to the "epicenter of AIDS" in central Africa.

I derived all medical facts and statistics from published medical reports and periodicals, newspaper articles, *The New England Journal of Medicine,* and *HIV/AIDS Surveillance,* the U.S. Department of Health and Human Services publication for the Center for Disease Control and Prevention.

I am deeply grateful, and probably lost without their knowledge, to my editors Laura Wallace-Smith and Mayapriya Long.

My unabated thanks to my family for their faith and loyalty and for putting up with me during the long hours of completing this novel. I love you all.

And last, but not least, I want to thank my lifelong friend, Joe Kolkowitz, President of Players Talent Agency in Los Angeles, for his unwavering support and conviction in me as a writer and a buddy.

Thomas C. McCollum III founded and was Chairman of the Board of HML Medical, Inc., a California based company that manufactured coronary angioplasty balloon catheters and a patented balloon catheter for diagnosing bronchial problems in AIDS-infected patients. He was also an investor, director, and chairman of the audit committee for Kallestad Laboratories, Inc., an American Stock Exchange immunodiagnostics company. He traveled three continents and spent over two years researching and writing this, his first novel. Over the past twenty-five years he has authored numerous medical articles for the business world. He retired in 1990 and moved to Marbella, Spain.